GOD ON MAYHEM STREET

A LEO TOWNSEND NOVEL

*For Tricia —
Soon you'll be signing your book over to me!
Enjoy!*

LITTLE CREEK PRESS®
AND BOOK DESIGN

Mineral Point, Wisconsin USA

Copyright © 2016 Kristin A. Oakley

Little Creek Press®
A Division of Kristin Mitchell Design, Inc.
5341 Sunny Ridge Road
Mineral Point, Wisconsin 53565

Editor: Karyn Saemann

Book Design and Project Coordination: Little Creek Press

First Edition
September 2016

All rights reserved.

No part of this book may be used or reproduced
in any manner whatsoever without written
permission from the author.

Printed in Wisconsin, United States of America

For more information or to order books:
www.kristinoakley.net or www.littlecreekpress.com

Library of Congress Control Number: 2016951391

ISBN-10: 1-942586-17-5
ISBN-13: 978-1-942586-17-3

Author's Note: *God on Mayhem Street* is a work of fiction. All characters and events are products of my imagination as is my fictional town of Endeavor, Wisconsin.

To Clyde and Elizabeth Oakley who have always been proud of me. I love you.

And to Caitlin and Jessica. Always.

1

Leo Townsend clenched the flowers in his hand when he spotted his father hunched over a grave a dozen yards away. He had hoped he wouldn't see Frank Townsend until the funeral lunch, when the house would be full of mourners and avoiding him would be easy. But more than that, Leo had wanted to be alone to say goodbye.

He smoothed his rumpled black suit and forced himself to walk on the gravel path past crumbling, century-old headstones to the newer section of the Merritt's Landing Cemetery, where the crosses gleamed white in the early afternoon sun and plastic flowers stood sentry.

When he stepped onto the grass still damp from the earlier rains, water beaded on his Italian loafers. He didn't bother to wipe them off. He didn't care if the moisture ruined the handcrafted leather. His mother would have been horrified. If she were alive.

Leo slowed as he approached his father. Frank stood alone by the mound of fresh dirt, staring vacantly at the Isabella Renata Salvatori Townsend funeral program in his hand. Frank's six-foot frame seemed to have shrunk from grief. The sleeves of his borrowed black suit covered his hands. The pants were too long, the cuffs, like Leo's shoes, damp.

When Frank noticed Leo his vacant eyes filled with rage. "You walked out of the funeral!" Lines etched his forehead, and his jaw clenched.

"You didn't attend the graveside service. How dare you dishonor your mother?" Tears in his eyes magnified his grief.

Leo knew that no matter what he said, his father wouldn't hear him. So he studied the grave, trying hard not to think of his mother buried under six feet of dirt.

"You couldn't be bothered with the funeral arrangements, attending the wake," Frank continued.

The yellow narcissus and white crocuses trembled in Leo's hand. He'd wanted red poppies to complete the bouquet, but the florist near O'Hare didn't carry them so she'd tied a red ribbon around the flowers, instead.

At this time of year, crocuses, narcissus, and poppies carpeted the gentle slopes of the Castelluccio di Norcia near his mother's Italian hometown of Norcia. She had wanted to take her children there, treat them to Prosciutto di Norcia, black truffles, and lentil soup, attend mass with them in the Basilica of San Benedetto, and run with them through the plain when it exploded in color. But that never happened because the farm kept the Townsends shackled to Endeavor, Wisconsin.

Isabella had hoped, once she and Frank retired, to take their grandchildren to Italy. But there was no retirement and there were no grandchildren. None of Leo's relationships had lasted long enough. And Leo's brother, Eddie, would never be able to father a child. Now it was too late. That morning, Isabella had been buried in this cemetery five miles from the farm.

"When you finally showed your face at church," Frank said, "you didn't even stick around to pay your respects."

Leo glanced up at the cloudless sky. *Sei la stella del mio cielo*, his mother always told him. *You're the star of my sky.* Sighing, he bent to place the bouquet on Isabella's grave. The bow fell off. He collected it, wiping bits of dirt off the satin.

He hated leaving her here.

Throat burning, tears welling, he shoved the ribbon in his jacket pocket, whispered, "Sei la stella del mio cielo," and started for his car. He'd be damned if he cried in front of his father.

"Explain yourself. Stop running away from your responsibilities."

Leo hesitated. He traced his finger over the scar on his chin that cut a smooth path through his habitual stubble. The two-year-old scar was a souvenir from the Chicago Triathlon mob stampede that had paralyzed Eddie from the waist down and left him in a wheelchair. Leo had fought the mob to get to his brother but had been unable to reach him, protect him. Frank couldn't forgive Leo for that. Hell, Leo couldn't even forgive himself.

A robin sang from its perch on the marble curl of a cherub on a nearby headstone. The red-breasted birds had been Isabella's favorite.

Leo finally turned to the man he'd so deeply disappointed. The wrinkled skin on Frank's face and neck was red and blotchy, in stark contrast to his starched ivory collar. The ring of white hair circling Frank's scalp glistened with sweat in the late-morning sun.

When did he get so old?

"Dad, we've been over this. I worked in San Francisco on assignment Monday and Tuesday. I couldn't get here until today."

"You breeze in from writing some asinine story about fag rights barely in time for the funeral and then leave in the middle of the service." Frank shook the program at Leo. "What the hell is wrong with you?"

"I couldn't sit through the Catholic Mass. I know that's what Mom wanted but it doesn't mean I have to listen to it."

"You refuse to honor her memory."

Leo moved to within an arm's length of his father and studied the old man's watery, bloodshot eyes. No whiskey fumes, just Old Spice aftershave, moth balls, and sorrow. "Sitting in a dark, dank church while an apathetic priest rambles on about sin and the afterlife doesn't honor Mom's memory. Becoming the successful, decent, honest man she raised me to be does."

Frank's face softened for an instant, and then he turned his back on Leo and marched down the hill to a waiting sedan.

"I'll be at the house," Leo muttered.

A breeze scattered Leo's flowers across Isabella's grave. He gathered them and tucked their fragile stems into the cool dirt, anchoring them in place. He was sorry they'd argued over her grave, but arguing had been their only form of communication for years.

"Sei la stella del mio cielo," he repeated, dusting off his hands and then trudging back to his Mustang. As he flung his suit coat onto the passenger seat, the ribbon flew out, hit the dashboard, and dropped to the floor mat. Retrieving it, he was reminded of the scarlet dress his mother wore the last time she'd ridden in this car only a few weeks ago.

He had won the Pulitzer Prize for his *Chicago Examiner* article on Carpe Diem, Illinois and had driven home to give his family the good news. Eddie cooked a celebration lunch of minestrone and garlic bread. Isabella praised Leo's achievements and ignored her food. Frank encouraged her to eat, interrupting her praises, but when she waved him away he glared at Leo and stormed out of the room.

After lunch, Leo took his mother for a ride in the Mustang. Oncologists had given Isabella chemotherapy in an attempt to stop the spread of breast cancer but were only successful in giving her nerve damage that made walking difficult. So he'd carried her to his car, shocked at how little she weighed.

He settled her in, tucking his car blanket around her shoulders. She smelled of menthol. Every morning Frank had rubbed her skin with ointment to increase her circulation and ease the pain. Leo then placed her purse next to her. Stuffed with Kleenex, a water bottle, Q-tips, Vaseline, morphine lollipops, lozenges, and heat packs, Isabella called the purse "her personal pharmacy".

"Grazie," she'd said, as she sunk into the leather seat. "Music please, Leonardo."

Leo flipped through stations until he came to WPR playing the fourth movement of Beethoven's Ninth Symphony. The crescendo of the strings and woodwinds carried them over the low bridge spanning the swollen Wisconsin River. A few boats clung to the shoreline as fishermen threw their lines, ignoring the traffic on I-39. The radio chorus added their voices to the symphony as Leo maneuvered the Mustang over roads cracked from the recent, harsh winter.

As the last joyous note played, Leo swung back toward Endeavor and Isabella suggested they stop at Buffalo Lake. He parked by the small, sandy beach, giving them a good view of the calm water surrounded by newly-leafing birch and maple trees and greening marsh grasses.

"Do you remember the last time we picnicked here?" Leo shifted on the driver's seat to look at her.

"Sicuro! You fought with Eduardo over the last cannolo." Isabella's Italian-rolled "r's" cracked. "Your father shoved the entire dessert in his mouth."

Leo laughed. "Cream squeezed out between his lips but he managed to swallow it."

"Then he picked you boys up, one under each arm, and threw you in the lake." Her eyes sparkled with tears.

On the radio, the Chicago Lyric Opera began its production of *Carmen*. Leo turned the music off and held his mother's dry, bony hand. "Delicious lunch. You've taught Eddie well."

She squeezed his hand.

"You didn't eat, though."

Isabella sighed a deep, rattling breath. "Food has lost its appeal. In some ways, that's worse than the cancer." She pulled the blanket tighter around her shoulders.

Leo turned on the car's heater.

"I'm sorry Frank walked out on your celebration," she said.

"Don't be. But it's amazing how Dad blames me for your loss of appetite. Blames me for so many things."

She didn't say anything and after a few minutes Leo wondered if she had dropped off to sleep. Eddie had told him Isabella was extremely fatigued. Another fallout of the disease and the treatment.

He reached for the gear shift. She placed her hand on his, stopping him.

"You remind Frank of his father," Isabella began. "You inherited Sawyer's passion for writing, a passion your father doesn't understand."

"He's never tried."

"Your great-grandfather George," Isabella went on as if she hadn't heard him, "invested everything he had into his farm, hoping that someday Sawyer would take it over. But Sawyer wanted to move his family to New York to pursue his writing career. They argued bitterly. Sawyer packed but your father, who was only sixteen, refused to go. Sawyer left him behind."

Leo knew this. Sawyer later claimed he had no farming skills, that he would have reaped the land into a dust bowl in a matter of weeks. Leo had to agree. Sawyer Townsend was a master cultivator—of stories, not crops. His novel, *All Souls Die*, had been a *New York Times* bestseller and had won the Pulitzer Prize.

Isabella's fingers tightened around Leo's hand. He was surprised at the strength in them until her beautiful smile pulled into a taut grimace. Leo recognized that expression. It accompanied a sudden onset of extreme, breakthrough pain not controlled by the extended-release opioids she took only as needed—which was becoming more and more frequent. He rummaged through her purse for a morphine lollipop, ripped off the packaging, and handed it to her.

"Grazie," she mumbled through the lollipop in her mouth.

"We should go." He dug for the car keys in his pocket.

She shook her head. After a few minutes, her face relaxed and she continued. "It was difficult for your father when you followed in Sawyer's footsteps. Frank dreamed of working the land with you, hoping one day you'd take over the farm. He tried everything he could to get you to love a farming life—"

"Including putting me in the hospital," Leo said, and instantly regretted it when the little color his mother had left drained from her face. But he'd never forget that frozen January morning when he was twelve. Wind chill of twenty below, ice pelting his bedroom window, Leo had dreaded going out to the barn and, instead, burrowed under his covers. Despite a ticklish cough, he'd stayed up late the night before watching the made-for-TV movie, "Murrow."

Bedspread wrapped around him, Leo had trudged down to his eight-year-old brother's room and offered to pay Eddie to milk, feed, and water the goats. Frank had specifically assigned Leo those tasks to teach him responsibility and to instill a little pride in "a job well done." Leo told himself he'd be more responsible tomorrow.

As Leo handed his brother a ten-dollar bill—Eddie was a shrewd negotiator even at that young age—their father had walked in. Angrier than ever, Frank dragged Leo out to the frigid barn despite his protests and worsening, convulsive cough. Frank stood over him, ignoring the coughing until Leo finished the job.

Leo had shuffled back to bed feeling like he'd never get warm again. His limbs were heavy and he had trouble lifting his head. When he skipped breakfast and didn't come down for lunch, his father called him "lazy" but his mother took his temperature—103. When Leo gasped for breath they rushed him to the hospital where he stayed, battling pneumonia, for three days. Their mother had cursed their father in Italian all the way to Madison General.

Isabella finished the lollipop. "Frank's apologized for that." She wrapped the stick in a Kleenex and shoved it in her handbag.

"Not to me. I've been a disappointment to him and always will be. I can't do anything to change that." Leo put his left foot on the clutch, right on the break, and turned the Mustang's key. The engine answered with a deep purr. He shifted into first.

She touched his arm, stopping him from pulling away. "He put his hopes into Eduardo—"

"Until the accident. Which he blames me for."

"Not anymore."

"He can barely look at me."

"Leonardo," she brushed his chin with her cold fingers. "Do something for me."

He studied her high cheekbones and angular nose, which had become much too sharp. He would do anything for her.

"Make peace with your father."

He had fought the childish impulse to say, "Why should I?" and nodded.

Now, Leo pictured the sweat on his father's forehead, his red-faced anger as he stood over her grave. Leo started to toss the ribbon out the car window but held on to it. He'd promised.

He turned on the car's engine and drove through the cemetery, gravel crunching under the tires. When he reached the road he hesitated. He could hop onto I-39, head south to Chicago and be home in three and a half hours. Or he could take the back roads, through the village to the farm and the funeral luncheon.

Leo rubbed the ribbon between his thumb and forefinger for a few moments. Finally, he retrieved his leather bomber jacket from the back seat and tucked the ribbon in the inner pocket. He then steered the car toward Endeavor.

2

Driving on Lakeview Avenue, Leo realized it had been a long time since he'd been in downtown Endeavor. After graduating from high school almost twenty years ago, he had visited the farm many times but had never ventured into the village. The Lakeview Avenue he remembered had more boarded-up shops than thriving businesses. Other than Aunt Sally's Diner and a couple of seedy bars, this had been a ghost town when he left for college.

Not anymore. Al's Appliances, where Leo's dad had purchased a six-burner stove for Isabella, was now Landry's Appliance and Computer Center. The vacant Ace Hardware where a teenaged Eddie had stacked shelves after school had become Landry's Farm & Hardware Store. And the once-neglected library, where Leo had sat in ratty chairs on rainy summer afternoons reading Jules Verne, Umberto Eco, and Stephen King, now had fresh vinyl siding, a manicured lawn, and a new name: The Jacob I. Landry Public Library.

Fifteen years ago, the people of Endeavor had elected local businessman Jacob Landry village president. That same year, Leo's old high school on the hill, once a beautiful, three-story building built with red brick from the Endeavor Brick Yard, was condemned and slated to be razed. It had been rumored that Village President Landry had worked some kind of magic to save the school.

Leo glanced up the hill. His alma mater now had gleaming windows, a new roof, and a large, handcrafted Endeavor High School sign. Jacob Landry might be taking over the village, but that seemed to be a good thing.

Not for Leo's dad, though. Frank had had many run-ins with the village president over the years. Landry had offered to buy the farm numerous times. Each time Frank had refused. A few years ago, Landry had succeeded in convincing the village board to annex Frank's farm into Endeavor. But his subsequent attempt to get it rezoned for commercial use, which would have shut down the Townsend family's farming operation, was voted down by the farmers on the board. Endeavor was a farming community and farmers stuck together.

Leo passed the only empty building on the main street, the historic Soo Line depot that had once housed *The Marquette County Epitome*. The closed sign on the newspaper's front door added to Leo's sorrow. His writing career had begun at *The Epitome* when, at the age of twelve, he had submitted his first article titled "An Italian Woman in Endeavor." Old Man Morrison, the editor, published Leo's piece in that Sunday's edition and offered to pay him a penny a word. Leo worked for the editor all through junior high and high school, even writing a story about his graduating class.

What happened to Mr. Morrison and why hasn't Jacob Landry bought and repurposed this building?

Leo drove by the Landry Multiplex Cinema, once the tiny Reel Theatre where his father had treated Leo and Eddie to *Indiana Jones and the Temple of Doom*. Now the marquee announced *The Passion of the Christ*. Apparently, the village president's revitalization miracles didn't include local newspapers or the latest mainstream movies.

Reaching the end of the street, Leo slowed. He imagined the farmhouse full of relatives and forgotten high school friends offering condolences. He pictured taking his dad aside, telling him about his upcoming interview and how it would change everything. He wanted his father to be excited for him, proud. But that was like wanting the Cubs to win the World Series. Heading back to Chicago seemed like a much better idea.

But Eddie would be at the house, grieving, surrounded by distant relatives and nosy neighbors. Leo reluctantly drove on.

When he crested the final hill on County T, his father's farm spread out before him. It covered several hundred acres of rolling fields and pastures bisected by a meandering stream Eddie had named "Take a Leak Creek" after peeing in it. An ancient oak that once supported Leo and Eddie's tree fort still stood proudly next to the two-story, hundred-year-old house, the tree's new crop of green leaves contrasting with the white clapboard and black shutters. The once-red barn to the left of the house had faded to a dull pink, the paint chipping off in patches. The white cap of the concrete silo sported a large swatch of orange rust.

Leo turned into the gravel driveway and maneuvered around pickup trucks and minivans that lined every foot of the two-hundred-yard drive. He passed the wrap-around front porch where people mingled and a couple sat on the glider his father had carved from a red cedar tree. The bench had been his mother's favorite spot to drink cappuccino and read the newspaper after completing her morning chores.

Leo parked next to his mother's lilac bushes on the side of the house. The flowers' sweet scent reminded him of Isabella hanging fresh laundry outside. His legs wobbled. It took him several tries to get out of the car.

Inside, Leo hugged his brother and accepted condolences from Aunt Edna, his father's ancient sister.

"Your mother was lovely, Leo. Never quite learned the English language though…"

His mother had spoken Italian, Portuguese, Spanish, and better English than he ever had but whenever Aunt Edna visited, Isabella's Italian accent had thickened.

Leo made his way to the kitchen where their longtime next-door neighbor, Millie Branson, shoved a plate of rhubarb pie into his hands. He chewed on a forkful without tasting it and edged out of the crowded kitchen, down the hall, and into the living room. He told Father Murphy some bullshit about how nice a service it was then stepped aside when the Ladies' Auxiliary corralled the good-looking priest. Leo then abandoned the plateful of pie on the coffee table and studied the family photographs on his mother's upright piano.

In their 1975 wedding picture, Frank and Isabella faced each other under the oak in the front yard. Isabella wore her mother's Italian lace dress. Baby's breath dotted her mass of curly black hair instead of the traditional veil. She had refused to cover her face because she said she wanted to get a good look at her husband before marrying him. Frank looked sharp in a black tux, though the bow tie was askew, matching his grin. He had whispered something to his new bride which had made Isabella laugh, her hand touching her new husband's cheek.

A smaller photograph showed a teenaged Leo with a grin similar to Frank's, mussing his younger brother's hair, Eddie winking. To the right was *The Great Hunting Expedition* as Eddie called it. Flanked by his two teenaged boys, Frank held a double-barreled shotgun, his foot on the deer he'd just killed. Eddie had one hand on his father's shoulder; the other held his own shotgun. Leo's arms were crossed, matching his sour expression. He was dreading field dressing the deer.

Leo's favorite picture, a copy of which he carried in his wallet, was a close-up of Isabella and her teenaged sons. Isabella's head tilted toward Leo and she smiled, her dark Italian features evident in both her boys. He felt his chest tighten, regretting that Mary, his girlfriend, had never met his mother. Mary had wanted to come to the funeral to support him, but Leo convinced her that this wasn't the best time to meet his father.

Frank spied him and scowled, perspiration appearing on his creased forehead. He started toward Leo but the condolence-laden priest sidetracked him. Leo took this opportunity to dodge past his father and search for Eddie.

He found his brother in the den, talking to people Leo didn't recognize. Eddie wore black designer jeans and a black linen jacket over a grey dress shirt. He'd tucked Isabella's bright orange-and-yellow scarf in his jacket pocket. The wheels on Eddie's chair were unadorned. Normally, he decorated them with whimsical, abstract covers—replicas of Andy Warhol, Jackson Pollock, or Pablo Picasso masterpieces—but today the spokes were bare.

An obese man Leo thought was a distant cousin occupied most of the leather couch across from Eddie, and was explaining in a too-loud voice how he wouldn't vote in the upcoming presidential election because the candidates were devils incarnate.

"Once Mom became a US citizen she never missed an election," Eddie said.

Realizing she'd never vote again, Leo dropped into his dad's recliner.

Perhaps sensing his brother's melancholy, Eddie added, "In the last election she wrote in 'Stefani Germanotta'."

"Who?" the fat man asked.

"Lady Gaga." Leo squeezed his brother's shoulder, thankful for this happy memory. He then spent the next half hour hanging by Eddie's side.

They bumped into Aunt Edna. "You boys look like *her*. But that's actually a good thing. Why aren't you married?"

"I am." Eddie grinned. "She's chained to a wall in the basement."

Edna gasped and then shot Eddie her dirtiest look.

Leo decided to mention Mary. "My girlfriend offered to come but I was on the west coast until early this morning. I didn't know when I'd get here."

Frank, passing by, said, "Convenient. Now you don't have to be embarrassed by your old man. The farmer." He vanished into the kitchen, followed by Aunt Edna.

Leo started after him.

Eddie blocked the hall with his wheelchair.

"He keeps…" Leo stammered. "I can't believe he—"

"You've done your time. Go."

Leo hesitated until he heard his father say, "Don't know why he bothered to come at all." Shaking his head, Leo hugged his brother and took off for Chicago.

3

Four hours later, Leo collapsed on the lumpy couch in his boss's *Chicago Examiner* office. The room still smelled of onions and relish that had smothered the Chicago hot dogs Ted Nelson, his editor, liked to eat for lunch.

"How's your dad? Your brother?" Ted asked.

"They're hanging in there. Thanks."

"I didn't think you'd come to work today." Ted leaned back in his squeaky desk chair, locking his hands behind his head and crossing his legs. His scarred biceps strained against the sleeves of his white t-shirt. The lettering on the shirt proclaimed, *The only valid censorship of ideas is the right of people not to listen. ~ Tommy Smothers.*

"It was an early service," Leo mumbled, avoiding his editor's concerned gaze. "I wanted to update you about my successful San Francisco trip. Lots of great information and quotes about the changing face of gay rights. I'd like to tie it in with what's going on in Chicago—"

"Look, Leo," Ted cut in, his tone gentle, "I know you're excited about this assignment, particularly with this weekend's rally, but don't you want to take a break? Spend a few days with your family in Wisconsin? Give yourself some time, to, you know, grieve?"

Leo didn't have time for grieving, not since he'd scheduled the interview of his career. Or maybe it was easier avoiding the realization that he'd never see his mother again. He shook his head. "Thanks, but it helps to keep working." He loosened his tie and unbuttoned the top of his rumpled dress shirt. He looked at Ted and grinned. "I have an interview with Griffin Carlisle."

Ted straightened, bumping his knee on the desk. He rubbed his leg. "When?"

"Saturday at eleven thirty. *The Examiner* will be treating him to lunch at Café Spiaggia." His grin widened.

"Eleven thirty? That's three and a half hours *before* the rally! And a one-on-one interview? How the hell did you manage that?"

"Mary knows him. They went to law school together. She arranged it for me."

"Mary?"

"Evans. The mayor of Carpe Diem, Illinois. *My girlfriend.*"

"You're still seeing her? How long has it been? Five, six months?"

"Seven."

"That's some kind of record for you."

Leo shifted on the couch. "Getting back to my Carlisle interview."

Ted paced his cluttered office, skirting stacks of yellowed newspapers and piles of folders. In the windows behind him, afternoon sunlight piercing through dark clouds reflected off a neighboring glass skyscraper. "See if he'll divulge who he's dating. Rumor has it the relationship is serious."

"I'll try, but I doubt I'll get anywhere. Carlisle is doing his best to keep the man's identity quiet. It's understandable. Imagine the media frenzy when they discover who he is, the boyfriend of the front-running presidential candidate."

"It'll be chaos. World news." Ted leaned against his desk.

"Might scare the guy away," Leo added.

"You'll probably be seen at Spiaggia's. You'd better watch yourself. The press would love to peg you as Carlisle's boyfriend."

Leo laughed. "I doubt it. The press is aware of my... reputation." When word got out that he'd had a relationship with Raegan Colyer, chief of staff to the Illinois governor and the woman he'd help land in jail for murder, mainstream newspapers became tabloids overnight.

Leo reached in his leather jacket for his pen and note pad, eager to brainstorm interview questions with Ted. A red ribbon lodged in the pad's spiral wiring. Grief sucked away his excitement.

"You okay, buddy?" Ted asked.

"What?" Leo realized he was rubbing the soft material. He shoved it back in his pocket. "Sure, sure." He tapped his pen on the note pad and forced himself to focus. "Instead of concentrating on who Carlisle's love interest is, I want his take on why he's leading in the polls. His ratings show him ahead by ten points."

"Even with all the anti-gay sentiment in this country, the guy actually has a shot at the presidency," Ted agreed. "Be sure to ask him about his motives. I mean, we know he's a businessman, not a politician. What about his schooling and work experience led him to run for office? And not just any office, but the presidency. Why does he think he's experienced enough to run the country?"

Leo jotted down notes. "I also want to know his plans to win over the religious right. See if he has a strategy to get past their condemnation of his lifestyle."

"He's been sticking to the issues, saying his private life is private, but he's going to have to address it sooner or later. If Carlisle wins, and his relationship is serious, will his boyfriend be living in the White House? Will he be called the First Life Partner? If they get married, will he be the First Husband? How will he be presented at state dinners?"

"More importantly," Leo said. "How will he and his partner deal with the leaders of countries where homosexuality is illegal? But I don't know how much information he'll be willing to give me."

"Who?" Beth Connor asked as she hustled into the office, carrying a stack of section budgets for that evening's editorial meeting. The young intern had recently been promoted to staff reporter, based upon Leo's recommendation. She handed the budgets to Ted, who tossed them on the nearest pile of papers on his desk.

"Griffin Carlisle."

Beth's bright eyes widened, then she smiled. "No problem. Turn on your charm. He won't know what hit him."

GOD ON MAYHEM STREET

4

When the CTA bus pulled to his stop on Michigan Avenue Saturday morning, Leo hesitated, hoping for a reprieve in the sudden downpour. No such luck. He sprinted to the entrance of Café Spiaggia. Inside, he shook rain off his leather jacket, leaving a puddle on the porcelain floor tiles. He straightened his multi-colored Jerry Garcia tie, finger-combed his damp hair, and rode the elevator to the second-floor restaurant.

Griffin Carlisle sat in a corner booth underneath a fifteenth-century Italian mural reproduction. Two men dressed in black suits, wires dangling from their ears, sat at a nearby table. Carlisle's security detail, no doubt.

Diners drinking wine at tables by the windows or relaxing in other red-couched booths glanced in Carlisle's direction and whispered, but left him alone. The room smelled of seared filet, Italian seasonings, and sweet perfume.

"Leo Townsend." Griffin Carlisle stood as Leo approached. "It's great to meet you." He held out his hand.

Leo's cell phone vibrated in his pants' pocket. *Probably Ted with some additional questions.* He ignored it. He had plenty to work with.

"Good to meet you too, Mr. Carlisle."

Carlisle had a firm handshake, commanding but not intimidating. His hand was larger than Leo's, the hand of a musician. He was known for playing the piano as well as any concert pianist.

"Please, call me Griffin."

Griffin matched Leo's height of six-three, though he was thinner and more angular. At forty-two, he was five years older than Leo and young for a presidential candidate. His short, black hair framed his deep-set blue eyes and had a tousled look to it, in sharp contrast to the precision haircuts the other presidential hopefuls preferred.

Griffin had taken off his suit coat and pushed up the sleeves of his white shirt, probably in an attempt to look like a regular Joe. It didn't work. Their young waitress, apparently recognizing the candidate, blushed when she introduced herself and stumbled when asking for their drink orders. Both men declined alcohol and stuck with water.

"I really appreciate your meeting with me," Leo began, as the waitress left. His phone vibrated again. "I know you're busy planning for this afternoon's rally."

"It's my pleasure. I would do anything for Mary Evans." Griffin leaned in closer, smiling. "Without her tutoring, I wouldn't have passed the bar." He picked up his menu.

Leo's phone stopped vibrating, thankfully. "You earned a dual degree at Northwestern. Isn't that right?"

"A Ph.D. in marketing and a law degree at their Kellogg School of Management."

"And you practiced law, but only for a few years."

"The funny thing about the law," Griffin leaned his elbows on the table, "it's nothing like what you see on TV. I realized that in my first year of law school and concentrated more on the marketing degree. But I'm stubborn. I don't like to throw away opportunities. So I practiced corporate law with Duncan and Murray in Chicago for a few years. Made some money. Then I quit to go into business. Founded Carlisle Websites, my website design company."

"Before websites were common."

"Yes. They were hard to market at the time. Individuals and even some companies didn't really see the need. But I can be very persuasive. Within a year, we were making more money than we could spend. I never opened a law book again."

While examining their menus, Griffin added, "But I'm sure you already know all this."

"Yes."

"You're looking for the 'inside scoop', as they say. You're hoping that you might find out more about my personal life."

"I'm also interested in your take on the issues and your political strategy."

"I appreciate your honesty. So I'll be honest with you." Griffin set his menu aside. "I agreed to this interview because I wanted to meet Eduardo Townsend's brother."

The menu slipped from Leo's hands. "How do you know Eddie?"

"Excuse me." The maître d' approached their table. "We've received an emergency call for you, Mr. Townsend."

"Who is it?" Leo asked.

"A Mr. Eddie Townsend."

"Speak of the devil," Griffin said.

"Did he say why…?" Leo began.

"No. But he sounded upset."

"Take your call," Griffin insisted. "I'm not going anywhere."

"I'm sorry. I won't be long." Steaming, Leo followed the maître d' to the reservations desk and picked up the phone.

"Eddie?"

"Dad's had a heart attack."

"Jesus." Leo closed his eyes and pictured the beads of sweat glistening on his father's forehead.

"We're at Madison General." Eddie's words came out in a rush. "When can you get here?"

"I'm in the middle of an extremely important interview. How about I leave in a few hours?"

"Christ Leo! Dad might not make it!" Eddie's words were edged with desperation.

"Of course. You're right. I'll leave now." He ended the connection, his mind racing. *Shit!* He tried to convince himself that an hour or so wouldn't make a difference, but he remembered his father's red face and heavy breathing earlier that week. At the time, Leo had passed it off as rage.

There was no way around it. He'd have to abandon the most important interview of his career. Leo pulled out his cell phone and punched his editor's number. "Ted, send someone to Spiaggia's as soon as possible. My dad's had a heart attack. It doesn't look good."

"Geez Leo, I'm sorry."

Leo heard a muffled, "Barnes, get your ass over to Café Spiaggia and fill in for Leo." Ted's voice came back clearer. "He's grabbing a cab. Should be there in five minutes." The line went dead.

Leo shot a glance across the restaurant to where Griffin Carlisle stood by their table, shaking hands with someone. The man turned. Rahm Emanuel, the mayor of Chicago.

"Goddamnit!" Leo cursed under his breath. He knew it was ridiculous, but he couldn't help wondering if his father had suffered a heart attack just to sabotage his career.

5

Jacob Landry kneeled on the prayer bench at the foot of his king-sized bed. The bench's red velvet cushion had two permanent indents caused by years of use. His sixty-three-year-old joints argued against kneeling but he ignored the pain, almost took pleasure in it. It brought him closer to the suffering of his Lord.

Holding his palms together in reverence, Jacob began his prayers. He asked for a bull market so he could sell some stocks and put a down payment on the land next to the Church of Our Beloved Savior. Spurred by Rev. Wallace's compassionate sermons and Jake's keen marketing strategies, the congregation had grown. Once he financed the much-needed addition, the elders wouldn't hesitate to rename the building The Landry Church of Our Beloved Savior. Maybe if he cashed in enough stock he could build that badly needed children's wing, too. Then they'd change the name to The Church of Our Beloved Savior Landry. He stifled a chuckle.

His prayers shifted to Mrs. Whitford, a Sunday school teacher at Our Beloved Savior and one of the church's biggest benefactors. The poor dear was at Madison General having tests for chest pains. Familiar with the old broad's eating habits, Jake knew it was indigestion, but he'd visit her later this afternoon just the same.

Next, he prayed for Red Carmichael, a longtime member of the Endeavor Village Board, to finally kick the bucket. That infuriating man fought progress in Endeavor every inch of the way. Jacob felt it his duty as village president, a title he held dear, to quash Red's efforts. If it weren't for Jacob's well-placed monetary inducements, Red would have succeeded in blocking construction of the new Jacob I. Landry Bowl Haven. Imagine depriving people of Friday night leagues simply to save a few scrawny trees in Bailey's Woods. Jacob's prayer wasn't purely vindictive, though. Poor Red had prostate cancer and had become a shriveled prune. Better to have him die quickly than lose the use of his pecker.

Finally, Jacob said a few words for Isabella Townsend, asking God to embrace her in heaven. He had loved that woman for forty-five years, from the moment she drove down Lakeview Avenue thinking she'd arrived in Portage. But the Lord let her stray into the arms of Frank Townsend. Now God had seen fit to take her home. At least Jacob would be spared the pain of seeing her Sophia Loren good looks every time she ventured into the village, and the pain of having her rebuke his advances.

And with Isabella gone, it'd be easier to finally get his hands on the Townsend farm, easier to pressure a grieving, disheartened Frank to sell.

Two years ago, the village had annexed Frank's property. Frank screamed at the village board the night they approved the annexation and condemned their actions. His screams were futile. Jake promised to reward vacations to the most influential board members with the extra tax revenue. Their decision to annex had been quick.

Now it was obvious that Frank was increasingly weighed down by the higher tax burden. His buildings were dilapidated and his fields untended. The man himself looked ragged. Soon Jacob would own the Townsend farm and all of his financial prayers would be answered.

The smell of apple-smoked bacon and buttered toast wafted up from the kitchen. His wife, Grace, was frying bacon for his favorite lunch of BLTs, fried new potatoes, and freshly-squeezed lemonade. His growling stomach drowned out his whispered *Lord's Prayer*, something he recited when his mind drifted.

Willing his thoughts back on track, Jacob began his most important prayer. Every day, Jacob prayed to God to help him combat all the threats to Christianity.

Jacob fought such threats on a daily basis as Endeavor village president but now there were national threats all the way to the US presidency. Optimistically, Jake had hoped that his information was wrong, that Griffin Carlisle wasn't going to run for president. When that homo announced his candidacy on national television, Jacob had run to the toilet and thrown up a healthy portion of Grace's onion-glazed pot roast. His wife sympathized but didn't clean up after him until *Wheel of Fortune* ended. The special report on Carlisle interrupting Grace's game show had upset her more than some queer running for national office.

The downstairs telephone rang.

"Jake," Grace called from the kitchen.

"Dammit, woman. I'm praying!"

"Tell that to Vernon. He's on the phone."

Forty-one-year-old Vernon Smith was built like a linebacker for the Green Bay Packers and had the brains to keep up with Jacob's elaborate schemes. He was Jake's right-hand man and co-conspirator. Jacob loved him like a son.

"Vern. You're interrupting my noontime prayers."

"I'm thinkin' those prayers may be answered. Old Man Townsend's been MedFlighted to Madison General. Rumor is it's a major heart attack. Guess his wife's passing was too much for him."

Jacob wiped his chin. *Shit, was that drool?* He stifled a laugh. "You be ready in five minutes. We're leaving for Madison."

6

"When Dad came in from the fields," Eddie said, his dark hair disheveled, his black Art Institute of Chicago t-shirt drooping over his torn jeans, "he looked like hell. Red face, perspiring, shirt untucked." A blue, white, red, and black-splattered replica of Jackson Pollock's *Summertime* covered the spokes of Eddie's wheelchair. The rubber tires squeaked on the hospital tile as he turned a corner.

"He looked like that on the day of mom's funeral." Leo tried to ignore the sterile smell of antiseptic that failed to mask the sick body odors of patients.

Even with the rain, Leo had made good time getting to Madison. But the minute he saw the anguish in his brother's chiseled face he wished he'd been there sooner, and immediately felt guilty for wanting to stay in Chicago. "I assumed it was because he was mad at me for missing the service."

"I thought the same thing this morning," Eddie said. "He asked if I'd heard from you. I gave him some bullshit about your workload. He broke out in a cold sweat and I thought, 'here comes the swearing.' But then he—" Eddie's voice faltered. He cleared his throat. "—he clutched his left arm. Swayed. Fell on top of me. Trapped me under him." He stopped wheeling.

Was Eddie remembering the triathlon tragedy? The claustrophobic crush of the mob? Was he reliving the anguish of his legs breaking, his spinal cord snapping? Leo squeezed his brother's shoulder.

Eddie cranked on the wheels and rolled down the hallway toward the waiting room. He had refused to buy an electric chair, declaring that if his legs couldn't get a workout at least his arms would. "Luckily, the weather cleared so my bedroom windows were open. Johnny was in the barn but he heard me shouting. Came running. Lifted Dad off me. Started CPR while I called 9-1-1. I've never felt so goddamned helpless."

"I'm sorry." *It's my fault you're helpless. No. The shooter's fault. He scared the crowd into stampeding. I couldn't have done anything to prevent it.*

Would Leo ever believe that? He rubbed the scar carved into his jaw, a memento from a panicked spectator's diamond ring as she punched him. "What do the doctors think?"

"There are blockages. Three or more. They're going to try an angioplasty. Stents. But he might need bypass surgery."

"Damn." Leo collapsed onto the nearest waiting room chair; the stiff, utilitarian cushions not at all comforting.

His dad was in bad shape, his brother trying to hold it together. Leo needed to be here. Still, he couldn't shake the image of Barnes barging into Spiaggia's with a broad grin on his coal-black face, like a kid on Christmas morning. Griffin Carlisle had expressed his concern for Leo's father and promised another interview down the road, but that would be a side note. Barnes would get the scoop of a lifetime and Leo, well…

None of that mattered now.

"Do they know how long the operation will take?"

"No," Eddie said. "Not until they know the extent of the damage."

Eddie's usual what-the-hell attitude had been replaced by a vulnerability Leo hadn't seen since the triathlon stampede. "How are you holding up?" Leo asked.

Eddie shrugged.

"Wait, did you say *Johnny* performed CPR. What about Ron?"

"Left a few months back for better wages."

"On a factory farm?"

"In Illinois."

"Ron had been with Dad for twenty years."

"He's got a family to support and Dad couldn't offer more money or benefits." Eddie scratched at the stubble on his face. "Anyway, MedFlight came. Landed behind the house, where Mom's tomatoes used to be. I was a mess. Johnny drove me to the hospital."

He must have been in bad shape. Eddie never let anyone drive the car Leo bought him after the accident, a Ford Focus ZX3 outfitted with swivel seats and hand-held controls.

"Where's Johnny now?"

"Had to get back to the farm. Man, I'm glad he was around. Shit-covered boots and all." Eddie managed a smile.

For years, Isabella had pleaded with Johnny to wipe his boots before coming in the house but he'd always forget. Then, one day, she made a batch of chocolate cannoli and refused to give him a taste until he left his boots on the back steps. Johnny never forgot again. Until that morning.

"So now, what? We wait?"

"Yeah."

Leo drummed his fingers on his leg, itching to check emails on his phone, but decided anything he read wouldn't register. "Can I get you something? Coffee?"

"Already drank five cups. I'm wired. What I really need is a shot of Dewar's."

"I hear ya. As soon as Dad's out of surgery," Leo cleared his thick throat, "and everything's fine, we'll head over to State Street."

"Deal." Eddie managed a smile. "So who were you interviewing?"

"It's not important."

"Bullshit. You almost didn't come. Who was she, some leggy model?"

"Griffin Carlisle."

"*What?!*"

"Look, I know how you feel about gays," Leo said. "That they flaunt their lifestyle too much, but you're wrong."

"Wrong? Have you seen the news coverage of the gay pride parade in Chicago?"

"What we think doesn't matter. Griffin Carlisle could be the next president." Leo glanced at the clock. "Carlisle's rally is starting." He took

GOD ON MAYHEM STREET

stock of the other waiting room visitors. A family deep in conversation. A couple absently flipping through magazines. An elderly woman consulting with a nurse. No one paid attention to the *Criminal Minds* rerun on the flat-screen TV. He flipped through the channels to CNN.

Thousands of people, dressed in everything from conservative street clothes to pink boas, had converged in Millennium Park under a slate-grey sky. The giant metal bean sculpture reflected their squished image. Men in khakis and women in long denim skirts clutched Bibles and signs that read: God Made Adam & Eve NOT Adam & Steve; God Condemns Homosexuals including Griffin Carlisle - Leviticus 18:22; and AIDS Is God's Answer to Homosexuality.

Others wore rainbow scarves, hats, t-shirts, and jean jackets. Griffin Carlisle had asked the gay community not to bring signs. Apparently one young man didn't get the memo. Cameras zoomed in on his Jesus Had Two Daddies placard. A woman brandishing a Children Need a Mom & a Dad sign didn't find it funny. A policeman on horseback steered his gelding between the two, defusing the situation.

"See? Crazies," Eddie said.

"The religious activists or the gay community?"

"Both."

The camera cut back to Griffin Carlisle, waving as he sauntered over to the podium. "Good afternoon, Chicago!" Carlisle's voice boomed. "Thank you for coming out—"

Laughter and cheers.

"—to hear what the next president of these United States plans for the future."

More cheers and a few jeers. Leo wondered if Carlisle would get through the whole speech without inciting a riot. Leo had written an article about the extra cost to the city of Chicago for police protection. The bill was expected to be three times more than when Carlisle's opponents had come to town.

"I am an unusual presidential candidate in many ways, but probably the most unusual is that I—"

"Here it comes," Eddie said.

"Shh."

"—believe government should stay out of people's wallets as well as their bedrooms."

Shouts and applause. Carlisle smiled, raising his hands for silence.

"Taxes are a necessary evil, but where your tax dollars go should be your choice. If you are a pacifist, you should not have to pay for war. If you are an environmentalist, you might want your tax dollars to go to the national parks and the EPA and not to foreign aid. When I am president, you will dictate how your tax dollars are spent. Using new tax forms, you will specify exactly where your money goes. You'll have the power, not the IRS!"

A roar from the crowd.

Carlisle let the applause die down before he continued, "My opponents, particularly those who are career politicians, couch unlimited government spending under the guise of providing quality education. What they do not say is that every year we spend more money on public schooling, and every year the quality of education in this country declines. No more. When I am president, I will turn control of education back to your local schools where it belongs. The bloated US Department of Education will look like a one-room schoolhouse."

Cheers, even from some of the far-right activists.

"Additionally, when I am president, I will uphold the Supreme Court's decision granting you the freedom to decide whom to marry."

A roar from the rainbow crowd.

"And you will decide how you will live and die without interference from Big Brother, the federal government.

"When I am president, our national defense policies will be strong and clear. We will guide only those governments who ask for guidance. We will respect foreign governments with the same amount of respect they afford us. We will defend the United States of America against any form of aggress—"

"Well, well, if it isn't the Townsend brothers," a voice bellowed from the hospital hallway. Jacob Landry, carrying a vase full of pink carnations, strutted toward Leo and Eddie. Vernon Smith hulked behind. Smith had been a senior at Endeavor High School when Leo was a freshman, and had enjoyed bullying Leo's scrawnier classmates.

"Christ," Leo said.

"Satan," Eddie amended.

"What unfortunate circumstance brings you to this neck of the woods?" Landry asked. His hand shot out. Leo shook it. Eddie kept his hands folded in his lap. Surprised by his brother's rudeness, Leo gave Eddie a questioning look before answering, "Dad's had a heart attack."

"I am sorry to hear that," Landry replied. "And so soon after Isabella's death."

"He's not dead," Eddie hissed.

"No, no, of course not. I didn't mean…"

"What brings you to Madison, Mr. Landry?" Leo asked.

"Dear boy, call me 'Jacob'." Landry's grin was too jovial for the occasion. "Vern and I are visiting Mrs. Whitford. Brought her flowers." He held up the vase. "Poor old angel thinks she has heart issues, so she's having tests. My guess is indigestion. She certainly can pack in the brats and baked beans. Isn't that right, Vern?" Landry glanced at the mountain of a man who crossed his arms over his massive chest.

"Nice of you to visit her," Leo said, to be polite.

"I like to do my part for the widows of Endeavor—"

"I'll bet," Eddie said.

"—and anyone else who might need a helping hand," Jacob continued, apparently not hearing Eddie.

Leo turned back to the TV.

The television crowd cheered again.

"What's goin' on?" Smith asked.

"Griffin Carlisle's—"

Landry punched the television off.

"Hey! I was watching that." Leo started for the TV.

Landry snagged Leo's arm. "You'd think a hospital of this caliber wouldn't allow such trash on their television set." He steered Leo to the couch. "Why don't we sit down? It's been awhile since we shot the breeze."

Leo couldn't remember ever shooting the breeze with Jacob Landry. He sloughed off the village president's hand and headed for the TV.

Vernon Smith, who had been the largest middle linebacker in

Endeavor High School's football history and looked like he could still bench three hundred and fifty pounds, blocked Leo. "Don't mess with Jake." He sprayed Leo with spittle that stank of stale beer.

Leo's instinct was to back away but his pride rooted him. "Mr. Smith, it's been a very bad day. Don't make it worse."

"I don't give two shits about your day. You shouldn't shove people."

"Vernon, it's quite all right." Landry patted Smith's back. "Leo didn't mean anything. People's manners go awry when they're distraught."

"*My* manners?!"

"Leo," Eddie interrupted.

"*What?!*"

"The doctor's coming."

7

The doctor shed her surgical cap, revealing matted brown hair. Dark circles underlined her eyes. She wore no jewelry or make-up and her blue uniform was wrinkled. She frowned, but Leo told himself that might not mean anything. Surely she was exhausted from the two-hour operation. "Your father's surgery took longer than expected but it went well," she said to Eddie. He relaxed back into his wheelchair.

"That's great!" Leo said.

The surgeon glanced at him and started to speak, but couldn't find the words. When Leo was younger, he'd gotten a kick out of seeing girls flustered by his good looks. Later, it had annoyed him. He'd tried friendly smiles, which usually made things worse. Eventually, he learned to ignore women's reactions.

"Leo Townsend." He held out his hand.

The doctor regained her composure. "Nice to meet you. I'm Dr. Pierson." She eyed Landry and Smith.

Leo had no intention of introducing them. "Is there somewhere we can speak privately?"

"My office is around the corner."

"Yes, you go on—" Landry began.

Leo turned his back on the village president and his henchman and followed the doctor down the hall.

Afternoon sunshine poured in the windows of her private office, a welcome relief after the earlier rain showers. The windows supported a makeshift greenhouse; ferns, cacti, and a blooming hibiscus took over half of the room. A desk, a few bookshelves, and a coat rack holding a white lab coat filled the other half.

"Good news," the doctor began as she sat behind her desk, tossing her cap next to her computer. "Open-heart surgery wasn't necessary. Instead, we performed a coronary angioplasty and placed three stents in his arteries. He's tolerating them well and is currently under observation in the recovery room. But with all the blockage, I'm wondering—did Frank complain of discomfort before his heart attack?"

"Not to me," Eddie said. "But he had slowed down."

"This morning you mentioned that your mother recently died of breast cancer," the doctor said. "That must have taken its toll."

"He did everything for her," Eddie said. "Leo and I suggested hiring a nurse but Dad insisted on doing it all himself. He fed her, when she'd eat anything. Gave her sponge baths, read to her. I offered assistance but he'd brush me off. Told me it was his duty as her husband." Eddie choked on his words, coughed. "Mom knew her care drained him. She finally convinced him it was time for hospice." Eddie's voice trailed off.

Then he cleared his throat. "But there must have been something going on with Dad even before Mom's cancer diagnosis. He never harvested the soybeans last fall. He kept telling our hired hands not to bother, that he'd get to it."

"That's not like him." Leo wondered why this was the first time he'd heard of it.

"Definitely," Eddie agreed. "And Dad may have screwed up the cows' rations. They've been losing weight. Doc Krueger, our vet, can't pinpoint the cause."

Leo had no idea this had been happening. He knew his dad wouldn't say anything to him. Hell, they rarely spoke. But why hadn't Eddie told him?

"Did he complain of heartburn? Dizziness?"

"He didn't mention being dizzy, though that would explain why he neglected the farm. Heartburn? Yeah, he mentioned that a few times."

"It sounds like he had coronary issues for a while," Dr. Pierson said. "In any case, the angioplasty was successful. However, because this was an emergency procedure due to his heart attack, he'll have to stay in the hospital for several days. We'll monitor his heart rhythm. Watch for complications."

"And once he's home?" Leo asked.

"His bedroom's upstairs," Eddie said. "Should we move him downstairs? To my bedroom?"

"No," the doctor said. "He can manage stairs at a slow pace. He'll have to take it easy for at least a week, no strenuous activity, no heavy lifting."

"He's going to love that," Eddie said.

Dr. Pierson reached into her desk drawer, selected a pamphlet with pictures of hearts and vegetables, and handed it to Eddie. "He'll have to take clopidogrel and aspirin to thin his blood. Also, he'll have to change his eating habits. Avoid foods high in saturated fats. Stay away from dairy products, other than skim or low-fat milk."

"Good thing Dad's no longer a dairy farmer," Leo kidded.

"Mr. Townsend, this is nothing to joke about."

"What I'd really like to know," Eddie said, coming to Leo's rescue, "is will Dad be able to manage the farm again?"

"He's sixty-seven. Maybe it's time he retired."

"I asked him to consider retiring," Eddie said. "One of the few times he yelled at me. Farming is his life. It's all he's ever wanted to do."

Leo agreed. It would be like someone telling Leo he could no longer write. How could his father give up something he was so passionate about, that defined him?

"Farming is strenuous," the doctor said. "And for Frank—particularly dangerous."

"Shit," Eddie said.

"I'm sorry. It's important that you realize how grave the situation is." Her pager beeped. "I have to go."

Leo offered his hand. "Thanks for saving his life."

Dr. Pierson finally managed a small, tired smile.

As Leo followed Eddie to the office door, he glanced over the plants and out the window at Wisconsin's gleaming white state capitol and the backed-up traffic on Park Street. He wondered if Dr. Pierson had ever set foot on a farm.

8

Leo trudged beside his brother's wheelchair down the sterile hall, past nurses barking orders on phones and hunched over computers at their stations. One bleary-eyed attendant pulled away from her screen long enough to grab a Styrofoam cup of coffee. She drank the dregs, crushed the cup, tossed it in a trash can, and resumed tapping on the keyboard without missing a beat. Over the public announcement system, an urgent male voice paged a Dr. Singh.

Leo and Eddie passed rooms where curtains were pulled back, exposing blanketed patients hooked to beeping machines. One elderly man moaned while a frail woman bent over his bed, holding his hand. Leo looked away, dreading what they'd find in his father's room. He braced himself. Thankfully, they didn't run into Landry and Smith again.

When they entered Frank's room, Leo realized nothing could have prepared him for seeing his father prone in a hospital bed. Sheets crumpled around his legs and chest. His thin gown hung low over one shoulder, exposing heart monitor wires among grey chest hairs. The wires snaked over to a monitor on a table to the left of the bed. The forefinger of Frank's left hand wore a blood pressure gauge. Clear tape over a white gauze bandage covered the spot where an IV entered his hand. It trailed up his arm to a bag of clear liquid hanging on a pole. The window blinds were drawn. Only the overhead fluorescent light illuminated the room, accentuating the creases in Frank's ashen face, making him look shriveled. His head had lolled to the side. His mouth hung open, and a bit of drool ran down his chin.

Leo felt nauseous and weak. He leaned on Eddie's chair for support.

"Whoa, big guy," Eddie said. "Grab a seat."

The monitor beeped frantically for a few seconds, startling Leo, then resumed a regular pace. Frayed, he made it to a chair in the corner and tried to adjust to this new image of his father.

Eddie reached out and touched Frank's calloused hand, careful not to disturb the IV.

Leo remembered those large hands lifting him into the tractor cab on the morning of his sixth birthday. An eerie fog had blanketed the fields of green sprouts. Isabella protested the trip, afraid it was too dangerous, but his father had ignored her. His mother's fears scared Leo but thrilled him, too. He never liked the farm animals, the barnyard smell, the chores, but he'd dreamed of riding in his father's new, shiny red, International Harvester tractor.

When Frank turned the ignition, the engine had roared to life and the cab vibrated, shaking the image of Clark Kent on Leo's pajama top and making the tiny Superman images on his pajama bottoms quiver. The tractor climbed over dirt mounds and dipped into ruts. The tread lugs on the tires kicked up clumps of mud. Hitting a particularly deep rut, Leo bounced off the seat and onto the cab's metal floor. His dad braked and reached for him. "Are you okay?"

Leo's bottom ached and he'd scratched his arm on the right brake pedal. "I bounced!"

And then his father had laughed, big and uninhibited. Leo wrapped his arms around his father's neck, the laughter shaking his small body.

Now, his father might lose the tractor, the house, the farm. He'd already lost his wife.

Leo's journalistic instincts kicked in. He wanted to know everything about the farm's situation, whether the land could be managed without his dad or whether they had to sell it. But as Eddie squeezed Frank's hand he let out a shaky sigh as if on the verge of tears, so Leo postponed

GOD ON MAYHEM STREET   39

that discussion. Instead, he decided to clear the air. "How angry was Dad when I left Mom's funeral lunch?"

Eddie studied Leo for a moment as if he'd forgotten he was in the room. Then his watery green eyes brightened. "Shittin' bricks. But then Sally from the diner arrived with her famous triple-fudge brownies. Did you know Mom worked at Sally's Diner when she first came to Endeavor?"

Leo shook his head.

"Sally told some great stories, like the first time Mom made the coffee. The thickest, blackest sludge Sally had ever seen. Mom had attempted to make espresso but the diners preferred Sally's bitter, watered-down American coffee."

Leo remembered when his father bought his mother an espresso machine for her birthday. "Finally," she'd said, "real coffee."

"Dad relaxed," Eddie continued. "He reminisced with Sally and even cried a little."

"Good." Leo now felt the decision to leave early had been the right one. "Hey, what ever happened to Gerald Morrison? The building that housed *The Marquette County Epitome* was boarded up."

"Landry," Eddie said. "He didn't like Morrison's editorial honesty, particularly when it pointed out the village president's dishonest tendencies. Landry bought out the paper and shut it down."

"So much for freedom of the press. Why didn't Landry develop the property? He's redeveloped everything else in town."

"He left it vacant as a lesson to anyone who crosses him."

"And yet people re-elect him."

"They look at the vacant newspaper building as one of Landry's weird eccentricities. It's something they put up with because they credit him with Endeavor's newfound prosperity."

"You don't like him," Leo said.

"Hell, no. I don't trust him. He's a pure politician driven by power. Acts only if it benefits himself."

They listened to the beep of the heart monitor then Eddie asked, "Speaking of politicians, what did you think of Griffin Carlisle?"

Deep in thought about the farm, the question caught Leo off guard.

"Oh. I, um, I didn't really get a chance to talk to him."

Eddie waited.

Leo loosened his tie as he remembered his first impression of Griffin. "He didn't seem like a pure politician. Quite the opposite of your buddy, Landry." Leo thought his brother would scoff at this but instead he inexplicably grinned.

"I've interviewed a lot of politicians," Leo continued. "They draw you in immediately. As if you've been friends for years. Eventually you realize that it's all show. You're a tool for them." He leaned forward, resting his elbows on his knees. "But Carlisle didn't try to draw me in. He didn't flatter me."

"There wasn't time."

"True. But in my experience, politicians start their conversations with false praise. Not Carlisle. He did mention you—"

"I Shot the Sheriff" rang from Leo's jacket. Glancing at his phone, he said, "It's my editor. I'd better take it."

"Sure, go ahead," Eddie said.

Leo ducked out into the hall.

"How's your dad?" Ted asked.

"Good." Leo passed the nurses' station and found a vacant family lounge. Someone had left yesterday's *Wisconsin State Journal* on the table. He glanced at the headlines, then walked over to the window. "The angioplasty was successful." He pulled aside the vertical blinds to get a good view of the Wisconsin State Capitol, an almost exact replica of the United States Capitol in Washington, D.C. "How was the Carlisle interview?"

"Terrific, though Barnes hasn't told me much. I'd put him on the line, but he's writing like a madman trying to get it done for tomorrow's edition. Front page material, he's promised me. Oh wait, here he comes with a big, shit-eating grin."

"Leo." Barnes' baritone voice came over the phone. "How's your dad?"

"He's going to be fine. Thanks. Tell me about Carlisle."

"I've got the full take on his platform. A social liberal as you might expect, but a conservative fiscally because of his business background. Probably one of the easiest interviews I've ever done."

"He talked about his personal life?"

"Well, no, not in so many words. But for the first time he's released vital details about his platform. The political pundits will eat it up. Here's Ted."

Great, instead of writing an exclusive about those details, I get to read about them in the paper.

"Barnes will cover your other assignments with Beth's help," Ted said. "Until you can get back."

"No need. I've got my computer. I can make a few calls—"

"Beth's already on it. Though she might call you if she can't read your scribbled notes. Keep me posted on your dad." The line went dead.

Leo stared at his iPhone. *Damn, am I that easily replaced? What the hell, those other assignments are routine. But the Griffin interview—that was the assignment of the century.* He opened the small refrigerator, grabbed two water bottles for himself and Eddie, and trudged back to his father's room.

Eddie seemed mesmerized by the beeping machine and drank the water absent-mindedly.

Leo wanted to know the condition of the farm and how soon he could get back to Chicago, but even though their father slept, it didn't feel right to talk about it in front of him. "Dinner?"

The hospital cafeteria's white walls and tile flooring matched the sterility of the rest of the building. Greasy fish smells came from the kitchen. A techno music mix droned from the sound system. Plastic tulips standing in Dollar Store vases on ersatz wooden tables added some color to the room, but instead of being cheery they were depressingly dusty. The chrome chairs around each table seemed designed for discomfort so people wouldn't linger over their food, which proved as uninspired as the room.

Leo grabbed a tray and loaded pizza slices and two large glasses of Diet Pepsi onto it, then followed Eddie in search of a handicap-accessible table. All were occupied, including one where four able-bodied businessmen argued over a stack of papers and ignored Eddie as he wheeled past. Leo bumped the shoulder of the closest man, spilling most of his soda onto the table. The men cursed as they frantically blotted their papers.

"Nicely done," Eddie said, when Leo caught up to him.

They claimed a vacant table in the corner farthest away from the businessmen. Leo pulled a chair out of the way and Eddie maneuvered as close as he could, then they dug into their pizza. The pepperoni on Leo's slice left puddles of grease in the semi-melted mozzarella. He ate around the burnt sections of crust then washed it down with the remainder of his flat Diet Pepsi. "How bad are things on the farm?"

Eddie picked a piece of pepperoni off his pizza, ate it, and wiped his fingers on a paper napkin. "Not sure. Dad pretended he had everything under control. I guess he didn't want me to worry. When he did admit to a few problems, he told me not to tell you." He crumpled the napkin and tossed it on the tray.

"Yesterday I overheard Johnny say the cows were doing better," Eddie continued. "But we've lost the soybean crop. Without that income, I don't know how Dad will make payments on his loans. And if he defaults on those loans—"

"He'll lose the farm."

"Everything. The house that great-grandpa built and that giant oak he planted. You know, the one Grandpa Sawyer defaced by carving his and Grandma's initials in it. Our pet cemetery, Tadpole Creek, and the well Dad dug that we'd double-dare each other to climb into—"

"Isn't that where you lost your virginity?"

Eddie laughed. It was good to hear.

"I'm still not sure how you managed it. That sucker was deep."

"We didn't actually make it into the well…" Eddie massaged his stubbled chin. "She said the huge pile of dirt reminded her of a beach."

"Some beach. Rocks and chunks of dirt."

"And that crystal you found."

"I'd forgotten about that. Did you know I gave it to Mom for Mother's Day?"

"You cheap bastard."

"Hey, I sprung for a velvet pouch to put it in. You know Mom, she loved it." Leo sighed. "Damn, I miss her."

"Me, too." Eddie's voice was thick. He took a drink of his Diet Pepsi. "Everything will be gone.

GOD ON MAYHEM STREET

"After my… accident… there were a lot of medical bills. Before that, the village annexed the farm, and the taxes skyrocketed. Dad took out a second mortgage. Or was it a third? Sold a lot of equipment. When my graphic design business became successful, I offered to pay him back for the medical bills but he refused. And he insisted I keep you out of it. Guess I should've gone over the books with him months ago. But I'm not good with numbers. I always left the finances to him."

"He wanted it that way. You said yourself how stubborn he is." Leo took another bite of soggy pizza, dropped it on the chipped plate, and shoved it aside.

Eddie finished his slice and placed his empty dish under Leo's. "He's proud of us. You at the paper. And even though I couldn't physically help him, he's proud that I established my own agency. He didn't want us distracted by the farm."

Leo found that hard to believe. His father was resentful and far from supportive. But if Eddie wanted to believe otherwise, he wouldn't correct him. Instead, he went into plan mode. "Let's get a hotel in Madison tonight. I'll drop you back here at the hospital first thing tomorrow morning before driving to the farm. You can make sure Dad's getting the care he needs. I'll stop back tomorrow night—"

"Don't drive back and forth. We'll get a nearby hotel. I'll use the Green Cabs. They're handicap accessible."

"I don't know—"

"Jesus Leo, I'm in a wheelchair, not a stroller."

"Obviously." Leo pointed to the Pollock splatter painting covering the wheels.

Eddie ignored him. "Get to the farm. Get it straightened out. You can pick us up when Dad's released."

"Okay, but I'll be back on Monday. You'll need a break from the hospital by then."

9

Leo made the mistake of grabbing a copy of *The Chicago Examiner* from the hospital gift shop and reading it before he left Madison on Sunday. The headline read, "Griffin Carlisle Uncovered. By Staff Reporter Travis Barnes." The article and a flattering picture of Griffin shaking the hands of Iowa voters filled most of the front page. The story took up all of pages six and seven, with a few pictures of Griffin giving speeches and meeting people in rural town halls and city conference centers.

The article was good. Damn good.

Leo spent the hour-long drive up I-39 to Endeavor mentally reviewing it and periodically glancing at the folded newspaper on the Mustang's passenger seat. It included the essentials of Carlisle's foreign and domestic policies without being bogged down in dry details and quoted political pundits who praised his stances. Predictably, Carlisle's rivals panned it as extreme liberalism, which added terrific conflict to the story. Barnes had written a prize-winning piece.

Leo tried hard to convince himself he'd have other opportunities. Maybe even another interview with Carlisle. After all, Carlisle hadn't yet divulged the name of his boyfriend.

By the time Leo turned his Mustang onto the long gravel driveway to his childhood home, he felt optimistic. But when he had to maneuver around a black sedan and a baby blue '58 Cadillac Coupe DeVille parked in front of the house, his sour mood returned.

When Leo was eight, he'd seen Jacob Landry's vintage Caddie for the first time. Coming out of Baker's Ice Cream Shoppe on Lakeview Avenue with a double-dip chocolate ice cream cone, he caught sight of the blue car and stopped in mid-lick. It was the first time he had fallen in love.

Landry put a strong hand on his shoulder and offered him a ride, once Leo finished his cone, of course. Tempting, but Leo barely knew the man and his school principal had lectured just that morning about being wary of strangers. Leo had thanked Mr. Landry and walked away. His first regret.

So what is that car doing here now? Is Landry stopping for a neighborly visit? Eyeing the black sedan next to the Caddy, Leo didn't think so. He parked and got out. The Cadillac's hood felt cool to the touch.

Leo vaulted the steps two at a time, whipped open the screen door, and tried the door knob. Locked. He walked the length of the porch, his dress shoes scraping the wooden floor boards, and peered around the corner of the house. Across the yard, several men stood by the silo. One pointed at the fields. Landry. *At least they didn't find a way into the house.* Leo pictured Landry rifling through his father's file cabinet and his mother's lingerie drawer.

He turned and bumped into Johnny. "Jesus. You scared the crap outta me."

"Sorry, didn't mean to." The wiry, middle-aged man shoved his hands in his Wrangler jeans. "Surprised to see you. Thought you'd be in Madison a few days."

"Dad's doing well and Eddie's keeping him company. I decided to check on the farm." Leo pointed at the cars. "What the hell's going on? What's Landry doing here? Who are those men?"

"They're from the bank." Johnny looked puzzled. "You didn't know they were comin'?"

"No."

"Mr. Landry said he talked to you yesterday." The farmhand shoved an electronic cigarette into the corner of his mouth. "Geez, Leo, I'm really sorry. If I'd known you were—"

Leo patted Johnny's back. "Don't worry about it. But do me a favor?"

"Sure."

"Go into the office and pull all the financial and operational records from January of last year until now." Leo handed Johnny a house key. "Livestock, feed, equipment, everything. Check it over. Make sure it's accurate. Take notes if you have to. I'll be there soon."

Leo jogged down the steps and around the house, past the lilac bushes and Isabella's barren clothesline. Avoiding puddles and mud, he caught up to Landry, Vernon Smith, and a business-suited pair of men as they entered the cattle barn.

"Jacob Landry!" Leo yelled above the bellowing cows. He gagged at the stench of animal urine.

Landry waved. The cuff of his pale blue shirt slid down, exposing a gold Cartier watch. "Leo, my boy, good to see you. How's Frank?"

"Fine. What the hell are you doing here?"

One of the businessmen, a tall, good-looking black man, started to answer, but Landry cut him off, "This is Oliver Tenney from Chicago. Standing next to Vernon is Emmett Everson, Endeavor Bank president." Landry put his hand on the back of the banker, who fidgeted with the brass buttons on his navy suit coat.

"I don't give a damn who they are. Get them off my property."

"*Your* property?" The village president smirked. "A few, shall we say, discrepancies have occurred with your *father's* loans. We thought we'd stop by to take a look. You don't mind, do you?"

"I do. Your timing couldn't be worse. Or was that intentional?"

"Oh, no, nothing like that." Landry shook his forefinger. "We were driving to the Branson place and thought we'd stop by."

"Uh, huh. Well, I'm sure the Bransons are wondering where you are." Leo gestured toward the driveway. "And about those so-called discrepancies, I'll stop by the bank tomorrow. During business hours."

"There's no rush—" Everson said in a high, thin voice.

"Listen," Landry interrupted, "we've had a chance to look around. We've noticed burdock and ragweed covering the fields. Fields which should have been plowed and planted by now. Some of the cattle are looking a little under the weather. With your dad in the hospital, it'll be

GOD ON MAYHEM STREET

tough to manage the farm. There'll be his medical bills. The mortgages. And the property taxes, of course. Those, as you well know, are due July thirty-first."

"What's your point?" Leo gritted his teeth.

"I'm prepared to make Frank another, very generous offer on the farm." Everson started to interject but the village president stopped him with a raised hand. "It's my way of helping him out of a difficult situation. 'Let each of you look not only to his own interests but also to the interests of others. Luke 6:38.'"

"Excuse me?"

"Simply assisting a neighbor. Look, I know farming's not your thing. Heck, you left as soon as you could."

"It's time *you* left." Leo began ushering them to the driveway.

Vernon Smith growled.

"Son," Landry continued as he followed Leo across the yard, "I meant that as a compliment. I've always admired the way you went after your dreams."

"Selling's out of the question." Leo crossed his arms and leaned against his car.

"Oh sure, sure, I understand. Just giving you that option." Landry flicked a ladybug off the Caddie's shiny door, then opened it. "If you're not prepared to sell, there are several financial issues we need to settle. We'd hate to see the bank foreclose… those things happen… when bills and taxes aren't paid." Landry's solemn face broke into a sneer. "I'd be happy to meet with you first thing tomorrow morning. Come on boys," he said over his shoulder as he slid into his vehicle. "Let's see what kind of pie Millie Branson has for us today."

Watching the cars pull away, Leo wondered if he'd heard Landry right. Had the village president actually threatened foreclosure? As far as Leo knew, Landry wasn't even on the bank board. He tried to shake off the threat and control his anger as he climbed the porch steps.

Before he went inside, he checked the soles of his loafers, making sure he didn't bring the farm into the house. He'd have to go into town in the next few days for jeans, t-shirts, and toiletries, things he'd left in Chicago in his hurry to get to the hospital.

He found Johnny sitting at the dining room table in a cloud of menthol vapors. The farmhand puffed on his e-cigarette as he sifted through cardboard boxes overflowing with paper. A spring breeze blew through the open windows, fluttering the sheer curtains and scattering several documents across the cherry-wood surface.

Leo gathered the wayward papers, his fingers running over the deep gouge he'd carved in the tabletop at age five. When his mother discovered his handiwork, she'd sent him to his father. Instead of spanking Leo, Frank spent the afternoon teaching him how to whittle wooden toy soldiers.

Vaguely wondering what happened to those soldiers, Leo took off his jacket, tossed it on a chair, and began sifting through the nearest box.

Several hours later, he assessed the assorted piles of bank statements, tax documents, and livestock and crop records. "We've made some good progress. How 'bout a lunch break?"

Johnny followed Leo into the kitchen and retrieved dishes and silverware. Leo opened the refrigerator and took out Tupperware containers half-full with salads, cold cuts, and sliced cheeses, and the remainder of a cherry pie—leftovers from the funeral.

He took slices of Wonder Bread out of the plastic bag, missing the crusty loaves his mother baked, and then threw together a ham and Swiss sandwich. When he lifted the lid off a container of fruit salad, a sickening ripe smell hit him. He quickly dumped the contents in the compost pail under the kitchen sink and rinsed the plastic dish. Next to the sink browning lilies and faded roses wilted in a crystal vase—funeral flowers. Leo knew he should throw them out, but not yet.

He sunk into a chair at the kitchen table, pushed aside the stack of syrupy condolence cards and thank you notes waiting to be written, and dug into his sandwich. Leo couldn't believe how going through mounds of paperwork could make him so hungry. Hungry like the look in Landry's eyes when he offered to purchase the farm. "Why does Jacob Landry want to buy our farm?"

"He's not interested in the farm, just the property," Johnny answered, chewing on his sandwich. "Word is he's lookin' to build a mega church out here. He's got townsfolk all excited. A mega church would bring lots of paying customers to town after Sunday services. Might even double Endeavor's population."

"God almighty."

"Around here, that's just another name for Village President Landry."

"I don't care if he's the president of the United States. Hell will have to freeze over before we sell to him."

"You sound just like Frank." Johnny set down his empty milk glass, a moustache of white on his upper lip.

Leo finished his ham sandwich, then asked, "Is Landry a member of the bank board? Does he have the power to foreclose on the farm?"

"He ain't on the bank board so, no, he can't do that… at least not officially. But he used his money to, uh, *persuade* village board members to annex your farm. No doubt he's got the Endeavor Bank Board in his back pocket, too."

Leo shook his head and collected their empty dishes. The cobalt blue plates were heavy and chipped. His mother had eaten off of them as a little girl, brought them with her from Italy, and could never part with them. "That bastard's not getting our place."

"Is that what you're gonna tell Jake tomorrow?"

"Tomorrow? Hell no. I'll be in Madison. Mr. Landry will have to wait."

10

"I'm coming to see you. That's all there is to it, mister." Mary Evans' rich voice came through the Mustang's Bluetooth. He heard clinking glasses and laughter in the background from the Monday morning crowd at Mary's bed and breakfast. He had thought he didn't want her in Endeavor, dealing with all these family issues, a family she hadn't even met. But at the sound of her voice, he knew he needed her.

"I've missed you," Leo admitted, as he pulled into Madison General's parking lot.

"It's settled. I'll meet you on the Union Terrace for dinner."

A few minutes later, Leo walked into his father's antiseptic hospital room. He patted Eddie on the shoulder and then asked his father how he was feeling. Frank grunted over a half-eaten bowl of cherry Jell-O. His eyes appeared sunken and grey bristle covered his chin.

Leo pulled a chair next to his brother as Dr. Pierson entered the room dressed in her white lab coat. The dark circles under her eyes were gone but the frown remained. She told them that while Frank's vitals were good, the hospital staff wanted to keep him until Wednesday. Frank resumed his grunting.

Leo and Eddie spent the morning attempting small talk with their father. Then, while Frank channel surfed and dozed, they answered emails on their phones. After another forgettable lunch in the cafeteria, Leo insisted that Eddie leave the hospital to enjoy the beautiful May afternoon. Uncomfortable with having so much attention, Frank agreed they should go.

With the University of Wisconsin's finals week in full force, it was quiet on the Memorial Union Terrace. Middle-aged business people relaxed in the signature green, yellow, and orange metal sunburst chairs. Only a few study groups clustered around tables attempted to ignore the beautiful lake and review their notes or finish their projects. Some students embraced the sunshine and sunbathed on the pier while sailboats and kayaks drifted lazily by.

With his over-stuffed computer bag slung over one shoulder, Leo weaved through the tables past a tattooed-covered guitarist playing "Baby Please Don't Go." He stopped at the outdoor grill for a pitcher of Spotted Cow while Eddie found a picnic table by the waterfront. The smell of frying brats made Leo's mouth water. He looked forward to eating one or two of the sausages once Mary arrived.

Leo set the pitcher and plastic cups on the wooden table. He opened his computer bag, and lifted out a large accordion folder stuffed with farm documents and a smaller envelope containing condolence cards and thank-you notes. "Sorry we have to do this on such a beautiful day."

Eddie poured them each a beer. "This will ease the pain."

They spent the next hour writing thank-you cards while the guitarist serenaded them with the blues. Memorial money, they decided, would go to the American Cancer Society. Then, with that sad task done, they moved on to crunching the farm's financial numbers. The predominance of red ink was depressing.

"What did you say the man's name was?" Eddie poured himself another beer, the guitarist singing "Stand by Me." "The black guy with Landry?"

"Oliver Tenney." Leo placed the folder on a nearby chair. "From Chicago."

Eddie searched on his iPhone. "Of Tenney, Ulysses, and Danforth? Is this him?" He handed Leo his phone.

An attractive African-American in a three-piece suit smiled at Leo from an architectural website. The guy looked like he should be on the cover of GQ. "Sure is. Who is he?"

"Heads one of the largest architectural firms in Chicago."

"What kind of work does he do?"

Eddie skimmed the website. "Churches, meeting houses, religious structures. He's also created some celebrity mansions."

"Johnny thinks Landry wants to build a mega church on the farm."

"I'm not surprised. I knew annexing Dad's land was about more than just tax collection. And Landry's conquered the business and political aspects of Endeavor, why not move on to the religious? He belongs to the Church of Our Beloved Savior in Endeavor, but Rev. Wallace is in charge there. Landry doesn't get to run things. You remember Rev. Wallace?"

Leo shook his head.

"Sure you do. You and Laurie Sue Harris disappeared during the homecoming dance—"

"Oh, geez, is he the one who found us in the janitor's closet?"

"He went looking for a mop—"

"And found a topless Laurie Sue. My pants around my ankles."

"She's his niece!" Eddie roared.

Leo laughed, almost spilling his beer. "The whole thing is kind of a pants-grabbing, yelling, tripping over something, probably the mop, blur. Thankfully he didn't have a gun."

"Good thing Mom dragged us to the Catholic Church in Merritt's Landing every Sunday. We were blacklisted from all seven of Endeavor's protestant churches."

"I didn't know Wallace had that much pull."

"He had some back then, and now he's second only to Landry."

Leo tilted his cup as he re-filled it to avoid getting too much foam. "So Landry's butted heads with Rev. Wallace and now wants a church of his own?"

"Looks like it." Eddie ran his hand over the battered file.

"Landry mentioned the possibility of foreclosure. And Johnny says Landry controls the bank board."

"The bastard controls the whole village." Eddie gazed out over Lake Mendota and then looked at Leo. "Are we going to have to sell the farm?"

Leo watched a boat glide by, wind filling its sail, and wished he was on board. "I don't know how Dad's going to pay the property taxes in July, let alone the mortgages. We need to get crops in the ground, generate some income. But even if we found someone to help with the planting, the cattle could be too much for us to handle. They might have to go."

"I've thought of that. I talked to Bill Stevens, you know, down the road."

"Is he interested in buying cattle?" Leo leaned forward.

"No, but he did contact an auctioneer for us. Someone he's familiar with. The auctioneer is available on May twenty-first. We could sell the healthy cows. The junkers, we'll unload at Equity."

"Johnny pointed out the sick ones. He's separated them from the rest of the herd."

"That should satisfy the quarantine requirements. And the timing would be perfect. If we sell enough—"

"Wait, did you say Monday, May twenty-first? A week from today?"

Eddie set his cup down and crossed his arms. "Why, do you have a hot date? Another high-profile interview?"

"A hot date, actually. With Mary. In New York City."

"Your Pulitzer Prize Luncheon! I'm sorry, Leo. With everything else going on, I completely forgot. We'll find a different date."

"Hold that thought," he said, as he spotted Mary exiting the Rathskeller.

Mary's long, floral dress billowed around her thin, six-foot frame, a strand of blond hair caressing her face. Her canvas purse was slung over one shoulder and she held a large, rectangular, brown-paper package in her hands. She wove around tables and chairs and stood at the top of the terrace, searching the crowd.

Leo waved.

Her face glowed when she saw him. She hurried down the stone steps, lifting the package above her head. When she reached him, she leaned it against her leg and kissed him.

"I didn't realize how much I needed that." He touched her soft cheek. "Needed you." He kissed her.

"Okay, get a room," Eddie kidded.

"Right, sorry. Mary, this is my brother, Eddie."

Mary shook Eddie's hand. "It's great to finally meet you."

"You, too. The woman who's stolen my brother's heart."

Mary placed her hand on Leo's chest and kissed him again. "I come bearing gifts." She searched in her bag, emerging with a ragged, dog-eared copy of *Because of Winn-Dixie*. "On loan from young Jimmy Edwards. He insists you read it."

Leo laughed. "Jimmy's a resident of Carpe Diem," he told his brother. "And a precocious reader. Tell him I certainly will."

Mary then handed him a copy of *The Carpe Diem Daily News*. "Check the byline on the front-page story."

The headline stated, "Leo Townsend Wins Pulitzer! By Assistant Reporter Natalia 'Tali' Shaw."

"Tali's writing for the paper?"

"She's fierce when it comes to interviewing."

He read the story.

"Right to the point without being melodramatic. This is good."

Mary handed him the brown-paper package, her fingernails tinged with blue paint. "I hope you like it."

Leo gently tore back the paper exposing his mother's smiling face, her head tilted toward Leo, Eddie on the other side of her. "You painted…" the words caught in his throat.

"I might have stolen that photograph you keep in your wallet."

"It's beautiful," Eddie said. "Oils? The lighting is well done. And you've manage to capture Mom's personality. Her warmth. It's really good."

"I enjoyed painting it," Mary said. "In a way, I now feel like I know her."

Leo studied the painting, amazed at how Mary had captured the curve of his mother's lips which created the dimple in her left cheek, the fine smile lines around her almond-shaped eyes, and the tenderness in those eyes as Isabella looked at the photographer—her husband Frank. "You have no idea what this means to me."

"I think I do." She wiped a tear off his chin.

Leo gently rewrapped the portrait and set it securely against the bench. Pouring Mary a Spotted Cow, he asked about her trip from northern

Illinois. She scooted closer as she recounted being stuck behind a giant farm rig dropping clumps of mud on the highway. "I couldn't get around it and for a second debated driving under it. My SUV would've fit—that's how big it was. But then it turned off the road right before Monroe."

"Did you see any deer?"

She leaned against him. He smelled her lavender lotion and felt the warmth of her body. "There were five or six in a field south of New Glarus but thankfully they were running away from the highway."

Leo put his arm around her and she sunk into him, making him feel whole. "So how's my favorite little town?"

"Carpe Diem's bustling. The Bradbury Inn—"

"Mary's not only mayor of Carpe Diem, she also owns a bed and breakfast," Leo clarified.

"A few weeks ago," Mary continued, "the inn was booked solid because of the teachers' convention. But now things have slowed down. I closed the inn for some badly needed plumbing repairs which should be completed before the tourist season begins. My concierge is overseeing the work while I'm gone."

"And how are things at the town hall?"

"After hosting the teachers' convention, we've had a lot of calls about families interested in unschooling." She turned to Eddie. "Child-led learning. It's how the people of Carpe Diem teach their children." Then she sighed.

"The phone calls are a good thing, aren't they?"

"We'll see. I'm concerned about a mass immigration." She sipped her beer. "Many families have called asking about the town, job opportunities, shopping."

"Don't you want people moving to Carpe Diem?" Eddie asked.

"Some people have a hard time understanding or embracing our town's unschooling lifestyle."

"But if they're interested enough to move to your town, won't they research it first?" Eddie asked.

"You would think so," she said casually, though she sounded worried. "Anyway, enough about me. How are you doing? Your dad's operation was successful?"

"It was," Eddie answered. "So I'm good."

"We were talking about the farm," Leo said. A breeze off the lake ruffled the papers. He shoved them back into his computer bag. "There are some financial issues. Eddie mentioned something about a cattle auction."

"We could have it right on the farm," Eddie said. "Bill Stevens, our neighbor, recommended an auctioneer who could hold it on May twenty-first. But since Leo will be in New York, I'll look into rescheduling. Hopefully, we'll only have to postpone it a week."

"Sounds good." Leo finished his beer. "The quicker we get some cash from the sale of the cattle and get this season's crops in the ground, the better we can protect ourselves against Landry."

"Landry?" Mary asked.

"Jacob Landry, Endeavor's village president," Leo said. "He's pushing Dad to sell the farm. We think he wants to build a mega church."

"And if he can't buy it," Eddie poured the last of the beer into Leo's glass, "he's got the power to get the bank board to foreclose."

"So you need to make the farm as solvent as possible," Mary said. "Raise enough money through cattle sales to pay the mortgage and taxes, and get a crop planted to cover future expenses."

Leo combed his fingers through his hair. "A cattle auction is a major undertaking. Plus, we'd have to pull it off at the same time we're tackling the planting—"

"You know," Mary said. "I happen to have an uncle who's an expert farmer."

"John. Of course!" Leo kissed Mary's cheek, then turned to Eddie. "John Holden runs Carpe Diem's communal farm."

"Plus, I'm sure I can find a few extra farm hands," Mary said.

"But are they available? Can they take a few days off? It's a lot to ask."

"After what you did for Carpe Diem, the townspeople will be lining up to help."

11

Wednesday morning, Jacob scanned the Townsend property with binoculars from the passenger seat of Vernon's pickup. He focused on the cattle yard as Vern parked the truck at the end of the driveway. Spotting Johnny filling the feed bunk with silage, Jacob texted "Call Caldere now" to his good-for-nothing, white trash niece, Dahlia. Caldere was sweet on Dahlia and for a hundred bucks, she had promised to keep the farmhand... occupied.

Within minutes, Caldere pulled out his phone, texted, and then opened the gate to the stockyard. The cows, those that took notice, ambled across the pasture to the yard. Caldere watched the animals for a few minutes and then closed the gate and climbed into his pickup.

"Go!" Jacob ordered.

Vern took off on County T away from the farm, gravel pinging the truck's fenders.

Behind them, Caldere tore down the driveway and spun onto the road in the opposite direction.

"Don't think he saw us," Jacob said. "Let's go dump this stuff before the cattle get there."

Vern whipped a U-turn, then raced up the driveway.

"Pull behind the barn." Jacob struggled into a pair of boots. "If anyone driving by sees us they'll think we're making a delivery, but I don't want them recognizing your vehicle."

Vern parked the truck behind the cattle barn, out of sight from the road. He hefted two fifty-pound bags of urea out of the bed while Jake grabbed the feed scoops. They walked into the barnyard, trying to avoid manure. Large, seemingly-healthy cattle trudged toward the feed bunk as emaciated cows wobbled behind. Jacob had never seen cows so lackadaisical about eating but was thankful for it. Their listlessness would make poisoning the feed that much easier.

"Drop the bags here." Jacob pointed to a dry patch of ground next to the trough. Vernon sliced open the first bag, then took one of the scoops from Jake. They sprinkled the white granules on top of the silage, careful not to spill it outside the feed bunk.

"Once they eat this, they'll drop like flies."

Vernon ripped open the second bag, tearing the top off and tossing it and the knife aside. A gust of wind lifted the plastic and settled it on the back of the largest cow. He lunged for the piece as Jacob's cell phone called, "Thank you, Jesus!"

Jake read the text message from his niece. "Johnny just left."

"Holy Mother of God," he said. "That's got to be the quickest screw in history. That girl can't do anything right. We gotta go. NOW!"

They finished spreading the urea, kicked mud over the few granules scattered around the bunk, and reached for the empty bags and stray piece. They raced to the truck, slipping in mud and manure.

Not bothering to take their filthy boots off, they climbed in. Jake stuffed all the plastic under the cab's seat while Vernon gunned the Dodge around the house.

"Easy does it, boy," Jacob said. "I know we're in a hurry, but we don't want to be leaving tire ruts."

Vern slowed until he got to the road and then spun the wheel, fishtailing the pickup onto the blacktop. The bags flew toward Jacob's open window, spraying urea granules in his face. Sputtering, he snagged them before they escaped. He shoved the bags back under the seat.

"No, no. Not this way," Jacob said. "We'll pass Caldere for sure."

"But if I turn around now it'll look suspicious. I say we keep going."

GOD ON MAYHEM STREET

"No. Turn around. Turn around!"

"Too late. Here comes Caldere's Chevy."

Jacob slid under the dashboard. "When you pass him, act natural. Wave. No, don't wave, nod."

Vernon nodded.

"He didn't even glance at me," Vern said. "Looked a little bombed."

"That's the effect my niece has on men." Jacob slid back onto the passenger seat. "That and the crushed Valium I dumped in her Bloody Mary mix."

12

At two o'clock Wednesday afternoon, Leo drove his father's Caprice up the farm's driveway, relieved to finally arrive. During the hour-long ride from Madison, Frank had slumped in the passenger seat, grunting at any attempts at conversation. He did admire Mary's painting and admitted he wished he had something similar. When Leo offered to loan it to him for a few months, Frank had managed to thank him, saying it would look nice hanging over the living room fireplace. Then he went back to grunting.

Eddie, sitting in the backseat, tried to pass the time by talking about his latest design projects but exhausted that topic when they left Madison's city limits. Leo switched on the radio, tuning in to Q106, Frank's favorite country station. Johnny Cash sang "Folsom Prison Blues." *Appropriate.*

As Leo parked in front of the house, Johnny bounded down the steps and opened the car door. "Let me lend ya a hand, Mr. Townsend. Sure is good to see you."

"Good to see you, too, Johnny. Good to be home," Frank said without grunting. "How are the cows today?"

Johnny shot Leo a nervous look. "Um…"

"Dad." Leo came around the car to help. "How about something to eat before you take a nap?"

"Dammit, Leo. If you're planning on treating me like an invalid, you can just go back to that city of yours."

Leo let out an exasperated sigh as Johnny escorted Frank into the house. He retrieved Eddie's wheelchair from the trunk, helped his brother maneuver onto the chair, and followed him up the side ramp into the house.

Johnny stood at the granite countertop opening a jar of mayonnaise. "I'd wanted to have sandwiches made 'fore you got home. Got sidetracked." He slathered the spread onto a piece of bread. A blob of mayo dropped onto the slate floor, turning the terra cotta white.

Leo remembered the day his parents had the tile installed. Isabella had finally gotten his father to agree to remodel the room in a style resembling her mother's Italian kitchen. The remainder of their farmhouse could be pure Wisconsin but she had wanted a piece of Italy with her as she cooked.

Leo snatched a paper towel. "Let me get that."

"Thanks," Johnny said.

Frank told Johnny to add lettuce and pickles to his ham-and-cheese sandwich as he popped the cap off a Leinie's.

"Dad, do you think it's wise to drink beer what with all the medication—," Leo said.

"Tell me about the cattle, Johnny," Frank interrupted.

Leo shook his head. If the guy wanted to kill himself, let him. Walking past Johnny to the refrigerator, he caught a whiff of the farmhand's cologne and wondered what he had planned for the day. Leo opened the refrigerator to search for a beer of his own.

Johnny fumbled with the mustard bottle, gave it a good squeeze, and splattered mustard all over his t-shirt. He took the dishcloth from the sink and tried to mop up the mess.

"Let it go," Frank said. "Answer me."

The farmhand sighed and tossed the rag in the sink. "They didn't want to come to the feed bunk this morning. Barely moved, as if they were drained of energy." He collected the plates of mustard-less sandwiches and a bag of potato chips and placed them on the table. "Three cows aborted 'round noon."

Leo glanced over the top of the refrigerator door. "Did you say 'aborted'?"

"Yes, sir." Johnny pulled out his fake cigarette and gnawed on it. "When I came across the fetuses, I called Doc Krueger. Had to leave a message. Haven't heard back. I've checked the rest of the cattle. They don't look so good, Mr. Townsend."

"Where are they?" Frank rose.

"The north pasture. I kept them away from the south field because I thought they might be getting into a poisonous plant or somethin' else there."

"I should check on the cattle. See for myself." Frank's legs wobbled.

"After you've eaten something," Leo said. "Slept—"

"Goddamnit, I'm not tired." He collapsed back onto the chair.

"Dad," Eddie said, "let Leo take you upstairs. I'll get ahold of Doc Krueger. We'll wake you when he arrives."

"There's too much to do." Frank put his head in his hands.

"I can put you at ease," Leo said. "Mary is coming tomorrow morning. She's bringing John Holden, a very successful farmer, and several friends to help."

Frank's eyes narrowed. "You seriously think I'd want a bunch of strangers running my farm? You must be outta your mind." His face reddened. "You've always thought of me as some stupid, hick farmer who never lived up to your city standards. Well, I don't need your charity."

"It's not charity." Leo ran his shaking hands through his hair. "Look, I admit I've never liked farming, but just because you do doesn't mean I think less of you. And I've never thought of you as a hick farmer. You've always been a very successful businessman."

"Until now, you mean."

"You've had a few rough months, that's all." Leo looked at his brother, who nodded for him to continue. "These aren't strangers, they're my friends. They want to help."

"Dad," Eddie said, "nobody's taking over the farm. These people are coming temporarily, until you get back on your feet. Let Leo and his friends do this."

GOD ON MAYHEM STREET

Frank shook his head, apparently about to protest, but instead pushed himself into a standing position and shuffled out of the kitchen.

Leo started after him but Eddie said, "Let him go."

"Fine." Leo exhaled, sitting at the table. He bit into one of the sandwiches. "I should drive into town, anyway. Buy work clothes."

"Don't drive. Run." Eddie helped himself to a handful of chips. "I'll loan you my sweats and old Nikes."

"Good idea. It's been awhile since I've stretched my legs."

Twenty minutes later, Leo had changed, retrieved his high school backpack from the depths of his closet, threw it over his shoulder, and jogged down the driveway. He breathed in the cool spring air as he turned onto County T and marveled at how different running in the country was. No people to dodge, no bus exhaust to inhale, only the sound of his feet against the blacktop and the occasional screech from a red-tailed hawk. Clouds blocked out the sun but didn't threaten to rain.

The road wound around farmsteads, each with the ubiquitous mobile home used for winter hunting retreats. As Leo ran up a hill, a Chevy Tahoe towing a fishing boat passed. It headed toward Buffalo Lake where Frank, Leo, and Eddie had caught walleye on the rare afternoons Frank took a break from farming.

As the road leveled, Leo ran past Heames Marsh, full of cattails blowing in the spring breeze. Farther down County T, he circumvented Churchill's Pond, famous for its clay used to make Endeavor bricks. He passed Jacob Landry's mansion, one of the dozen or so historic homes built with the beautiful, deep red stones.

Arriving in town, Leo slowed his pace and then pushed through the glass door of Landry's Department Store. He threw his backpack into a shopping cart and added t-shirts, a pair of work boots, and bib overalls. Shuffling through a rack of jeans, he pictured all the pairs he had back in his Chicago apartment when a woman's voice drawled behind him.

"Aren't you a sight for sore eyes."

He turned, nearly bumping into Jacob Landry's niece. "Dahlia Toole. It's been a long time."

Dahlia had been homecoming queen to Leo's king. Back then, girls envied her lustrous blond hair but the boys only wanted her body. With long legs and perfect curves, she always showed just enough cleavage to entice. His senior year, Leo had the opportunity to see where that cleavage led, but he didn't go any further. Dahlia had been a tease and Leo didn't have the patience to be that persistent.

"Oh, honey, I haven't been a Toole for over fifteen years," Dahlia cooed, still looking good at thirty-six. Her low-cut t-shirt exposed slightly lower and less perky cleavage. "I've been a Turner and a Benson. Now I'm back to Landry. Finalized my third divorce last December."

"I'm sorry to hear that."

Dahlia's hot pink t-shirt matched her large handbag, both studded with rhinestones. Her faded jeans were torn in strategic places. As she moved closer to him, her long, French-manicured fingernails stroked his bare forearm. He backed away and reached for the nearest pair of jeans.

"Don't be sorry. Ralph was no good for me. Felt it the second after I said 'I do.'" She inched closer. He could smell cigarettes, hairspray, and men's cologne. "You look like you ran here."

"I did."

She stared at him, then continued, "I'm sorry about your mom. Such a nice lady. Heard your dad had a heart attack. How's he doing?"

"Much better, thanks."

"Is that why you're back in town?"

"Helping out."

"And you're needing farm duds." She glanced at the jeans he held in his hand. "You're in the wrong section, honey. You're a tall hunk of man. Those would barely go past your knees." She reached across him to a pair of larger pants. Her breasts grazed his arm. "Let Dahlia help you out." She stumbled on her spiky heels and fell against him.

Leo seized her arms, holding her away from him as if she was contagious. He was used to women coming on to him, but this was ridiculous. He moved her to the side and took a pair of jeans from the larger section. "Thanks for your help. Good to see you again," he lied as he walked away.

"Honey, I didn't mean to scare you off. How about heading over to Isaiah's for a cold one?"

"Sorry. Gotta go."

The backpack's straps chafed Leo's shoulders and his muscles burned as he crested the final hill to the sound of rolling thunder. He slowed his pace, stopping at his father's rusty mailbox to collect its contents—an AARP flyer and a few bills. As he walked toward the driveway, something scrunched underfoot. A piece of plastic with the word "urea" on the label. *Urea? Like in urine?*

Curious, he stuck the label in his backpack and jogged the rest of the way to the house, making it inside as the first raindrops fell.

Except for the rain pelting the roof, the house was quiet. Leo went upstairs, avoided the creaky floorboard outside the master bedroom, and walked into his old room, dropping the backpack on the floor next to his bed. A University of Illinois pennant and Meat Loaf, The Rolling Stones, and Cars posters covered the blue walls. Leo's diplomas sat on the bookshelf next to his football and track trophies. Photographs of high school graduation, prom court, and the Endeavor football team gathered dust on his dresser. The room still smelled of Brut cologne.

Leo considered tossing the retro paraphernalia before Mary came but decided she'd get a kick out of it. He studied the prom picture and marveled at how little Dahlia had changed. Then he noticed a black velvet pouch on his desk next to the lamp he had made in shop class. He dumped the pouch's contents. A translucent crystal the size of his thumbnail and two folded pieces of paper spilled onto the desktop.

Leo examined the oily-feeling crystal. White-and-yellow-tinged, it resembled a translucent piece of polished glass. Its edges were rounded and the sides were smooth but speckled with irregular pits. Leo set the crystal aside. He unfolded the yellowed paper and read his teenaged scrawl. *Mom, this crystal reminds me of you—unconsciously natural, mysterious, and strong. I love you, Leonardo.*

He unfolded the other note and saw his mother's beautiful handwriting. *Leonardo, when you gave this crystal to me, you were embarrassed that you hadn't bought me a gift. But I love it even more because it came from our land. I've treasured this crystal always, as I've treasured you. I love you, Mom.*

Leo ran his fingers over the words and wiped his damp eyes. He folded the notes and put them and the crystal back into the bag and then placed the bag securely in the breast pocket of his bomber jacket. The floorboard in the hall creaked. Frank shuffled past Leo's room mumbling "gotta check on the cows." Leo collected his new jeans and a clean shirt and headed for the shower.

13

Jacob sat in Carl Kenyan's best chair, appreciating the pinup of Scarlett Johansson while the barber trimmed his ears. He considered chiding Carl for having something so pornographic in his establishment but, he reminded himself, Miss Johansson was one of God's creations. Made as a companion for man. No, God wouldn't mind him admiring her beauty.

Jacob took in her pouty lips and full curves. She really did have a nice pair of—shoot, now he was getting aroused. Quickly he pictured Grace, his wife, as a pinup, all two hundred jiggly pounds of her. His arousal faded. Yes, sir, that always did the trick.

He glanced over at Vern sitting in the next barber's chair, starting to doze. Not quite ten o'clock on a Thursday morning and the boy was spent. Maybe Jacob shouldn't work him so hard.

"What's on the agenda for today?" Carl lifted the smock off of Jacob and dusted stray hairs from the back of his neck.

"I've got some business down at the bank. Looking to acquire the Townsend property." He slid out of the chair and adjusted his Smith & Wesson .38 revolver in its waistband holster. He'd worn the concealed gun so long it felt like a body part, but on rare occasions like this morning it shifted uncomfortably.

Carl stopped folding the smock. "I didn't know Frank put his farm up for sale."

"It's not on the market yet, but it's definitely for sale. Townsend owes so much money on his mortgages, and in taxes, he'll be lucky to break even." Jacob admired his short hair in the mirror. He had gotten a close cut his entire life, though now the black had been replaced by white. He liked the white better; it made him look more *presidential*, more sincere.

"But he's had a run of bad luck is all, surely you don't want to kick him when he's—"

Vernon loomed over the barber. He was twice the short, scrawny man's size and in much better physical shape. "Buying farms, it's just business. Isn't that right, Jake?"

Vern was alert after all. Jacob admonished himself for doubting his right-hand man.

"More than that, Vern, we're helping Frank out. He can't handle a farm that size in his condition. In fact, that farm is on the decline. Think of it as lending a helping hand and providing progress for the community. The land can be put to better use." He tossed a fifty-dollar bill on the counter next to the bottle of talc powder. "Thank you, Carl, for the wonderful cut."

Jacob pushed through the barbershop door, the bell tinkling overhead, and hustled onto the damp sidewalk. The morning's rain had stopped but the dark skies and heavy air threatened more showers. Across Lakeview Avenue, cars occupied all the parking spaces in front of Landry's Department Store. He recognized several of them, pleased to see that the good people of his village loved to fill his pockets.

Vernon followed him out. "To the bank?"

"You have the paperwork?"

"Shoot, I left your case inside. Hang on, I'll—"

A Harley roared onto Lakeview Avenue. It drove two blocks and pulled into the empty parking space directly in front of Jacob. The motorcyclist dropped the kickstand and removed his helmet, exposing a long, brown ponytail streaked with gray and a matching goatee. His face was weathered but his blue eyes were alert.

Jacob assumed the man was on his way to the barber; Lord knew he certainly needed one. Jake then glanced at the man's passenger. Her silvery blonde hair escaped from underneath her helmet and her leather jacket couldn't hide her curves. Curves that Scarlett Johansson would envy.

"I'm wondering if you might tell me where I could find Jacob Landry," the man shouted over the idling engine.

"You're looking at him," Jacob said. "Who are you?"

"No shit?" the hippy said. "Ain't it my lucky day." He switched off the engine, nodded to his passenger, who dismounted, and then he limped over to Jacob. Taking off one fingerless glove, he held out his hand. "I'm Patrick Holden, Mr. Frank Townsend's attorney. Pleased to meet you."

Jacob found himself shaking the man's scarred hand. "His attorney?"

"That's right. So if you or that bank of yours have any concerns, please contact me directly." Patrick reached inside his leather jacket. "Number's right here." He handed Jacob his business card and then mounted the motorcycle. His passenger straddled the bike behind him.

"Oh, and the next time you step foot on Mr. Townsend's land, we'll take it to the sheriff. In case you're not current on Wisconsin law, trespassing is a Class B forfeiture. Cost you two hundred bucks." Holden yanked his glove on. "Have a nice day." Adjusting his helmet, he backed the bike into the puddled street and roared down Lakeview Avenue, spraying mud.

Jacob swiped at a splatter on his white shirt, smearing it brown. "Vernon," he hissed as he handed the younger man the business card. "Find out everything you can about Patrick Holden. Everything. Start by contacting the state bar association. See if he actually has a license to practice law in Wisconsin."

"Now, or do you want me to come down to the bank with you?"

"Now. I can handle those idiot number crunchers." He walked toward the barbershop's door to retrieve his briefcase. "Once I'm done at the bank, I'll meet you back at my office. Lord, a mercy, what a day this is turning out to be."

14

Leo stood on the front porch, playing the part of a farmer in his white t-shirt, Lee jeans, and heavy work boots. He tugged on the stiff pants. His feet sweated in the boots. Next to him, Frank fidgeted in a wicker chair in his button-down shirt, brown slacks, and loafers. He'd grudgingly agreed to dress for company when his sons had refused to let him pitch in with the farm work.

A large, custom van with the words "The Bradbury Inn" painted on the side turned into the driveway and honked a hello.

"Christ, where will they sleep? Who's going to feed them?" Frank said as Eddie wheeled out the front door. A replica of *American Gothic* covered the spokes of Eddie's chair in homage to Leo's new attire. As if on cue, Johnny sauntered around the side of the house carrying a pitchfork.

"I've told you." Leo concentrated on keeping an even tone. "It's all been taken care of. Mary with me, John Holden on the sleeper sofa in the den, and Patrick Holden and his friend Charlotte in the guest bedroom. Johnny cleaned out the old dairy barn. The kids will camp there in the hayloft."

As the van splashed through puddles and parked, Leo added, "There's plenty of food. We still have casseroles from the funeral and Mary's son, Will, is a fantastic cook."

Leo hugged Mary as he helped her out of the van. Her hand lingering on his chest. The blue underneath her fingernails matched the paint smear across the front of her yellow sweatshirt. "I could get used to your new look," she said. She'd pulled her hair back into a ponytail, though a few blonde strands framed her face.

"You're looking good yourself." His hand rested on her left hip where green paint merged with purple on her sweatshirt. "Even your work clothes are artistic." He kissed her.

John Holden strode around the van's hood and shook Leo's hand, a breeze tossing his mane of white hair.

"I can't tell you how much your coming means to me," Leo said. He gestured to the men behind him. "To us."

"Honestly," John pushed up the sleeves of his brown cotton sweater, "the whole town wanted to be here, but I convinced them to remain behind and attend to things while we're gone."

"How long can you stay?"

"At least through the weekend. Maybe longer if you need us."

Mary opened the van's sliding door with a *whoosh*. Quinn, Mary's eighteen-year-old daughter, climbed out. Spiky hair dyed black, black sweater over black leggings, black high tops, Canon camera around her neck, Quinn hadn't changed much in the last month and Leo was glad for it. She fist-bumped him, revealing *carpe diem* inked on her right hand.

"When did you get the tattoo?" Leo asked, after she gave him her condolences.

"End of April. Soon after we saw you in Chicago. Mom was against it but I told her, this way, if I drop dead in some back alley in Italy, they'll be able to identify my body."

"Oh, Quinn." Mary feigned exasperation.

"When is the big trip?" Leo asked.

"June first," Quinn answered. "We can't wait to tell you all about our plans."

"We're even thinking of stopping in Norcia." Will, Quinn's younger brother, hopped out. "Visit some of your relatives." *Had he grown another inch?*

Leo shook Will's hand. "Good to know. I'll warn them to be on the lookout for a computer-hacking chef and his shutterbug Goth sister."

"Don't forget about me," Tali said, joining them. Several inches taller than Quinn, her older half-sister, with blonde hair rather than inky black, she had the same dark, intelligent eyes.

"You're going, too?" Leo hugged her.

"Yep," Tali answered. "I've been working two jobs—writing for the *Daily News* and serving at Joan and Dan's Diner while their son is at Oxford—so I've saved some money. Mom's pitching in half but I'm determined to pay her back."

"How's that boyfriend of yours?" Leo asked.

"Josh is good. He's in North Carolina, working temporarily as a NASCAR technician."

Leo whistled. "Sweet gig. How'd he swing that?"

"Chief Billiot's brother-in-law works for NASCAR and needed someone to replace him for a few months while he recovered from a back injury."

"Is Josh going with you to Italy?"

"No. He's not sure how long he'll be down there. He's hoping it'll turn into a permanent position."

John reached into the front seat and handed Leo a box of Italian wines from the Umbrian region. "I thought we should drink to the memory of your mother."

Leo glanced at the labels. "These are terrific, John. Very thoughtful. Thank you."

Leo introduced John, Mary, and the kids to his father, brother, and Johnny. After they offered Frank and Eddie their condolences, the kids complimented Eddie on his choice of wheel covers. Quinn asked Eddie if she could pick his brain about graphic design and he readily agreed. Then Leo asked Mary, "Where are Patrick and Charlotte?"

In the distance, they heard the revving of a motorcycle and soon the bike rumbled up the long driveway and parked alongside the Bradbury van. Patrick cut the bike's engine. He took off his helmet, revealing a broad grin, and waited for Charlotte to dismount. He limped over to hug Leo. "Sorry I was delayed. I had a talk with Landry."

"Oh?"

"He won't be dropping by anytime soon." Patrick gave a hearty laugh, then sobered as he shook Frank's hand. "I'm sorry to hear about your wife's passing. But I'm glad to see you're well, sir."

Frank grunted, with a hint of a smile. "So, I've been told you're my attorney."

"Only if you agree."

"What did Landry say?" Leo asked.

"Didn't say a thing. Though I caught him wiping off his shirt as we left. Damn if my bike didn't kick up some mud."

Frank's smile broke into laughter. "You're hired."

"Thanks for taking time away from your law practice, Patrick," Leo said, as they unloaded the van. "And your fair trade store, Charlotte."

"Our pleasure." Charlotte slung her duffle bag over her shoulder. "I was due for a vacation. And the Illinois state legislature needed a break from Patrick."

"Causing problems?"

"No more than usual." Patrick hefted bags of groceries.

Leo led everyone, laden with groceries, sleeping bags, and suitcases, into the house. He helped them unpack, thanking Will for bringing plenty of pasta makings and homemade cheeses, and showed them to their rooms. Eyeing the comfortable guest bedroom, Patrick and Charlotte declared they'd never leave. But the kids argued that they'd gotten the better deal when they climbed the ladder to the barn's loft. As they claimed their cots, they discovered the rope swing.

"Easiest way down," Leo explained. "Put your foot in the loop and hang on. When you get to that pile of hay at the other end, jump."

As Tali and Will took turns, Quinn snapped pictures. She then set the camera down to give the swing a try. Letting go at the last possible moment, she flew a few feet then disappeared in the pile. "We could use you as a scarecrow," Tali said, as she picked pieces of alfalfa from Quinn's hair.

Everyone followed Leo back into the kitchen for sandwiches and instructions from Johnny. "We borrowed a couple of tractors from the neighbors, fueled 'em, and are ready to plow the rotten soybean field. We'll drag the offset disk through and use the finisher to prepare the soil.

As soon as that's done, we'll plant corn."

"Isn't it late for that?" John asked.

"Yeah," the farmhand admitted, chewing on his e-cigarette. "But we've planted late before cuz of long winters and things worked out okay. We're pushing our luck, is all."

"And what about the cattle? How are they doing?"

"Some are pretty sick. Frank got fed up with Doc Krueger telling us there wasn't anything wrong with 'em. And then he didn't even show up last night like he said he would. So I called that Doc Stork, the Merritt's Landing vet. He left right before you all got here.

"Doc Stork's sending blood samples to the Veterinary Diagnostic Lab at Iowa State. They'll test for fertilizer poisoning. Urea. Strange thing is we haven't used the stuff since last fall. He's also testing the cattle feed. He put stomach tubes in the cows to relieve the bloating, and filled them with water. Doc's hoping it'll save 'em. Says he'll be back tonight to do more of the same."

"Did you say 'urea'?" Leo asked. "Hang on." He bolted upstairs to his bedroom and fished inside his backpack. He returned to the kitchen and showed Johnny the piece of trash.

"I found it down the road yesterday afternoon on my way back from shopping in Endeavor, near that stand of birch trees—"

"Vernon Smith," Johnny cut in, his brow furrowed, the electronic cigarette now in his mouth.

"What about him?"

"Yesterday morning I, well, I..."

"You were here, on the farm," Leo prompted.

"In the early morning, yeah, to feed the cattle. After that I went into town to visit... a friend."

"Dahlia Landry?" Frank asked.

"Yeah." Johnny resumed chewing on his e-cigarette. "I... we..."

"We get the picture," Leo said. "Tell us about Smith."

"Coming back here, I passed his truck on County T. Thought for a moment he had come outta your driveway but figured that couldn't be. No one was home. Anyway, I saw something white, this piece of trash, fly out his window. Pissed me off. Thought he was littering. But he's a big guy, not one to tangle with. I let it pass and drove on by."

"Are you sure this trash flew out of his truck?" Leo handed Johnny the piece.

"Yes, sir."

"Leo, are you suggesting that Vernon Smith snuck onto our farm yesterday to dump urea in our cattle's feed bunk?" Frank asked. "That's crazy."

"Someone did. And we know exactly why Smith would poison the cattle."

"We should check into this," Patrick said.

"Go. Find out what's going on," John Holden said. "We've got everything under control here."

Leo grabbed his bomber jacket and his car keys. "Come on, Patrick. Let's pay Mr. Smith a visit."

15

Leo and Patrick found Vernon Smith sleeping on a wooden bench outside the village president's office. His snores echoed around the vacant hall.

"Not quite noon and the guy's completely passed out." Leo leaned over the large man. "He doesn't smell of alcohol."

"What does he do for a living?"

"Some sort of bodyguard for Landry."

"Not a very stimulating job, apparently."

Leo kicked Smith's outstretched Adidas. Easily a size seventeen.

Smith stuttered awake. "What the hell?!"

"Didn't see your foot. Tripped right over it. Sorry," Leo said.

Smith grumbled while settling back into nap position.

"You're Vernon Smith, right?" Leo asked. "Played defensive tackle for the Endeavor Eagles?"

"So?"

"Man, you were great." Leo held out his hand. "Leo Townsend. I ran into you at the hospital in Madison."

Smith's hand completely engulfed his.

Leo continued, "I played on the football team, too, second-string quarterback. Hell, I was really just a bench warmer my freshman year, when you were a senior."

"Sure, I remember you. Tall, skinny. Better suited for the basketball court."

Leo turned to Patrick as if he'd just noticed him. "Oh geez, my manners. Vernon Smith, this is Patrick Holden."

Patrick held out his hand.

Smith stood. Six inches taller than Patrick, he outweighed him by at least a hundred pounds of pure muscle. At forty, he'd obviously maintained his build. Leo imagined Smith ate raw steaks for breakfast.

Patrick grinned up at the large man and continued to hold out his hand.

Smith debated a moment and then shook it. "You're the attorney, that right?"

"In town to help out on the Townsend farm." Patrick slapped Leo on the back. "This city boy doesn't know much about cattle and soybeans."

"Sadly true," Leo said. "Even though I was raised on that farm, I spent more time warming a football bench than feeding the cows. But if I remember right, Vern, you worked on two farms back in high school. Your dad's and the Bransons'."

"Started working my daddy's farm as soon as I could walk," Smith said. "Detasseled corn on Hugh Branson's farm for beer money."

"Then maybe you could answer a question for me." Leo produced the torn piece of plastic and handed it to Vern. "I found this at the edge of our property. Would someone use this on a farm?"

Smith's sleepy eyes widened as he read the label. "Um, sure," he croaked. "This here's urea fertilizer. Contains nitrates which are good for crops."

"Nitrates?" Leo turned to Patrick. "Didn't the vet say that Dad's cattle had nitrate poisoning?"

"He sure did."

"This stuff can be tricky to use," Smith said. "Best to keep it far away from cattle."

"I'm sure you're right," Leo said. "Funny thing is I've never seen this stuff before."

"Your dad probably uses it all the time."

"Not lately. Dad hasn't done any farming for months. Fields are overgrown with weeds. My mother, um, anyway, he's been distracted and not feeling good."

"Right, his heart attack," Smith said. "How's he doing?"

"Good, thanks. The cattle aren't doing so hot, though. Strange how they can get nitrate poisoning when the fields haven't been fertilized since last fall."

Smith said nothing.

Patrick glanced at his watch. "We should go, Leo. Our appointment with the chief of police is in a few minutes."

"Oh, sure. Well, nice talking to you, Vernon." Leo held out his hand.

Smith shook it again, his hand damp, and eased down onto the bench as if afraid he'd break it, a distinct possibility.

"One more thing," Leo said. "You didn't happen to drive by my dad's farm yesterday morning, did you? Out on County T?"

Smith froze halfway to the bench. "Not that I recall."

Leo smiled. "Of course. You'd have no reason to be on that side of town." "I Shot the Sheriff" rang from his pocket. "Have a nice day." He took out his cell phone as he walked down the hallway.

"Nice to meet you, Mr. Smith." Leo heard Patrick say. "I'm sure I'll be seeing you again."

Leo clicked on his phone. "Townsend."

"It's Griffin Carlisle. How's your father?"

"He's happy to be home. Thank you for asking." Leo was surprised to be hearing from the candidate.

"Glad to hear it. Listen, I'd like to do a follow-up interview. With you. Tomorrow morning if possible."

Leo froze in the middle of the hallway. He tried to control his excitement and to think of a more professional response than "you're shitting me." He finally said, "I could make that work."

"I understand you're in Endeavor, at your family's farm."

"How did you—"

"I'll explain later. I've discussed my schedule with my press secretary. We've rearranged a few things. I'll be in Minneapolis this weekend. My opponents are making the rounds at the Minnesota Businessmen's Convention on Saturday and we need to crash their party. Endeavor's on my

GOD ON MAYHEM STREET

way. Is there a local restaurant where we could meet?"

Finally, Leo would get the interview he dreamed of. He pumped his fist in the air, almost punching Patrick. Then he pictured the commotion on Lakeview Avenue as the candidate's motorcade drove to the Swampside Bar and Grill. The whole village shut down while a helicopter flew over. No doubt people would line the sidewalk and press against the restaurant's windows to get a glimpse of Griffin. It would be comically distracting.

Without thinking, Leo blurted, "We should meet at the farm. It would give us more privacy."

"I don't want to inconvenience your family, your father—"

"I insist," Leo said, as he tried to reassure himself that this was the best option.

"Okay. Listen, I won't bring my whole entourage. I'll send them on ahead. In fact, I'd rather come by myself, but my campaign manager will insist that my two-man security detail come along."

"That's fine."

"I'll see you tomorrow morning. Ten o'clock. Or would eleven be better?"

"Ten's perfect. Thank you, Griffin."

"I'm looking forward to it."

Leo ended the call and then glanced back down the hall. The bench was vacant. He turned to Patrick. "I'll be interviewing Griffin Carlisle out at the farm tomorrow."

"Nicely done." Patrick high-fived him.

"I've got to make a quick call to my editor."

"Meet you in the police chief's office."

Leo ducked into the empty men's room and called Ted with the good news. But as he clicked off his phone, his excitement turned to dread. He imagined his homophobic father and brother trying to hide their disgust as they shook Griffin's hand.

Maybe he should call Griffin back, suggest meeting in town.

No. He'd find a way to deal with his family.

16

Jacob tapped the papers on his massive desk while staring at his phone and asking God to make it ring. Emmett Everson had promised to call him once the bank board meeting adjourned.

The board was considering whether to begin foreclosure procedures on the Townsend farm. Jacob had done a lot of wrangling and a bit of bribing to get them to consider it, but he knew it would pay off. All he needed to hang over Frank Townsend's head was the threat of foreclosure. A proud man, Townsend would, at all costs, avoid losing his farm in such a humiliating way. His only alternative would be to accept Jacob's lowball purchase price.

Vernon burst through the door.

"You can't just barge into my office, Vern. Can't you see I'm busy?" Jacob's hand waved over the Townsend file.

Vernon slammed the door. The framed photograph of Jacob's swearing-in as village president rattled on the wall. "Leo Townsend knows we poisoned his dad's cattle. He and that hippy lawyer are headed to Chief Grey's office right now." Vernon's body quaked. "I can't go back to jail, Jake. I'll take that sawed-off shotgun of yours and end myself."

Jacob pushed back from his desk. "I don't doubt it. But no one's going to jail." *Especially me.*

Jake could picture it. He'd be sitting in his favorite front-row pew at The Church of Our Beloved Savior, kneeling in prayer with the rest of the congregants as the choir sang its glory to God. Police Chief Morris Grey, whom Jacob stole money from during their weekly poker games, would march up the aisle with his men, just for show. He'd grab Jacob, drag him out of his pew, slap handcuffs on him, and march him out of the church, taking great delight in the shocked and horrified faces of the congregants.

Not one of the bastards would come to his defense.

Jacob paced the room, his Ferragamos sinking into the plush, wall-to-wall carpet. Surely God would never allow him to be arrested. "Vernon, sit down. You'll give yourself a coronary. Don't want to end up like Old Man Townsend, now do you?"

Vern slumped onto the overstuffed chair Jacob had bought exclusively for him. The other two respectable, stiff chairs were too small. Those were reserved for citizens who wanted governmental assistance and could offer Jacob something in return.

"Tell me exactly what Townsend said." As Jacob listened, he relaxed. "They have no credible evidence."

"They have a piece of the bag. Probably has fingerprints on it."

"Fingerprints only prove that we bought fertilizer and that maybe we littered, unintentionally of course. They have no way of proving when it got there or how. And it certainly doesn't explain how any fertilizer from that bag made it all the way down the driveway, across the front yard, and into the feed bunk."

"But they said they were going to the police chief's office."

"They were bluffing. They wanted to see your reaction. You didn't panic, did you?"

"I was surprised, but no. I played it cool." Vernon sunk deeper into the chair. The poor boy looked relieved and exhausted all at the same time.

"Why don't you go home?" Jacob offered his hand to ease Vern out of the chair. "Grab some lunch. Take a nap and meet me at the bank before it closes. If I haven't heard back from Emmett soon, I'll go see him in person. Make sure he understands the importance of the situation."

Vern lumbered over to the office door, reached for the knob, and then stopped. "Do you know anyone named Griffin?"

Jacob thought a moment. "I think that fella down in Jamison is named Griffin. Sam Griffin. Runs that large feed store."

"Huh, I wonder why he'd be coming here," Vern muttered.

"What are you talking about?"

"Townsend got a call on his cell. Some guy named Griffin is coming to their farm tomorrow morning. Ten o'clock. Townsend seemed excited about it."

"Maybe he's agreed to lend a hand. Lord knows they need it. Doesn't matter. Nothing will help them now, especially after I nail things down with Emmett."

Vern left, quietly closing the door behind him.

Yes, sir, Jacob thought as he sat at his desk and opened the Townsend file. Glancing at all the red on the balance sheet, Jacob knew God was definitely on his side. Buying Frank's property would be like eating one of Grace's BLTs, easy and delicious. His stomach growled. He debated heading home for his noontime prayers and Grace's cooking, but remembered the expected call and the sack lunch his wife had packed for him. Hopefully a BLT, though BLTs were better with crispy, hot bacon.

He reached for his desk drawer, marveling at how smoothly it opened. The desk had cost him over ten thousand dollars, but it had been well worth the money. Underneath his lunch lay *The Wisconsin Chronicle*.

Jacob spread the front page of the newspaper out on the desk and emptied the lunch bag. *Shoot, no BLT.*

Leftover pot roast sandwich? No. Peanut butter and jelly!

What is the woman trying to do, kill me?

He hated peanut butter. Then he remembered the crack he'd made about her burnt pot roast the previous night. Several Bible passages came to mind about a wife being obedient to her husband.

As he leaned over to toss the sandwich in the trash, he read the paper's headline: "University to Raise Fees, Students Protesting." *Uppity rich kids with nothing better to do.* He dug an orange out of his lunch, glancing further down the page. Peeling the fruit, the sweet citrus smell making his stomach growl again, he read, "Presidential Candidate Griffin Carlisle Met with Wisconsin Leaders at Capitol Today."

He set the orange down. Any story about that homosexual ruined his appetite. *People like Griffin Carlisle shouldn't be allowed to exist, let alone run for office.*

Wait a minute.

What had Vern said about Townsend's phone call? A guy named "Griffin" coming to town. Wasn't Townsend a reporter?

Jacob switched on his iMac. Sure enough, *The Chicago Examiner* staff list included Leo Townsend, Metro/Government Reporter. Jacob located Townsend's last story, "The Changing Face of Politics." It featured a head shot of Griffin Carlisle.

Hell.

Townsend wasn't excited about some feed king coming to the farm. He was going to interview a presidential candidate.

That fag is coming here. To my village!

Jacob's empty stomach churned until he remembered that, in addition to running the bank, Emmett headed the local chapter of the Protect Marriage Movement. Perfect. A few words in the right ears to get anti-gay folks riled might give the Townsends one more reason to sell. He'd talk to Emmett.

But would that be enough? More information, that's what he needed. Jacob reached for his phone. "Vern, I've got another little job for you."

17

Leo entered the small lobby of the Endeavor police department. Patrick was leaning against the counter and chatting with the desk sergeant about the Brewers' chances. Two other officers holding steaming coffee mugs stood by the community bulletin board cluttered with yellowed village meeting notices, discussing the high price of gasoline.

"You can go in." The sergeant waved a *Sports Illustrated* in the direction of the chief's office.

Leo introduced Endeavor Police Chief Morris Grey to Patrick and thanked him for seeing them on such short notice. The police chief was seven or eight inches shorter than Leo and numerous inches wider, the buttons on his brown uniform stretched to their limit. But his six-star badge and the brass buckle on his belt gleamed, and his navy blue pants were sharply creased.

"You're expecting an important visitor tomorrow." Chief Grey sat behind his metal desk. Only a telephone, a plastic pencil holder with one yellow pencil, and a picture of the chief with his wife and three kids adorned the desktop.

"How'd you—"

"Griffin Carlisle's campaign manager called. Protocol."

"I'd appreciate it if we could keep this to ourselves."

"We're a small town. Word gets out. But I'll do my best." The chief settled back into his chair. He clasped his hands over his protruding belly. "What can I do for you?"

"Someone's poisoned our cattle," Leo said.

Startled, Grey knocked over the pencil holder with his elbow. The lone pencil rolled onto the floor, clicking as it bounced on the linoleum tile. He left it there. "How do you know?"

"The vet from Merritt's Landing—"

"Why not use Doc Krueger?"

"He's been hard to get a hold of. When several cows aborted, we called Dr. Stork. He found high nitrate levels in their blood, most likely from urea fertilizer. My dad hasn't fertilized in more than six months."

"Why would someone poison your cattle?"

"To get us to sell the farm."

Chief Grey assessed Leo. "It's well known that Jacob Landry wants to buy your farm. You're not suggesting he's behind this?"

"I am. Johnny Caldere saw Vernon Smith driving past our property yesterday morning. Johnny said this flew out Smith's window." Leo placed the piece of fertilizer bag on the chief's desk. "It's no secret that Smith is Jacob Landry's right-hand man."

The chief examined the piece without touching it. "If you could prove that this came from Smith's pickup, I might be able to get him for littering. Not much else. If Caldere caught him on your property with the bag in hand, then we'd have something to work with. But I'd still need evidence to connect his actions to Landry."

"Agreed," Patrick said, rising. "We simply wanted to make you aware of the situation and our suspicions."

"Understood. If anything else occurs, be sure to let me know."

As Leo and Patrick left the village hall and walked down the sidewalk, Patrick said, "How much do you want to bet Chief Grey already got the word out—"

A solid mass slammed into Leo's back. He lost his footing, struggled not to fall. "What the—"

"My apologies," Caleb Toole said, grabbing Leo's bomber jacket to keep him from falling. "Didn't see you."

Toole had been in Vernon Smith's high school class and had played tackle on the football team. He was still large but unlike Smith, he'd let himself go. His enormous gut spoke of fried food and too many beers.

Leo found his footing. He tried to pull away but Toole wouldn't let go. "What the hell?!"

Toole yanked Leo closer. "I heard you're entertaining that fag politician on Friday. Didn't know you swung both ways, Townsend." He let go of Leo's jacket and wiped his hands on his jeans. "Wouldn't want to catch anything."

"You're outta line."

"You're outta your mind if you think folks 'round here will let you bring that, that—"

Leo moved to within inches of Toole's face, vaguely aware that a small crowd was gathering. "Who I invite into my home is none of your goddamned business."

Toole didn't back down. "It is my business when you bring a bomonation of God here to our nice Christian community."

"Wrong word, moron." Leo headed for the car. Patrick followed.

Behind them several people in the crowd gasped.

Leo spun around in time to see Toole's fist. He bobbed to the left and received a glancing blow on his chin. He punched Toole hard in his soft underbelly.

Toole let out a whoosh of hot, sour air and doubled over. Leo bent close to the large man's ear and whispered, "You're the abomination."

A trio of middle-aged women with shopping bags shook their heads, then walked away, muttering to each other. Two businessmen looked impressed and nodded their approval. Carl and his customers had watched the show through the barbershop's picture window across the street. Carl scratched his nearly bald head and frowned. But from her diner's entryway next door, Aunt Sally clapped.

18

After grabbing a quick sandwich, Leo found Frank and Eddie talking in Eddie's first-floor bedroom, a Bach violin concerto playing in the background. The bedroom doubled as Eddie's studio. Definitely not farmhouse-typical, the room was decorated in urban chic. The blonde floorboards contrasted with the dark wood of the platform bed and side tables, which were topped with sleek, silver lamps. Vertical blinds bookended a wide picture window that offered a panoramic view of the backyard and fields beyond.

Frank was relaxing in the leather chair, a mug of steaming coffee in his hands. Eddie sat in front of his computer table, which was covered with an odd mix of high-tech gadgets and old-world implements. His twenty-seven-inch iMac monitor displayed a Chicago skyline screensaver with the Townsend farmhouse nestled in Millennium Park. What Eddie called, "The best of both worlds." Next to the computer lay his digital Cannon camera. On the corner of the table, two scrunched tubes of paint lay beside a glass jar holding an eclectic array of brushes and drawing pencils. Eddie fingered the bristles of one of the brushes as Frank discussed the rotted soy bean crop they would have to plow under.

"There's fresh coffee in the kitchen." Frank raised his mug.

"Maybe later." Leo sat on the edge of the bed.

"How did it go with Chief Grey?" Eddie asked.

"Nothing he can do, but at least he's aware of the situation." Leo hesitated. "So… I'll be busy tomorrow morning… Griffin Carlisle is coming here for an interview."

"That gay guy?" Frank asked.

Eddie's face paled.

"The presidential candidate." Leo tried to keep his voice calm. "I'm writing an article about him. He's offered to stop here on his way to Minnesota."

His father laughed without humor. "Homeschoolers, gay politicians, what next?"

"I'll interview him in the study. We'll be out of your way."

"Sure, why not? Have him join the party." Frank slammed his half-empty coffee mug on the table, making the paintbrushes jump, and shuffled out of the bedroom.

Eddie's face drained of color.

"Are you okay?" Leo asked.

Eddie bit his bottom lip and reached for his cell phone. "Gotta make a call. Hope I can get a cell tower signal."

That's something Endeavor has in common with Chicago. In the country, the lack of cell towers made it hard to get reception while Chicago's numerous skyscrapers actually blocked signals. "Who are you—"

Eddie waved him angrily away.

Leo closed the bedroom door behind him as Eddie yelled, "No goddamned reception!"

Thursday evening, the sun shone through the farmhouse's dining room windows, warming Leo's back. His sore body welcomed it. He'd spent the afternoon mending fences, using muscles he didn't even know he had. He and Johnny had also helped Doc Stork tube the cattle to relieve their bloating and hydrate them. Disgusting treatment but it worked. The cattle's health was improving.

Leo finished his chicken parmigiana and considered seconds. He'd had Will's food before but this was better than anything he had tasted, even at Spiaggia's in Chicago.

"You've outdone yourself, Will."

"I can't take all the credit," the teenager said. "I found your mom's recipe box. I hope that's okay."

Leo raised his glass of wine. "It's a wonderful tribute." He smiled at Eddie, expecting his brother to agree, but Eddie had been uncharacteristically quiet during the meal.

"What's for dessert?" Patrick asked, surprising Leo. *How does such a skinny guy pack in all that food?*

"Isabella's tiramisu," Will said. "Her recipe called for dark rum. I've included dark chocolate, too."

"Sounds incredible. But I'd better pass." Frank collected his empty plate. "Doctor's orders." Will had made him a low-fat dish of baked chicken breast and fresh vegetables. "I'll be in the den watching the news if anyone needs me." He shuffled off toward the kitchen.

"You didn't tell us what happened in town." Mary said, as Quinn and Tali rose to help Will clear the dishes.

"Didn't want to say anything in front of Dad."

"Did Vernon Smith admit to something?"

"No. Though he squirmed when I showed him that piece of fertilizer bag."

Will and the girls brought out the tiramisu on Isabella's Italian china. Leo tasted the sweet dessert. "Will, this is amazing. I only wish my mother was here. She would have tried to adopt you."

Patrick inhaled his dessert and then said, "We had an interesting talk with Police Chief Grey. He seemed sincerely concerned about the cattle but said his hands are tied. I have to agree. Without an eyewitness, poisoning is pretty hard to prove."

"Why couldn't you mention this in front of Frank?" Mary asked.

Leo finished his dessert and pushed his plate aside. "After we left Chief Grey's office, a man named Caleb Toole threatened us, me."

"Oh, my god."

"Word got out that I'm interviewing Griffin Carlisle here at the farm tomorrow morning."

"Interviewing a presidential candidate?" Tali cut in. "How cool is that?"

"Very cool. But Toole made it clear that some of the locals aren't too keen on my inviting such a *'bomonation of God'*—his words—to Endeavor."

"What did you do?" Mary asked.

"Leo slugged him in the gut." Patrick laughed. "Doubled him over."

"Awesome!" Will said.

"The guy hit me first." Leo rubbed his jaw. "A glancing blow, thankfully. Toole's a big guy." He waited for a witty comment from his brother—something about the dangers of taking on the local redneck.

Eddie just studied the contents of his wine glass.

"I doubt he'll bother us again," Leo said.

Mary looked unconvinced. Eddie said nothing.

"After we clean up, how about a nightcap on the front porch?" Patrick said, in an obvious attempt to lighten the mood.

"You all go ahead." Leo rose to help. "I've got to do some prep work for my Carlisle interview."

As Leo rinsed the last of the dirty dishes and arranged them in the dishwasher, he reconsidered following everyone outside. Patrick's brandy would loosen his sore muscles. But he wanted to review Barnes' article and his notes, jot down some questions, and do some additional research. He'd like to broach the subject of Griffin's boyfriend—

"Leo." Eddie wheeled into the kitchen, interrupting his thoughts. "Can we talk?"

Leo closed the dishwasher and flipped it on. The machine murmured to life as he sat down at the kitchen table across from his brother.

"There's something I've wanted to tell you," Eddie said, "…should've told you years ago. It never seemed to be the right time…"

Eddie took a deep breath, which didn't calm his shaking hands.

Someone screamed.

"Mary!" Leo ran past Eddie and out to the porch. His feet slid in something slimy and he fell hard in a mass of what appeared to be bloody intestines. The spongy coils reminded him of the one and only time he'd gutted a deer. The stench was overwhelming.

"*What the hell?!*"

Leo's fingers touched a severed snout. He gagged, then grabbed the railing to pull himself up, his hands slipping on the rungs. He shouted a warning to Frank, Eddie, and the kids as they prepared to bolt out the front door.

"Ew," Quinn and Tali said in unison, recoiling.

"Gross," Will added, holding his nose.

Patrick and John were racing down the driveway, cursing the rearview lights of three pickup trucks. The drivers honked and whooped with laughter. The last truck stopped at the end of the driveway. The driver shouted something that sounded like "faggot."

"What happened?" Leo asked.

"Trucks roared down the driveway straight at us," Mary said. "Men with buckets piled out even before the trucks stopped. Tossed this mess. It's amazing no one got hurt."

John rejoined them, Patrick limping behind. Both were breathing hard.

"The lead truck had a Protect Marriage Movement sign in the back window," John said. "Does that mean anything to you?"

"That's an organization that fights same-sex marriage legislation," Eddie said. "Leo's *friend*, Caleb Toole, is a member of the local chapter."

Leo turned to Patrick. "Did you see Toole in any of the trucks?"

"No."

"Toole isn't the major problem," Eddie said. "Emmett Everson, president of the local chapter of the Protect Marriage Movement, is also president of the Endeavor Bank—the bank that holds our mortgages."

"Christ," Leo said. "Maybe I should call Griffin. Postpone."

"Hell, no," Frank said. "I won't let a bunch of religious nuts dictate who I can and can't have in my house. You tell Carlisle we're looking forward to his visit."

"I agree," John said. "But inform Mr. Carlisle of the situation. He might want to increase his security."

"I'll visit the police station again tomorrow." Patrick massaged his leg, which had never fully recovered after his near-fatal motorcycle accident the previous fall. "File a formal complaint. Maybe Chief Grey can at least keep those assholes out of our hair while Carlisle is here. Quinn, could you take some photos before we clean up this mess?"

Quinn left for the barn to retrieve her camera. Moments later, she reappeared and started clicking. After snapping pictures for about ten minutes, she reviewed them. "That should do it."

Frank began to move a wicker chair out of the scum.

"No, Frank," Charlotte said. "You go on to bed. We'll take care of it."

Frank hesitated, nodded, and went inside.

"I'll get a bucket and some rags." Eddie wheeled into the house and soon returned with cleaning supplies.

Leo wiped his hands on the rag Eddie offered him. "You wanted to tell me something?"

"Tomorrow," Eddie said and then handed the rest of the supplies to Charlotte and Patrick.

Leo turned to Mary. "We need to talk." He ushered her down to the driveway, careful to avoid the gore.

As their shoes crunched on the gravel, a whippoorwill called. Leo gazed at the night sky, amazed at the number of stars he could see—stars blotted out by city lights in Chicago. On the western horizon, clouds thickened and began to cover the starlight. "Maybe it would be best if you and the kids left in the morning. I don't want to put you at risk."

"We just got here. We'll be fine. We survived that anti-homeschooling riot last year, didn't we?"

"True…"

"John, Patrick, and Charlotte are taking Frank and the kids to the cattle auction in Richland Center in the morning. They won't even be here during the interview."

"What about you and Eddie?"

"I'd like to see Griffin after you've talked to him. Eddie mentioned that he has some work to do. Griffin's Secret Service men will be here. We'll be perfectly safe." She kissed him. "But I'm worried about you. What will happen once the article's published?"

"I've written about controversial figures before. Threats go with the job."

Mary placed her hand over his heart, a look of concern in her eyes.

"I'll be careful. I promise." He tucked a strand of blonde hair behind her ear. "Wait with me while I give Griffin a call?"

"So you're on a first-name basis with a presidential candidate, huh?"

"He insisted. He's not like any other political candidate I've known. I actually trust him."

"Normally, I'd say you shouldn't. He's a politician, after all," Mary said. "But I've known Griffin a long time. I'd trust him with my life."

After several connection attempts, he got through. "Griffin, this is Leo."

"Is everything okay?"

"The local anti-gay organization found out you'll be in town. The bastards paid us a visit tonight. They threw buckets of pig guts and blood. Then sped off."

"I'm so sorry. Was anyone hurt? Should we cancel?"

"Everyone's fine. And I'd still like you here. But I'm worried about your safety."

"I've been an openly gay man for over twenty years," Griffin said. "Pig blood is the least of my worries. I'll alert my security team. We'll be fine. But I don't want to bring any problems to your family."

"My father's determined to have you here."

"I really appreciate this, Leo. It's very important that we meet. I'm giving you a scoop, if you want it."

"Yes, of course I want it. But a story of mine almost destroyed a whole town last year—"

"My story," Mary corrected, whispering teasingly in his ear.

"—and I don't want that to happen again."

"Do you think those idiots will return tomorrow? Do they know what time I'm arriving?"

"I'm afraid they do." Leo pictured Griffin accosted by Landry and his thugs. "I have an idea."

19

"Drinks on me!" Jacob yelled as Caleb Toole and the others barged into the tavern. They high-fived and fist-bumped as Jacob tapped beers and Blake Shelton sang "Boys Round Here" on the jukebox.

Jacob loved owning Isaiah's Tavern. The sleek, mahogany bar lined with carved beer taps, the gleaming liquor bottles reflected on mirrored shelves, the honky-tonk jukebox, the crushed leather chairs and oak tables, the private booths lit with Tiffany lamps, the small stage where he showcased local talent and even strummed on his guitar a few nights every month—he loved every inch of it.

He especially loved serving the townsfolk as they blabbed their secrets over one too many whiskeys. His teetotalling Christian friends complained when he opened the place but he referred them to scripture, Isaiah 55:1, *Yes, come buy wine...* And after all, Isaiah was his middle name.

"How did it go?" he asked Caleb, as the younger man took a frothy mug from Dahlia. Dahlia's breasts threatened to dislodge from her hot-pink tank top. Jacob had to remind himself that she was his niece.

Caleb downed his beer, then replied, "I wish you could've been there." He winked at Dahlia. She flipped him the bird.

"Yeah, 'specially when Townsend came running out onto the porch and landed in a pile of pig guts. On his ass," Artie Potts added, wiping foam from his top lip. The others roared. Artie belched.

"That would've been a sight! Sorry I missed it."

"Will it stop that Carlisle faggot from coming to town?" Dahlia set a heaping plate of fried cheese curds in front of Jake.

"I sure as hell hope not!" Jacob selected a clump of curds and bit into the gooey cheese.

"Why not?" his niece asked.

"I'm planning an impromptu press conference on County T, using the Townsend farm as the backdrop." He wiped his mouth on a paper napkin that read: *Come to Isaiah's ~ We'll Answer Your Praiahs.*

"We'll welcome Griffin Carlisle to our beautiful little village," Jacob continued. "Open the meeting to questions.

"I figure Emmett, as president of both the bank and the local Protect Marriage Movement, will want some answers. I think a few hundred congregants from the evangelical churches in town might want to hear those answers, too." He took a long swig of Guinness. "We'll all be respectful, of course. Listen to what the man has to say. When he spews forth the filth of his lifestyle, we will be vindicated. He will bring about his own destruction."

"You're delusional." Dahlia crossed her arms.

"How so?" he asked coolly.

"That man's been on the campaign trail for almost a year and is close to winning his party's nomination. Have you ever heard him discuss his personal life other than to admit he's queer? You won't get him to say a goddamn thing."

"Dahlia, sometimes it amazes me how many times you can be wrong," Jake said. "First, politicians can never turn away admiring voters. We'll simply meet his limo at the end of the Townsends' driveway, cheering, clapping, lending support. And now that I think of it, why stay in the road? We'll follow him all the way up to Frank Townsend's front door. By then, it'll be too late to stop us."

"Couldn't if they tried," Artie grunted, his mouth full of fried cheese curds, his lips greasy.

"That's right, my boy." Jacob slapped him on the back.

The front door opened. A burst of sunlight backlit Vernon Smith's massive silhouette. When the door closed, Jacob could see Vern grinning so wide it was amazing he got through the door.

Jake winked at Vern, then continued, "Carlisle is coming to our little neck of the woods for the sole purpose of granting Leo Townsend a *Chicago Examiner* interview. Why do you suppose that is?" He didn't wait for an answer. "He's going to tell Townsend the name of the man he's screwing. Give him an exclusive."

"Yeah. So?" Dahlia filled a boot of beer for Vernon and handed him a fresh basket of deep fried pickles.

"We'll hear the whole thing," Jacob said, as the jukebox played OneRepublic's "Secrets."

Vern added, "While the rest of you vandals were throwing pig guts at the Townsends, I snuck in their back door." He chugged the whole boot, then belched. "Bugged the place."

"No way!" Dahlia playfully slapped his arm.

"Sure as shit." Vern stuffed a fistful of pickle slices into his mouth. "Managed to plant three of those babies before Frank Townsend came back in. Thought he'd catch me in the living room but he went right upstairs without a glance in my direction. I high-tailed it to the kitchen, planted the last one, and managed to get out without anyone seeing me. Hiked it to my car parked in their back forty."

"Great job, Vern," Jacob said. "By this time tomorrow we'll know who Carlisle's *boyfriend* is." He sneered.

"Ya goin' to tell the press?" Caleb pried open a few peanuts and tossed the empty shells on the floor.

"Nope, we're keeping it to ourselves until the time is right." Jacob put his arms around Vern and Caleb, the shells cracking under his loafers. "We'll destroy Carlisle—and the Townsends—all in one fell swoop."

"What've you got against the Townsends, other than them hosting a fag?" Caleb asked before downing a shot of whiskey and chasing it with his fourth beer.

"Yeah." Artie wiped grease from his chin with his sleeve. "And why are you so obsessed about buying that farm? It's not like it's profitable."

Jacob silently disagreed, picturing the contents of the safe in his office down the hall.

"I know a good business deal when I see it," he said.

20

Leo went for a quick run Friday morning, happy to see that the previous night's rain had washed all remaining traces of pig's blood from the front porch steps. Then, he showered and dressed. As he threw on his bomber jacket and grabbed his reporter's notebook and digital recorder, Eddie appeared in his bedroom doorway.

"I need to talk to you." Eddie's words were little more than air, as if it took too much effort to make a sound.

Leo checked the time on his phone: 9:07. "I'm really sorry, but it'll have to wait. Landry's crew might make an appearance here." Leo squeezed past the wheelchair, the spokes bare. "I'd like to get to town before anyone spots me leaving."

Jacob's sixty-five-year-old vocal chords were tired of shouting, "God Condemns Carlisle," and "Queer Candidate," though he couldn't stop because his faithful loved it. He was proud of the creative chants but disappointed by the low turnout. At nine thirty Friday morning, half an hour before Carlisle's expected arrival time, barely twenty-five God-fearing Endeavor townies had gathered on County T at the end of the

Townsend's rain-soaked driveway. Not much of a rally. Police Chief Grey had driven by to check things out, saw the straggling group, and didn't even bother to stop.

Emmett had promised that everyone from his local Protect Marriage Movement chapter would be available but most begged off at the last minute, claiming they were busy with crops, jobs, children… whatever. Jacob had taken his frustrations straight to God, asking the Almighty why He would forsake him at this most opportune time. God answered by instilling enthusiasm in the small band of protestors. They more than made up for the lack of numbers.

After the chants, the hymns began. These were Vernon's idea. Who knew the guy could sing? Course the rest of them couldn't hold a tune, but nobody cared. The off-key songs rallied the folks even more and got great coverage from the newly-arrived Madison and Milwaukee TV broadcasters jockeying for the best camera angles. Jacob was glad he'd called them and couldn't wait to watch the nightly news.

Leo sat in a corner booth at Aunt Sally's Diner, directly across from Griffin Carlisle. The restaurant smelled of bacon and fried donuts and the countertops gleamed.

Sally had promised that at ten o'clock on a beautiful Friday morning in May there'd be few customers in the place. By that time, the breakfast crowd would be gone, headed back to the village hall, the bank, or local places of business to start their day, out to the fields for the spring planting, or down to Buffalo Lake to get a jump on the weekend fishing.

True to Sally's word, Leo, Griffin, and the two Secret Service agents were the only customers. Leo guessed that anyone who might have lingered over their breakfast was out at his father's farm, hoping to catch a glimpse of a presidential candidate.

Aunt Sally poured a steaming cup of coffee into Griffin's blue mug, age spots covering the papery thin skin on her right hand. Sally had already been elderly when a teenaged Leo frequented the diner, stopping in with his buddies for chocolate malts after Saturday matinees. His memories of her extended even further back, in fact. When seven-year-old Leo asked Isabella if Sally was his aunt, his mother had replied, "No, Leonardo. The people of Endeavor simply call her 'Aunt Sally' because she's so good to us."

As Leo thanked Sally and introduced Griffin, she set the coffee pot on the Formica table and patted him on the cheek. "I'm so sorry about your mom, sweetie. Such a wonderful woman. I miss her. And I'm sorry to hear what happened out at your place last night. Those men are animals."

Before Leo could respond, she turned to Griffin. "Candidate Carlisle. It's a pleasure to meet you." She smoothed her crisp white apron over her floral dress and shook his hand. "I'll get you one of my cinnamon pecan morning buns. Hot out of the oven." She grabbed the coffee pot and headed for the kitchen, her skirt swishing.

"Sally," Leo called after her, "thanks again for not telling anyone we're here."

"By anyone do you mean Jacob Landry? Oh, sweetie, I'd rather bathe in a tub of cow shit than talk to that S.O.B." She pushed through the half-doors to the kitchen, making them swing.

"Sally doesn't mince words, does she?" Griffin laughed.

Leo smiled, but couldn't shake an ominous feeling. The last time he'd sat in a restaurant with Griffin, Eddie had called with the news of their dad's heart attack. And then moments ago, Eddie had wanted to discuss something that he found difficult to say. But there hadn't been time. Leo checked his phone for messages. No connection.

"This was a brilliant idea to meet here." Griffin sipped the coffee, blanched, and then pushed it aside.

"I knew most of the town would be at our place. Your arrival is the most exciting thing that's happened in years."

"How's the farm? Did you get that mess cleaned up?"

"Yes. With everyone pitching in, it didn't take us long. And last night's downpour helped."

"Have the police caught the vandals?"

"No. Their license plates were covered in mud so we didn't get the numbers. And the police chief claims it's impossible to find specific pick-ups because Endeavor has more trucks than people." Leo raised his coffee cup to his lips, then remembered Sally's knack for burning coffee grounds and set it back down. "One of the trucks had a Protect Marriage Movement sign in the back window. The police chief questioned members of that illustrious organization. Not surprisingly, those folks claim their signs were stolen."

Griffin shook his head. "Frustrating."

"Phone reception is tricky in Endeavor, but I did manage to talk to Mary before you arrived." Leo decided to give the coffee a try and found it hard to swallow. Small town diners were said to have the best coffee in the world, but while Aunt Sally made the best omelets, chicken pot pies, and triple-fudge brownies, she never had been able to brew a good cup of coffee.

He dumped in a couple of packets of sugar and poured a splash of cream into the mug. "Mary and our hired man are relaxing on the front porch. There's a group of people out in the road chanting but they're harmless. A few reporters came but without you there, they won't stay long."

Griffin followed Leo's lead by adding sugar and cream to his coffee. After blending the liquid, he took a drink and winced. "How long before those people realize we're here?"

Sally marched over to their booth. "They'll never know if I have anything to do with it." She set down two plates topped with large hunks of hot cinnamon-and-pecan rolls. "Enjoy." She waved her hand and hunkered off to deliver bakery to the Secret Service men.

"That crowd will eventually give up and head back into town," Leo said. "We have some time, though. Patrick should be arriving there in the limo soon." He took a bite of the roll, warm sugar, cinnamon, and roasted nuts filling his mouth.

"Ah, yes, the decoy. Okay, then, I should get to the point."

Leo turned on his digital recorder and set it on the table.

Griffin studied his hands holding the coffee cup. He drew in a deep breath. "As you know, I am in a serious relationship with your brother, Eddie."

Leo froze for a few seconds. *Had he heard right?* He fumbled with the

GOD ON MAYHEM STREET

recorder, suddenly unable to find the "off" button.

"Everything okay?" Griffin asked.

"Doesn't seem to be working," he mumbled. He finally pushed the right button but continued to mess with it, giving himself time to process that Eddie was gay. Why hadn't he considered this before? Eddie was good-looking, intelligent, and creative, yet once he'd graduated high school, he'd never mentioned girlfriends.

"Sorry, recorder's not working." He shoved the machine aside and fished his notepad and pen out of his jacket pocket.

"I realize Eddie just recently told you," Griffin said. "It can be a lot to process."

You have no idea. "Not at all." Leo hoped he sounded unfazed.

"Good, good." Griffin laid his hands on the table. "So when I met Eddie, I wasn't looking for a relationship. In fact, I had talked myself out of any long-term commitments. It's difficult pursuing a political career and having a serious relationship, even for a heterosexual male. Do you know how many politicians' wives stay with their husbands only for the sake of the campaign? Oh, well, I guess that's obvious; just look at the Clintons.

"Anyway, I hope you don't mind me telling you this but I was attracted to Eddie right away. His sense of humor, talent. The way he's completely comfortable with his disability. He uses his wheelchair as a tool, as an extension of himself. It's almost balletic." He cringed. "That sounds like I was turned on by his chair. Please believe me, it's nothing like that. I don't have any weird fetishes, although that would make for an interesting headline." Griffin laughed.

Leo managed a smile as he struggled to wrap his head around this new image of his brother. Then it occurred to him that Ted would take him off this assignment. Journalistic ethics kept reporters from writing about family members. While it was goddamned disappointing not to get the scoop, he had to admit it was also a relief. Leo didn't want to be the one to tell the world his brother was gay.

"My campaign manager," Griffin continued, "had heard about a particularly talented graphic artist, Eduardo Townsend, so we went to Eddie's Chicago office. We like to see who we're dealing with, to find out everything we can. You can tell a lot about someone by visiting their workplace.

"We sat in the fifteenth-floor conference room with an incredible view of the boats drifting down the Chicago River. I looked around for a portfolio or an easel with examples of his work, anything, but there was nothing. I had outlined what I wanted when I set up the meeting, so I assumed Eddie would have a few drawings, at the very least.

"Eddie asked me, 'what is the first thing you would do as president?' The question surprised me. I remember kidding about redecorating the China Room until I realized that he was serious. So we discussed my plans, goals, and political aspirations. Well, I should say, I discussed, because Eddie simply listened." He paused as if picturing Eddie's face.

"Anyway," Griffin continued. "This went on for about forty-five minutes. Finally, my manager said that we had another appointment. He thanked Eddie and rose from his seat.

"I realized that this meeting had not gotten us anywhere, other than for me to ramble on to a complete stranger. I was embarrassed. Angry.

"Eddie said, 'Give me a minute.' He reached into the credenza for a large sketchpad and fine-tip marker. He began to draw. Amazing to watch. When he finished, my face looked back at me, very presidential, patriotic, but hopeful, visionary. Somehow he captured not only what I looked like, but what I imagine my presidency will look like. Well, you know, you've probably seen the posters."

"Yes, they're incredible," Leo agreed. Always something vaguely familiar about the sketches, he'd wondered who the artist was. He should have recognized them as Eddie's work.

"We hired him immediately. I took him out to a celebration dinner that night. We've been together ever since." Griffin hesitantly took a bite of his bakery. "This is good." He sounded surprised.

Leo jotted a few notes and then asked, "So you want me to tell the world you're dating my brother?"

"No. I plan on making the announcement after the national convention this summer, assuming I'm my party's nominee. In the meantime, I'm sure both sides will continue to make it an issue. My manager wants to use that to our advantage. Get the sympathy vote but also keep people guessing. What is important is to keep Eddie's identity a secret for as long as possible. I'd appreciate it if you could help us with that."

Sally appeared, and before either one could stop her, she topped off their coffee then visited the Secret Service agents.

"I can't keep it quiet that long. The press—hell, my editor will demand to know."

"If we could just hold off." Griffin tapped his long fingers on the table. "I'll assure the voters that my boyfriend has been vetted by the NSA, CIA, FBI, the Department of Homeland Security—and my mother—and that they have no reason to fear him. I'd like to focus on the issues and not my love life." Griffin sighed.

"I don't think Eddie's aware of the impact this will have," he continued. "He's hidden his homosexuality his whole life. This is much more than coming out to your family."

Which he has yet to do.

"It's coming out on national television. You wouldn't believe the number of death threats I get on a daily basis. It's unnerving—even for me—and I have bodyguards. Do I really want to put Eddie through this?"

"It sounds like you're thinking about breaking up with him."

"Honestly, I have tried, for his sake. Eddie claims that I'm worth anything we may have to deal with."

Leo pushed his roll and coffee aside. "I'll keep Eddie's identity a secret but when you want to divulge his name, I can't write the article. It's a conflict of interest."

"I've considered that. How about an editorial? An exclusive. Tell your editor that I don't want anyone else writing this. It's you or no story."

An editorial is a possibility. But could he write it? Normally, Leo wouldn't hesitate. The country was entitled to know who their presidential candidates associated with. Some would argue that it was a matter of national security. And if he wrote the exclusive, he'd have his pick of jobs. Maybe even land a top position at the *Wall Street Journal* or *New York Times*.

But what would the publicity do to Eddie? He'd lived his entire life pretending to be someone he wasn't and now the world would know. Was a job worth exposing his brother?

No.

He looked at Griffin's hopeful face. "I'll discuss it with my editor when the time comes," he said, knowing he wouldn't take the assignment. He glanced over Griffin's shoulder at the vintage Mickey Mouse clock on the wall. 11:30. "We'd better go."

As they slid out of the booth, Aunt Sally approached them and handed Leo a large paper bag. "A few morning buns for Frank. Don't tell his doctor."

When he reached for his wallet she waved him off. "My treat."

He leaned down and kissed her weathered cheek. She smelled of baking powder biscuits and butter.

She shook Griffin's hand again. "I'll be famous in Endeavor," Sally said. "I've shaken the hand of the next president of the United States, twice."

Jacob was having serious troubles. At ten thirty Carlisle still hadn't shown at the Townsend farm. Ten thirty turned into ten forty-five, and Jacob assured his group that politicians were always late. When eleven o'clock came and Carlisle still hadn't made an appearance, Jake's faithful turned on him. Artie led the charge, claiming he'd lost a whole morning of planting for nothing. Spit flying from his mouth, he questioned why Carlisle would come to some podunk village like Endeavor.

Endeavor, a podunk village?

Artie pointed out that serious candidates hit the big cities and college towns and didn't bother coming out to the sticks. Others shouted in agreement, their words putting a stop to the few still singing hymns. Artie shoved past Jacob to steer the Bransons toward their car.

"Hang on," Millie Branson said. "Is that a limo?"

Carlisle's black limousine—*who else could it be?*— drove down County T, slow and sure as if it owned the place. The sides were splattered with mud but the license plate clearly read *Washington, D.C.* Rather than intimidating anyone, the large vehicle ignited the crowd more than Jacob's chants or Vernon's hymns.

As the car turned into the driveway's entrance, Vern played linebacker and blocked it. Caleb, Artie, and Buddy Howard joined in. They shouted, pounding on the hood.

Jacob walked to the driver's door, surprised to see a beautiful blonde woman behind the wheel, a chauffer's hat on her head.

She rolled down her window and leaned out. "Back away from the car. Let us pass."

The chauffer was dressed in what looked like a man's white shirt, modestly buttoned to the hollow at the base of her throat. But the shirt didn't hide her curves. Patrick Holden's motorcycle partner. Jacob smelled a trick.

"Take off your shirt and we'll consider it," Jake suggested.

Buddy whooped. Artie and Caleb whistled.

The limo's passenger door flew open, slamming into Caleb and knocking him in the mud. Patrick Holden exited, climbed over Caleb, and pushed his way through the crowd to Jacob.

Jake backed away. The hippy was wiry but certainly strong if he could flick three-hundred-and-fifty-pound Caleb away like a bug. Jake cringed, expecting a fist to impact with his jaw. Then Vern appeared. He shoved Patrick against the car.

"Get your goddamned hands off me!" Patrick yelled.

Vern obliged but blocked the hippy's path to Jacob.

"Hey." Artie peered into the limo. "There ain't no one in this car but the driver. Goddamn it, Jacob!" He slammed the passenger door shut and yelled to the crowd. "Carlisle's not here and he ain't comin'."

"It's a decoy," Jacob yelled. "I tell you, Carlisle will be here."

"You're full o' shit." Caleb wiped the mud off the seat of his pants. "I actually think you're losin' it. Come on, boys, let's go home."

Crowd members grumbled as they walked to their trucks. Jacob felt his face flush. He hadn't been so humiliated since the summer he turned fifteen and lost his swimming trunks diving into Buffalo Lake.

21

The Secret Service men ushered Leo and Griffin into the back seat of Frank's Caprice, a less conspicuous and roomier car than Leo's Mustang. Leo directed the driver down a rutted, one-lane back road to avoid running into any townspeople. The car's tires kicked up gravel and clumps of mud. Bouncing, Leo held onto the back of the passenger seat's headrest to steady himself as the driver circumvented potholes deepened by the spring rains. Griffin held onto his door handle. As they swerved to miss a deep rut, the Chevy's right front tire popped.

"Damn, I'm sorry," Leo said, as they watched the hissing tire deflate. "We shouldn't have taken this road."

"Not your fault." Griffin crouched by the flat. "We needed to avoid detection. But we're running out of time. I wanted to talk to your family."

"It won't take that long to change," the driver said, opening the trunk of the car.

"How far away are we?" Griffin asked, standing.

"The farm's over the next hill." Leo pointed to the rusty white cap of the concrete silo.

"Lead the way."

Even sidestepping mud, it didn't take Leo, Griffin, and the second Secret Service man long to reach the top of the hill and the barbed wire fence ringing the Townsend farm. Leo lifted the wire, making a gap for the two men to maneuver through. They trudged down the hill, slipping and sliding in their dress shoes but not falling. As Leo reached the bottom, he took his leather jacket off and threw it over his shoulder, the spring breeze cooling his skin.

Griffin followed Leo, trudging around mud and clumps of upended grass. "What's this?" He tapped a concrete ring with the toe of his shoe.

"Our original well. It dried up a few years ago so Dad had it sealed off." Leo moved closer, his feet sinking into the damp earth. "That's strange. Someone's been digging here. Must be a leak. Dad didn't mention it." *But he hadn't mentioned dying crops and sick cattle, either.*

As they started across the field, Leo said, "When they dug the well, Eddie and I were teenagers. We used to goof around on the pile of dirt." He reached in his jacket pocket for the black velvet bag. "I found this." He handed Griffin the smooth crystal.

Griffin stopped to examine the stone. "What is it?"

"No idea."

"I have a geologist friend who could identify it. In fact, Mary knows him. Oliver Tenney. We went to law school together. He's on my campaign committee."

"Oliver Tenney from Chicago? The architect?"

"Do you know him?"

"He was here on Sunday with Jacob Landry, inspecting the farm."

"Really?"

"Landry's pushing the Bank of Endeavor to foreclose so he can buy our land. We think he wants to build a mega church."

"Eddie mentioned the possible foreclosure and I was sorry to hear it. Oliver is the top architect in Chicago, especially when it comes to churches. Small world." He rubbed the crystal between his thumb and finger. It sparkled as it caught the sunlight.

Ten minutes later, Leo led Griffin and the Secret Service agent up the wooden steps to the farmhouse's back porch. They left their muddy shoes beside the screen door and entered the neo-Italian kitchen. A package of cracked-wheat wafers with a note taped to it lay on the hardwood table. *Hi, Leo and Mr. Carlisle! There's a plate of aged cheddar and smoked sausage for you in the fridge. Enjoy! Will.*

"Mary's son?" Griffin asked.

"He's an amazing chef." Leo tossed his jacket on the back of a kitchen chair and took the hors d'oeuvres out of the refrigerator.

"What is he now? Fifteen?"

"That's right." Leo removed the plastic wrap from the tray. "I'm guessing he made the cheddar and smoked the sausage himself." He bit into the peppery meat. "Something to drink? Will's homemade lemonade or something stronger?"

"Lemonade. Better be sharp when I meet your father."

"Nothing for me," the Secret Service agent said. "If you don't mind, Mr. Townsend, I'd like to take a look around. If we're all clear, I'll position myself on the front porch."

"Certainly. Whatever you need to do."

Griffin thanked the man and pulled out a kitchen chair. He examined the woven seat. "Beautiful."

"My mother said they reminded her of her mother's kitchen in Italy."

"When I first met you," Griffin said, sitting down and helping himself to cheese and crackers. "I had a hard time picturing you living on a farm."

Leo poured the lemonade into one of his mother's Italian crystal glasses. "I hate farming, much to my father's disappointment. I take after my grandfather. The writer Sawyer Townsend." He handed Griffin the glass.

"No kidding! His book, *All Souls Die*, is one of my favorites. Not a fan of organized religion, was he?"

Leo laughed. "No, particularly small-town evangelical churches. My dad claims Sawyer left Endeavor because he didn't want to farm, but I wouldn't be surprised if the local ministers ran him out of town."

Mary breezed into the kitchen, smelling of fresh lavender. "Griffin Carlisle, it's been a long time."

An ashen-faced Eddie wheeled in behind her.

"Too long, I'm afraid." Griffin embraced Mary.

"And now it's Presidential Candidate Carlisle." She gave him a peck on the cheek. "Congratulations."

"Thanks. How have you been?"

"Got me a new man." She kissed Leo.

Damn her lips are soft.

Griffin bent as if to hug Eddie, glanced at Mary, and then shook Eddie's hand. "Nice to see you again." He said to Mary, "Eddie's created all the beautiful artwork for my campaign. Logos, posters, everything."

"That's an amazing coincidence," Mary said.

"I'd like a moment with Leo," Eddie cut in, and then added softly, "If you don't mind."

"Certainly," Griffin said. "Mary and I have some catching up to do."

Leo followed Eddie into his bedroom. The bedsheets and blanket were rumpled, dirty clothes littered the floor, and beer bottles filled the waste basket. One bottle had rolled under the desk, leaving a trail of drips across the wooden floor. Mozart's *Requiem Mass* resounded from the speaker on Eddie's desk.

The minute the door clicked shut, Eddie said, "Did Griffin tell you…"

Leo grabbed the wayward beer bottle and tossed it in the basket. It clattered when it hit the other empties.

"I'm sorry you found out this way," Eddie said.

Leo shoved the mass of tangled sheets aside and slumped on the bed. "Why didn't you say anything?"

"When Griffin said he was giving you the exclusive I assured him I'd talk to you before your meeting today. The last couple of days, I've tried. We kept getting interrupted."

"You've had years."

"I… I feared that you… felt the same way Dad did. I didn't want you to think less of me." His voice faded as he looked at his hands in his lap. His fingers tore at a frayed nail on his left thumb.

"That's not possible." When Eddie's moist, bloodshot eyes met his, Leo added, "You should've had more faith in me."

A tear grazed Eddie's grizzled cheek. "I'm sorry."

"When did you first realize…"

"Remember I told you I lost my virginity on the dirt pile by the well?"

"That's what you said."

"I lost it all right. And to beautiful, perfect Dahlia Landry. But the experience felt like shaking hands. No passion." He angrily wiped the tear away. "The whole time I kept picturing her brother. I had always suspected I was gay. That moment I knew."

"But that was what, fifteen years ago?"

"Eighteen."

"Why didn't you tell me then?"

"You'd just left for college. I had high school to deal with. When you graduated from U of I, you began reporting for the *Examiner*. I was studying at the Art Institute and working on the farm during summer breaks. We were both so busy. Kind of lost touch, you know? When we began training for the triathlon two years ago, I almost told you."

Eddie looked hopeful, and more than a little worried. "I'm so sorry I didn't tell you sooner. Trust you."

Leo hugged Eddie, held onto him until Eddie's tense muscles relaxed and then gave him a sad smile. "I'm sorry you've felt you had to keep this a secret." He sat back on the bed. "I have to say I'm a little relieved. You never mentioned dating anyone. I worried that you wouldn't find someone to spend your life with. I'm happy for you. But..."

"What?"

"He's what... ten years older than you?" Leo kidded.

"Isn't Mary five years older than you?"

"Touché. But wait a minute. When we saw Griffin's rally on TV you complained about gays flaunting their lifestyle."

"I may have exaggerated, but some in the gay community do take it too far. I don't believe in shoving my sexuality in other people's faces."

"No, you're the master of hiding it."

Eddie wheeled over to the desk and turned off Mozart's melancholy music. "I almost told Dahlia."

"*Dahlia?*"

"When she divorced her second husband a couple of years ago, I took her out to dinner. She read the signs wrong, came on to me. She was shocked when I turned her down."

"Does Dad know?"

"I haven't told him. But on some level I'm sure he does. Are you going to report who Griffin Carlisle's boyfriend is?"

Leo shook his head. "My editor will take me off the story. Ethics. It's impossible to be objective about family members."

"But if Griffin gives you an exclusive your editor won't have a choice. Right?"

Leo paced the room. "Griffin suggested an editorial. My editor might agree to that. It's the exclusive I've been waiting for," he admitted. "You can't imagine what it would do for my career."

"Oh, really?" Eddie raised an eyebrow.

"Okay, maybe you can. Newspapers would pay a lot of money for a clue to the man's identity. Your identity." He turned to face his brother. "But Eddie, it's not about the story. It's your life. I can't do it."

"I'll be named eventually."

"I don't want to hurt you."

"The story's going to come out. I want you to write it."

Leo studied his brother's handsome face, a more youthful version of his own.

"Please."

Leo took a deep breath and exhaled. "Okay."

Eddie's shoulders relaxed, then shuddered. "So I guess I need to tell Dad I'm gay." He chewed on the frayed thumbnail. "I'm dreading that more than becoming national news."

"If he already suspects it, it'll be a relief to have it out in the open. You're his favorite son, it'll be okay."

Eddie wheeled toward the bedroom door. "I'll talk to him as soon as he gets back from the cattle auction."

Leo followed him into the kitchen.

"Hey, you two," Mary said. "Griffin was asking me about Quinn and Will." She turned back to the candidate. "They're planning a trip to Italy this summer."

"Wonderful," Griffin said. "And how is that little town of yours? Your inn?"

"Both are keeping me busy, particularly the town. We have several new families who don't understand our unschooling, child-led learning lifestyle. One couple spanks their child in public. The town council, led by Patrick, is drafting rules of public conduct."

"What does John say?" Leo asked, as he poured Eddie a glass of lemonade.

"He finds it sad that Carpe Diem residents are now the intolerant ones."

"Why didn't you tell me?" Leo asked.

She caressed his face. "You've got enough problems of your own. It'll sort out."

"I'm sure you'll be able to handle it," Griffin said. "You've always thrived on conflict."

"A little peace and quiet would be nice for a while."

"I wonder what that would be like," Griffin said.

Eddie coughed and set his glass down. "I didn't see the car."

"We drove on the back roads and popped the tire," Leo said. "We trudged through the mud."

"It wasn't that bad." Griffin clinked the ice in his glass. "Felt good to walk."

"And we discovered that someone's been digging around the abandoned well."

"That's odd," Eddie said.

"Do they know about your crystal?" Griffin asked Leo.

"Eddie does but I haven't shown it to Mary. Hang on." Leo reached for his coat. When he pulled out the pouch, a red ribbon dropped to the floor. He rubbed the soft fabric tenderly and replaced it in his pocket. He handed the stone to Mary and explained its origin.

She held it to the light. "It looks like a piece of glass but there's more of a brilliance to it. What type of crystal is it?"

"I don't know. Griffin suggested I ask your law school friend, Oliver Tenney." Leo turned to Eddie. "Apparently he's an architect *and* a geologist."

"Mary and Griffin know Tenney?" Eddie said. "Amazing."

"I'd forgotten about Oliver." Mary handed Leo the crystal. "Does he still work out of Chicago?"

"In the Loop," Griffin answered.

"We could stop by his office on Sunday before we go to O'Hare. It'd be nice to see him. It's been years." She put her arm around Leo.

"We probably won't have time. But I'll keep the crystal in my jacket just in case." Leo placed the stone back in its velvet bag and slipped it in the coat's pocket, next to the ribbon.

"You're taking a trip?" Griffin asked.

"To New York City. For the Pulitzer Prize Luncheon."

"Ah, yes." Griffin held up his glass. "Congratulations, Leo."

"Thanks. I'm looking forward to it. How were things here?"

"People gathered at the end of the driveway," Mary said. "Other than their singing painfully off key, not much happened until Charlotte and Patrick arrived in the limousine. Then the crowd got a little rowdy. Lots of shouting, mostly at Landry, and then car doors slamming and engines revving as they left."

"Where's Patrick now?"

"He and Charlotte went to talk to the police chief. Again. I'm not sure it'll do any good. I hope he doesn't get himself into trouble. You know how he can be."

"Yep, the last time he tried persuading a government official, he almost got himself killed."

The front screen door screeched and then slammed. Quinn, Will, and Tali burst into the kitchen with news about fast-talking auctioneers, mammoth-sized cattle, and juicy steak sandwiches. Leo introduced the kids to Griffin Carlisle. They quieted, visibly in awe of meeting a presidential candidate. John Holden entered the kitchen followed by Leo's father, who was polite but quiet during the rest of the introductions.

But as Frank joined them at the table, he grilled Griffin about his views on the Middle East. Frank's command of the facts and the depth of the discussion impressed Leo. Leo had always assumed his father only cared about the weather and local farm reports.

When Frank and Griffin agreed about what should be done in the region, Frank said, "This man's got my vote."

"My job here is done," Griffin laughed.

Frank said to Leo, "I like this guy. I'm glad you invited him here."

Leo winked at Eddie, who rolled his eyes.

"*I'm* glad to hear that," Griffin said, then he became serious. "Frank, I'm wondering if you and I could talk privately."

"Come on, kids. Let's get to those farm chores." Mary ushered them out of the kitchen.

"Why don't we go to my office?" Frank suggested.

"I'd like Eddie and Leo to come, too."

As the four men started down the hall, Eddie had a hard time getting enough traction on his wheels to make them turn, his hands slipping. Leo reached for the wheelchair's handles, but Eddie waved him off.

Frank led them into the study and yanked back the curtains, exposing the windows and a sweeping view of the hill Leo and Griffin had climbed. He offered Griffin his recliner and sat on the leather couch next to Leo. Eddie managed to wheel across the braided rug and settle beside Griffin.

"Frank," Griffin began. "I want to tell you how sorry I am to hear about your wife. I understand she was an incredible woman."

"She was," Frank said.

"I also want to apologize for the problems my visit has caused you."

"I appreciate you saying that."

"Frank." Griffin looked down at the rug and then directly at Leo's father. "I have something rather important I need to tell you."

"No, wait," Eddie said. "I'll tell him."

Griffin glanced at Eddie, his right hand starting to reach for him and then dropping back into his lap.

"Dad," Eddie croaked. "Griffin and I are in a relationship."

The only sound in the room was the solid ticking of Isabella's Italian grandfather clock in the corner.

Then Frank laughed. "Is this some kind of joke?"

"No, Dad. It's not. In fact, I'm in love with Griffin."

Frank stared at his son, his face turning red. He glared at Griffin and opened his mouth, but no words came. He stood, his feet unsteady, but he waved off Leo's help. Then he stomped out of the room.

"At least he didn't slam the door," Leo said.

"Actually," Griffin said, "that was better than the reaction I got from my dad. When I came out to him at sixteen, he slugged me."

"Seriously?"

"He asked my brother to hold me down. Said he wanted to beat the fag out of me."

"What did your brother do?" Leo asked.

"He refused."

"Good."

"Said he didn't want to touch me."

"Jesus." Leo leaned his elbows on his knees, clasped his hands. "But now that you're successful, things must be better."

"You would think so. My mother and I keep in touch, but my father and brother actually hate me more because I've told the world of my 'deviant nature'. So much for familial love."

Griffin took Eddie's hand.

"Give Dad some time to digest this," Leo said. "When you do talk to him, I'll come with you. Lend support."

"Thanks."

"I should get going." Griffin leaned over to kiss Eddie.

Leo diverted his eyes, not ready to see this display of affection between his brother and another man.

"Stay for lunch," Eddie said.

Leo rose from his chair. "We've got plenty of Will's excellent food."

Griffin glanced at the antique clock. "My campaign manager is expecting me at the hotel in Minneapolis by six. We have some prep work to do before tomorrow's convention and then there's a campaign donor reception."

"It's a four-hour drive to the Twin Cities," Eddie said. "We'll feed you and get you on the road by two."

"Deal," Griffin said. "And what about our friend Landry? Any chance he'll make another appearance?"

"Doubtful," Leo said. "He didn't catch you. His followers have turned on him. And we're on to him about the cows. He's done harassing us."

22

Jacob relaxed in the passenger seat of Vernon's pickup as they rumbled through the streets of Endeavor. Vernon pounded his fist on the steering wheel, shaking the truck. "We missed our chance. If Carlisle was here, he's gone!"

Jacob hummed "The Battle Hymn of the Republic."

"Why're you so calm?"

"Carlisle's not gone. I have a hunch he's at the Townsends."

Vernon whipped a U-turn.

Jacob gripped Vern's arm. "No, Vern, let it go. There's been enough chasing for today."

Vern slid the truck into a vacant spot in front of Aunt Sally's Diner and threw the car into park, jolting them to a stop. "You're giving up?"

A black limo crawled past. For a moment Jacob thought they'd caught Carlisle after all. Patrick Holden waved at him from the driver's seat. *That damned hippy lawyer.*

Jake pictured his daddy's sawed-off shotgun hanging over his living room fireplace. He thought about how nice it would be to cock that gun and feel it kick back into his shoulder, to watch the pellets leave the double barrel—and then pulverize Patrick Holden's face.

"I never give up," Jacob said. "Let's go to your place. If Carlisle has been at the Townsends', your little recording devices might have found something interesting."

Twenty minutes later, Jacob and Vernon sat in what passed for a kitchen in Vern's mobile home. The place smelled like a locker room after a five-hour football game played in sweltering heat. Dirty laundry spilled out of a basket, spreading all over the threadbare couch. A soiled sock hung on the corner of the flat-screen TV.

Four years earlier, Vernon had lived in a comfortable, three-bedroom split-level with a two-car garage in the Rolling Acres subdivision on the edge of Endeavor. But his wife had complained that he spent more time with Jacob than with their two toddlers. She'd accused him of loving Jake more than he loved her. Vern acknowledged the first accusation—taking care of children was woman's work, after all—but he and Jacob vehemently denied the second, insisting they were true-blooded heterosexuals.

When Vern avoided his wife's incessant complaining by spending even more time with Jacob, she filed for divorce. The house sold at a loss and his wife emptied their bank account, packed the kids, and took off. She left Vern with barely enough money for the trailer. It sat at the end of Shady Lane, next to perpetually-full dumpsters and a disintegrating 1975 Datsun pickup truck.

Jacob searched in the fridge for a cold Budweiser. He needed a stiff drink, but Vern only bought cheap beer. He found a takeout pizza box with three limp slices of sausage, a half-eaten sub sandwich, a garlic dill pickle jar with one spear, three cans of Red Bull, and a sour smell—probably from the sandwich. He slammed the refrigerator shut then sat across from Vern, pushing aside cords, plugs, and a small box that looked like a flash drive.

Jacob inspected the box. "What's this?"

"Equipment I didn't need. Didn't have time to plant that last bug."

"Might come in handy." Jacob pocketed it. He slipped headphones over his ears as Vern plugged the cord into the iMac Jake had bought him for his fortieth birthday.

"The bugs are voice-activated," Vern explained. "Saves batteries. I rigged the computer with a splitter jack so we can use two sets of headphones at the same time." Vern adjusted the second set over his ears.

Within minutes of eavesdropping on the Townsends, Jacob praised the Lord and fought the urge to dance around the cramped room. Instead, he continued to listen as Griffin Carlisle told the Townsends he had to go.

"Oh, sweet Mary Magdalene." He yanked off the headphones. "I think I heard those two boys kiss. Glad I didn't have to see that. Though I sure wish I could have been there when Eddie told old man Townsend he was gay." He rubbed his hands together. "Would have liked to have seen that old codger's face."

"What do you think Frank'll do?"

"If Eddie were my boy, I'd take matters into my own hands. A beating like the one Griffin's father proposed might be in order. He'd no longer be allowed anywhere near Carlisle, of course. I'd keep a watch on him 24/7."

"And there's that homosexual cleansing course Emmett teaches," Vern added.

"Yep, he'd be going to that. Clean him right up." Jacob pushed back the chair, scraping it against the yellowed linoleum. "This is incredibly good news. Wraps everything up in a nice, neat package."

Why had he ever doubted the Lord's methods? He hoped God would forgive him his doubts. But of course the Lord had forgiven him. He'd snared both the Townsends and Griffin Carlisle in one perfect plan and He'd selected Jake to carry out that plan. Jacob looked down at his hands to see if they glowed with the light of God. *Was this how Moses felt when he carried the Ten Commandments?*

Jake's cell phone praised Jesus. "Emmett, thanks for returning my call. Now's as good a time as ever." He turned off his phone and headed for the door. "Be back later. Got me a banker to persuade."

Jacob strode into Emmett's glass-and-chrome office again, feeling like a fish in a goldfish bowl. The room was large, sterile, airy, but Jacob preferred cave-like offices where transactions remained private.

Emmett offered him one of the utilitarian chairs but he declined. Instead, Jacob remained standing, forcing the banker to look up at him.

"Emmett, I know there are foreclosure laws that dictate a time frame, but with a little creativity there are ways around them."

"I have no idea what you're talking about." Emmett picked a piece of lint off his lapel.

Jacob often wondered about the banker's sexual tendencies. The guy had a wife, but no children. *Did they have sex?* And though Emmett ran the homo-cleansing program at the Church of Our Beloved Savior, what man in his right mind preferred the Milwaukee Symphony over a Packers' game?

"Sure you do," Jacob said, with a good-natured chuckle. "That place down by the river you bought out of foreclosure. You got quite a good deal. It belonged to Johnny Caldere before you snagged it at the sheriff's sale. Start to finish, the whole process only took what, a month?"

"Three and a half months—totally within the law."

"You bought it and then Caldere actually had to pay you. Least that's what I heard." Vernon had been bonking the head bank teller at the time. She had been a fountain of information.

"It was a deficiency judgment." Emmett's face grew red. "The foreclosure sale price wasn't high enough to cover what was left of the mortgage, so the court issued a judgment against Mr. Caldere. He had to pay the bank for the remainder of the loan after deducting the fair market value of the property. Paid the bank. Not me."

Same thing. Jacob decided to ratchet it down a bit. "My mistake." He managed a self-effacing smile. "I'm not big on all the legal proceedings." He had some experience with foreclosures; many of the properties he owned in Endeavor had been bought through sheriff's sales, but he'd always let the bank handle the proceedings.

This time, though, Jacob was in a hurry. Leo Townsend might wonder why he was fixated on buying the Townsend farm and do a little investigating into things that were none of his business. Jacob had to buy that farm before Leo stumbled upon the land's true value. "My point is that it can be done right quick."

"The quickest time," Emmett said, "is six months if the bank waives the right to a deficiency judgment. From what you tell me, the property's value has decreased measurably. Therefore, the bank will want to exercise its right. Waiving that right is unlikely, just as it was with Johnny Caldere."

Jacob waved his hand. "Waive away. I'll make up the difference."

"The board of directors would never agree."

"You let me worry about that." Eight of the bank's thirteen directors owed Jacob for various favors. The others wanted something from him and would happily negotiate. "So now we're down to six months. How can we make it quicker?"

"It isn't possible unless the property is abandoned. In the case of abandonment, you cut the time in half."

"Three months, now you're talking."

Emmett looked at Jacob as if he were an idiot. "But the Townsends live there."

Not for long. "True, true. Six months, then."

"If you don't mind me asking, what's your hurry?" Emmett leaned back in his office chair.

"The property is too much for Frank Townsend to handle. The man's wife just died and he's had a heart attack. Who knows when he'll get back on his feet. This will give him the chance to retire. Give me a chance to build a mega church. Bring more God-fearing Christian families to Endeavor. It's a win-win solution."

It was partially true. Jacob had once wanted to build his church on the property. But the Lord had other plans. Those plans had been revealed, and his financial prayers answered, when Dahlia appeared at his front door in tears two and a half years ago.

Drunk, she'd ranted to Jacob about throwing out an old keepsake from the Townsend farm. She'd handed him a cloudy yellow crystal; said she'd discovered it as a teenager in the dirt pile next to the Townsend's well. She'd held on to it for years.

It was easy convincing her to give Jake the rock. Hell, she'd practically thrown it at him.

The next morning, Jacob had sent Vernon to see Oliver Tenney in Chicago. The man was not only a world-class architect but also a pretty decent geologist. Oliver called later that day with incredible news. Dahlia's crystal was a natural diamond, and if properly cut, might be worth ten thousand dollars. Jacob immediately stowed it in his office safe at Isaiah's Tavern and devised plans to own Townsend's pile of dirt and uncover more.

Since then, he'd succeeded in annexing the farm into the village, which spiked Frank Townsend's property taxes. He'd enjoyed knowing how much that had squeezed Frank financially. Lately, he'd focused on destroying the farm. With Vern's help, he poisoned the cattle. This worked; they were sick and, coincidentally, so was Frank, thanks be to God. Soon Townsend would have no choice but to sell or face foreclosure.

And then last Sunday after a tour of the Townsend farm, Oliver Tenney had confirmed the geological formations there were ripe for a diamond mine. But how long would Tenney be able to keep this to himself?

"A mega church is commendable, Jacob," Emmett said. "Though I don't know what Rev. Wallace would think."

Jacob didn't give a rat's ass what Wallace thought. "You've got the ball rolling on the foreclosure, right?"

"No, not yet." Emmett examined his fingernails. They looked manicured. "I wanted to give the Townsends a little time, you know, get Frank home. Settled."

"Frank's been back a few days. Let's get this thing going."

"I'll file the complaint and the lis pendens with the Circuit Court before the end of the month."

Jacob reached across the banker's desk but stopped short of grabbing the man by the collar. Instead, he picked up the framed picture of his homely wife. "Take you only a few minutes to fill those forms out now. It'd be doing me a great service if we'd get this taken care of first thing Monday morning."

"I'm sorry, Jacob, but I simply can't. Not yet."

Jacob put the picture down, opened his wallet, and fished out a few hundred-dollar bills. "Buy the wife something pretty." He slid the money across the desk.

Glaring, Emmett slid the money back to Jacob. "You dropped this."

Jacob shoved the bills in his wallet. "What can I do to get you to speed up that foreclosure?"

"Nothing." Emmett crossed his arms, obviously enjoying watching Jacob beg. "As I've already told you, these things take time. But hey, you're the village president. Why not look into eminent domain? Surely you can make an argument that acquiring the Townsend farm is for the village's greater good. No one could argue that a mega church isn't for everyone's benefit."

"Eminent domain will take too long."

Frustrated, Jacob considered telling the banker about Eddie and Griffin Carlisle. He knew Emmett would sign the foreclosure papers without hesitation if it meant throwing a homosexual out of town. While the bank board couldn't discriminate against Eddie for his abnormality, the banker would do everything in his power to expedite the foreclosure. And he'd assist Jacob in harassing the Townsends until they abandoned the place. After all, Emmett had helped Jacob rile the boys to deface the Townsend front porch simply because Griffin Carlisle was coming to visit.

But Jacob kept the Townsend/Carlisle relationship to himself. He wanted to sell that valuable information to the press. Now was the time to call FOX News.

"I'm sorry," Emmett said, not sounding sorry at all. "I can't expedite this."

"We'll see." Jacob stormed out of Emmett's office and through the bank's lobby, nearly knocking Aunt Sally over as she entered the building. He climbed into his coupe and drove back to Shady Lane.

"Vernon, give me some good news," Jacob said, as he entered Vern's mobile home.

Vernon was bent over his computer at the kitchen table with headphones gripping his ears. He shoved a headphone off one ear to hear Jacob.

"Emmett won't help us out on the Townsend foreclosure," Jacob said. "Looks like I'll be calling FOX News."

"There's something you need to listen to." Vern pushed buttons on his laptop as Jacob slid on the headphones. "This is from the bug in Townsends' kitchen."

GOD ON MAYHEM STREET

"It looks like a piece of glass but there's more of a brilliance to it," a woman's voice said. "What type of crystal is it?"

"I don't know," Leo answered. "Griffin suggested I ask your law school friend, Oliver Tenney. Apparently he's an architect and a geologist."

Jacob yanked off the headphones. "Leo's got a diamond."

"The good news is he doesn't know it. Yet."

"But he has a connection to Oliver Tenney. We've got to get that diamond from him before he finds out how valuable it is."

"It's in his jacket pocket."

"There's got to be a way." Jacob paced the small room. When his foot skidded on a bare patch in the carpet, his hand shot to the window sill for support and became entangled in bug-infested spider webs. Disgusted, he wiped his hand on his shirt. "Keep eavesdropping. Follow Leo's movements. Let me know when he heads to town."

23

Leo, Mary, Eddie, John, and the kids said their goodbyes to Griffin and watched his limo drive away. Frank hadn't come downstairs but Griffin quietly assured Leo and Eddie he wasn't offended. "He just needs some time," he'd whispered.

As the car turned onto County T, it veered to make room for a motorcycle pulling into the driveway. The cycle stopped at the bottom of the porch steps.

"Was that Griffin Carlisle?" Charlotte asked, pulling off her helmet.

"Yes," Mary answered. "I'm sorry you missed him."

"That's okay." Patrick threw his gauntlets into his helmet. "I'm not in the mood to meet anyone. It's been a hell of a day."

"It didn't go well at the station?"

"Apparently Police Chief Grey despises Landry. Mentioned something about the village president cheating at cards and stealing his money, though he couldn't prove it."

"That's good," Leo said.

Patrick shook his head. "Chief Grey dislikes gays even more than he dislikes Landry. He noted our concerns but won't lift a finger. Says there's nothing he can do because the protestors were on County T—public property. When I pointed out that they unlawfully blocked access to the driveway, Grey claimed that was a minor issue. Asshole's not budging."

"Thanks for trying," Leo said.

Charlotte put her arm around Patrick. "Come on, babe." She led him into the house. "I'll buy ya a beer."

"First dibs on the rope swing," Will hollered, racing away. Quinn and Tali chased him to the barn.

"Leo, I think we should check on Dad," Eddie suggested.

"Right."

"I've got to call my concierge," Mary said. "See how things are at the inn."

Leo gave Mary a kiss and had a sudden desire to grab her and drive off to Chicago's opulent Palmer House hotel with its champagne room service, leaving the farm and all this small-town drama behind. Sighing, he followed his brother inside.

Eddie shifted himself and his wheelchair onto the lift Leo had installed at the bottom of the staircase. Leo followed him up the stairs and then down the hallway to the master bedroom. They passed Eddie's black-and-white photographs of Isabella kissing Frank on the front porch glider, Leo leaning against the weathered barn doors, a romping newborn calf, and geese flying in a V-formation over dried fields. The photos always evoked in Leo a feeling of home.

Out of habit, Leo walked around the floorboard kiddy-corner from the master bedroom door. That board had alerted his parents that fourteen-year-old Leo was sneaking in three hours past his curfew. Frank punished him by giving him a month's worth of cleaning out the calf pens. Leo had avoided that board ever since.

He paused at the door, ran his fingers through his hair, and knocked.

"Come in."

Fifty-year-old red Damask curtains covered the bedroom's large windows, blocking out the world. Grandfather Townsend had preferred a dark bedroom, better for sleeping, and had invested in the expensive material. When Frank and Isabella moved into the bedroom, Frank had refused to replace them despite the faded material and frayed edges. Isabella acquiesced when he had her parents' four-poster bed shipped from Italy.

A brass lamp on the bedside table illuminated him. He sat on the edge of the bed, his head in his hands.

"Dad." Eddie wheeled over to the bed. "I'm sorry I didn't tell you sooner. I'm sorry it came out this way."

Frank walked over to the vanity table and touched Isabella's sterling silver hair brush. "Your mother knew." He ran his fingers over the brush's engravings. "She told me her suspicions years ago. Hoped you'd trust us enough to tell us. She loved you." He looked at Eddie. "I love you. No matter what."

Eddie's body relaxed.

"But now that I know it's true," Frank said. "I'm having a difficult time wrapping my head around it. It changes things. You're not who I thought you were. And I feel like I've failed you because you were afraid to tell me."

Frank turned to Leo. "You're going to write about this? Why am I asking? Of course you are. It's a big story. It'll do wonders for your career. And we all know you'll write about anything, no matter whose life you ruin."

"Dad, that's not true." Leo balled his shaking hands into fists. "You know it's not true."

"No, I don't. Didn't your story destroy Mary's town?"

"That wasn't my article. And Carpe Diem, Illinois wasn't—isn't—destroyed."

"Be that as it may, you're now determined to ruin your brother."

"Next you'll blame me for his homosexuality." Leo headed for the door.

"Well, maybe if you'd been around more instead of abandoning us as soon as you turned seventeen…"

"I didn't abandon you." Leo faced his father. "I went to college. My being around more wouldn't have had any effect on Eddie's sexuality. It's not a choice."

Eddie grasped his father's hand. "This is who I am, Dad. And now that I've met Griffin, fallen in love with him, I wouldn't want to change even if I could."

Without another word, Frank pushed past them and out into the hallway.

"Unbelievable," Leo said. "You tell Dad you're gay and you're dating a politician, but not just any politician, a presidential candidate. He hates politicians, yet, he gets mad at me. I'll never figure out why he hates me so much."

"He doesn't hate you."

"Yeah, he does."

24

Saturday morning, Jacob swung by Vernon's place to see if there were any more eavesdropping developments. He knocked on the yellowed front door and checked his knuckles for grime as he waited. No sounds from inside the trailer. Had Vern gone out? Jake jimmied the door. The latch stuck but with a push, it opened. Vernon was slumped over his kitchen table, the headphones still attached.

"Vern!" Jake yanked the headphones off.

"Wha—?" Vern wiped saliva from the corner of his mouth. "Musta fallen asleep." He glanced at the recording equipment. "Not much excitement over at the Townsends."

"Come on. I'm taking you out for breakfast."

As Jacob and Vernon entered Aunt Sally's Diner, Jacob smelled biscuits and gravy, his favorite. He nodded to the only other customers, an out-of-town couple seated at the counter, as he walked past them to a corner booth. He was thankful the place was empty. After the disaster out at the Townsend farm, he'd had enough of that ungrateful crowd.

"Jacob Landry, what the hell are you doing in my diner?!" Sally exploded out of the kitchen.

"Now Sally, don't be mad. You and me go way back. Let bygones be bygones."

"Bygones my ass. You take your shit-eating grin and your gorilla and get the hell outta my diner." She advanced, rolling pin in hand.

Jacob laughed as he slid into the booth. "Oh, dear, what are we going to do Vern? We simply came in for a country breakfast. Surely our money's as good as anyone's. Some would say better."

"I want you outta here."

"In fact," Jacob continued calmly, "Sally's grandson, what's his name Vern?"

"Devon Hass."

"That's right, Devon. Devon loves my money. Particularly when he needed it last night to bail himself out of jail."

Sally's raised rolling pin hung in the air.

"So you see, Sally, you actually owe us. It'd be real neighborly if you could serve us some coffee and your breakfast special—two for Vern. And I won't say a word to that boy's mama."

Sally's lip quivered as she lowered the rolling pin. She stammered for a moment and then stomped into the kitchen. Soon there was metallic crashing, banging, and scraping as if an army of soldiers were searching the kitchen for a hand grenade.

Vernon laughed. "You sure have a way with women, Jake."

"One of God's gifts, my boy."

Sally returned, slammed two cups and a coffee pot on the table and hurried back to the kitchen. Jacob chuckled. He took a sip of the coffee and frowned at the bitter taste. He pushed the cup away as he watched the out-of-town couple leave a wad of bills on the counter and saunter out of the diner to a parked Toyota Prius. *Probably from Madison.*

Vernon gulped his coffee without grimacing. Jacob shook his head. Vern could drink battery acid and enjoy it.

"So Griffin Carlisle's banging Eddie Townsend," Jake said. "How do you think the folks of our good village will take it when they find out that a well-known politician has been dallying with one of our own?"

"Yeah, I can't believe it. Homos in Endeavor."

"My guess is Carlisle came here to meet Eddie's family before he announces it to the world."

"Once he spills the beans our information isn't worth shit," Vern added, stating the obvious.

"True, though we still have the issue of homosexuals living in our midst. That should give us some traction with the bank board." Jacob tapped his fingers on the table.

"Go to the media with it. Let's destroy Carlisle and the Townsends and be done with it."

"Now hold on, Vernon. This information is valuable. Let's get something for it first."

Sally dropped their heaping plates on the table. A sausage link jumped off Jacob's dish. "I appreciate what you've done for my grandson," her voice quivered. "Enjoy your breakfast. Then leave."

Vernon growled.

Jacob, in an especially good mood, decided to reward her. "You bet, honey. We'll eat and be out of your hair."

She tossed their bill on the table and stalked off to the kitchen.

They ate in silence, the biscuits disappearing quickly. Then Vernon started in on his second helping and asked, "When you say 'get something for the Carlisle information,' are you thinking of selling Eddie's name to the press?"

Jacob swallowed the last of his sausages before answering. "It has crossed my mind. But first I think I'll let Emmett know exactly what the bank is dealing with. I'd bet my granddaddy's Bible that once he hears, he'll want to rush the foreclosure as soon as possible. Kick the Townsends out of Endeavor.

"But I don't want to play my cards too early." He selected a fifty from his wallet, threw it on the table and slid out of the booth. "Once you're finished here, go home and put those headphones back on." He patted the big man on the shoulder. "Let me know if you hear any more secrets."

25

After a long morning run, Leo actually cleaned the isolation pens in the loafing shed. Once he got used to the odor he didn't mind it so much. In fact, the manual labor gave him a chance to think about his Griffin Carlisle article, to work it out mentally. Once the shed was clean, he spread fresh straw. Finally, a smell he didn't have to get used to. As Leo finished with the last section, he heard Mary giggle.

She stood next to the open barn doors, taking pictures of him with her iPhone. He glanced down at his white t-shirt and bib overalls covered in bits of hay, pants tucked into heavy-duty work boots. A far cry from his leather jacket, designer jeans, and Italian loafers. "If you post those pictures on Facebook, I'll never forgive you." He pretended to be offended. "It'll ruin my reputation."

"I can read the headlines now." Mary watched him put away the pitchfork. "Casanova falls in love with heifers."

He snatched two handfuls of straw and ran toward her. She squealed, barely making it out of the barn before he pummeled her with it. He threw his arms around her and kissed her. "No cows," he said, when he came up for breath, "Casanova's in love with Mary."

She looked at him, her eyes wide. She touched his face, ran her fingers over the scar on his chin. "I love you, too."

He kissed her again, wanting to take her then and there, until he heard the rumbling of a tractor and teenaged shouts of laughter.

"I have an idea," he said. "Why don't I treat everyone to lunch in town? We've all been working so hard."

She shook straw out of her hair. "You get cleaned up and I'll let them know."

"Or better yet," he grabbed her around the waist, "let's leave them a note and get cleaned up together."

"Are you sure you don't want to come into town with us, Eddie?" Leo asked, as he walked into his brother's bedroom. "It's a beautiful day. So warm I'm leaving my jacket here."

"Can't." Eddie took a folder out of his desk drawer. "Buddy Howard and Artie Potts will be here in a couple of hours. They hired me for a design project weeks ago. With everything that's happened... well, I forgot about it. Anyway, I've got to pull together some sketches before they arrive." He switched on his computer. "I'm surprised Dad's going with you but I'll admit it's a relief. It's hard to face him."

I always have a hard time facing Dad. "He wants to pick out the supplies we need." Leo checked over the list. "Doesn't trust me to get it right, I suppose. I tried to talk him out of it. Thought it would be too much for him. Christ, he just got out of the hospital, but that of course made him even more determined to come. It's probably a good thing. Give you both a little time." Leo slipped the supply list into his wallet. "See you later."

Eddie started a Google search on his computer. "Bring me back one of Aunt Sally's brownies."

As they entered Landry's Farm & Hardware Store, Leo smelled rubber and freshly-cut wood. The shelves were packed with livestock feed, tractor parts, and horse tack. Frank picked out the specific fencing supplies he needed while barking at Leo to buy the livestock supplements the vet recommended. Tali squealed when she found four-packs of Sprecher's root beer, so Leo added a few to their cart.

They loaded the Bradbury Inn van with their purchases and then Leo led the exuberant troops three blocks down Lakeside Avenue to Aunt Sally's Diner. As they walked, Frank engaged in a lively conversation with John Holden about the benefits of grass-fed cattle and free-range farming. *Hard to believe the man just had a heart attack.*

Leo introduced everyone to Aunt Sally. Wearing a blue apron over her yellow-checkered dress and a wide grin, Sally ushered them to her favorite two booths. "I could get an early start on my famous fish fry if anyone's interested." She tightened the strings on her apron. "My grandson, Devon, caught two buckets of walleye this morning. They'd go great with coleslaw and home fries."

"Perfect," Leo said, and Sally left for the kitchen.

Locals occupying neighboring tables told Frank how good he looked. Carl Kenyan kidded that his problem was not his heart but his shaggy hair. Bill Stevens asked if he could borrow Frank's farmhands. Mrs. Whitford gave him a kiss on the cheek. "Still handsome as ever," she told him, causing him to blush.

Then Jacob Landry walked in.

"So, kids." Leo turned to the booth behind him, trying hard to ignore Landry's presence. "How're your plans for Italy?"

Landry stood in the doorway, taking stock of the place.

"Good," Quinn replied. "Since Will's our foodie, he's picking out the restaurants in Florence and Rome. Tali's using her research skills to track down your ancestors in Norcia."

Landry spied Leo.

"And your job?" Leo asked Quinn.

Landry shook Carl and Bill's hands and asked Mrs. Whitford how she was doing on this fine day. Then he walked toward Leo.

Leo gritted his teeth.

"Be cool," Mary whispered in his ear.

"I'm the money behind the operation," Quinn said, and the kids laughed. "Actually," she continued, "I'm working on our budget, which is hard to do because Will's—"

"If it isn't Leo Townsend," Landry interrupted. "Frank, glad to see you're up and about." He reached out to shake Frank's hand. Frank turned to John Holden and asked him about cattle prices in Illinois.

After an awkward moment, Landry rested his outstretched hand on Leo's shoulder. "You've got quite a crew here. But where's Eddie?"

Leo moved out of Landry's reach. "What do you want, Jacob?"

"My, my, the Townsend boys sure aren't in the mood to be social." When Leo didn't take the bait, Landry said, "Fine. I'll be on my way." He made his rounds to the other patrons as Sally came out of the kitchen with a fresh pot of coffee.

She steered clear of Landry and approached Leo, leaned over and whispered, "I need to talk to you."

"What's on your mind?" Leo asked.

"Not here." Sally glanced at Landry. "In the kitchen."

Landry eyed Sally suspiciously, then sauntered out of the diner.

"What was that about?" Patrick asked. "Landry didn't even order takeout."

"Seemed like he wanted to make an appearance," Mary said.

"Agreed." Leo exited the booth. "And where is Vernon Smith? I didn't think Landry traveled anywhere without that goon."

Outside Aunt Sally's Diner, Jacob slid into his Coupe DeVille, closed the door, and called Vernon. "Leo's in town. He's not wearing his jacket. Looks like the Lord gave us a break."

"Buddy Howard and Artie Potts are out at the Townsend farm now," Vern reminded him. "Eddie's done some design work for him."

"I'll call Caleb. He can join them. You head over there right away. Search for that diamond while the boys occupy Eddie. Keep an eye out for Johnny. Don't let him or anyone else know you're there." Jacob fingered the mother-of-pearl cross dangling from the Caddie's rearview mirror. "I'll stay here. Let you know when Leo's headed your way. And Vernon—"

GOD ON MAYHEM STREET

"Yeah?"

"I'm counting on you."

"Landry gone?" Aunt Sally asked as Leo entered the kitchen. Pans of raw fish, egg wash, and breading lined the counter. A large metal bowl filled with raw fries sat next to the fryer.

"Until I saw Jacob, I'd forgotten about this morning. My pantry needed restocking and I had to run to the store. Only after I filled my cart, did I discover I'd left my wallet at home. Had to rush home then back to the store—quick—to prepare for the lunch crowd. Don't know where my mind is these days."

"What about this morning?" Leo asked.

"Jacob and Vernon were here for breakfast. I overheard them talking." She paused. "Okay, all right, I eavesdropped. Normally I don't listen in on my customers but he's got me so peeved that I wanted revenge. The nerve of him coming into my place and treating me like that."

"Treating you like what? Did he hurt you?"

"No, nothing like that. It's… oh, never you mind." She took a deep breath. "Landry knows that Griffin Carlisle's boyfriend is your brother. He's going to sell that information or use it in some other evil way. Eddie's like a son to me and I like Mr. Carlisle. I'd hate to see either of them get hurt."

How on earth did he find out? "Thanks for letting me know. I owe you."

"No need for that." She hesitated. "Well… there is something. If there's a way you can get Landry out of my hair, and everyone else's for that matter, I'd appreciate it."

"I'll try."

"You do that, sweetie. Now join your party. I've got fish to fry."

As he walked into the dining room, Leo considered the last two days. Yesterday at the diner, Griffin had told Leo he was seeing Eddie, but Sally hadn't said anything to Landry. Then, Eddie had admitted to Leo he was gay and Griffin had talked to Frank about their relationship. But that was at the house. He stood next to the table but didn't sit down even after Mary slid over to make room.

"Is everything okay?" Mary asked.

Suddenly it was all so clear. Jacob Landry had poisoned their cattle, arranged to vandalize their house with pig guts, blocked their driveway with an anti-gay protest, and intimidated Charlotte. He'd trespassed on their land; had he been in the house as well? Had Landry bugged their conversations?

"Leo?"

He took Mary's hand, led her out of the diner, down the sidewalk away from Landry sitting in his car, and past a group of teenagers inspecting a brand new pickup, its engine revving. They walked another block, then stopped in the dank doorway of the abandoned depot. "Sally overheard Landry say he'd discovered that Eddie, that he's… well—"

"Gay?" Mary asked.

He stared at her.

"Come on, Leo. Eddie's good looking, smart, successful, in his early thirties, and not dating? But what does that have to do with Landry? Why does he care?"

"Because Eddie's seeing—"

"*Griffin?!*" She covered her mouth. "Well, that makes perfect sense. But how did Landry find out?"

"He bugged our place."

Mary shivered. "That gives me the creeps."

"Eddie's home alone. And Landry knows it." Leo took out his phone and punched his brother's number. Thankfully, he got a connection and the phone rang.

"Johnny's there," Mary said.

"Johnny's out in the fields." The phone continued to ring. "Come on Eddie, pick up!"

GOD ON MAYHEM STREET

26

Leo reached Eddie's voice mail the two times he got through.

"Didn't he have a meeting with someone?" Mary asked, as they hurried back to the diner.

"Buddy Howard and Artie Potts."

"There you go. He won't answer or call back until those men leave."

Of course, she was right. Maybe he was being paranoid, but he had a bad feeling. "I'd like to get back to the farm."

Mary held his hand, her fingers intertwining with his.

When they entered the diner, the room smelled of fried fish and everyone was eating. Leo slid into the booth and announced, "I'd like to leave as soon as possible."

"Why?" Frank asked.

"Just need to get back." Once home, Leo would make sure Eddie was fine—of course he was—then he'd explain everything to them when he found that bugging device. He cut into the walleye and shoved a forkful of it into his mouth but had a hard time swallowing.

Twenty minutes later, Frank shifted on the van's passenger seat, a bag of triple-fudge brownies in his lap. "I don't know what your hurry is. We were having a nice afternoon."

Leo glanced in the rearview mirror at Mary. She stared out the window and chewed on her bottom lip. When she met his eyes, she stopped chewing but didn't smile.

As he pulled the van up to the farmhouse, he took inventory of the vehicles. His Mustang and Patrick's motorcycle were parked out front, Frank's Caprice in the back, but there was no sign of Buddy Howard's car. *Why hadn't Eddie called him back?* Leo scanned the fields and found a dot on the far hill. Johnny riding the old red tractor.

Frank got out of the van and wobbled. "I'm a little tired."

Leo and Mary helped him to the porch as the kids followed Patrick and Charlotte to the barn with the bags of supplies. Quinn called first dibs on the rope swing. Tali moaned. Will said he wasn't interested in swinging, he wanted to get into the kitchen to figure out Aunt Sally's triple-fudge brownie recipe.

Frank handed Will the bag of brownies and patted Leo's shoulder. "I'm fine now, thanks." He climbed the steps and let himself in.

"Eddie, we're home," Leo called as he and Mary entered the foyer. They walked down the hall, started past the living room, and then froze. The coffee table was overturned, the rocking chair on its side, couch cushions slashed and scattered about. *"What the?!"*

"Leo!" Will yelled.

As they raced into the kitchen, Leo felt something crunch beneath his shoes. Pieces of his mother's china. Kitchen drawers lay overturned on the floor, spilling silverware and pots and pans. Dishes, glasses, boxes of cereal, and spilled cans of coffee littered the countertops and the floor. Bags of flour had been sliced open and shaken, covering everything with white powder.

"Eddie!" Leo shouted as he ran to his brother's bedroom, Mary behind him. He pounded on the door.

A moan.

Leo tried to open the door but something blocked it.

Another moan.

"Mary, help me. Slowly."

They pushed until they made a gap large enough for Mary to squeeze through.

"His wheelchair is blocking—" she said from inside the room. "Oh, my god!"

"Leo," she shouted. "Call 9-1-1!"

Mary shoved the overturned wheelchair aside, giving Leo enough room to push through.

Eddie lay sprawled on the hardwood floor, his useless legs bent at weird angles, his bloody, beaten face barely recognizable. *Oh, Jesus.*

Leo yanked the quilt off of Eddie's bed, laid it on his brother, and dropped to his knees. "Eddie. It's going to be okay. The ambulance is coming." *Not again. Not again.* "I'm sorry. I should have been here." His tears mingled with the blood oozing from his brother's mouth. "Protected you."

"Look." Mary pointed a shaking finger at the wall above the ransacked bed. NO FAGS! was spray-painted in bright red.

Frank ran into the room. "Eddie?"

Leo attempted to block Frank from the scene.

Frank shoved Leo out of the way. "Oh, my god, Eddie!" Then he saw the spray-painted words and rounded on Leo. "You bastard!" he screamed. "Who did you tell?!"

"No one. I—"

Frank's fist smashed into Leo's mouth.

Leo staggered back, tasted blood as his lip split. "What the hell—" A second punch connected with the right side of Leo's face, hammering him to his knees. Pain shot through his cheekbone.

Patrick stormed into the room, yanking Frank back. "Get a grip, man!" Patrick roared, dodging another of Frank's punches.

"This isn't helping Eddie!" Mary shouted.

Spent, Frank stopped swinging and cried.

"Leo, are you okay?" Mary asked.

"Yes." He staggered to Eddie's side.

She turned to Frank. "Let's get warm water. A wash cloth, towels."

"Kids!" Patrick called in the hallway. "Eddie's been beaten. Run down to the road. Keep an eye out for the ambulance. The police."

John appeared with towels and offered Leo a pillow. Leo gently slid it underneath Eddie's head. Blood soaked the white pillow case within minutes.

"Goddamn it!" Leo yelled, his swelling lip giving him a slight lisp. "Where the hell is the ambulance?"

27

Leo paced the waiting room of Madison General. The late-afternoon sunlight shining through the windows couldn't warm him. He absently touched his swollen lip, which matched his swollen right eye. He winced as his fingers grazed the shiner.

When Leo first got to the hospital, his blood-smeared clothes and battered face had alarmed the nurses. They tried to clean him up but he waved them off. He was numb to the pain and didn't give a shit how he looked.

He shuffled past Mary sitting on one of the couches with her arm around Frank. She held out her other hand to him. Leo took it, squeezed it gently.

She touched the blood stains on his shirt. "I brought clothes." She reached around the side of the couch and handed him his leather jacket and a duffle bag. "And your computer. I figured you'd go crazy without it. But I left it in the car."

When he took the jacket from her, flour billowed off it, causing him to sneeze.

"It was turned inside out in the corner of the kitchen," Mary said. "Covered in flour but in good shape."

Leo folded the jacket over his arm as "I Shot the Sheriff" rang out from his jeans pocket.

"We found four bugs," Patrick said, through the phone.

"Holy shit—four!"

"Yep. As you described, they were small, rectangular and black, and resembled computer flash drives." Leo had reported on politicians who'd been bugged, so was familiar with the devices and had explained what to look for. "I found one attached to the back of Mary's painting. Quinn found one in Eddie's bedroom on the base of his lamp, Tali discovered one at the foot of the grandfather clock in the study, and Will removed the last one by the kitchen phone. We fought the urge to smash the damned things. We've sealed them in a plastic bag."

"They couldn't have been planted very long ago. I hung Mary's painting Wednesday evening."

"Probably Thursday night. We think while those goons were splashing us with pig guts out on the porch, someone else came in the back door and planted them."

"Of course," Leo said. "They knew Griffin Carlisle was coming out to the farm Friday."

"Leo," a voice called from the hallway. Chief Grey in full uniform.

"Thanks, Patrick. Gotta go." Leo turned off his phone and shoved it in his pocket.

"What happened to you?" The chief shook Leo's hand.

"This?" Leo touched his lip. "A misunderstanding."

Grey studied him but didn't question further. "How's Eddie?" He took off his cap.

"In surgery."

"I see." Grey hesitated, apparently hoping for more news, but when Leo didn't offer any, he went on, "I wanted to let you know, in person, that we've arrested Caleb Toole, Artie Potts, and Buddy Howard for ransacking your place, and for beating Eddie. They're in the county jail for the weekend. They'll stay there until a bail hearing can be held. That won't happen until Monday at the earliest."

"How are they connected to Jacob Landry?"

"They work for him over at the bowling alley. Why? Do you think Jacob's involved?"

GOD ON MAYHEM STREET 143

"Yeah, I do." Leo decided not to mention the bugging devices. Instead, he listed Landry's other harassments. "Pig guts, protests, and now this."

"I'll look into it."

"How did you catch them so quickly?" Frank asked, standing.

"They went to Dahlia Landry's place drunk and bloody," the chief answered. "They told her they hit a deer and decided to gut it right there on the road but didn't realize it would make such a mess. They wanted to use her shower. She wouldn't let them in. When they drove away in Caleb's pickup, Dahlia noticed the empty truck bed—no deer. She gave me a call. I hauled them in. They've admitted to being at your place but haven't confessed to anything else.

"Buddy and Artie claim they hired Eddie to design a logo for the new charity they're starting. According to Buddy, Eddie hadn't done any work though they'd already paid him quite a lot of money. Said he refused once he found out the true purpose of the charity. And he refused to give them a refund."

This caught Leo off guard. "What charity?"

"It's called The Way to Sight."

"An organization for blind people?" Mary asked.

"That's everyone's first guess. No. They help homosexuals become heterosexual."

Mary laughed.

Chief Grey frowned.

"Oh," Mary said. "You're serious."

"Eddie told them he'd donated their money this morning to GLAAD: The Gay & Lesbian Alliance Against Defamation."

"And I thought I had balls," Leo said.

"Will they be charged with attempted murder?" Mary asked.

Grey hesitated. "I don't know about that. Misdemeanor battery, maybe. Those boys were a little drunk, is all. They just got carried away."

Leo threw his jacket on top of the duffle bag and lunged at the chief. Frank blocked him.

"Morris," Frank said. "They left Eddie for dead."

The police officer put on his cap, straightening the brim. "I'm not condoning what those boys did. I'm just not all that surprised it happened. Having a homosexual presidential candidate in your home probably wasn't the smartest idea."

"Are you shitting me?" Leo gently pushed his dad aside and looked down at the squat chief. "Who the hell we invite into our home is none of your fucking business."

Grey backed away. "Now, Leo," he said. "You misunderstand me. You have to remember where your Dad lives. This isn't Chicago. People in these parts aren't too keen on Griffin Carlisle running for office. Or on you inviting him here." He replaced his cap. Leo was tempted to swipe it off his head.

The chief glanced at the wall clock. "I've got to be heading back. When Eddie's well enough, I'll need his statement." He tipped his hat to Frank. "I really am sorry."

Frank sank back onto the couch as Grey walked away.

Bob Marley sang about shooting the sheriff again. Leo pulled out his phone.

"How is Eddie?" Griffin's voice shook.

"He's in surgery."

"I'm sorry I didn't call sooner. I was in the middle of a goddamned speech. We're leaving Minneapolis now. I missed the last flight to Madison so we're taking the limo. Driving like a bat out of hell. We should be there in a few hours." The line went dead.

"Griffin's on his way." Leo picked at the dried blood on his shirt. "I'm not so sure it's a good idea, Griffin coming here."

"It'll be fine," Mary said. "They've caught the guys who did this."

"You think they caught everyone involved? You honestly don't think Jacob Landry was behind this?"

"I'm sure he was but I doubt we'll have a way to prove it. Even so, Griffin will have his security team."

"Mr. Townsend?" A doctor in blue scrubs walked up to Frank. "I'm Dr. Sikdar," he said with a subtle British accent, and shook Frank's hand. "Your son is stable. Three of his ribs are cracked but luckily none of them punctured his lungs. We've set his broken nose and stitched the laceration under his right eye. It'll scar, but with proper care it won't be disfiguring. At first we thought he might be a candidate for the ICU, but that doesn't seem necessary. We're settling him into a regular room. If he remains stable, he can go home tomorrow."

"Terrific news." Leo was so weak with relief he collapsed into the nearest chair. Mary leaned over and kissed him.

"Can we see him?" Frank asked.

"In an hour or so." The doctor scanned Leo's black eye and swollen lip. "You've had a row. Did the men who attacked Eddie do this?"

"No."

The doctor hesitated. When Leo didn't explain any further, he said, "I'll stop by his room in a few hours."

Another hospital room with beeping machines and antiseptic and latex smells. Eddie's lips were split and bloated. His eyes were swollen shut and a miniature railroad track of stitching ran under the puffy skin of his right eye. The bruising from his broken nose colored his face in a purple so deep it was almost black. His body, covered by white, clinically clean and pressed hospital sheets, accentuated his battered face.

At the first glimpse of his son, Frank swayed. Leo reached out to steady him, but Frank shook him off. "Get out!" he bellowed at Leo, his face red.

"I didn't tell anyone… It's not my…" Leo looked at his brother, tears blurring his vision. "I'm sorry." He shuffled down the hall to the waiting room, where Mary took him in her arms.

He pulled back. "I shouldn't have left him…" Leo's voice trailed off as he saw his father weaving toward them. Sweat glistened on Frank's crimson face. His breathing came in short, quick gasps.

Leo ran to him and eased him onto the floor. "Dad!"

"My chest." Frank clawed at his shirt.

"I'll get a doctor." Mary took off for the nurses' station.

"His cardiologist is Dr. Pierson!" Leo called after her. He cradled his father's head and shoulders in his lap. "It's going to be okay. It's all my fault."

Frank shook his head. "Don't blame you, not really. Too much. Can't…"

28

Leo hunched over a cup of cold coffee in the hospital cafeteria. He'd been sipping at it for hours. Nurses, doctors, and patients passing by stared at his bloody clothes, which he hadn't bothered to change. People usually stared at him because of his good looks; now they couldn't take their eyes off his train wreck of a face.

Leo smelled roasted chicken, pizza, and chili coming from the kitchen but he had no appetite. Mary played with the plastic straw in her iced tea.

She reached across the table and took his hand. Her hands were soft and warm. "I've been trying to figure out why Jacob Landry wants your father's farm."

"He supposedly wants to build a mega church."

"Mmm. Why is he pushing for the bank to foreclose so quickly?" Mary took a sip of her tea. "When I practiced law, I handled a few foreclosures. In Illinois, a foreclosure takes almost a year. There are very specific parameters and timelines that must be met. I would guess Wisconsin law is similar. Even if your dad had recently missed mortgage payments or doesn't pay his property taxes this July, the bank can't legally take the farm until next year."

"Legalities won't stop Landry." Leo shoved his coffee cup aside. "If he's bribing the bank board, well, screw the rules. And Emmett Everson, head of the Protect Marriage Movement, runs the board. Eddie's relationship with Griffin is just what Landry needs to convince them to foreclose."

"But foreclosure is just one option," Mary said. "Landry's already succeeded in annexing your farm into the village. If he can show that taking it is for the public good, say for the development of a church, then the village of Endeavor can take the land through eminent domain."

"And if the people of Endeavor decide they prefer a mega church on our land rather than having a gay man in their community," Leo said, thinking out loud. "They'll back Landry."

Feeling chilled, Leo grabbed his jacket off the back of his chair and shirked it on. The soft leather comforted him but the chill remained. He rubbed his arms. The jacket emitted a puff of flour. He pictured the coat lying on the kitchen floor, turned inside out. Suddenly, he remembered his crystal.

Leo searched for the black velvet bag. "My crystal. It's gone." He checked both inside pockets again and found only the red ribbon. "Did you see the bag on the kitchen floor?"

"No. But the kitchen was a disaster."

"Hang on." He replaced the ribbon and dug his phone out of his jeans. "Patrick?"

"How's Eddie?" Patrick asked. "Your father?"

"Nothing new about either of them yet. How's the clean-up coming?"

"The place looks great."

"Did you find a small, black velvet pouch in the kitchen? It had a crystal inside."

"Will cleaned the kitchen. Let me ask him."

In a moment, Patrick returned. "He didn't find anything like that. You think those assholes stole it?"

"Definitely."

Patrick sighed. "Even if you could prove it was stolen, I doubt those guys have it anymore. I'm sorry. I'm heading over to the police station with the bugs. I'll mention it."

"No, ship the bugs overnight to my friend, Chicago Police Sgt. Zachary Davies. There's a FedEx Office in Portage. I'll text you his address."

"You think Chief Grey will tell Landry?"

"Possibly. I'll call you as soon as we hear from the doctors." He clicked off his phone. "Landry had those guys steal my crystal. I'm sure of it. Or maybe he sent Vernon Smith in there while those bastards beat Eddie. Anyway, with the place bugged, Landry knew where to find it."

"That's why Landry came into the diner," Mary said. "To see if you had the jacket with you."

"That crystal must be valuable. And if there are more, that would explain why Landry's desperate to get our land. Not because he wants to build some goddamned church."

Mary fumbled in her purse. "I'm calling Oliver. He might know something about this." She did a quick search on her phone, then tapped in a number. "Oliver Tenney, please. He's not? When will he back?"

Dr. Pierson entered the cafeteria. Leo stood as she approached.

Phone glued to her ear, Mary rose and walked a few feet away.

"Frank's going to be fine." The doctor's stern mouth cracked into a small grin. "His heart is in good shape. He just overexerted himself today."

"But he complained of pain. He couldn't breathe."

"He thought he was having another heart attack, which made him anxious, and he hyperventilated. His pain was caused by the stents stretching the arterial walls. Not by a heart attack. We've given him some pain killers. He's resting comfortably but we'd like him to stay overnight for observation."

Mary rejoined them. "Good news?"

"Dad's going to be fine."

The doctor frowned. "However, I'm now certain that Frank won't be able to farm full-time. And I'm not sure part-time farming is even a good idea… we'll have to see how he does in the next few weeks."

"All right." The words came out thick. Leo cleared his throat. "We probably should have insisted on hiring more help when Mom got sick. I just…" *What? Had better things to do?* "Thank you, doctor."

Dr. Pierson nodded and left.

"I spoke to Oliver's assistant. He's at an architectural conference in

Philadelphia until tomorrow," Mary said. "He's flying into O'Hare in the evening. She'll arrange to have him meet us at the Chicago Cubs Bar & Grill in the terminal tomorrow night."

"Perfect. In the meantime, let's figure out how to get that crystal back."

29

Jacob sat at a corner table with Vernon at the Swampside Bar & Grill, swallowing his last bite of bacon cheeseburger and chasing it with a swig of Point Special Lager. Vern had single-handedly devoured one of the bar's sixteen-inch sausage and pepperoni pizzas and most of Jacob's home fries, and talked about ordering a double portion of deep-fried cheese curds.

"I swear, Vernon," Jacob said. "If this table wasn't bolted down, you'd eat that, too."

"Nah. The table's made of wood. I don't eat vegetables." Vern picked his teeth with a splintered toothpick.

"Except for my fries." Jacob laughed, then whispered, "Good work today."

Vern shrugged. "Like taking candy from a baby." He handed Jake the black velvet pouch.

Holding the pouch under the table, Jacob loosened the drawstring and reached in for the diamond. It was larger than Dahlia's. "And you're sure no one saw you?" Jacob rubbed his thumb on the smooth facets. "Particularly Eddie?" He returned the diamond to the bag and pocketed it.

"Caleb and the boys were… keeping him busy."

"Thank the Lord."

"But Leo's still meeting with Oliver Tenney. What's to keep Tenney from spilling the beans?"

Jake slammed his hand on the table. "I completely forgot about Tenney." He took a swig of his lager. "But he shouldn't be a problem. I'll place a few phone calls. Make sure Oliver's suddenly unavailable." He raised his bottle to Vernon. "See, Vern, this is why I pay you the big bucks."

Vernon snorted.

Jacob glared.

Vern ignored the glare and downed his Budweiser. "Did I mention that Chief Grey called? Told me that Eddie Townsend got beat up pretty bad. Asked if I had anything to do with it."

"And you said you were at the lake fishing, right?"

"Of course. He even believed my bit about catching half a dozen blue gills. He has no idea I robbed the Townsends." Vern peeled the label off his beer bottle. "I sure was tempted to join Caleb and the others and beat the shit out of that crummy little fag."

"Shh. Keep your voice down." Jacob peered around the bar. Few tables were occupied, but all the bar stools were taken. A middle-aged couple was trying their luck at the electronic slots.

The jukebox played "Born This Way" by Lady Gaga. Jake gagged on his beer. "Damn fag music. You couldn't pay me to put that on my jukebox." He wiped his mouth on his crumpled paper napkin. "You had more important work to do. And beating the shit out of Eddie Townsend serves another purpose."

"Oh, yeah, what's that?"

"Bringing Carlisle back to town." He finished off his lager and waved Tammy Erickson, the waitress, over. She took his order for another Point beer and Vern's order for cheese curds, chicken wings, and bread sticks. As she collected the empty beer bottles and dirty dishes, she bent over the table, exposing ample young cleavage. She winked at Jacob and left.

"Once Eddie's released—"

"Might be awhile," Vern said. "Sounds like he's in pretty bad shape."

"I told those idiots to just knock him around. They took it too far." Jake stopped talking as Tammy delivered their beer. As she left, he slapped her on the butt, making her giggle.

"You'd better cut that out," Vern warned. "Tammy's daddy's walking in with some woman."

"That crazy son of a bitch would probably sell me his daughter if the price were right." He drummed his fingers on the table. "You still friendly with that nurse at Madison General?"

"Yeah."

"Have her keep an eye on things for us. No, you go and take Dahlia with you. The more eyes the better, particularly if Carlisle shows at the hospital. As soon as you get wind that Eddie's been released, I'll sell his name to the media. They'll pay plenty to find out who Carlisle's boyfriend is. And think what will happen when word gets around Endeavor." Jacob smiled, imagining the uproar.

"It'll be crazy here, and out at the Townsend farm."

"Which will throw the village board and, more importantly, the bank board, into turmoil." So excited by the possibilities, Jacob started to get a hard-on. He reached under the table and adjusted himself as Tammy arrived with the bottles of beer and Vernon's wings.

"Mr. Landry." She watched him fumble with his pants and stopped short of the booth. "What the hell are you doing?"

"Adjusting my concealed weapon." He smirked. The sight of her pouty, twenty-something lips made his pants even tighter.

Her eyes narrowed. "Ya mean your gun. Right?"

"Of course. My .38. I never leave home without it." He grinned. "Cocked and ready to go."

She shook her head while trying not to smile and set the food down. When she turned toward the kitchen, Jacob snatched her hand.

"When's your shift over?"

She glanced at his firm grip, her eyes lingering over the gold Cartier watch on his wrist. "Eleven."

"I hear they've got a new bedroom suite over at the Tomahawk Inn in Briggsville." He caressed her palm with his thumb. "Even has a hot tub. Thought I'd check it out. Care to join me?"

Her hand moistened but she didn't pull away. Instead, she scanned the restaurant. Jacob followed her gaze to where her old man sat sharing a pitcher of beer with a woman who was definitely not Tammy's mother.

GOD ON MAYHEM STREET

"Sure, why not?" She sauntered back to the kitchen.

Vern laughed as he watched her go. "Jesus, Jacob, women sure do adore you."

Jake slammed his hand down on the table again, making both the wings and Vernon jump. "Vernon Elmer Smith. Don't you take the Lord's name in vain. Not in my presence. *Ever*."

30

Leo and Mary were sharing a couch in the waiting room and discussing crystal-recovery scenarios when a rumpled Griffin Carlisle appeared with his Secret Service agents in tow. The presidential candidate gaped at Leo's split lip and blood-smeared shirt. Griffin reached for him as if to give him a hug but stopped when he noticed the elderly couple in the corner. The pair had been arguing politics a moment ago. They had puzzled expressions on their faces as if trying to place Griffin.

"Let's go somewhere private," Griffin said.

Leo led the men into the hospital's vacant chapel. Stained glass artificially lit from behind colored the wooden pews orange and gold, and the room smelled faintly of incense. Thick carpet muffled their footsteps. The Secret Service men checked the room, found it secure, and went out into the hallway. The instant the door closed, Griffin asked, "What happened to you?"

"My dad took his anger and frustration out on me." Leo fingered his swollen lip. "But I'm fine."

"How is Eddie?"

"His surgeries went well. But he looks like shit."

"I need to see him."

Leo had been dreading this moment. "I talked to the hospital staff, told them Eddie's boyfriend would be coming to see him. Of course I didn't give them your name. They asked if you've registered as domestic partners in Wisconsin or elsewhere. You haven't, have you?"

"No. We'd have to be living together."

"Then you can see Eddie only if he designates you as a visitor. Right now, he's unconscious so that's impossible."

Griffin collapsed on the nearest pew. He buried his face in his hands.

"Maybe there's a way." Leo phoned Mary. "Could you bring my leather jacket, clothes, and any make-up you have to the chapel?" He clicked off his cell.

Twenty minutes later, Leo and Mary stood in the chapel's doorway and watched Griffin walk down the corridor, his two Secret Service men ten paces behind. The turned-up collar on Leo's bomber jacket covered the lower half of Griffin's face. He wore Leo's faded blue jeans and sunglasses, and his black, tousled hair had been finger-combed back in a style matching Leo's longer hair. He replaced his normally purposeful stride with a saunter remarkably similar to Leo's as he passed by the waiting room and nurses' station, receiving only disinterested glances.

When Griffin reached Eddie's room at the far end of the corridor he ducked in, then came out a few seconds later to give Leo a thumbs-up before disappearing back into the room.

Leo and Mary sat in a pew in the chapel, the cushioned seat far more comfortable than the couch in the waiting room. Instead of torn magazines and crumpled newspapers strewn on coffee tables, Bibles, Korans, and hymnals filled the pews' book racks. Leo thumbed through a hymnal, vaguely wondering if it included both "Amazing Grace" and Muslim chants.

"Griffin will want to stay with Eddie through the night," Mary said. "Maybe we should head back to the farm."

Leo shook his head.

She laid her hand on his chest. "There's nothing you can do for him right now except take care of yourself. You need a good night's sleep."

Leo shoved the hymnal back in the rack. "I want to stay a couple more hours, then get a hotel room close by. Don't think I can sleep but with a shower and clean clothes, I'll be as good as new. You should go, though."

"No way, mister. I'm staying with you." She kissed him.

"I hoped you'd say that."

"A couple of the nurses mentioned that this is UW-Madison's graduation weekend, so getting a room might be tricky but I'll take care of it."

Griffin pushed through the chapel doors. His Secret Service men surveyed the room, then retreated back into the hall.

"Leo?" Griffin swayed.

Leo caught the candidate as his legs buckled under him, then helped him to a seat.

Griffin's deep-set blue eyes were moist. "What those men did…" His expression darkened. "I could kill them." He studied the carpeted floor, obviously trying to compose himself, then angrily wiped his eyes. "I don't want to wait. Write that exclusive now. Get it in tomorrow's Sunday morning edition, if possible. I'll hold a press conference in the afternoon."

Leo doubted he had the energy to write even a word or two, let alone the piece that would change his brother's life. "I don't know…"

Griffin glared at him. "If you're not up to it…"

"Hey, I'm as angry as you are. But it's a lot to ask of Eddie. I know he wanted me to write the article but things have changed. I don't know if he'd want to be the poster boy for anti-gay violence."

"He'd agree to this."

"How can you be sure?" Mary asked.

"I've been with Eddie for almost a year. Our only arguments have been about being seen together in public. Eddie had had enough of sneaking around and wanted to dine in restaurants, catch a movie, see Broadway shows in Chicago, or go to the Lyric Opera. When I'd tell him that wasn't possible, he'd get so angry." He managed a smile.

This didn't fit with Leo's image of his younger brother. Eddie could be indignant if he came across an injustice but he rarely lost his temper, even at their infuriating father. "I've never really seen Eddie mad."

"One night he whipped a book at me. Missed my head by this much." Griffin held his forefinger and thumb an inch apart. "Smashed the Limoges vase on the mantle." He tilted his head toward the chapel doors. "Those guys barged in, guns raised. It was tense until I reassured them everything was fine."

"Didn't Eddie know you were protecting him?" Mary asked.

"That's my point," Griffin said. "He didn't want that. He wanted people to know. Eddie said that in today's society, our relationship shouldn't be an issue."

"Sounds naïve," Leo said.

"I like to think of it as visionary," Griffin replied. "But more than that, Eddie may have thought I was ashamed of him." He struggled with the next words. "That he didn't mean as much to me as I did to him. Which is so far from the truth. I've never felt like this about anyone, ever. He is everything to me."

"So," Leo began, "my editorial would prove to Eddie how much he means to you?"

"Exactly."

Leo needed a moment to think. He pushed his tired body off the pew and wandered over to the lectern, which was devoid of any religious symbols. One spiritual pamphlet lay askew on the wooden surface. On the pamphlet's cover was a photo of a man, a woman, and two small children, looking heavenward toward a light with the words: *Comforting Your Family in Your Time of Need.*

Leo sighed and walked back to Griffin. "I'm beyond exhaustion. But if my editor wants me to write Eddie's story, I'll give it my best shot."

31

My brother, Eduardo Salvatori Townsend, "Eddie," is an award-winning graphic designer and a wickedly funny yet quiet soul. Like most younger brothers, he knows how to both get under my skin and calm me. Almost two years ago, Eddie was one of the victims of the Chicago Triathlon mob stampede and is now permanently confined to a wheelchair. While that accident robbed him of the use of his legs, it didn't rob him of his spirit, of his enthusiasm for life.

This afternoon, three men thought they could beat the gay out of my brother. Eddie now lies in the hospital. He never flaunted his homosexuality. In fact, until a few days ago I had no idea he was gay. But even flaunting a gay lifestyle is no justification for violence.

Eddie loves me and our father and his boyfriend, Griffin Carlisle. Presidential Candidate Griffin Carlisle. Eddie had wanted to tell the world about his relationship, but Mr. Carlisle wanted to protect Eddie. That didn't work.

I've also fallen in love. I once had a reputation as a womanizer, but that's no longer the case because of her. I would go mad if society prevented me from being with her. And yet our society does that every day to homosexuals. Some are minor slights, using "gay" as a deroga-

tory term, others are horrific acts, savagely beating gentle souls and leaving them for dead.

Leo reread his words. They were so emotional, probably due to his exhausted state. Definitely not his usual style. What would Ted make of it? At this point, it didn't matter. It was a few minutes past eleven and Leo would have to get this story to the paper as soon as possible to make it into the midnight printing.

He glanced around the hospital cafeteria, glad that it was still open and glad that no one else seemed to know this. He needed to be alone. Mary understood. Before Leo left to retrieve his computer from his car, she had suggested that he write in the cafeteria while she stayed in the waiting room, close to Eddie's room.

Leo looked back at his computer, amazed it hadn't given him any trouble this evening, despite its occasional knocking. The ancient laptop had been a gift from his Grandfather Sawyer. Ted had offered to buy him the latest model but he couldn't part with this one, even though it ran at a glacial pace.

He skimmed several more paragraphs and then added:

So let me be the first to introduce to the world my brother, Eddie Townsend, lover of Pablo Picasso, Johann Sebastian Bach, peanut butter and banana sandwiches, Chicago's Montrose Beach, his Ford Focus ZX3, and presidential candidate Griffin Carlisle.

And when you see his battered and bruised face, remember that this is the price he paid for falling in love.

Leo paused, his fingers poised over the keys, but a clicking noise continued.

"*I said, 'What happened to you, honey?'*" Dahlia Landry sat across from him, her French manicured fingernails tapping the table.

Shit. Why in the hell is she here? He touched his bruised cheek. "A misunderstanding."

"Well, I hope the other guy understands better than you do." She laughed, her cleavage jiggling. Then her smile faded. "I'm sorry about Eddie. How's he doing?"

"Hanging in there. There's a possibility he might be released tomorrow. Hey, thanks for calling Chief Grey. Turning those bastards in."

"Glad to do it. Skinned a deer, my ass."

He studied his computer screen.

"I saw you working away and thought you might need a cup of coffee." She pushed a mug toward him, her silver bracelets clinking against the table top. "Lord knows you look like you could use it."

He ignored the mug.

"Whatcha working on?"

"A story. Got a deadline." He resumed typing, hoping she'd take the hint.

"Strange place to be writing."

He had no time nor patience for this. "Why are you here, Dahlia?"

"Well, let me tell you." She ran her finger along her lower lip, then rested her hand on her chin. "I'm meeting a girlfriend. She's a nurse here. Once she gets off her shift, which should be any minute now, we're checking out Madison's nightlife. Heard there are some pretty intense bands in town. Maybe you could join us?"

"No, thanks. I've got to get this article to my editor tonight. If you'll excuse me—"

"Oh, sure, don't let me stop you. I'll be as quiet as a mouse." She pursed her red-lipsticked lips and pretended to lock them with a key. She rummaged in her large pink handbag, found a *People* magazine, and flipped through it.

Leo tried to get back to his story but her heavy, flowery perfume and the rustling pages distracted him. And he was so incredibly tired. He reached for the coffee and downed it despite its bitter taste. "I could use another cup." He raised the mug. "Would you mind?"

"Not at all." Dahlia took the mug from him but not before caressing his hand with her painted nails. She slung her bag over her arm and sashayed away.

Leo refocused. He thought about reworking the article, embarrassed by the lack of professionalism, but remembered Ted telling him that an editorial should be from the heart. Barnes would write the straight journalistic piece with all the cold, hard facts.

Leo reread his words several times, tweaked them in a few places, and then changed them back, keenly aware that Ted was holding the presses for this story.

"Here you go, honey." Dahlia placed a hot mug of coffee in front of him, running her hand along his back.

He glanced around the empty cafeteria as he sipped the coffee. This cup was bitter, too, and salty. Probably the bottom of the pot.

Doing his best to ignore Dahlia humming "All the Single Ladies" while checking Facebook on her iPhone, he typed a few more paragraphs, rearranged others, and read the article before saving it. He attached it to an email to Ted and then moved the cursor to "send." He debated whether to send the email now or take it back to the waiting room and review it one last time.

When Dahlia dragged her chair over, Leo decided it was time to leave. He reached for his computer bag.

"You're going?" Dahlia asked. "You haven't finished your coffee."

He drank some more and grimaced at the briny taste. Placing the mug down, he stood. Or tried to. His legs wobbled. *How long have I been sitting there?*

"Geez, I'm more tired than I thought." He tried to say "I'm really woozy" but it came out, "I'm... weally... woozzze."

Leo reached for his computer, his fingers pushing several keys, trying to type something. Or send something. *Which was it?*

He shook his head to clear the dull fog in his brain, and lost his balance. Grabbing the table, he pulled it on top of himself as he fell to the floor. His laptop hit the tiles, splintering on impact. Pain smacked the back of his head. Stars burst across his eyes then faded to black.

32

"Damn, Dahlia. How much of that shit did you give him?" Vernon asked, as he settled Leo onto the motel's stained bedspread and then jerked the heavy polyester curtains across the grimy window.

It had been easy to kidnap Leo with just a wheelchair, a blanket, and Dahlia's floppy hat. The doctors and nurses were either too busy or too bleary-eyed to notice them, and hospital security gave them only a passing glance as they wheeled Leo out of the lobby and into the parking ramp. They dumped him into the bed of Vern's truck and drove off.

When they arrived at the Mad City Motel, Dahlia had stayed in the truck with Leo as Vernon checked in. One lonely street lamp lit the motel's parking lot, throwing shadows on the row of doors and curtained windows. A man Uncle Jacob's age passed in front of the truck, his arm around the waist of a twenty-something woman. She wore a skimpy red halter top and a jean skirt so short the bottom of her cheeks jiggled out. Laughing, the couple stumbled into a room.

Vern left the motel office, waving to the college-age attendant. When Dahlia exited the truck, she caught the kid staring at her through the motel's front window. Embarrassed, he suddenly found his computer very interesting.

Hefting Leo out of Vern's truck bed had been tricky but they'd managed without attracting any more attention from the attendant, who remained glued to his computer.

"I might have gotten carried away." Dahlia wiped her hand across the motel room's battered, dusty desk before setting what remained of Leo's computer on it. The machine rattled. The lid hung at an awkward angle. Some pieces had broken off, others were loose. "But he's a big guy. I wanted to make sure I gave him enough." She wiped her hand on her jeans and plugged in his laptop. "Damn, it won't turn on. Totally busted."

A woman moaned in the room next door, followed by loud, rhythmic thumping. Vern pounded on the wall. The thumping stopped.

"Save a Horse (Ride a Cowboy)" rang out from Dahlia's handbag. She fished for her phone.

"Hi, Uncle Jacob."

"Where are you?" Jacob asked.

"Some pay-by-the hour motel down the street from the hospital." Dahlia absently opened the desk drawer and found a torn Bible and a used condom. She slammed the drawer shut, her skin crawling.

"Townsend's with you?"

"Yeah. He's zonked." She walked over to Leo, prone on the bed, and caressed his swollen lip and rough chin. "Won't be goin' anywhere for a while."

Vern sat in one of the shit-brown chairs by the window and read through a stained and dog-eared Chinese takeout menu someone had left on the table.

"Excellent," Jacob said. "And you're sure he was writing an article about his brother and Carlisle?"

"One hundred percent. He said he had a deadline to meet. Had to get the article to his editor tonight. What else could it be?" She studied the geometric pattern on the bedspread and started to sit down until she remembered the used condom.

"Didn't you read it?" Jacob asked.

"Can't. His computer's busted. It hit the floor the same time Leo did."

"Did he send the article?"

"He pushed a few keys right before he passed out but the drugs hit him hard." She studied Leo's beautiful face, then thought *oh, what the hell*, and sat down next to him. "Don't think he was able to send anything."

"At least that's something," Jacob said. "And having a broken computer will delay publishing the article."

Vernon crumpled the menu, tossed it in the trash, and sauntered into the bathroom.

"There's more," Dahlia said, ignoring the sound of Vern peeing. "Griffin Carlisle's at Madison General. He came in several hours ago with two Secret Service agents. Went right to Eddie's floor. And it looks like Eddie will be released tomorrow."

"Good news. Put Vern on the line."

"Vern! Uncle Jacob wants to talk to you."

The toilet flushed and Vernon appeared, his hand held out.

Dahlia gave him her phone, hoping he had washed his hands. Under her breath she said, "Asshole didn't even thank me."

Another moan and more thumping from next door. It didn't feel right leaving Leo alone in this shithole in his condition. But Uncle Jacob wanted to keep him from spilling the beans about Eddie and Carlisle. Dumping him here where he could sleep off the pills was the best way to do that.

"Yep, course." Vern chuckled. "It'll be fun. When do you need us back in town?... Okay. See you then." He tossed Dahlia's phone to her.

"What would be fun?"

"You finally get to fuck Mr. Townsend."

"*What?!*"

"Jake wants a video." Vern shook his iPhone. Thump, thump, thump from next door.

"Christ, Vern, I'm not raping the guy. Besides, there's no way in hell he'd be able to get it up." Dahlia had always wanted Leo, but not like this. *Right?* She placed her hand on his chest, felt it rise and fall with each breath. He was so gorgeous. *If only he wanted me.*

"All I need is one short video. We'll use it as leverage. Get Leo to talk his old man into selling the farm."

"Blackmail him, you mean."

"Convince him, blackmail him. Call it whatever you like; just get to work."

She pushed off the bed. "No."

Vernon grabbed her by the front of her blouse, lifting her off her feet. The collar dug painfully into the back of her neck.

She cried out. The thumping next door stopped momentarily, and then intensified.

The seams in her sleeves ripped.

"You're hurting me," Dahlia whimpered. "Let me go."

"Do what I say and enjoy it." He tore open her shirt, buttons popping off. "Make it look good." Then he threw her on top of Leo.

33

Jacob pounded on Emmett Everson's front door, taking some of his sexual frustrations out on the heavy mahogany. He'd waited an hour, but Tammy hadn't shown at the Tomahawk Inn in Briggsville. *Stupid bitch; her loss.*

He pounded harder, turning his knuckles red, raising a little blood. Finally, the yellow porch light turned on and the door opened, revealing an angry Emmett dressed in lavender pajamas, his hair matted to one side of his face. His wife peered from behind him. A rat-like dog yipped in her arms.

"It's after midnight, Jacob." Emmett pushed onto the front stoop. "What the hell—?" The light highlighted dark bags under his eyes.

"Not here." Jacob shoved past Emmett and into the banker's dark foyer. Emmett's wife backed against the carved spindles of the staircase, shushing the dog. Its barks turned to shrieks that blasted around the room.

"You can't come barging in here. Who do you… quiet, Tinkerbelle!"

His wife clamped the mutt's mouth shut.

"Eddie Townsend's fucking Griffin Carlisle," Jacob said.

Emmett gasped. So did his wife. He hustled Jacob into his den, closing the door behind them. "Are you sure?"

Jacob sauntered over to a cabinet underneath an oil painting of

Tinkerbelle. The banker's stash of alcohol included red and white wines and a cherry Port. No hard liquor, much to Jacob's disappointment. A red would have to do. He uncorked the bottle with a wine opener that read: *Banker by Day, Opera Lover by Night*. He poured two glasses and handed one to Emmett.

"I have proof," Jacob said, after taking a gulp of the tart liquid. "I'm announcing it to the press."

"Do you think that's wise?" Emmett plopped down on a chintz chair. "Consider what that news will do to our wholesome little community."

"I've given it a lot of thought." Jacob sat in Emmett's leather desk chair and put his feet on the desk, his Ferragamo oxfords looking good on the distressed wood. "That boy is diseased and a menace to our community. His disgusting lifestyle could spread to our impressionable young boys. The people of Endeavor should be aware of this threat so that it can be eradicated. The Townsends have to go."

Emmett considered for a moment, then downed his wine. "You're right, of course."

Jacob controlled his excitement. He needed more from this man. He put his feet down, reached into his pants pocket, and slid an envelope across the desk. "And you're the man to get the ball rolling, Emmett. Foreclosing on the Townsend property is the first step."

Emmett hesitated and Jacob thought the banker would again reject his bribe, maybe take offense. Then, Emmett grabbed the envelope and shoved it into the pocket of his bathrobe. "I'll file the foreclosure papers first thing Monday morning. The bank board won't protest."

"Excellent." Jacob swirled the wine in his glass. "But that's not enough. We have to expedite matters." He threw back the rest of his drink. "Once the press gets wind of this—"

"When are you talking to them?"

"As soon as Eddie Townsend's released from the hospital. Looks like that'll happen today. In the meantime, call the bank board and tell them to be available for a meeting this afternoon."

"It's Sunday."

"It'll be after church. They'll balk at getting together, but as soon as my statement is aired and the chaos begins they'll beg for that meeting." He poured himself one more glass of wine.

34

Dahlia ran her hands through Leo's hair, something she wanted to do every time she saw him. Goddamnit, he was beautiful, even with a bruised face.

She'd had a crush on him since high school. They'd dated, but she blew that when he caught her with Caleb Toole. Probably her greatest regret. When she couldn't have Leo she'd made love to Eddie, but that relationship went nowhere and now she knew why. Later, all her husbands couldn't compare to Leo. Ralph, her last husband, was almost as good-looking but he lacked Leo's charm and was dumber than a dairy cow.

Now, at last, she had her chance with Leo. But not like this. Not with him passed out.

Dahlia had sent Vernon to the nearest liquor store for booze, telling him she needed something to relax her before… before what? She hoped that by the time Vern came back, Leo would be somewhat aware of the situation. At least enough to enjoy it.

Leo moaned.

Dahlia bent over, traced the scar on his chin with one French-manicured fingernail and gently kissed his lips just as Vernon returned, loaded down with two six-packs of Miller and a cheap bottle of Chianti.

"I see you've gotten started." He closed the door with his foot. "Don't need the booze after all?"

Dahlia snagged the wine and unscrewed the cap. "Hand me that glass over there."

She downed two glasses before Vern shoved her back onto the bed and told her to get busy. She unbuttoned Leo's shirt.

"Show us more of your titties." His cell phone was poised.

"As long as you promise not to get my face in the picture."

Vern laughed.

"Please, Vern?"

"All right. I suppose people don't need to know who he's fooling around with."

Dahlia shrugged off her torn blouse, revealing her lacy, pink Victoria Secret bra. Well, if there had to be pictures, at least she still had a great figure. She pushed open Leo's shirt and kissed his neck, feeling the stubble prick her lips. When she ran her hands across his chest, Leo raised his fingers to touch her, his eyes closed.

Vern pushed the pause button. "He's coming out of it. Hurry."

Dahlia no longer needed any encouragement. The years of wanting this man took over. She unhooked her bra, grinning when she noticed Vern's eyes widen as he turned his phone back on. She shimmied out of her jeans, revealing her pink G-string.

"Oh, that's great," Vern whispered huskily.

Dahlia ignored him and unbuckled Leo's belt.

Leo's hand touched her hair.

Dahlia took his fingers, sucked on each one, and felt him harden underneath her. With his other hand he caressed her face, a tenderness she hadn't felt in years. She checked to make sure he was still drugged and then kissed his lips. She unzipped Leo's designer jeans and started to pull them off.

"Wha?" Leo's eyes were tiny slits as he struggled to sit.

"Shh, honey, it's okay," Dahlia cooed. "We gonna have a little fun."

She kissed him again. Damn, he was irresistible.

"Mary?" Leo mumbled.

Dahlia froze.

"Don't stop," Vernon hissed.

Dahlia pushed herself off Leo, fighting back tears. "You've got enough." She scooped up her clothes and handbag and ran into the bathroom, slamming the door behind her. She looked at her reflection in the cracked mirror. Excess mascara had smeared under her eyes, dark roots creeped into her bleached-blonde hair, and her large breasts sagged without the support of her bra. She closed her eyes, remembering the taste of Leo's lips.

"Jake called," Vernon said, from the other side of the door. "Wants us to dump Townsend at a bar. Make him think he tied one on."

"Gimme a minute!"

"Hurry," he whispered, through the door. "Townsend's waking up. We gotta get him outta here."

Dahlia splashed water on her face, dried off, and then dressed, finding three buttons still hanging on her blouse. Fastening them was enough to make her decent. She ran a brush through her hair, more out of habit than vanity, as she avoided her reflection. Entering the bedroom, she saw Vernon standing awkwardly over a prone Leo.

"I don't want to touch him." Vern pointed to Leo's pants bunched around his ankles.

Dahlia dropped her purse next to the bed and dressed Leo as gently and quickly as possible. It was like dressing a drunk.

Vern lifted Leo into a standing position. He shifted Leo's right arm over his shoulders and put his left hand around Leo's waist.

"Where to?" Dahlia kept her voice soft as she stuffed Leo's computer into its bag, swung her purse over her shoulder, and opened the motel room's door.

"There's a bar a few doors down. We'll prop him in the back. Hopefully, it'll be packed so no one will notice."

"You'd better hope nobody notices," she hissed. "We're dragging a guy with a battered face and bloody clothes."

At midnight on the Saturday after finals week and midway through graduation weekend, college kids, some wearing black caps and gowns, packed the Red and White Pub on Park Street, many looking in the same shape as Leo. The bouncer, if the pub had one, had vacated his stool by the door so sneaking Leo in was easy. No one noticed them in the dimly lit, beer-saturated room. Kids danced at the other end of the bar to the music of a local band, the drumbeat vibrating in Dahlia's chest. The music roused Leo enough that he stumbled beside Vern, but not enough for him ask where he was or who half-carried him.

Dahlia helped prop Leo up in a vacant booth loaded with empty plastic beer cups. She handed her purse to Vern and set Leo's computer bag next to him. Just as she wondered whether they should stick around to make sure he came to, her elbow hit a full beer, dumping its contents into Leo's lap. His body jerked. Dahlia and Vern raced for the door, her spiked heels slipping in a puddle of spilled beer. As she righted herself, she glanced back. Leo was trying to wipe the beer from his pants, looking confused and lost.

35

The pounding wasn't in his head; someone was beating drums, jamming on an electric bass. Leo shook his head, trying to clear it. Pain shot through his temple. He closed his eyes and drew in several deep breaths.

Beer cups littered the table. Leo wiped his damp jeans, releasing beer fumes. Had he been drinking? Binging? His tongue stuck to his cracked lips but he didn't have any lingering beer taste in his mouth.

Where am I?

He slid to the end of the booth, pushing something off the bench. His computer bag. He reached for it when the lead singer in the band started to sing—or rather, shriek. Leo put his hands over his ears before he remembered they were covered in beer. He wiped them on a dry spot on his shirt and then collected the computer bag and slumped back in the booth.

There was no way in hell he'd intentionally come into a bar that had a screamo band. Leo liked alternative forms of music but he couldn't take the screeching assault. Had he gotten here earlier, before the band started? Where had he been before that?

The hospital. The article. Mary, his dad, Eddie.

Leo checked his soaked pants for his cell phone. Nothing but wet bills. He unzipped his bag and found his phone—dead. His computer was in pieces. "Oh, shit." He threw a few bills on the table, hoping they would cover whatever he'd had to drink, then shouldered his computer bag and wobbled out.

The cool May air and silence helped to sober him. He leaned against the bar's red-and-white-striped front door and glanced around, happy to see Madison General only a block away. He started down the sidewalk but his legs wouldn't cooperate. Several times he tripped, so he slowed his pace. He dreaded Mary seeing him like this. She'd never seen him drunk and he was proud of that. In fact, he hadn't been drunk for over a year. *Until now. Jesus, what had happened?*

As Leo stumbled into the hospital lobby, the admissions attendant rose to help him. Leo waved her off. Thankfully, the hospital was otherwise deserted at this time of night. *Or was it early morning?* As he waited for the elevator he gulped water from a drinking fountain, wishing he could soak his head in it. At least he'd gotten rid of his cotton mouth.

Moments later, he exited onto Eddie's floor and shuffled into the waiting room.

"Leo!" Mary hugged him. "Where have you been?" She backed away, her nose wrinkling. "Have you been drinking?"

"I'm sorry," was all he could manage. He didn't want to admit that he'd passed out.

Mary touched his face and gave him a sad smile. "It's okay. I just wish you'd asked me to join you. I could have used a drink or two myself."

"I'm sorry," he repeated, wondering why he hadn't asked her along. Why couldn't he remember the last few hours? Maybe it would come back to him after he'd gotten a good night's sleep. He certainly had more important things to think about. "Any news about Dad? Eddie?" He made his way over to a couch, needing to sit down.

"Your dad's sleeping comfortably. But Eddie woke up."

He stopped short of the sofa and held his breath.

"He's good. Griffin's with him."

Leo started towards Eddie's room. "I need to see him."

Mary touched his arm. "It's almost one a.m. He's sleeping and you're not exactly in the best shape."

Leo looked down at his saturated jeans. "I guess you're right." He sighed, then remembered the article. "I've got to find my computer."

"Um... it's hanging on your shoulder."

"Oh... yeah." He dropped onto the couch and shoved the magazines on the coffee table aside to make room. As he lifted the computer out of its bag, it rattled.

"Oh, no," Mary said.

Leo opened the laptop. Cracks spider-webbed across the screen. Keys were missing; he found several in the bottom of the bag. He hit the computer's power button. Nothing. And it had been months since he'd remembered to save anything to an external drive. Months of writing, articles he hadn't published yet, interviews and research on gay rights. All gone. Suddenly he felt nauseous.

"What happened?" Mary asked.

He closed his eyes and swallowed several times. The queasiness in his stomach dissipated. He took a deep breath and opened his eyes. "I don't remember." He dug in the bag, looking for the brass nameplate that said, *"To Leo, let your fingers take flight. Love, Penman."* Penman had been his grandfather's nickname. The nameplate wasn't there.

"I'm so sorry." Mary's voice cracked as she sat next to him. "I know how much that computer meant to you."

Leo shoved the busted machine back into the bag.

"But the good news is, Ted has your article."

"Really? How... I must have sent it before I..." *What? Took the first drink? Of what?* He remembered drinking coffee while he drafted the article, nothing stronger.

"Ted called me when he couldn't reach you," Mary said. "The article hasn't been published yet. He wants to talk to you before he runs it. He admitted he'd been burned once before when he printed a story without confirming it with you." She gave a sly grin.

"Ted's been overly cautious since your Carpe Diem article." Leo managed to smile back. His cracked lips were sore and his head ached, though it wasn't as bad as it had been earlier, right after his father's beating. If he'd drank enough to pass out, why wasn't he hung over? He glanced at his cell phone's black screen. "Can I use your phone? Mine's dead."

"That explains why you haven't returned my calls." Her eyes were sympathetic yet tinged with anger.

Leo quickly called Ted. He was, characteristically, still up. Despite his better judgment, Ted had taken a chance and sent the article to press without confirmation from Leo. It would be in that morning's edition.

After ending the call, Leo took Mary's hand. "I remember sitting at a table in the hospital cafeteria. Writing the article on my laptop. I remember someone joining me."

"Who?"

Leo closed his eyes and tried to picture the person's face. "A woman. Someone I know." He looked at Mary. "The next thing I remember is waking up in a bar down the street, my pants soaked in beer. I have no idea how I got there."

Mary kissed him lightly then looked at him, puzzled. "I don't taste beer. Are you sure you've been drinking? This woman, is it possible she drugged you?"

"How long was I gone?"

"Almost three hours. You left for the cafeteria around ten."

"If I'd had enough alcohol to pass out for several hours, I would be puking my guts out now or at least have one hell of a hangover. I only have a slight headache." Leo snatched his computer bag and crossed the hall to the nurses' station. Mary followed closely behind.

"Excuse me," he said to the nurse behind the counter, as he pushed aside a display of nutrition pamphlets. "Would you be able to run a drug test on me?"

The nurse stopped typing on her computer, raised an eyebrow, and frowned. "Do you have the doctor's orders?"

"No."

She straightened in her office chair and resumed tapping on the keys. "I can't."

"But there's a good possibility I've been—"

"No orders, no tests."

Leo slammed his hand on the counter. The pamphlets jumped, several fell to the floor.

She glared at him but continued typing.

"Sorry. Look. I know this is a strange request. But I think someone slipped me something a few hours ago."

She took notice of his bruised face and the blood stains on his collar. "You mean like a date rape drug?"

"Exactly."

"That's a simple urine test. But without a doctor's order I'm hesitant to—"

"Can you page the on-call doctor?"

The nurse glanced back at her screen and the stack of paperwork next to her computer. Then, she turned to the whiteboard roster on the wall behind her and reached for the phone. She hesitated. "You don't have a lot of time. The drugs won't be in your system for long." She set the phone back in its cradle and opened a cabinet behind her. She handed him a sterile cup and pointed to a nearby bathroom.

When he gave the nurse the vial a few minutes later she said, "The lab will run the test ASAP but won't release the results until office hours. They open at eight a.m."

"Thanks." Exhausted but no longer wobbly, Leo put his arm around Mary.

"After some finagling," she said. "I managed to get us a room nearby."

"Great, let's get out of here. But first I want to see Eddie, even if he's sleeping."

When Leo entered his brother's hospital room, Eddie was staring at the ceiling. Griffin was fast asleep in a lounge chair beside him.

Eddie grinned wearily through his bruises.

"Damn, it's good to see you smile," Leo said.

"You look like shit," Eddie whispered.

Leo tried to smooth out his damp shirt. "Long story. I'll tell you over beers when you get out of here." He nodded toward Griffin. "Did he mention the article?"

"You finished it?"

"It'll be in today's paper. But there's a chance I can still yank it."

"Print it."

36

Leo woke Sunday morning in a rumpled hotel bed with Mary's arm draped across his bare chest. He tried again to piece together what had happened the previous night. He knew he'd been drugged, or maybe he wished it were true. The alternative, that he'd drank so much he'd passed out, was something he didn't want to face.

Frustrated, Leo checked the digital clock beside his charging phone on the nightstand. It was 7:32 a.m. The Sunday edition of *The Chicago Examiner* would be on doorsteps and in newsstands by now. Once the news hit, his day would be even crazier than yesterday. He eased himself out of bed, careful not to disturb Mary, and looked for his computer bag. Then he remembered his destroyed laptop in the trunk of his dad's car, parked behind the hotel. A sick feeling of loss washed over him. Could his data be retrieved? Why hadn't he listened to Ted and backed up his files every day? He collected his duffle bag and went into the bathroom.

Despite not getting to bed until almost two a.m., the disturbing events of the previous night, and his ruined computer, Leo felt energized. And not just because of the hot water beating down on him from the showerhead. He always felt energized when his articles were published and this was a big one. More importantly, Eddie and his dad would be released from the hospital today.

He turned off the shower. As he toweled himself dry, he heard voices coming from the bedroom. He pulled on a clean pair of jeans before venturing in.

Mary sat on the edge of the bed in panties and an unbuttoned nightshirt, her blonde hair tousled around the collar. The sight of her made Leo consider postponing their visit to the hospital.

"You clean up nicely," she said.

"Thanks," he replied, sitting next to her.

She touched his face. "The swelling's gone down."

"I'm almost human."

She pointed at the TV. "They received advanced copies of your article."

Photographs of Leo, Eddie, and Griffin appeared on the screen with the caption: *Breaking News.*

"Once they figure out that Eddie's at Madison General," Leo said, "it's going to be a zoo."

"Which is why I called room service."

"Good idea." Leo watched the screen as Endeavor Police Chief Morris Grey answered questions. When the news cut away to a commercial, he asked, "What did you order?"

Mary turned to him, her shirt opening even further, revealing the curve of her breast. "Two breakfast specials and a pot of coffee. I hope you're hungry."

"Starving." He noticed the sheen of her lips as she smiled.

He opened her blouse more. "How long before it gets here?"

She leaned into him, letting his hand cup her breast, and whispered in his ear, "Oh, I think we have time."

37

Jacob breathed in the heavenly scent of Rev. Wallace's hyacinths as he bent down to retrieve his Sunday edition of *The Chicago Examiner* off the sidewalk. As he straightened, his bathrobe parted to reveal his favorite red silk pajamas. The cool morning air caressed his face.

He glanced across the street at the Kruegers' ranch house and caught the vet looking at him through his picture window. Doc Krueger knew the Townsend cows had been poisoned but had kept that to himself. In return, Jacob had sent the vet and his wife tickets for a two-week Caribbean cruise. Doc Krueger help up an envelope and mouthed "thank you." Jacob waved.

He walked back inside to the smell of coffee brewing in the kitchen's automatic coffee maker. In a particularly good mood, he hummed "The Battle Hymn of the Republic" as he opened the editorial section of the paper. Griffin Carlisle's smarmy face covered much of the page with the headline, "Griffin Carlisle's Boyfriend! By Staff Reporter and Columnist Leo Townsend."

Dear Lord, how could this be? How had Townsend managed to write this, let alone get it published? Dahlia said she'd drugged him before he had a chance to send the article. Said that his computer had smashed when he passed out.

Jacob cursed himself for not going with his instincts and contacting FOX News. How much money had he lost by hesitating?

He stumbled across the Oriental rug, stubbed his big toe on a leg of the rosewood coffee table, and collapsed onto the couch. He rubbed his toe while reading the article, a sickly diatribe of sentimental, pro-homosexual crap. He cinched the robe's belt around his belly and plucked his cell phone off the table.

"Hullo," came Dahlia's sleepy voice.

"I'm guessing you haven't seen *The Chicago Examiner*."

Scuffling noises. "It's seven thirty a.m. On a Sunday!"

"Haul your ass outta bed. Read the paper." Jacob hung up and pushed Vern's number.

"Morning," Vernon said, bacon sizzling in the background. "Read *The Examiner*, did ya?"

"How in God's great name did this happen?!"

"Bad luck."

"I'm gonna beat the shit outta Dahlia."

"*You're* going to beat the shit out of her?" Vern asked.

"Okay, I'll have one of the boys do it."

"Who? Caleb, Artie, and Buddy are locked up."

"You could…"

"No, I couldn't," Vern replied. "I don't have a problem messing with a scumbag or a fag but I draw the line at beating up women. Besides, Dahlia did do something right. She posed in some great booty shots with Townsend."

"I forgot about the video. Vern, you're a genius."

"You want me to post it on the internet?"

"Not yet." Jacob jogged through the living room and took the stairs two at a time. "I've got a better idea."

"There's something else," Vern sounded serious. "This morning I listened in on the Townsends again."

Jacob stood on the landing. "Whadya hear?"

"Ordinary conversations that continued until about seven last night. Then, some weird crunching noises. I checked all the equipment three times. I got nothing."

"You think the bugs' batteries ran out?"

"Nah, they're voice-activated. The recording only came to a few hours. They're good for at least a hundred. My guess is the Townsends found the bugs and destroyed them."

"How the hell did they even know to look for them?" *What had happened yesterday that tipped them off?* Then Jacob remembered seeing Aunt Sally whispering to Leo. "Sally. She must've overheard us talking. Told Townsend and he put it together. I'll deal with her later; right now we've got to act quickly. Come get me in ten minutes."

Jacob bolted into the master bedroom. He retrieved the first shirt and pair of slacks he found in the closet. He shrugged them on, leaving his silk pajamas and robe in a heap on the floor.

Then he shook his snoring wife. "Grace, honey, I'm heading out. I'll meet you at church for the eleven o'clock service."

"Jacob Isaiah Landry, today's the Lord's Day," Grace muttered, her eyes closed. "You and Vernon stay out of trouble." She turned away and resumed her snoring.

Grabbing his phone, wallet, and handgun off the dresser, Jacob spotted Vern's extra listening device. He shoved it in his pocket as he closed the bedroom door behind him.

38

Leo held Mary's hand while they walked the few blocks from the hotel to Madison General, the Sunday newspaper tucked under his arm. The morning air was crisp and smelled slightly of fish from Monona Bay. Groups of happy college kids in black caps and gowns passed them with proud families trailing behind. A pack of bicyclists in Lycra jerseys serpentined between parked cars and vehicles on the road. Church bells chimed in the distance.

"So, I've been thinking about your computer," Mary said.

"Me, too. I can use the desktop computers at *The Examiner* for now but I'll have to get a new laptop."

"Talk to Will before you buy one. He ordered the computers for the inn. Got an amazing deal. Hopefully, he can retrieve your files."

"I hope so."

A convertible cruised past, making Leo miss his Mustang. He had left it in Endeavor in favor of his father's larger Caprice.

As they rounded the bend, they came within sight of Madison General. The parking ramp, main street, side streets, and even the non-emergency entrance to the hospital were clogged with reporters and TV vans.

"Didn't take them long to find Eddie," Mary said.

"There must be a side entrance." Leo surveyed the scene.

"Well, hello," a voice came from behind. Leo recognized it before he even turned around. Jacob Landry. "Join Vernon and me for Danish Kringle at that bakery a few doors down? Lane's Bakery, isn't that right, Vern?"

"Yep," Smith replied, not taking his eyes off Leo. "Got something to show you."

Leo's first impulse was to attack Landry. He knew he'd get pummeled by Smith but it would be worth it. Mary put her arm around his waist and pulled him toward the hospital.

"Where ya going, Leo Townsend?" Smith almost shouted Leo's name.

Several reporters glanced in their direction. Leo quickly turned back to Landry. "Leave me and my family the hell alone," he hissed.

Landry shook his head. "Can't do that. I've got a business proposition—"

"We're not selling the farm."

"Just ten minutes of your time. Otherwise, Vern would be happy to tell those reporters exactly who you are."

If that happens it'll be a free-for-all. "Let's get this over with." He whispered to Mary, "Go to the hospital. I'll be there soon."

"Not a chance, mister. I'm coming along."

Leo and Mary trailed Landry and Smith into the bakery. The smell of chocolate, coffee, and cinnamon hit Leo, but rather than comforting him, the aromas churned his full stomach.

"This will work," Landry said, choosing a corner table and pulling out a gold-plated money clip. He shoved a small wad of bills toward Smith. "Buy us coffees and some of that Kringle they've got in the display case."

"We're not eating or drinking anything that passes through Smith's hands." Leo glared at Landry. He pulled out a chair for Mary and sat down next to her.

"Fair enough. Just for us then, Vern!" he hollered at Smith, who was hungrily eyeing the contents of the display case.

Landry sat across from Leo and grinned. "Check your cell phone."

Leo placed the newspaper on the table and looked at his phone. There was an email from an undisclosed account, with a video attached.

"You might want to turn the volume down." Landry pointed at an elderly couple sipping coffee nearby.

Leo adjusted the sound and hit play. Mary peered over his shoulder.

As the footage rolled, Mary's hand shot to her mouth. Leo dropped the phone.

"Who??" Mary asked, her voice catching.

He didn't answer as he retrieved the phone from the floor and watched to the end. But he knew that body. *Dahlia.* Her large breasts caressed his bare neck. "You asshole."

"No, not an asshole. An opportunist." Jacob sipped his coffee. "A word of advice. Sex outside of marriage is a mortal sin. It'll land you in hell."

Leo pushed the edit button but decided against deleting the email. "Let me guess. Sell the farm or you'll post this sleaze on YouTube."

Smith rejoined them. Landry took a bite of his Kringle. Pastry flaked off onto his open hand. "I've offered your father a fair price considering the state of the farm." A blob of fruit filling lodged in the corner of his mouth.

"He's not going to sell," Leo said. "Especially to you."

"Then, I'll use the video to help persuade the Endeavor Bank Board to foreclose." Landry licked the fruit off his mouth. "I'll invite the board over for movie night. Might even make popcorn.

"The bank board justifiably condemns premarital sex. More importantly, it abhors the idea of homosexuals living in our wholesome community." He slapped Leo's copy of the Sunday *Examiner.* "Your disgusting video together with Eddie's immoral lifestyle will convince the board to shove your father off that farm.

"It's time Frank moved on… and took you and your fag brother with him."

Leo's phone sang "I Shot the Sheriff." He checked the screen. Ted.

"I forgot to mention," Landry said. "I sent the video to your editor."

Leo clicked off his phone. He'd deal with Ted later. "This is blackmail."

"You can't prove that."

"I have the video." Leo held up his phone.

"Check again."

Leo glanced back at his messages. The email was gone. "What the—"

Landry chuckled. "Vern encrypted the email. Watch it once and it's gone. But of course, we still have the master." He casually brushed crumbs off his slacks and then locked eyes with Leo.

Leo pushed back from the table.

The village president checked his gold watch. "I'll expect your call within the hour."

Leo tried to steady his voice. "We can't make a decision like this so quickly."

"You're not in a position to bargain, Townsend," Smith growled.

Landry put a hand on the big man's shoulder without taking his grey eyes off Leo. "It's Sunday. I'm in a generous mood. I'll give you until seven o'clock tonight. But for every minute after seven, the price drops a thousand bucks."

He grinned.

"You fuckin—"

The elderly couple gasped.

Mary snatched the newspaper and took Leo by the hand. "Let's get out of here." She guided him through the bakery and out the door.

"He can't get away with this." Leo paced the sidewalk. "There's no way in hell we're selling him the farm."

Mary didn't say anything.

"The woman in the video is Dahlia Landry," Leo said. "Jacob Landry's niece."

"She's the one in your prom picture."

"She drugged me—"

"What are you going to do?"

"I'm not sure. Let's get inside the hospital." Leo looked for a way to sneak past the cluster of reporters. He pointed out a man unloading a laundry truck. "I think we can get in unnoticed." He headed for a steel door at the back of the loading dock, hiding his face behind the newspaper.

They made it to the metal door without incident, pushed through, and almost bumped into the back of the truck driver. Unaware of their entrance, the driver hummed along to a song piped into his ear buds as he wheeled a trolley loaded with bundles of fresh laundry. Leo pulled Mary across the hall and into the stairwell. The metal door clicked shut behind them. They climbed as Leo's cell phone sang "I Shot the Sheriff."

"Ted."

"What's going on?!" the editor yelled, his words blasting through the phone and bouncing off the stairs. Leo turned the volume down. "Why on earth did you send me that video?"

"I didn't—"

"If the press gets hold of this you're the story," Ted continued. "Not Griffin Carlisle. You. Is that what you want?"

"I never—"

"Your article gave all the attention to Carlisle. Are you trying to grab some of that back? Christ, Leo, I thought you'd gotten rid of your demons. Left the bottle and the loose women behind."

"Stop!" Leo's voice boomed off the steps.

Silence on the other end.

"It was a set-up. I was drugged." Leo took a few deep breaths. "The woman in the video is Dahlia Landry. Her uncle is Jacob Landry, the village president of Endeavor who's trying to take our farm."

Ted whistled. "Can you prove it?"

"Last night I gave the hospital a urine sample. I'll get the test results back soon."

"And you've got the video."

"Not anymore. Landry wiped it. I'm sure it's gone from your phone, too."

"Hang on." Pause. "It is. Um, look, I'm sorry…"

"With my track record, I could see how you'd jump to conclusions."

"Still, I'm sorry. Let me know about the test results. If you're positive, you should go to the police."

"The police won't believe me. If the video's posted online, they'll watch it and then ask me what I'm complaining about. Anyway, why would the media care? I'm not a national public figure."

"You weren't until you wrote about your brother and Griffin Carlisle."

Leo glanced at his hand holding the newspaper, his fingers underlining the headline, "Griffin Carlisle's Boyfriend! By Staff Reporter and Columnist Leo Townsend," and knew Ted was right. Then he remembered Dahlia sucking on those very fingers.

"I'll call you back." He ended the connection and Googled on his phone for a number. The newspaper slipped from under his arm and fell to the floor with a slap.

"Dahlia. It's Leo Townsend."

Mary grabbed the paper and started for the stairs. He seized her hand and pulled her back. He put a finger to his lips and clicked on the speaker phone.

"Oh, shit!" Dahlia's words reverberated in the stairwell.

"Don't hang up. I watched our video and, well, I'd like to, um, get together."

"You're kidding, right?"

"I'll admit, at first I was pissed."

"But you're not now?" Dahlia asked, in a puzzled voice.

"I got to thinking about you. You see, my girlfriend and I, we haven't, um, seen eye-to-eye lately. She's older. Kind of set in her ways."

Mary slugged him playfully.

"I'd like to be with someone who's not so uptight." Leo grinned at Mary, remembering their adventure under the hotel sheets and in the shower earlier that morning. "Anyway… the video. It made me want to see you again." He hoped he sounded eager.

There was a long pause.

Leo held his breath.

"Yeah. I'd like to see you, too."

"Excellent! Is today for lunch too soon?"

"I can meet you at Dotty Dumpling's Dowry at eleven thirty."

"Dotty's what?"

She laughed. "It's a pub on North Frances, about a half mile from Madison General."

Not too far from the hospital but far enough away from the news hounds. "Sounds good. See you there."

"Smooth," Mary said, as Leo clicked off his phone. "But once you meet her, then what?"

"Remember my digital recorder we used to nail Christopher Shaw?"

"When Chris tried to strangle me?" Mary rubbed her neck. "Kind of hard to forget."

"I'm going to put it to good use again."

188   KRISTIN A. OAKLEY

"What if the hospital releases your dad while you're with Dahlia?"

"Chances are Eddie will be released after Dad so you two could wait in Eddie's room. I'll meet you there."

They climbed the four flights to Eddie's floor. Leo cracked open the door. A doctor checked a clipboard as he strolled down the hall. Two orderlies wheeled a sleeping man on a gurney around the corner. A couple chatted with a nurse who nodded, then escorted them into a patient's room. There weren't any loitering reporters in the corridor. Leo went to the nurses' station.

"I'm Leo Townsend," he said to the attending nurse. "How's my brother, Eddie, doing?"

"Fast asleep. You might want to wait. Visit him later."

"We'll go to the cardiac unit first. See my dad. Is there a test result for me?"

The nurse sifted through the stack of manila folders next to her computer. "Here it is."

Leo opened the folder as he and Mary climbed the stairs up to the cardiac floor. "I've tested positive for Gamma-hydroxybutyrate. GHB. It says this drug is commonly used for DFSA, Drug Facilitated Sexual Assault."

"There's your evidence."

Leo shoved the folder under his arm as they entered Frank's stuffy hospital room. Breaking news shouted from the TV.

Frank's gray bangs grazed the deep wrinkles in his forehead, and the bags under his eyes were heavy.

Leo turned off the set and sat on the edge of his father's bed. "They're releasing Eddie today."

Frank grunted. "Will he be strong enough to deal with being 'The Man Behind Griffin Carlisle,' as the media's calling him?"

"He approved the article."

Frank shot Leo the same incredulous look he'd given him when Leo was twelve and had paid Eddie to feed the goats.

"Eddie wanted me to print it, Dad. He insisted."

Frank turned to Mary. "The doctor hasn't made her rounds yet, but the nurse is confident they'll release me after lunch."

"Terrific," Mary said. "You've spent enough time in this hospital."

"Hell, yes. Gotta get to the farm. Protect my home because of that goddamned article." Frank glared at Leo. "Take us home," his eyes narrowed, "and then leave."

Leo stood. "This isn't something we can hide from."

"You've made sure of that, haven't you?" Frank gestured angrily at the blank TV.

Leo kept his voice calm and in control. "I was drugged last night." He handed his father the test results.

Frank opened the folder, his voice softening. "Who would drug you?"

"Dahlia, on Landry's orders. Vernon Smith then made a video of a semi-naked Dahlia… um… kissing me."

"Why?"

"Landry's threatened to post the video on YouTube if we don't sell him the farm."

Frank tossed the folder to the foot of the bed. "So now that bastard's attacked both of my sons? Just to build a church on our land?"

"Not for a church." Leo filled his dad in on the stolen crystal. "Mary and I hope to talk to a geologist in Chicago tonight. Find out what it's worth. My guess is there are more crystals on our property, which is why Landry's hellbent on you selling."

"Damn." Frank closed his eyes.

Leo sat back down on the bed. "Call Landry. Agree to sell the place—"

Frank straightened. "What?!"

Leo raised his hand. "Tell him you need until four o'clock Tuesday afternoon to sign the paperwork. If he gives you a hard time, say I'll be out of town until then and you won't sign anything until I'm there. And, because it's still hard for you to get around, you want to conduct the transaction at the farm."

Frank clenched his fists, looking like he wanted to punch Leo again. "I won't sell."

"Hell, no. But Landry won't know that."

Frank's glare softened as did his fists. "I might like this plan." Then he raised an eyebrow. "As long as it's not for another sensational story you intend to write."

Mary handed Leo's father the folded *Examiner*. "You should read it, Frank."

Frank hesitated, then unfolded the paper. His eyes widened, surprised at the large headline. He took his time reading. When he finished, there were tears in his eyes.

Leo reached for his father and felt Frank's arms enclose him. For the first time in years, they hugged.

39

Just before eleven o'clock, Jacob exited Vern's truck outside the Church of Our Beloved Savior. Normally, the trip from Madison took an hour but Vern had driven like a madman to get him back to Endeavor in forty-five minutes, in time for the Sunday service.

Parishioners greeted Jacob as they climbed the church steps. He flashed them his best politician smile and patted the side of Vern's truck. "I'll see you later."

"Dahlia's trying to get your attention." Vern pointed across the parking lot.

"Uncle Jacob!" Dahlia stood by her silver Corolla and waved, her pink purse jiggling on her arm. "I need to talk to you."

"That girl has some nerve coming here," Jacob said to Vern. "And right before church."

"Murdering her might not be the best idea." Vern chuckled and drove off.

Jacob sauntered along the church's brick path that he had hired men to lay, past the aromatic Adam roses he had hand-selected, and through the newly-paved parking lot he'd paid for. Spaces were filled with pick-ups and minivans. By the time he got to Dahlia, his urge to beat her had diminished.

"Came in person to apologize?" Jacob asked. "I admire that."

"What?" Dahlia's eyes were vacant. "Nah, I already apologized."

The urge to hit her was back. "Then why in God's name—"

"I've got a lunch date with Leo Townsend." Her words came out in a rush. "In about an hour. He called me this morning." Dahlia bit her bottom lip. "I thought he'd be really pissed at me. He said he was at first, but then seeing the video kind of turned him on."

"Huh, I'm not sure what to make of that." Jacob fingered the listening device in his pocket and switched it on.

Dahlia frowned. "I think he honestly likes me."

Jake put his arm around his niece. "I'm happy for you, honey." He gave her a slight squeeze and in one quick movement slid the bug into the corner of her handbag. "You go, have fun."

She wrapped her arms around him. "I'll tell you all about it when I get back."

No need to. I'll be listening.

When Jacob entered the church, Bill Stevens was playing the last stanza of "Jesus Comes with Clouds Descending" on the organ. Jake shook hands with several parishioners and slid into his pew beside a scowling Grace. For the rest of the service he wondered why he'd bothered racing back to church. Rev. Wallace rambled on about Luke 6:37: "Judge not and ye shall not be judged." One of Jacob's least favorite verses and one of the few he disagreed with the Lord about.

If he was a disciple of the Lord, surely he could judge on the Lord's behalf. People needed to know when they'd transgressed and Jacob was the man to do it. Hadn't God revealed that to him on numerous occasions, in numerous ways? How could he be village president and have so much influence over the people of Endeavor if it wasn't for the Lord's blessing?

"Many of you no doubt read the newspaper before coming to church this morning," Rev. Wallace said to the packed congregation. "I'm sure you were as shocked as I was. Let me rephrase that. Surprised. At my age and in my profession I find that there are very few things that shock me."

The parishioners chuckled.

"But it is surprising that one of our own—"

"Is a faggot?" Jacob said. Grace jabbed him with her elbow.

"—has such political connections," the reverend continued. "Doubtless this will bring a lot of media attention to our little village."

"It already has, Reverend," Emmett shouted from the back of the church. "We passed several news vans on our way out here."

Murmuring broke out among the congregation.

"Going to the Townsend farm, I expect," the reverend said. "The Townsends have been through a lot these past few weeks. First the Lord took Isabella, and then Frank suffered a heart attack. As good neighbors, let's do what we can to lend our support." He opened the Bible on the pulpit. "Let's take some advice from our heavenly Father—"

"Now wait just one minute!" Jacob yelled, unable to control his anger. Grace slapped his arm. "What I meant to say, Rev. Wallace," Jacob stood, trying to maintain a calm and steady voice as he continued, "is that with all due respect, you're missing the point."

Rev. Wallace snapped the Bible shut. "Am I?"

"Yes, sir," Jacob said. "The Townsend boy is a homosexual. He's violated God's laws."

People around Jacob nodded their heads. Some shouted their agreement. Grace tried to shrink into the pew. *Hard for a woman of her size to do.*

The reverend raised his hands, asking for quiet. "Only God can judge—"

"That's bullshit," Carl Kenyan said.

Several members of the Ladies' Auxiliary gasped.

"It's all right," Rev. Wallace said. "What would you like to say, Carl?"

"Excuse me, Reverend," Carl said. "I'm sorry for the bad language. But there's no judging. It's obvious. Eddie Townsend is a corrupted soul."

It pleased Jacob to hear Carl change his tune. A few days earlier, Carl had defended the Townsends.

"He's a threat to the young, impressionable people of Endeavor," Emmett said.

"And think of the diseases!" a woman shrieked from the back.

"AIDS!" added someone else.

Rev. Wallace raised his hands once again. "Please, let's have some semblance of order. Remember we are in a house of God."

Jacob sat down and put his arm on the pew behind his wife. Pleased with the turmoil he'd created, he squeezed her shoulder. She looked at him in surprise and he winked at her. After a few minutes of watching Rev. Wallace's frustrated attempts to calm the congregation, Jacob stood again.

"QUIET!" he bellowed, shocking everyone into silence. "The reverend is right. This is neither the time nor the place for this type of discussion. I'd like to hold a community meeting later today. Not an official village meeting, we don't have time to deal with the legal requirements of that, just an opportunity for discussion. I know it's Sunday, the Lord's day, but this is an emergency. So please, bring any concerns you have to Isaiah's this afternoon. Two o'clock."

"I really don't think this calls for a—" the reverend said.

"Laurie Sue." Jacob turned to the very pregnant church choir director. "How about 'Onward Christian Soldiers'?"

Laurie Sue raised her arms. The choir rose.

"That's—" Rev. Wallace said, "not what we had planned—"

Bill Stevens played the first few chords, drowning out the reverend's words. On cue, the congregation rose and sang. When the hymn ended, conversations burst forth and congregants shuffled down to the basement for coffee and donuts.

Jacob caught sight of Aunt Sally leaving the church. "I'm gonna skip the small talk," he said to Grace. "Meet me by the car in twenty minutes."

Jake caught Sally at the bottom of the church steps. "I've got to talk to you," he whispered. He took her arm and steered her over to her battered pickup.

Sally shook loose of him. "You get your stinkin' hands off me."

"Everything all right?" Carl Kenyan said, as he passed on the way to his sedan.

"Fine, fine." Jacob nodded and turned to Sally, his face inches from hers. Her breath smelled of stale coffee and peppermint gum. "Seems there's been some complaints about your establishment. Bugs in the pancake batter, employees not washing their hands."

"My place is spotless," Sally said. "Health inspectors should take courses from me."

"Ah, but health inspectors take money from me. While Vern and I were guests in your filthy diner, you listened to our private conversation. You passed along what you overheard to the Townsends.

"You're a sinful snitch. Now you're going to pay with your business. One call from me and the county health department will shut you down by Friday."

"You can't." Her bottom lip quivered. "I love that diner. It's everything to me."

Jacob patted her arm. "At least I'm giving you until Friday." He sauntered across the parking lot to his convertible, humming.

40

Leo leaned against the hard windowsill in Eddie's hospital room and finished reading his *Chicago Examiner* article out loud. The story was so saccharine it embarrassed him. How could Ted have published it? He would be the laughing stock of the newsroom.

He glanced over the top of the page at his battered brother in the hospital bed and at Griffin Carlisle seated beside him.

Eddie coughed to clear his throat. "Damn, it's good." His still-swollen nose made the words sound nasally.

"An amazing article." Griffin handed Eddie a cup of water.

Eddie drank deeply and handed the empty cup back to Griffin. "What did Dad say?"

"The TV news reports pissed him off." Leo tossed the newspaper onto the bed next to his brother. "He wanted me to take him home and then to leave, never come back."

"But then Frank read Leo's article," Mary said. "It's going to be okay."

Leo filled Eddie and Griffin in about the positive drug test, described the video, and explained his lunch date with Dahlia.

"You should go to the police," Griffin said.

"I'd like to handle it quietly, if possible." Leo took a deep breath. "The good news is Dad's being released early this afternoon. How about you, Eddie?"

"Dr. Sikdar recommended I stay another day for observation and rest. I told him, I'm observed so much here I never get any rest. And, as Grandpa Sawyer used to say, the food could puke a buzzard on a gut wagon."

They laughed.

"He agreed to release me today, too."

"He wants to get rid of you. And it's obvious you're feeling better." Leo put his arm around Mary, feeling the curve of her hip through her soft cotton dress. "If I'm at lunch when Dad's released, Mary will bring him here until I get back. If you're both released—"

"We'll drive back to Endeavor without you." Eddie smirked. "Get your sorry ass running."

"Funny," Leo said as the nurse bustled in. She took Eddie's temperature and blood pressure and then removed the IV from his arm. "Doctor says you don't need the antibiotic intravenously anymore." She placed a Band-Aid where the IV used to be. "Everything looks good." She smiled, peeled her gloves off, and dropped them in a receptacle.

Griffin pulled back the curtain over the doorway for the nurse as she left.

Leo glanced at the digital clock on the wall. It was 11:00 a.m. "Our flight leaves O'Hare at eight thirty tonight. And Mary wants to meet Oliver Tenney at the airport before that. I don't see how we can get you and Dad back to Endeavor, settle you in, and make it to O'Hare in time."

"I'll have my helicopter pick you up at the farm," Griffin said.

"I couldn't ask you to do that."

"After this article," Griffin tapped the newspaper, "it's the least I can do."

"That's very generous, thank you." Leo turned to Eddie as Griffin phoned his pilot to make the arrangements. "I've talked to Dad about selling the farm to Landry."

"No!" Eddie held his side and grimaced.

"Hang on," Leo said. "Dad and I agree that we'd rather torch the place than sell it to that asshole." He filled them in on his plans.

"I Shot the Sheriff" rang from his pocket. He clicked on his phone. "Hey, Johnny. Is everything all right at the farm?"

"More than all right," Johnny said. "Corn's planted. Doc Stork just left. Tell Mr. Townsend that the cows are perking up. But that's not why I called."

"Oh?"

"There's word that Landry's planning a community meeting today at two o'clock at Isaiah's. Somethin' to do with your brother and Mr. Carlisle."

"Thanks for letting me know." Leo clicked off. "What time is your press conference, Griffin?"

"Five thirty, why?"

"Jacob Landry's holding a community meeting this afternoon in his tavern," Leo said. "A perfect opportunity to introduce yourself to the good people of Endeavor."

41

When Leo left Eddie's hospital room on his way to meet Dahlia for lunch, Mary stopped him and mussed his hair.

"Hey." He frowned, backing away from her. "What are you doing?"

"I'm not sure of the details of your plan but if you want to seduce a woman you need to look the part."

"With messy hair?"

"Shh. Hold still." She ran her fingers through his hair, positioning it just so, then rolled up his shirt cuffs. She unbuttoned the shirt halfway, her fingers lingering on his bare chest. "There. You looked good before, even with the bruises. Now you're irresistible."

He kissed her.

"But make sure she doesn't unbutton *her* shirt."

Leo headed to Johnson Street, passing a UW dorm. A groundskeeper mowed the lawn, a warm breeze carrying the sweet smell of freshly-cut grass. College kids ambled by in shorts and Bucky Badger t-shirts. Further down on Dayton Street, students were double-parked as parents helped them load boxes into minivans. The cap and gown-wearing graduates where absent. *Probably at their graduation ceremony.*

Turning left onto North Frances, Leo spotted a red brick building with large, green-framed windows and a Dotty Dumpling's Dowry sign in gold letters. He entered the restaurant, pleased he'd arrived ten minutes early. Dahlia wasn't there yet and neither was the noontime crowd.

The empty wooden booths gleamed in the lamplight. Vintage posters and photographs covered the walls and model airplanes hung from the ceiling. Leo asked for a booth underneath the stained-glass windows that depicted red barns, grazing cows, and the state capitol in the distance. He sat down facing the front door as his phone rang. "Sally? Is everything okay?"

"It's good to hear your voice." Her words dragged as if she couldn't find the energy to make the sounds. "Oh, Leo, my world's falling apart. Jacob Landry's closing my diner on Friday."

"What?!"

"He owns the health inspector. I don't see a way to hang on to my place. If there's something you could do..."

"Landry's not closing your diner. That's impossible to do from a jail cell."

"Oh, sweetie," Sally responded, despair thick in her voice, "people have been trying to get him jailed for years. His ass is too slippery."

"But now he's got me to deal with."

"You sound cocksure."

"By the end of today I'll have enough evidence to lock Landry away."

"I hope you're right."

"Trust me. And then we'll celebrate with some of your triple-fudge brownies."

"You've got a deal."

Leo pocketed his phone as he saw Dahlia walking toward the pub. Her bleached-blonde hair remained in place even as a breeze caught her pink leather handbag. She wore a tight-fitting, hot-pink blouse cut low enough to entice but not so low that she looked like a hooker. Her dark blue skirt hugged her hips and grazed the tops of her knees. She wore six-inch navy heels with deadly points.

The whole outfit looked like an attempt to be classy but missed the mark. The cigarette dangling from her hot-pink lips didn't help.

Dahlia stopped in front of Dotty's to drop the cigarette and stamp it out. A college kid held the door open for her, ogling her cleavage. She thanked him, patting him on the shoulder, her hand lingering a moment.

"Dahlia." Leo slid out of the booth as she approached. He kissed her on the cheek. She smelled of cigarettes and too-sweet perfume. "You look fantastic."

After a few words about the spring weather they glanced at the menu. Dahlia ordered the Heart Throb burger. Leo ordered the spicy Bayou. The waitress brought them each a bottle of Tyranena IPA.

Leo took a swig of his beer. "I was sorry to hear about your folks."

"Yeah, well, they weren't the best of parents." She wiped moisture off the side of her bottle. "Mom drank too much and Dad smoked anything he could roll. Amazing they lasted as long as they did."

"How's your brother Daniel?"

"You remember him?"

"Sure, I do. Had a good throwing arm."

"He left town as soon as he graduated high school. Moved to California, got a job in real estate, and is doing pretty good though I haven't heard from him in a while."

"Married? Kids?"

"Nope. Shares an apartment with a guy from his office."

Leo raised an eyebrow questioningly but Dahlia simply drank from her beer. "And how about you? Kids?"

"Jesus, no. Too much of a commitment."

The waiter dropped off their baskets of burgers and fries, the smell of charbroiled meat making Leo's mouth salivate.

"Speaking of kids," Dahlia popped a ketchup-covered French fry into her mouth. "Did you know that Laurie Sue Harris is on her fifth?"

"Phew, dodged that bullet." He bit into his burger. The meat was a perfect medium-rare, juicy and full of flavor. The special sauce added just the right amount of spice.

Dahlia laughed. "I'd forgotten you'd dated her." She cut her burger in half and took a dainty bite. "Yum."

"Who did Laurie Sue marry?"

"Oh, honey." Dahlia ran her manicured fingers across the top of his hand. "She's never been married."

Leo laughed, choking on his beer, and for a moment it was as if they were back in high school on a date. But now, like then, Dahlia's overdone makeup and French-tip manicure didn't do it for him. He preferred natural beauty.

Dahlia laughed as she reached across to pat his back. He coughed and then took another swig of beer.

"Unbelievable," he finally said. He wiped his mouth on a napkin and figured now would be as good a time as ever. He turned on the microcassette hidden in his jeans pocket, then reached across the table to stroke Dahlia's hand. She jerked but left her hand there, a slight smile forming on her lips.

"I want to talk about the video," Leo said. "About you drugging me."

She dropped her gaze to the table. "I wondered when you'd get to that."

"Why'd you do it?"

She pulled her hand away. "It wasn't planned. At least not entirely. At first, Uncle Jacob wanted me to completely stop you from writing your article. He said if *The Chicago Examiner* published it, Endeavor would become the next Provincetown or San Francisco. Ya know, a gay center."

Leo laughed. "That's ridiculous."

Dahlia shook her blonde head, her hairdo still not moving an inch. "Look, I've got nothing against the gays. It's just that competition for the last remaining men in Endeavor is pretty steep. Why add to it?"

She chewed on another fry, then continued, "When he realized he couldn't stop the article, Uncle Jacob told me to delay it. Buy him some time, even a day or two, so he could sell the name of Griffin Carlisle's boyfriend to the national press. Make some money. And by beating *The Examiner* to the story's release, put his own spin on their relationship. Smear your family's name and use that to speed up the foreclosure on your dad's farm."

Dahlia dunked another fry in ketchup, then set it back in the basket. "I couldn't believe how exhausted, and yet determined, you were last night. Christ, you couldn't keep your eyes open but you kept typing. So, I slipped you a little something. Thought I'd let you sleep off the night in the motel. Delay the article by a day."

"Why the video?" Leo asked.

"That wasn't my idea, honest." Dahlia glanced at the other customers, at her hands, anywhere but at Leo. "Uncle Jacob can be pretty persuasive."

"He was at the motel?"

"No. He called."

"How persuasive can he be from sixty-five miles away?" Leo asked. "I mean, you basically sexually assaulted—"

"—I thought you weren't mad." Dahlia shoved her basket aside. "I thought that's why you wanted to meet me. I thought this was a… date."

Leo breathed deeply. "I'm not mad. I'm simply curious as to what went down. It's not every day a guy stars in a steamy video with a half-naked, beautiful woman."

His praise worked. Dahlia went on, "Jacob didn't need to be there. Vernon was. He threw me on top of you. Didn't give me much of a choice."

This was all the evidence Leo needed. He studied Dahlia. She'd been straight with him. Time to be straight with her. "I'm sorry they put you through this."

"Really, I feel awful bad about it—"

"I know," Leo said. "Now, I need to be honest."

Dahlia looked out the window at a passing bicyclist. "This isn't a date."

"No, it's not," Leo admitted. "I'm sorry I misled you, but I'm in a serious relationship with someone else."

She looked at him. "Mary."

"How do you know her name?"

Dahlia shrugged and sighed. She bit into her burger, wiped the sauce from her lips. When she finished chewing, she surprised him by saying, "Back in high school, if I hadn't fooled around with other guys, been true to you, would we have—"

"Been a couple? Maybe."

She attempted a smile.

The waiter stopped at their table. "Dessert?" he asked. "A piece of our famous fudge-bottom pie?"

"Make that two pieces," Leo said.

"I forgot to ask," Dahlia said as the waiter left. "How's Eddie doing?"

"He looks like hell but he'll heal. He's going home today."

Dahlia played with her napkin. "Did Eddie, ah, tell you about the dinner date we had a couple of years ago, after my second divorce?"

"He mentioned it."

Dahlia's cheeks reddened. "I came on to him. When he turned me down, I was hurt. Of course, at the time I didn't know he was gay."

The waiter arrived with the pies. Leo thanked him, then dug into the rich chocolate and flaky crust.

After taking a bite, Dahlia said, "I went home, got drunk, then made my way to Uncle Jacob's house to vent."

"I wouldn't think you'd get much comfort there."

"Actually, I did. I know you think Uncle Jake's the world's biggest creep but he does have a soft spot. He made me feel better. Even took my love rock for safekeeping."

"Your what?"

Dahlia laughed. "My love rock. Years ago, Eddie and I, ah… fooled around near that abandoned well on your place. Afterward, something shiny caught my eye. A rock. More like a piece of glass, a crystal."

Leo dropped his fork, splattering whipped cream across the wooden table. "Sorry, it slipped." He retrieved the utensil. "Go on."

"I kept it as a souvenir. When Eddie rejected me, I wanted to smash it."

"Instead you gave it to Jacob. And he's still got it?"

"As far as I know."

"Jacob had our place bugged. Or did you know that?"

"Vern bragged about it. Followed Uncle Jacob's orders…" She stared into space, apparently recalling something, then looked to her shoulder and finally at her purse. She dug in the bag, pulling out what looked like a flash drive and tossed it on the table. It landed in a smear of whipped cream.

Leo chose his next words carefully. "Yeah, well, your uncle's actions no longer surprise me." He examined the device and then pried the back off of it. "Has he always been such an asshole?" He took a knife and prodded the device, trying to send static.

"Hell, yes." Dahlia grabbed the bug and left for the ladies' room before Leo could stop her.

She came back moments later. "Flushed that sucker," she whispered. *Evidence down the toilet.* At least they had the others.

Dahlia cleaned the whipped cream off the table, pushed aside their dessert plates, and dumped all the contents of her purse. She examined each pocket and seam, then replaced the contents piece-by-piece.

"I was naïve enough to think Uncle Jake cared about me." She wiped away angry tears. "I told him I was meeting you for lunch." She blushed. "He wished me good luck. Even put his arm around me. I thought that was sweet. But he was planting that bug in my purse. What an asshole."

"I have a confession." Leo held out his digital recorder.

Dahlia narrowed her eyes.

"I'm sorry. I needed evidence of Jacob's involvement." He pushed the recorder across the table to her. "Take it."

She studied the machine for a few moments, then pushed it back. "You won't need it. I'll testify against Uncle Jacob."

"I hope you won't have to. Anyway, Jacob discovered I also had a crystal and where I kept it in the house. He used the attack on Eddie as a cover to steal it."

Dahlia dropped her gaze.

"You know something," Leo said.

"Turn your recorder on again."

Leo flicked on the machine and set it on the table between them.

"Caleb called me. Wanted me to bail him out of jail. Something I'd never do. The best place for Caleb Toole is behind bars. Eddie's not the first person he's beat up." She rubbed a tiny scar under her left eye.

"But I wanted to tell him that in person. I was pissed that he and the boys came to my place lying about skinning a deer. Pissed that he hurt Eddie. He said Eddie deserved it, being a f—" She looked down again. "Caleb said he helped Artie and Buddy," she shifted uncomfortably in the booth, "teach Eddie a lesson under orders from Uncle Jacob. Caleb bragged that Jacob encouraged him to go and make sure 'that homo fulfilled his end of the bargain.' Jacob's words, not mine."

Leo felt sharp pains in the palms of his hands and realized he'd clenched his fists so hard he'd drawn blood. He blotted his palms with a napkin. "So while Caleb and the others… um, beat Eddie, Vern stole my crystal."

"But why go to all that trouble for a worthless rock?" Dahlia asked. "Mine wasn't even very pretty, kind of cloudy, brownish yellow. I only kept it for sentimental reasons."

"I've been wondering the same thing." Leo noticed the Bucky Badger pennant hanging on the wall above Dahlia. "We're on a Big Ten university campus. They'll have a geology department," he said, as the waiter cleared their dessert plates.

"Department of Geosciences." The waiter gave him the bill. "I've taken a few classes."

"It's graduation weekend and a Sunday. Would it be open?"

"Normally, no, but some departments have receptions. Plus, professors are grading papers and tests to report their final grades. So you might be in luck. Geosciences isn't far—Lewis Weeks Hall. Take a left on North Frances, cross over Johnson, then turn right on West Dayton. Five, six blocks."

Leo handed the waiter money and told him to keep the change.

Dahlia asked, "Can I tag along?"

Sliding out of the booth, Leo glanced down at her spiked heels. "Can you manage six blocks in those?"

She placed her hand on his arm. "Oh, honey, I could run a marathon in them."

42

The minute Dotty Dumpling's Dowry's solid oak door swung closed behind them, Dahlia lit a cigarette and inhaled deeply. "Ah, I needed that. I can't believe my goddamned uncle."

Leo led the way, making sure to walk upwind from the cigarette smoke. A group of talkative businessmen wearing name tags moved over on the sidewalk to let them pass.

When Leo and Dahlia stopped at the busy Johnson Street intersection, Dahlia continued, "I always knew he used me as a tool, but forcing me to make that video and then bugging me?"

As the light changed, Leo offered his arm. She gave him a shy smile as she slipped her hand in the crook of his elbow and let him lead her across the street.

Safely on the other side, she said, "The funny thing is I like bartending. I like mixing the drinks, making my own concoctions, chatting with the customers. I'm damn good at it, too. I can make a hundred a night in tips alone. Double that on weekends." She stomped the cigarette butt out with the tiny heel of her shoe.

They turned right on West Dayton and walked past the great lawn in front of the Kohl Center athletic arena. College graduates mingling with families crowded the lawn as they took pictures and showed off their diplomas.

"But I can't work for Uncle Jacob anymore," Dahlia said, ignoring the frivolity. "Not after what he's done to me. And I'm tired of Endeavor. Except for this past week, it's the same dozen customers. I know their life stories better than they do. Plus, I've married and divorced all the available men." She laughed.

As they passed the dorms, Leo said, "Why not move to Madison or even Chicago? Get a change of scenery."

"Oh, honey," Dahlia said. "Believe me, I've thought about it. But I'm almost forty. Who'd hire me? I've never bartended in a big city."

They walked past apartment buildings and what looked like a coal power plant and then arrived at Lewis Weeks Hall. When they entered the geology building, a blast of cold air hit them. *Why do Midwesterners feel the need to turn on the air conditioning the minute the temperature reaches sixty-five?*

Their footfalls echoed in the empty hall as they passed display cases showcasing the Great Lakes tectonic zone, Ice Age geology, and meteorites. They peeked into the small geology museum, Dahlia ooing over the purple quartz, and then bumped into the department administrator locking her office. She said the Geoscience graduation reception had been the day before so many of the professors were gone, but she thought Dr. Henry Arsenault was available.

"Take a left and follow the corridor," she said.

A few moments later, Leo knocked on the professor's door.

"Come in."

The room smelled of dirt and ancient tomes. Built-in shelves covered every wall, surrounding the small window and overflowing with books, rocks, bones, and maps. Debussy's "Clair de Lune" played through a wireless speaker on the window sill.

"How can I help you?" the surprised geologist asked, shoving aside a stack of papers. He had a hint of a French accent. Apparently he expected a student, someone fifteen years younger that Leo and Dahlia. His face was lined and deeply tanned and he resembled a younger, more mundane version of Harrison Ford. "Please, sit." He waved a brown hand at two chrome-and-black leather chairs in front of his desk.

"I'll get right to the point," Leo said, after introducing himself and

Dahlia. "We've discovered two crystals on my family farm in Endeavor, about an hour north of here. We were wondering if you'd know what they are."

The professor turned off Debussy and held out his palm.

"We don't have them."

"They've been stolen," Dahlia said.

"Which makes us think they're valuable," Leo added. "We can describe them."

Dr. Arsenault nodded.

"Mine was brownish-yellow and about the size of a shelled peanut," Dahlia said. "Like a piece of glass, but cloudier."

"The one I found," Leo said, "was more translucent and as big as the end of my thumb. White tinged with yellow. It also looked like polished glass."

There was a burst of laughter from the hallway as a group of students passed.

Dr. Arsenault shut his office door. "Were the edges rounded, sides smooth?"

"Yes."

Dahlia nodded. "But mine had pits in it."

"So did mine."

"And how did the stones feel to the touch?" The professor examined the bookshelves behind Leo.

"Oily," Leo and Dahlia replied simultaneously.

After a few minutes of searching, the professor selected a thick book titled *Rocks and Minerals of North America*, flipped through it, and showed them a photograph. "Is this what your crystals look like?"

The stone in the photo closely resembled Leo's. He read the page heading and sucked in a deep breath.

Diamonds.

"*Diamonds?!*" Dahlia said. "You're shitting me."

"C'est vrai," Dr. Arsenault said, grinning. "But without testing, we can't be certain." He handed Leo the book. "In what county is Endeavor?"

"Marquette."

"And they were lying in a field?"

"No," Leo said. "About twenty years ago my father dug a well. That's when we found these crystals, *diamonds*, in the dirt pile."

Professor Arsenault smiled, creasing his face further.

"But how is that possible?" Leo asked. "There aren't any diamonds in Wisconsin."

The geologist relaxed in his desk chair. "There have been a few finds. Many of them after a well was dug. The most notable diamond is the Eagle, found in Eagle, Wisconsin, which weighed sixteen point two-five carats." He held his fingers an inch apart. "It was stolen from the American Museum of Natural History in New York City in 1964 and never recovered."

"And a diamond the size of a peanut." Dahlia held her forefinger and thumb about half an inch apart. "How many carats is that?"

"That depends upon whether it can be cut into gem quality. Because both your diamonds are large there's a good chance they can be. Their value would also depend upon what flaws they have, their grade. But my guess is your diamonds could each be worth a few thousand dollars, maybe even tens of thousands of dollars."

"Now we know why they were stolen. How did the diamonds get there in the first place?"

"Originally it was believed they were pushed here from Canada by the glaciers. Geologists theorized that diamonds found here in the upper Midwest came from kimberlite pipes—carrot-shaped cones of solidified rock debris several hundred meters deep. These pipes were formed by violent volcanic eruptions which sometimes brought diamonds to the surface. Glaciers then scraped the diamond-bearing topsoil of the Canadian kimberlite craters and scattered the diamonds throughout the Midwest."

"But that's no longer the theory?" Leo asked.

"In 1981, geologists located the Lake Ellen Kimberlite in the Upper Peninsula of Michigan. It was the first evidence that kimberlites naturally existed in the Midwest. Structures similar to the Lake Ellen Kimberlite have been found in Wisconsin, including in the Glover Bluff Crater which is in—"

"Marquette County," Leo said.

"Exactly," Dr. Arsenault said. "And kimberlites tend to cluster so where there's one—"

"There might be more. So how do we know if there is a kimberlite pipe on our property?"

"There would be evidence of the greenish-gray, crumbly kimberlite and minerals such as garnets. Geologists could use magnetic and other surveys to explore the area. But of course, the best way would be to drill."

"A diamond mine. On our property." Leo whistled.

"You're getting ahead of yourself," Dr. Arsenault said. "Even if you discover a kimberlite pipe on your land, only one kimberlite in one hundred contains commercially valuable diamonds."

"But it's worth looking into?"

"Absolutely." The geologist handed them his card. "I'd love a chance to dig around."

Leo pulled out his business card and wrote his Endeavor address on the back. "Come up any time."

Once they were safely on the street Dahlia said, "Fucking Uncle Jacob. He knew all along. Said he'd keep my rock safe. Goddamn, him!" She fished a cigarette out of her purse. "Gonna take back what's mine." She lit it and puffed aggressively.

"That could be dangerous."

She touched the scar on his chin. "Uncle Jake would never hurt me. I'm family."

"I'll walk you back to your car."

"That's sweet, but I'm parked in the opposite direction." Dahlia kissed him and then wiped the lipstick off his cheek. "Thanks for lunch, for being honest, and for discovering we have diamonds." She sashayed down Dayton Street, attracting glances from a group of passing frat boys.

Leo pulled out his phone as he turned toward the hospital.

"Sgt. Zachary Davies."

"Zach, it's Leo."

"Got those bugs your friend sent me. As you anticipated, no fingerprints."

"Damn."

"However, we've traced them to a computer shop in Milwaukee. I've emailed Vernon Smith's photograph to the Milwaukee Police Department. They're checking it out. Of course, the shop didn't have a security camera but hopefully they'll come up with a witness. Smith's a hard man to miss. And he's got two previous felony convictions. If we can nail him on this illegal bugging charge, he'll go to prison for a long time."

"Excellent. But it's Jacob Landry I really want."

"What's Landry done?"

"Burglary. Kidnapping. Blackmail."

"Tell me more."

43

Jacob leaned against a stool on the stage at Isaiah's Tavern, fingering the microphone. A small table next to him held his granddaddy's jeweled Bible and a crystal glass of Glenlivet Scotch Whisky.

A cool afternoon breeze blew in from the front door, propped open with an untapped keg of Leinie's. The breeze brought the stink of cow manure recently spread over nearby farmers' fields. Ceiling fans above the bar stirred the "farm-fresh air," mixing it with bar fumes of spilled alcohol, perspiration, and deep-fried, beer-battered cheese curds.

Farmers, shop owners, school teachers, and stay-at-home moms occupied every chair, bar stool, and inch of hardwood floor. They gossiped about Griffin Carlisle and whispered about Eddie Townsend. Jacob had unplugged the flat-screen TVs above the bar so no one would be tempted to turn on the Brewers' game. Surprisingly, no one noticed.

Emmett, sipping a glass of white Zinfandel, sat at a nearby table with Endeavor Bank Board members who were sharing a pitcher of Leininkugel's and a jumbo basket of deep-fried pickles. Police Chief Morris Grey and several of his officers were wedged into a booth, drinking pitchers of Diet Coke. They were dressed in full uniform including nightsticks, which Jacob thought was ridiculous; this crowd might get rowdy but *violent*? There was nothing to fight about—everyone here was on the same anti-gay page.

Behind the bar, Vernon filled a frosted mug with Grateful Red IPA. He reached across the counter to slap Carl on the shoulder and laughed as he handed the barber the cold ale. Next to Vern, Dahlia filled a pitcher of Point beer, her hair drooping in tandem with her plastered-on smile. She looked as if she was desperate to leave.

Jacob tapped the microphone. "Let's call this meeting to order." Voices hushed and chairs scraped the wooden planks as people turned their attention to him.

"The purpose of this meeting," Jacob began, "is to address any concerns you might have about," he hesitated, took a swig of whiskey and continued, "homosexuality."

Several ladies from the Church of Our Beloved Savior choir wrinkled their noses and sucked on the straws of their Long Island Iced Teas. Laurie Sue Harris, sitting at a food-cluttered table with her brood, covered her preschooler's ears.

Why in the Lord's name did she bring her kids?

Rev. Wallace slid out of a booth in the back. Jacob had told Vernon to seat him there and was pleased to see that Vern never let him down. "As the main religious counselor to our community," Rev. Wallace shouted, a worn Bible in his right hand. "I feel that I should be the one to address any concerns."

Several people murmured agreement.

"That certainly is kind of you to offer, Rev. Wallace," Jacob said. "But I think you'll find that Pastor Guinness and Pastor Tully beg to differ. Yours is not the only church in town."

The two ministers nodded dutifully from their front-row table.

"The Bible says," Rev. Wallace continued, undaunted, "'For the entire law is fulfilled in keeping this one command: 'Love your neighbor as yourself. – Galatians 5:14.'"

Jacob rested his hand on his granddaddy's Bible, the embedded jewels and soft leather cool to his touch. "'Thou shalt not lie with mankind, as with womankind: it is abomination – Leviticus 18:22.'

"With all due respect, Rev. Wallace, we could quote Bible passages all day but in the end this is a village-wide matter. Something that concerns

GOD ON MAYHEM STREET

all of us in Endeavor. Of all denominations.

"So now, down to business," Jacob continued, pleased to see the reverend toss his Bible in the booth and slump down next to it. "It has come to our attention, actually to the attention of the world—"

This evoked several chuckles.

"—that Endeavor resident Eddie Townsend is the boyfriend of presidential candidate Griffin Carlisle—"

"How does that concern us?" a deep voice asked from the far corner of the bar.

Emmett scoffed.

"Excuse me," Jacob said, "who is asking the question?"

An old man with wild, Albert-Einstein hair and a faded plaid shirt appeared in the lighted doorway. "John Holden. I'm a friend of the Townsends from Illinois."

Another Holden?!

"Goddamned flatlander," someone in the back of the room murmured. Several people laughed.

Jacob held up his hand, silencing the crowd. "I see. Well, Mr. Holden, this is a community meeting. Since you're not from Endeavor, this doesn't concern you."

"Except for the fact that the whole country might be taking orders from a fag in the White House," Emmett said.

"Emmett, please." Jacob hoped he looked convincingly shocked. "That kind of language is not necessary."

"Sorry," Emmett murmured.

"You're right." Holden's words took command of the room, even without a microphone. "I'm not a member of your community. But this does concern me. Eddie Townsend is a friend of mine."

"Be that as it may, I'm sure you can appreciate that Mr. Townsend's lifestyle has directly affected the safety and well-being of the good people of Endeavor," Jacob said. "It's been chaotic here since the news broke of his sins."

"It's true," Chief Morris said. "I've had to deputize several new police officers to keep the peace."

Millie Branson rose from the booth behind the chief with her hand on her wide hip. "I've kicked reporters off my front stoop three times just this morning. All because my farm is next door to the Townsends."

"S'right," said her husband, Hugh Branson, lifting his frosty mug of beer. "I caught a couple of those slimy bastards in the bushes along our property line."

"What did you do?" Bill Stevens set aside his mustard-smeared brat. "I've been having similar troubles."

"I sicced Bruiser on 'em." The bar erupted in laughter. Bruiser, a Rottweiler-Great Dane mix, was twice the size of the average Rottweiler and twice as mean.

"Okay, okay," Jacob said into the microphone. "We've made it obvious that the Townsend situation affects everyone in this community." He glared at John Holden. "Let's discuss what we can do about it. Our goal is to show the Townsends the benefits of moving out of Endeavor, preferably far-away, to a community that is more, shall we say, appreciative of Eddie's lifestyle."

"Jacob Isaiah Landry," Aunt Sally said, sliding off a bar stool. Her skirt caught the top of the stool, pulling it down behind her and crashing it to the floor. Johnny Caldere reset the stool while she straightened her skirt, her face reddening. She took a deep breath. "Those boys have as much right to live in Endeavor as you do. In fact, there are many here who would be happy to see you go."

Johnny nodded in agreement.

"Most definitely," frail Red Carmichael said from his wheelchair.

"You're crazy!" Tom Franklin, Endeavor High School's math teacher, called from the back of the bar. "Endeavor's booming economically because of Jacob. If he left, so would our prosperity. Eddie Townsend's deviant behavior will destroy what Jacob built. Townsend needs to go!"

"How will I protect my children from molestation if Eddie Townsend is free to roam our streets?" Laurie Sue Harris clutched her toddler to her bulging belly.

"It's best for all concerned if the Townsends move on," Carl Kenyan said. "Why would they want to live in a place where they're not wanted, anyway?"

"This is their home." Sally's voice quivered.

Vern appeared by Sally's side, taking her by the elbow. "You should sit, Sally." She balled her hands into fists and for a moment Jacob thought she might slug Vernon. Instead, she shrugged off his touch and climbed onto her stool.

"The Townsends will never move." Holden crossed his arms. "That farm has been in their family for four generations."

"I see, Mr. Holden, that you aren't as close to the Townsends as you claim. This morning, I gave them a very fine offer for their farm. They're giving it serious thought." Jacob took another drink of whiskey, the liquor warming his throat as he let the news settle in. "If they refuse there's a good chance the bank will foreclose. If not, the village of Endeavor might acquire the property by eminent domain. One way or another, we'll soon be rid of the Townsends."

"What will become of the property?" Millie asked.

Picturing backhoes digging up diamonds, Jacob waved the question away. "If the Townsends leave peacefully, we'll give them a bonus. Isn't that right, Emmett?" Jacob offered the banker the stage.

"This should be interesting," Holden said.

Emmett took the microphone. "Free of charge, out of the goodness of our hearts, we'll arrange a one-on-one between Eddie Townsend and the Protect Marriage Movement. Offer him counseling, both psychological and spiritual. This boy needs help, and we will do everything we can for him."

Jacob leaned into the microphone in Emmett's hand. "Once he's safely out of town, of course."

People nearest Jake applauded. But the crowd in the back seemed preoccupied and then shifted as someone entered the bar.

"And if he doesn't accept your help?" Holden asked, over rising murmurs.

"The Protect Marriage Movement is very persuasive," Emmett said. "In our fifteen-year history, no one has refused this offer."

"Until now." Griffin Carlisle, dressed in a crisp black suit, pushed through the crowd. Two huge Secret Service agents followed and behind them, a buzzing cloud of reporters and cameramen tried to cram into the bar. Ignoring gasps from the townspeople and shouts from reporters,

Carlisle wound his way around the tables, his eyes drilling into Jacob.

"What do we do?" Emmett moaned, backing off the stage.

"Leave it to me," Jake said.

44

Griffin Carlisle was taller and better looking in person than he was on TV. Dahlia wondered whether she'd have an opportunity to flirt with the man, until she remembered he preferred men. She scanned the room. Everyone, including Uncle Jacob, had their eyes on the presidential candidate. The opportunity she'd been waiting for.

Dahlia wiped her sticky fingers and tossed the damp bar towel next to the sink. She tucked a few wayward strands of hair behind her ear, then squeezed past Vernon. Thankfully he, like everyone else, was glued to the scene up on the stage and didn't notice her exit.

Watching Carlisle walk through Isaiah's made Jacob's skin crawl. He'd have to get a sanitation crew in here after the man left. But that wasn't his biggest problem. How was he going to handle this homo? Normally, he'd tell Chief Grey to throw Carlisle out, but two huge Secret Service agents and a trio of cameramen from WKOW, WMTV, and WISC—the ABC, NBC, and CBS Madison television network affiliates—followed him. The lights on their cameras spotlighted Carlisle.

Jacob decided to play it cool, listen to what the fag had to say, and then rely on his own oratory skills. When Carlisle held out his hand, Jake gave him the microphone rather than touch his homosexual skin.

"Ladies and gentlemen of Endeavor," Carlisle began. "I'm sorry I've intruded on your community meeting but I understand that I may be part of your topic of discussion." He took off his suit coat and handed it to his Secret Service agent.

Please God, don't let him take off any more clothes.

"First," Carlisle said, "let me say that what many, if not all of you, read in the papers this morning is true. I am in a relationship with Eddie Townsend."

Murmurs from the crowd.

Emmett, now sitting safely with the bank board, looked as if he'd smelled something putrid. "Disgusting."

"It's also true," Carlisle continued, "that yesterday three men visited Mr. Townsend in his home on the pretense of doing business with him. They beat him, savagely beat him. Since this is an ongoing police investigation," Carlisle said, "that's all I can say about it."

Dahlia ducked into the hallway, paranoid that the clicks of her high heels on the hardwood floor would draw everyone's attention. She convinced herself that even if they noticed her, they'd assume she was headed to the ladies' room. She glanced over her shoulder at the crowd. Everyone was gaping at Griffin Carlisle.

Happy that the homo had nothing more to say, Jacob moved closer, expecting Carlisle to hand him the microphone. Carlisle shifted to block him. Jake backed away.

Carlisle said, "I kept Mr. Townsend's and my relationship a secret not because I was ashamed of it. I've been openly gay since I began dating as a teenager. And no one could ever be ashamed of Eddie."

Carlisle gazed over at Chief Grey and his men. "I feared what society would do to him once they found out about us." He looked directly in the cameras. "Unfortunately, my fears weren't unfounded.

"Eddie looks like hell but he'll come through. And when I am president, he'll be by my side. Together we'll change the face of American politics." Carlisle's last words were drowned out by an angry roar from the crowd.

Dahlia ignored the roar as she passed Tammy Erickson exiting the ladies' room. She nodded at the girl, stood by the restroom door for a minute, and then ducked into Jake's office.

Unlike Jacob's village hall office, this one was windowless and had barely enough room for his desk and leather chair, a flimsy plastic chair for employees who were being reprimanded, and a white marble stand for his granddaddy's Bible. Had Dahlia been devout she would have found a Bible in a bar to be sacrilegious. But she didn't give a shit.

Jacob's bar patrons shouted, shoved, and fist-pounded, reminding him of a Pentecostal tent revival he'd attended with his parents as a boy. It had scared him then, but this invigorated him now.

Emmett raised his fists and shouted, "You'll never be president! Never!"

Chief Grey and his men tried to extricate themselves from their crammed booth but Jake waved them off.

Carlisle held up his hand. After a minute, this small act silenced the room. He turned to Jacob, "I understand you have some concerns," and handed him the microphone.

Dahlia closed the door behind her, switched on the light, and went straight for the reproduction of Leonardo da Vinci's *Last Supper* that hung on the wall behind the desk. She removed the painting, exposing a wall safe, and pushed the numbers: 004110. This referred to Jacob's favorite Bible verse, Isaiah 41:10, "So do not fear, for I am with you; do not be dismayed, for I am your God. I will strengthen you and help you; I will uphold you with my righteous right hand." Throughout Dahlia's life, Jake had told her he was that righteous right hand.

Jacob accepted the microphone from Carlisle, holding it with his fingertips and keeping it as far away from his face as possible without losing the amplification.

"Thank you, Candidate Carlisle. Yes, we have many concerns. Endeavor is a Christian community. We refuse to tolerate a lifestyle—Eddie Townsend's lifestyle—that goes against the teachings of God. He must leave." He touched his Bible and caressed the supple leather.

"'Sodom and Gomorrah and the surrounding towns gave themselves up to sexual immorality and perversion. They serve as an example of those who suffer the punishment of eternal fire.' – Jude 1:7. Endeavor will not become the next Sodom and Gomorrah. Not while I'm village president."

"That's ridiculous—" Carlisle said.

"Not at all Mr. Gomorrah, excuse me, Carlisle. It is my duty as the village president of Endeavor to protect our community—"

"Then where were you when Eddie was attacked—"

"—against evil influences. It is my duty to escort the Townsends out of town. For good."

Carlisle reached for the microphone.

Vernon appeared and blocked him.

Carlisle's equally-large Secret Service men surrounded Vern.

"Get your hands off me!" Vern yelled.

Ignoring the scuffle, Jacob said into the microphone, "My message to the Townsends: sell me your farm and get out. Before we throw you out. Eddie's kind isn't wanted here." He hesitated, and then added, "A round of drinks for all who concur."

Dahlia found a cash box inside the safe with bills poking out from under its lid and several official-looking manila envelopes. She grabbed a fistful of tens and twenties, leaving the hundreds and fifties behind, and then lifted the documents. A black velvet bag lay underneath. She opened it and dumped two crystals, *diamonds*, into her hand. Crumpled paper remained at the bottom of the bag.

Dahlia smoothed the two small pieces of paper on the desk, reading the notes between Leo and his mother. Touched by their sentimentality, she felt a little guilty for taking his diamond. But he'd inspired her to leave Endeavor. The money from selling the diamonds would give her a great start.

She examined the stones. Her love rock seemed bigger than she remembered, but not as big as Leo's diamond and not as clear. Dahlia rubbed her smooth stone between her fingers and wondered how much money she'd get for it. A thousand bucks? Ten thousand? She had Googled Wisconsin natural diamonds but the few that had been found had been tiny compared to this.

A roar from the barroom, so loud that even Jacob's solid walnut door couldn't muffle it, startled Dahlia. She shoved the notes into the bag, dropped in the stones, and tied the drawstrings. She tucked the soft velvet pouch securely into her lacy bra. Then she replaced the envelopes in their original spots, closed the safe, and returned the painting, eyeing it to make sure it wasn't crooked.

"I'd like a word with you." Carlisle grabbed Jacob's arm. His bony fingers dug into Jacob's elbow.

Jake jerked his arm free. He could feel his face redden with anger. "There's nothing you could say that I'd want to hear."

"You'll want to hear this." Carlisle took in the cameramen. "Not here. Your office."

Jacob considered. Airing this fiasco in public had been successful, provoking the right amount of local panic. *And now a private discussion, excellent.* Jacob could leak it to the press and spin it to his benefit. He led Carlisle down the hallway to his office.

45

"Oh, my god." Mary stared at the TV anchorman summarizing the Endeavor community meeting, the Styrofoam cup of coffee in her hand forgotten. As the station cut to commercials, she said, "Jacob Landry is pure evil."

Leo punched the "off" button on the television. Eddie's hospital room with its antiseptic odor had suddenly become claustrophobic. He walked to the window and opened it to the sound of a jackhammer and the smell of concrete dust from the construction site across the street.

"Wait a minute," Frank said, from his chair by the empty bed. "Landry's pushing the bank to foreclose on our farm because..."

"Because I'm gay." Eddie stopped packing his duffle bag.

"There's more to it than that." Leo handed Eddie his jacket. "He's stirring up anti-gay sentiment in the community, saying you pose a grave threat and must leave, all as a convenient cover. He's doing this because he wants our land. But not to build a mega church. He wants our… diamonds."

Frank shot Leo an incredulous look. "Diamonds?"

Leo told them about discovering the recent digging around the farm's abandoned well, the disappearance of his crystal, Dahlia's revelation that Landry had hers, and what he and Dahlia had learned from Professor

Arsenault. "My guess is Landry didn't want us to know we have a diamond, and possibly lots of them. That's why he stole mine.

"Arsenault says we'd have to test to confirm there are more diamonds on our property. But Landry clearly thinks he'd strike it rich and is willing to do whatever it takes to get his hands on our farm." Leo crumpled his empty coffee cup and tossed it in the trash can.

"We need to play Landry's game for a few days," he said. "Let him think he's won. So, Dad, call Landry at seven o'clock tonight and tell him you'll sell at four o'clock on Tuesday at the farm. That should give Mary and me plenty of time to get back from the Pulitzer Prize Luncheon in New York—"

A nurse walked in, interrupting Leo. "The doctor's signed your release papers, Mr. Townsend. You're good to go." She handed Eddie his paperwork.

Eddie shoved the papers in his duffle bag.

"Would you like me to wheel you out?"

"Oh, geez," Eddie said.

"I'll do it." Leo winked at the nurse.

"Super. Take care," she said, and left the room.

Eddie shoved the rest of his things in his duffle bag as Leo continued explaining his plan, "I'm working with Sgt. Zachary Davies of the Chicago Police Department, trying to pull together enough evidence to prove Landry's guilt." Leo helped Eddie zip his bag. "Zach's been in contact with Brian O'Donnell, the sheriff of Marquette County, but we're keeping Chief Grey out of this. I don't trust him and I don't want any of this leaked to Landry." He threw Eddie's duffle bag over his shoulder.

"Hopefully, Zach and the sheriff will have all the evidence they need to arrest Landry while he's at the farm on Tuesday."

"That, I don't want to miss," Frank said, as they left the hospital.

46

Dahlia reached for the doorknob, then stopped when it turned.

"My office is small, but quaint, and very, very private." Dahlia heard her uncle say, his words muffled by the door.

She glanced down at her cleavage that peeked out from her V-neck t-shirt, relieved that the velvet pouch was well-hidden. As she adjusted her bra one more time, the door opened. The excited shouts of patrons enjoying a free round of drinks and Waylon Jennings on the jukebox, singing "I've Always Been Crazy," flooded the room.

"Dahlia," Jacob said, his brow furrowed. "What the hell are you doing in here?"

Griffin Carlisle, stony-faced, stood behind him.

Dahlia backed into the room, trying desperately to think of a plausible reason for her presence. She shoved her quaking hands into her pockets and felt relief when her fingers touched crumpled paper. "We were short on change." She showed the tens and twenties. "The petty cash drawer is empty. Thought I'd take care of it myself rather than bother you."

"Hustle your ass back to work. Vernon's alone behind the bar."

Dahlia shoved the money back into her pockets and slipped past the men.

As Jacob closed the office door, Dahlia leaned against the hallway wall and breathed.

When Jacob closed the door the room instantly quieted.

Griffin Carlisle stood in the center of the office, his arms crossed. "What will it take for you to leave the Townsends alone?"

"I could ask you the same question." Jacob cracked open the door, letting the chaotic noise blast in. "Hear what you've done to my village?"

"What *I've*—" Carlisle took a deep breath. "Tell me your price."

Jacob shut the door. He pictured mounds of priceless diamonds and laughed. "Great sense of humor. I see why they call you 'gay'." He walked behind his desk and opened the bottom drawer. "Drink? I've got some damn good scotch." Jacob set two crystal tumblers on the gleaming desktop, poured the liquor in each, and held one out for Carlisle. Carlisle ignored the glass. *Probably drinks pink champagne.*

"I'm serious," Carlisle said. "I know you want the Townsend property. I've heard you want to build a mega church. I'll give you the money to buy another piece of land. And enough for a building."

Jacob set Carlisle's glass down. "And in return?"

"Leave the Townsends the fuck alone."

"My, my, such language from such an elegant man." Jacob took a swig of the scotch. It burned and then warmed his throat. He'd thought he'd need the liquid to face Carlisle but now he found the man less than intimidating. "Does Eddie know you're buying me off?"

Carlisle didn't respond.

"Well, thanks kindly for the offer but no thanks."

"Take the money. Let them keep their farm."

"It isn't about the money. Endeavor is a wholesome village where honest, decent, God-fearing folk raise their children. Eddie Townsend's lifestyle is a disease. He needs to leave." Jacob waited for Carlisle to charge him, certain the man would throw a punch, hoping he would. Greeting all those reporters in the bar with a black eye fresh from Carlisle's fist would be a gift from God.

But Carlisle didn't move. Even his gaze remained steady. "You've got that speech down so well I almost believe you."

"Are you calling me a liar?"

Carlisle tilted his head.

Jacob slammed his glass on the table. "Why would I lie about eradicating your kind?"

"Because you're a smart man," Carlisle said, without a hint of sarcasm. "You must realize your actions are helping my presidential campaign. I couldn't pay for better advertising. You've built sympathy for me. My campaign donations have doubled in the last few days.

"Instead of eradicating Eddie," Carlisle moved to within inches of Jacob, forcing Jake to look up at him, "you've put him in the White House." He strode out of the office, not bothering to slam the door behind him. Pandemonium erupted in the bar.

Jacob drank the last of his scotch, formulating a plan in his head. Once the commotion in the barroom subsided, signaling Carlisle had left, Jacob marched into the bar and onto the stage. He grabbed the microphone.

"This party's moving to the Townsend farm."

47

Thunder rumbled as Leo drove his father's Caprice north on I-39 toward Endeavor. Roiling grey clouds shrouded the sun, darkening the road. Leo flicked on the headlights. "I hope we can get inside the house before the skies open," he said to Frank. His father rode shotgun, Mary and Eddie in the back.

Leo took the exit leading to their farm and soon realized he'd completely underestimated the impact of his story.

Fifteen or more TV and radio vans were parked along County T, joined by what seemed to be every pickup truck within a hundred-mile radius. Leo eased his car through the tunnel of vehicles. He maneuvered around people waving both pro and anti-gay signs and shouting, oblivious to the impending thunderstorm. Even with the Caprice's windows rolled up, the noise was deafening. Leo hoped that amid the chaos, no one would recognize them. He got within a hundred feet of their driveway when one of the journalists shouted, "It's Leo Townsend!"

Reporters engulfed the sedan. Cameras trained on Leo, Frank, Mary, and Eddie's faces.

A photographer took advantage of Leo's slow speed and jumped on the hood.

"Get the fuck off!" Leo yelled, while thinking how grateful he was they hadn't taken his Mustang.

The man slithered off the car but only after taking twenty or thirty shots of Leo and Frank.

"Where're the police?" Frank's shaking voice was barely audible above the commotion.

"There. Up ahead." Mary said, pointing at three scrawny officers. They were backed against two police cruisers parked at the end of the driveway, holding up their hands in an attempt to move the crowd aside. The surge overpowered them.

"We're almost there, Dad." It took every bit of Leo's reserve for him not to slam on the gas and drive straight into the crowd. He inched forward, nudging people out of the way. Finally breaking through the human barrier, Leo gunned the car.

As they pulled up to the house, John and Griffin came down to greet them.

When Leo opened the car door, the crowd roared from just two-hundred-feet away. "Quickly. Let's get inside."

"How long have they been here?" Leo asked Griffin, as he popped the trunk and John escorted Frank up the porch steps.

"Mary's kids saw the first TV van around ten this morning." Griffin took Eddie's wheelchair out. "A Madison station. It's been a constant stream of traffic all day." He bent down to kiss Eddie.

"I'm so glad you're here," Eddie said from the back seat, as he shifted closer to the car door.

"You might not be," Griffin admitted as thunder rolled overhead. "After the village meeting, I met with Landry in his office…"

Griffin moved the wheelchair within Eddie's reach. "I offered him money to leave you and your family alone. Oh, don't give me that look. He didn't take me up on it. Anyway, I may have ticked him off even more."

"Jacob Landry was born ticked off." Leo lifted the luggage out of his trunk. A cold downdraft billowed his shirt. He swung Eddie's duffle bag over his shoulder and handed Mary their bag.

Eddie struggled to shift onto the wheelchair from the sedan's back seat and winced. Griffin reached in and lifted him onto the chair with such tenderness that Leo looked away, embarrassed that he'd somehow invaded their privacy. As Griffin pushed Eddie's wheelchair up the ramp, struggling against the rising wind, Leo and Mary followed and tried to ignore the angry chants from the crowd.

"We've decided to stay a few more days." John held open the door.

"I can't tell you how much I appreciate it," Leo said. "And thanks for attending Landry's meeting. Stalling until Griffin arrived." The door closed behind him, blocking out the mob's cries but not the increasingly loud thunder. He bolted the door, something he'd never done before.

As Leo set Eddie's bag down, he smelled fresh bread and chocolate cake.

Mary smoothed her windblown hair. "Will goes into high-gear baker mode when he gets upset."

"He's also made some of that sun tea you like, Frank," John said.

Frank nodded and climbed the stairs.

Patrick limped toward them from the kitchen. "I just got off the phone with Chief Grey. He's called in additional police. Says he'll take care of the situation."

"When I talked to him he was, shall we say, less than cordial." John crossed his arms. "What made him change his mind?"

"I might have mentioned suing the police department."

Frank stopped on the fifth stair.

"Are you okay?" Mary started for him.

Frank turned to Mary. Tears shined his face.

"Dad?" Leo asked.

"I'm thankful you're here," Frank said.

Mary followed Frank upstairs with their duffle bag over her shoulder. "A hot shower and a long nap will do him good."

"Hang on a minute." Leo checked the hall clock. They had just enough time to catch their flight to New York. He pictured the columned rotunda in Columbia University's Low Library. Imagined himself walking to the podium to accept the Pulitzer in front of the best writers and journalists in the country. He heard himself reciting his speech about the power of the written word and paying tribute to his mother for passing on her intellectual curiosity and unconditional support.

And then he pictured the photographer throwing himself on top of his father's car.

"I'm canceling our trip. Mary and I are staying, too."

"No, Leo," Frank said, as thunder shook the house. "As long as it's safe to fly, go to New York. Collect your Pulitzer Prize."

48

Jacob threw back another beer as he watched Leo Townsend inch his father's Caprice through the mass of bodies on County T. Technically, drinking alcohol on this public roadway was illegal, but Jake had come prepared. Before leaving Isaiah's, he'd collected his handy street-use permit and temporary malt beverage license in case Chief Grey had a problem with his impromptu party. He'd wasted his time. The Chief was first in line for a beer.

Lightning cracked in the distance. Jacob prayed for the weather to clear.

"Slo-mo homo!" Vernon shouted at the Caprice.

Jacob laughed with a mouth full of Leinie's Red and sprayed beer suds on Hugh Branson's flannel shirt. Hugh, swaying, didn't notice.

The crowd echoed Vern's words in a thunderous chant. "Slo-mo homo! Slo-mo homo!"

A few out-of-town pro-fag protestors, and Rev. Wallace and ten or twenty other Endeavor townspeople who hadn't seen the light, tried to shout down Jake's crew. But Jacob and company handily drowned out the reverend's calls for equality and other such bullshit.

The wind increased and the thunder grew louder but the clouds held their rain.

Ignoring the weather, Jacob and his flock focused on the eager media. He thanked God for the paparazzi, who added to the festival atmosphere. The only things missing were balloons and cotton candy. He granted interviews to reporters while crowd members outdid each other with louder and more vulgar chants.

After Jake ended his fifth interview with his prayer to the Lord to cleanse Endeavor of homosexual pestilence, the sky darkened even more and there was talk of leaving. Jacob climbed into the bed of Vern's truck and tapped a third keg. "Can't leave now," he shouted, though his throat was strained and sore. "Just tapped the Spotted Cow."

People glanced at the thickening clouds, shrugged, and gathered behind the truck, cups held out. Then, over the sound of thunder, Jacob heard the distinct *whop-whop-whop* of helicopter blades. He instinctively ducked, spilling beer on his chinos. The helicopter pulsed over the Townsend farmhouse and landed on the back lawn. The crowd held its collective breath. A few minutes later the copter took off, heading south.

Griffin Carlisle has to be on board. With his fag boyfriend.

Jacob jumped down from the truck. "Come on." He led the crowd up the driveway.

Three young police officers attempted to block the swell, arms outstretched, looks of fear on their faces. Hugh and Carl slipped cups of Spotted Cow into the policemen's hands. The officers hesitated, glanced at each other, and then chugged.

The crowd had made it halfway to the farmhouse when Chief Grey shoved through with five additional officers in tow. "This is private property," he said. "You need to leave."

"What the hell, Morris?!" Jacob yelled.

"You're trespassing."

"A few minutes ago you didn't give a damn."

"Patrick Holden has threatened to sue the Endeavor Police Department if your people don't get off the Townsend's property. Now." Morris stood eye-to-eye with Jacob. Jake shifted to the left but the chief blocked him.

Jake could smell beer on the chief's breath.

"*Mr. President*, you've made your point. You can still hold your little party on County T." Morris and his officers again moved forward, further invading Jake's space.

"Help me out here, Jacob," Morris pleaded. "I don't want to arrest my own people."

Jacob relented. "Back to the road, everyone."

As the crowd grudgingly retreated, Morris thanked him.

"You disgust me," Jacob hissed in his face.

A streak of lightning lit the sky, touching down not a mile away. The accompanying crack of thunder rattled the windows of the vehicles parked along the road. Then God, in his infinite wisdom, opened the skies.

Instantly, a cold deluge drenched Jacob. Men shouted, women screamed. Everyone sprinted for their cars and trucks. Vehicles pulled away quickly, their tires spewing mud while reporters regrouped in their news vans. Rain beat the roof of Vern's truck as Jacob and Vernon huddled inside, damp and shivering.

49

As the helicopter flew into O'Hare, Leo welcomed the sight of Chicago's skyline. The John Hancock Center on the left and the Willis Tower on the right acted as giant bookends for the array of skyscrapers shrouded by the darkening sky. The helicopter had outraced the thunder and lightning, but the storm front chasing them had made for a bumpy ride.

When the helicopter landed, Leo took off his headset. Instantly, the noise from the beating blades assaulted his ears. He shook the pilot's hand, and then climbed out of the aircraft, thankful to be on solid ground. A torrent of dust and grit blown by the blades forced him to cover his eyes. Mary handed him their luggage and his leather jacket, then he helped her out. She struggled to control her billowing skirt, yanking the floral fabric tight to her body, but managed to stick close to Leo as they headed for the airport door.

Safely inside, Mary finger-combed her windblown hair. She took the duffle from Leo as he threw the garment bag over his left shoulder. They entered the main hallway and joined the stream of travelers from all over the globe walking to various destinations.

They wove their way down the American Airlines terminal to the Chicago Cubs Bar & Grill, where they planned to meet Oliver Tenney. The crowded bar smelled of grilled burgers and deep-fried onion rings.

They walked through the restaurant, catching bits of conversations in French, Spanish—and Farsi?—but didn't see the geologist.

Leo grabbed the only available table and ordered margaritas. "I've been thinking about Dahlia," he said. "I'd like to help her."

"Do what?"

"Leave Endeavor. Start a new life. I know a guy who might hire her."

"Call him. Oliver's flight must have been delayed. We have time."

Leo placed the call.

"Kasey's Tavern."

Leo heard conversations and clinking glasses. "Rob, it's Leo Townsend."

"Hey, man, where've ya been? Everything all right? Last time I saw you, you weren't looking too good. Staggered home." Rob's voice boomed through the cell phone.

Leo mouthed to Mary, "Right after Mom died." She took his hand and kissed it.

"I'm doing much better, thanks." Leo winked at Mary. "Hey, you still looking for a bartender?"

"Yep. Manny's last day was Wednesday. Asshole didn't even stay through the weekend."

Leo told him about Dahlia as their cocktails arrived.

"I don't know, man," Rob finally said. "Tending bar in downtown Chicago is a lot different than tending bar in some hick Wisconsin dive."

"You'd be doing me a favor."

Silence.

"I'll throw in my Cubs season tickets."

"Done."

As Leo ended the call and searched for Dahlia's number, Mary said, "Isn't Kasey's near your condo?"

Leo set his phone down. "That's right."

Mary studied him for a moment, frowning. With her index finger, she wiped salt off the rim of her glass.

"You're okay with this, aren't you?"

She didn't respond as she flicked the salt from her finger.

"It's the only lead I have on a job. I think she should leave as soon as possible. Who knows what'll happen on Tuesday." He hesitated. "I didn't tell you, but Landry's contacted the health department to shut Sally down simply because she told me he knew about Eddie and Griffin. Imagine what he'll do to Dahlia when he finds out she implicated him in my kidnapping."

Mary nodded but didn't look at him.

He leaned in close. "Even if you and I weren't together, I wouldn't be interested in Dahlia. She's not my type."

"What—buxom, blonde, and gorgeous?" she said to her drink.

"Actually," he grinned mischievously, "My type is boney, grey-haired, and masculine. Too bad I have to settle for you."

Mary shook her head, then laughed. "I've settled, too." She kissed him.

Leo pushed Dahlia's number.

"Leo?" Dahlia said, her voice shaky. "Hang on." There were shuffling noises and then thunder. "Okay…"

"Where are you?"

"Under the awning over Isaiah's rear entrance."

"It's hard to hear you."

"Raining like a son of a bitch. I should get back to work…"

"How does working as a Chicago bartender sound?"

"Are you fucking serious?"

"It's all set." He gave her the details. "And Rob knows of a vacant apartment across the street from Kasey's. He can get you a good deal on that."

She sniffed. "Thanks, Leo." Her words were thick. "You need anything? Any fucking thing? I'll testify against Uncle Jake," she whispered, barely audible above the pounding rain.

"No, I'm keeping you out of this. But promise me you'll leave Endeavor as soon as possible. Start a new life."

Silence.

"Dahlia?"

Silence then, "I'm sorry." It came out in a whisper.

"For what?"

"I, um…" Dahlia cleared her throat. "Thanks. For everything." The line went dead.

Mary's phone rang.

"Oliver, we're here…" she said. "Oh. I'm sorry to hear that… yes, I was looking forward to seeing you, too."

"He's not coming?" Leo held out his hand. "Let me talk to him. Ask him a few questions."

"Oliver," Mary said into the phone. "I'm going to hand you over to Leo Townsend. He's got a few… Oliver?" She looked disbelievingly at her cell phone. "He hung up. Or maybe I lost the connection." She tried the number. No luck.

"What did he say?"

"He sounded strange. He's usually so put together, quite a charmer actually, but he sounded flustered. Made some excuse about having to go into the office."

"On a Sunday?"

"I know, right?" Mary tried the geologist's number again. "Nothing. Not even voice mail."

"Landry got to him."

"Oliver would never let anyone *get* to him." She didn't sound entirely convinced, however. "But I am surprised he's blowing us off. We used to be good friends."

"Landry can be very persuasive."

"And yet you're not going to have Dahlia testify against him?" Mary asked. "How are you going to get a prosecutor to indict him without her testimony?"

"Dig up other evidence against him." He finished off his drink. "When we get back to Endeavor, I'll call the motels near Madison General. See if anyone remembers seeing me and Vernon Smith that night."

"You're both hard to forget."

"Exactly. I've got the medical records proving I was drugged and somewhere out there there's a video."

"What about the bugging devices?"

"Sgt. Davies said there's enough evidence to charge Smith but there has to be a stronger connection to Landry. Maybe I should stop by the Marquette County Jail and talk to Caleb Toole." He pictured Toole's angry face as he swung at Leo. "On second thought, he'd never admit to anything."

An image of sickly cows hit him as a waitress carrying a tray full of bacon cheeseburgers passed by. His stomach churned. "I wonder if Landry paid Doc Krueger to misdiagnose our cattle. Maybe we should talk to Doc Stork and pay Krueger a visit."

"We'll be busy when we get back," Mary said.

Leo pushed away from the table. "Let's go to the gate. Check in and get settled." He threw some crumpled bills on the table and slung the garment bag over his shoulder as Mary grabbed the duffle.

They wove through the terminal to the self-service check-in computer.

"Are the tickets on your phone?" Mary held out her hand as she touched answers to questions on the screen.

He reached in his jacket pocket and handed it to her.

"What's this?" She peeled a red ribbon off the phone's black plastic case and handed it to him.

Leo rubbed the satin between his fingertips and pictured his mother's face.

"Leo?"

He touched the 'cancel' button on the computer screen.

"What're you doing?"

He grasped Mary's hand. "The hell with New York." He led her toward the exit. "We're going back to Endeavor."

Dahlia retrieved the black velvet pouch out of her bra, feeling the stones and paper through the cloth. The awning above her pooled with rainwater, bulged, and then overflowed, soaking the front of her shorts and her bare legs. She backed against the door and dumped the diamonds into her hand. They caught the light from the street lamp, sparkled in the gloom. After a few minutes, she placed them back in the bag.

I should get in my car now. Leave. Never come back. Dahlia pictured Leo's pale-green eyes and chiseled, slightly scarred chin and held the pouch to her chest. She'd see him in Chicago. She stuffed the diamonds back in her bra, and then pushed through the door into Isaiah's.

Immediately, she was flooded with noise and the musky humidity that comes from damp clothes clinging to warm bodies.

"Where the hell have you been?" Vernon yelled at her from behind the bar. "Get your ass over here."

She patted her chest. A few more hours wouldn't make that much of a difference.

50

Jacob stood under his deluxe shower head, washing the grit off his body. Country singer Josh Turner's righteous song, "Me and God," played through the speakers embedded in the red-and-gold Italian shower tiles.

Jacob lathered his grey-haired chest with a bar of Irish Spring, releasing the fresh scent and immediately leaving him feeling cleaner. He wished steaming and soaping away his frustration and anger were as easy. First, that fag Carlisle had insulted his intelligence; they both knew that homos had as much chance of living in the White House as Jacob had of growing a pair of tits. Then, the disaster at the Townsend farm.

He rinsed the suds, turned off the spray, and opened the glass door to grab an embroidered towel off the hook.

As Jacob glanced in the mirror, the song "Flawless" came on, and he felt slightly better. He had a few wrinkles around his eyes and the beginnings of a jowl under his chin, but very little sagging around his arms and belly. He thanked God for good genes, because Lord knows he had no interest in exercising unless it was between the sheets with some young thing.

Then, the song was interrupted by a news report claiming that Griffin Carlisle was raised in a God-fearing, Christian home. Jacob punched off the radio. He jerked the bathroom door open. Steam escaped into the master bedroom. "Grace! Where in God's name are my clothes?"

"Laid out on the bed!" She shouted from downstairs. "Use your eyes!"

Dropping his towel on the plush carpeting, he yanked on his white dress shirt and crisp chinos. He didn't bother to dry his hair. He grunted a goodbye to Grace and left.

When he pushed through the heavy door into Isaiah's, Jacob's mood lifted. The storm had driven practically the whole village, and statewide and national media, into his little establishment. It seemed that every reporter who had ever walked the earth was in the tavern, asking about Eddie Townsend. Jacob had known the journalistic vultures would descend on Endeavor, but he was surprised they arrived so quickly. So much the better; it put even more pressure on the bank board to kick the Townsends off their land.

Jacob shook the rain off his shoulders and slipped on wet floorboards as he made his way through the sea of damp people. He stepped behind the bar to help a limp-looking Dahlia, her blonde hair sticking to her damp forehead. The ceiling fans struggled to stir the moist air and soon he was sweating, too. His white shirt clung to his body and emphasized the outline of his holstered Smith & Wesson .38. His concealed weapon was no longer concealed but he didn't give a shit. Everyone in town knew he packed a loaded gun. If they had a problem with it, they could get the hell out of his bar.

Jacob's hands grew stiff and sticky as he filled countless pitchers of Spotted Cow and Leininkugel's. And as the beer flowed, so did the Eddie stories. Seemed like everyone was debating gay rights. Not debating so much as agreeing that there shouldn't be such a thing. Again, Jacob felt pride for his little village as he tapped another keg of Leinie's Red.

"Jacob!"

"One minute." He wiped his beer-covered hands on a towel and looked for the caller. Emmett waved at him. *Excellent.*

"Emmett," Jacob said. "Why don't we go into my office?" He turned to Dahlia who held five mugs of beer in her left hand and a tray with mixed drinks in her right.

"You'll be all right for a bit, won't ya Dahlia?"

She shot him a look so foul he worried his pecker would shrivel up and fall off.

"Vernon," Jacob called, spotting the big man across the room.

The sea of customers parted as Vern made his way over.

"Help Dahlia out, will you? Emmett wants a private word." Jacob winked.

"Okay, Emmett." Jake closed the door to his office. "What's the latest?"

Emmett sat in the plastic chair across from Jacob's desk, grinning like the Cheshire Cat. "The bank board voted unanimously to foreclose as soon as possible, employing shall I say, legal acrobatics."

Jacob clapped his hands together. "That is good news. What's the timeline?"

"I'd say the foreclosure will be complete by the end of August." Emmett crossed his legs. "The place should be yours by September."

"Praise the Lord." Jacob walked over to his granddaddy's Bible and placed his right hand on it. "'Lazy hands make a man poor, but diligent hands bring wealth.' Proverbs 10:4. My prayers have been answered."

"And I have to tell you," Emmett said. "The bank board thinks of you as a hero. Calling the meeting here to address the homosexual lifestyle that's infecting Endeavor. Devising a plan to rid our village of this scourge. If not for your efforts and foresight, Eddie Townsend would remain here, corrupting our young men."

"I do appreciate the bank's support. How about a drink on me?"

"Normally I don't drink on Sundays except for communion." Emmett chuckled. "But today I'll make an exception."

Jacob opened a desk drawer. "What'll ya have? Bourbon? Or I've got some Dalmore single malt scotch, aged eighteen years. I've been holding onto it for a special occasion. This qualifies."

Emmett made a sour face. "White wine for me."

He almost asked Emmett if he was gay. No use, however, in alienating the banker when he was the key to getting the Townsend farm. But Jake made a mental note to have Vernon investigate Emmett's extracurricular activities. If the man was indeed one of those closet gays, that information would come in handy.

At six minutes past seven, Jacob stopped drumming his fingers on his desk and began pacing the braided rug in his office. He thought about pouring himself some more scotch, but he still had a buzz from the glass he'd drank almost an hour ago and wanted his head to be clear when Frank Townsend called.

His office door muffled the bar noises, but periodically Jacob could hear raucous conversations and laughter while the Oakridge Boys sang on the jukebox. He was dying to join the party. But Townsend would call any minute and then he'd really have something to celebrate.

"Thank you, Jesus," praised his cell phone from the desk. In his grab for the phone, he knocked over the photo of Wisconsin Gov. Scott Walker shaking Jacob's hand in the state Capitol rotunda. Jacob righted the photo and then breathed deeply to calm himself, letting the phone "Thank Jesus" one more time. Then, he pushed the button.

"Yes?"

Silence.

"Hello?"

"You're a goddamned bastard," Frank Townsend said.

Jacob swayed on his legs. *He's not going to sell.*

"I'm selling you my farm." Frank's voice was guttural, the words choked.

Jacob clenched his jaw, afraid he'd let out a whoop of joy.

Frank drew in a deep breath and continued quickly, "But tell Emmett I want to sign the papers at the farm. Tuesday afternoon. Four o'clock. Leo's out of town until then. He deserves to be here."

"Certainly." The word came out an octave higher than Jacob intended. He reigned in his excitement and lowered his voice. "I'll have Emmett—"

The phone went dead.

Jacob kissed his granddaddy's Bible then dropped to his knees on the rug, hitting the seams a little hard for his sixty-five-year-old kneecaps. He barely felt the pain. He put his hands together and thanked the Lord, then recited Philippians 4:19: "And my God will meet all your needs according to his glorious riches in Jesus Christ."

When he opened the office door, bursts of laughter and fiery arguments hit him. The crowd had swelled in the hour he had been in his office. He walked over to Carl, who sat at the corner of the bar talking to Bill Stevens. He put his hand on Carl's shoulder and shouted, "Drinks are on the house!"

Above the resulting commotion, Jacob heard Vernon groan. He joined the big man. "What's with you?"

"I've been running my fool ass off behind this bar."

Jacob collected a few glasses. "I'll help."

"So what's the occasion?"

"Frank Townsend's selling me the farm."

Vernon stared at Jacob and then jumped when ice-cold beer doused his hand. His attention reverted to the tap, which he immediately turned off.

"No shit!"

Jacob laughed, feeling giddy. He leaned in close and whispered, "That investigative reporter son of his is useless, praise the Lord. Didn't figure out that his father is sitting on a shitload of money."

"How'd Frank sound?" Vern dried his hands on a towel.

"Terrible, but who gives a damn." He laughed again, slapping Vern on the back. "He's asked me and Emmett to stop by the farm on Tuesday at four o'clock. Emmett still here?"

"Nope, told me he had to get home for Sunday dinner."

"I'll go to the bank first thing tomorrow morning, talk to him, get the necessary paperwork filled out. By this time Tuesday, the Townsend place will be mine."

"Did I hear you say you're buying the Townsend farm?" a man leaning across the bar asked. He held a pen poised over a spiral notepad.

"That's right."

"And you're Jacob Landry?"

"Yes, sir. And you're—"

The man pushed through the crowd and raced for the door.

"That was a reporter," Vern said.

"It would appear so, my boy. What the hell. I don't anticipate any problems with the sale." He took the full pitcher out of Vern's hand and poured himself a beer.

"You want me to come with you to the Townsends' Tuesday?"

"You bet your sweet ass." He slapped Vernon on the back. "This is your triumph as much as it is mine. I want you there when we send the Townsends packing once and for all."

51

"A red Camaro?" Mary walked beside Leo as they crossed the Enterprise car lot at O'Hare. Thunder cracked overhead.

Leo grinned, stuffing the rental agreement in his garment bag. "I want to see how it compares to my Mustang. And red is my color." He threw both bags in the trunk and climbed in as the sky let loose. "Damn, I wanted to ride with the top down," he shouted over the pounding rain.

The Camaro's windows were smaller than his Mustang's. The soft leather seats seemed lower. He turned the car on. It had that same great purr. He revved the engine. "The drive back to Endeavor should be fun." He backed the car out of the parking space, the wipers struggling to keep water off the windshield.

"Are you sure about this?" Mary rested her hand on his shoulder. "The Pulitzer Prize Luncheon is a once-in-a-lifetime event."

He pretended to look hurt. "Are you saying my writing's all downhill from here?"

"You know what I mean." She playfully shoved him. "I hate for you to miss it."

"I'll admit I am disappointed. Had one hell of a speech planned. Plus, the networking opportunities would have been incredible. But I need to be home."

Pulling to a stop sign, he connected his phone to the car's Bluetooth. "First call: my brother." He handed Mary the phone and then turned onto West Higgins Road and followed the line of cars making their way to I-90.

Mary punched in Eddie's number and turned up the volume as the rain pounded the car.

Eddie answered, but it was difficult to hear him.

"Talk louder," Leo said. "It's raining like crazy."

"Are you calling from the plane?" Eddie's raised voice was loud and clear.

"There's been a change of plans. We're heading back to the farm."

"Why? Everything's fine—"

"I know. But the farm's where I want to be. What's been going on?"

"Storm blew through. Lightning, thunder, the works. Drenched the protestors. Awesome sight, by the way. Bastards left in a hurry. There's a couple of TV vans still camped out on the road but they're huddled inside, probably for the next few hours. Doesn't look like the rain's going to let up soon."

"Excellent. How'd Dad's conversation with Landry go?"

"Dad sounded pathetic, angry, and desperate. All at the same time. The minute he hung up he laughed so hard he couldn't catch his breath. He said Landry sounded like he was going to wet his pants with excitement."

Leo and Mary laughed. "Damn, I'm sorry I missed that!"

Eddie's laugh turned into a dry cough.

"How are you doing?"

"Swollen, sore, and achy as hell. And—" This last word came out muffled as if Eddie was cupping his hand over the phone.

"And what?" Leo said, worried.

"Really, really happy. Griffin planned on leaving tonight, some rally in Iowa, but Dad insisted he and his Secret Service men stay. Told him we'd put roll-away beds in the study for his men. Griffin called his campaign manager, who agreed that a news leak about Griffin cancelling campaign appearances to be with his recuperating boyfriend would garner more votes than any rally."

"So he's leaking it?"

"As we speak." The smile was evident in Eddie's voice. "Dad and Griffin have been sitting at the kitchen table for the last hour talking over beers and Will's brat-and-beer-cheese nachos. Right before you called, Dad challenged Griffin and Patrick to a hand of Sheepshead."

Leo heard laughter and someone slapping cards on the table. "Congratulations," he said. "Griffin's passed the Frank Townsend Sheepshead test."

Eddie laughed.

"What about the kids?" Mary asked.

"They're on their computers in the living room with Mom's old photo albums spread out on the coffee table. They're researching our extended family in Italy, determined to visit them."

"Makes me want to go along," Leo said. The downpour relaxed into a gentle rain. Leo adjusted the windshield wipers.

"Where are you?" Eddie asked.

"We just left O'Hare. I want to make a quick stop in Madison. Then we'll head out to the farm. Be there in a few hours."

"What're you up to?"

"Digging Landry's grave."

"Hey, Leo." Eddie's voice had sobered. "I'm sorry you're missing the Pulitzer celebration."

"Thanks. But it feels like the right thing to do. See you later." Leo clicked off the connection and suddenly thought of Dahlia. "I'm sorry."

"About what?" Mary asked.

"No, that's what Dahlia whispered. I don't know why."

"Maybe she was apologizing for the video again?"

"I don't think so. She didn't sound like herself. More like a kid who's been caught with their hand in the cookie jar…" He pushed the gas pedal. "Not cookies. Diamonds!"

"You think she stole them back from Landry?"

"I sure do."

"If Landry finds them missing," Mary said. "He'll suspect Dahlia. And if he suspects that Dahlia knows they're valuable, he might assume you do, too."

"He'll sense that Dad's selling the farm is a trap."

"I'm plugging in her number," Mary said. "You've got to tell her to return them."

Dahlia's voicemail came on. "Honey, you've missed me. Tell me what's up." *Beep.*

"We'll try again later." Leo slowed the car back down to seventy-five as thunder shook the Camaro and the rain came back in full force.

Over the next forty-five minutes, Mary tried Dahlia several more times, with no luck.

"Something's not right," Leo said. "Call Patrick."

"Oh, man," Patrick moaned. "You took me away from a winning Sheepshead hand."

Leo heard Eddie yell, "Winning, my ass!"

Patrick chuckled.

"I'm calling about Dahlia." Leo filled him in. "Could you get over to Isaiah's?"

"I'm grabbing my coat."

Half an hour later, Patrick called from underneath the covered front entryway of Isaiah's, the sound of rain drumming around him. "She's in the bar, running her ass off serving drinks. The place is packed. Looks like the whole village plus all the out-of-town news media are here. I haven't had a chance to talk to her."

"Have you seen Landry?"

"He's here, helping out. Doesn't look like a man who knows he's been robbed. I'll go back in, keep an eye on the two of them."

As Leo pulled into Madison ninety minutes later, he received a text from Patrick "nothing 2 report." He drove the Camaro slowly down Park Street toward Madison General, the wipers struggling to clear the downpour.

"There," Mary shouted. "The next block. I bet that's it. See the neon sign that says Mad City Motel?"

Leo parked in front of the motel's office. He studied the squat, concrete building, trying to remember it. Nothing. Then he glanced down the street and through the rain saw the striped, red-and-white door of a pub. That he remembered. "This must be the place." They waited a minute for the rain to dissipate. When it didn't, they darted inside. In those few paces they managed to get soaked.

Shaking off the water, Leo walked to the chipped counter, the soles of his shoes sticking to the filthy tiled floor. He rang the bell. The wall behind the counter was covered in dusty walnut paneling. A vintage starburst clock hung crookedly, its hands stopped at 2:25.

Several minutes passed. Leo hit the bell again. A pimply college kid trudged in from a back room, a cloud of sweet pot smoke trailing him. "Need a room?" he mumbled, his eyes half closed.

"No," Leo said. "Just information."

The kid's eyes widened. He slouched against the wall. "Are you cops?"

"No. Mr...."

"Todd. So what d'ya want?"

"I think I might have been here last night but it was a rough evening, if you know what I mean."

"Don't remember you."

"How about the couple with me? A man about my height but sixty pounds heavier, all muscle, and an attractive blonde woman."

The kid thought a moment. "Big—" He cupped his hands in front of his chest, and then looked at Mary and blushed.

"The blonde woman has a full figure," Leo said.

"She's hard to forget. I remember the big guy, too." Todd picked at a pimple on his chin. "He hauled another guy into their room. Other guy was totally wasted."

Leo pretended to be embarrassed. "That would've been me. How did they pay?

"Cash. Everyone does."

"Do you remember what room we were in?"

"I think ten."

"Could we take a look? See if they left anything behind?"

"Sure, it's vacant." He handed them a room key. "But it's been cleaned. You won't find anything."

Leo and Mary darted back outside and down the sidewalk alongside the motel rooms, sticking as close to the building as possible to avoid the stream of water pouring off the eaves. A woman in shorts, a halter top, and spiky shoes skulked out of room 11, checking Leo over as he passed. "Sweetheart," she called as he unlocked the door to room ten, "I'd do you for free."

He pushed into the room.

Mary laughed as she closed the door. "I'd do you for free, too." She kissed him, her fingers running through his damp hair. Then she looked at the stained bedspreads and torn curtains. "But not here."

"Whadya mean?" Leo feigned disappointment as he turned on the lamp. The bulb flickered underneath the torn lampshade but managed to stay on. "We passed up a night at the Waldorf Astoria for this." He opened the desk drawer. Someone had ripped the cover off the Gideon Bible and left a used condom behind. "Cleaned? Should've brought gloves." He wiped his hand on his damp shirt.

Mary lifted the cushion off the easy chair. "Cockroach!" she squealed. She threw the cushion back. "I'll check the bathroom."

Leo lifted the bedspread on the first twin bed then got down on his hands and knees and inspected underneath. Nothing but dust bunnies and the smell of mold. He crawled over to the other bed, avoiding a dark brown stain in the threadbare carpet, and lifted the cover. More dust bunnies, a cocktail napkin with a smear of bright pink lipstick, and what looked like a piece of metal. A brass nameplate carved with familiar words.

"Got it!" Mary darted out of the bathroom. "I found a receipt from Steve's Liquor behind the trash can. Signed by Vernon Smith."

52

By nine o'clock Sunday night, Jacob felt no pain. He'd stopped helping Vern and Dahlia with the bartending an hour before to shoot the shit with Carl and Bill over pitchers of Guinness and a bottle of Death's Door White Whisky. Vern didn't seem to mind. He flirted with a trio of buxom reporters as he served them dirty martinis. They were laughing at Vern's dumb jokes, one leaned across the bar and kissed him on the cheek.

He'll get lucky tonight.

Dahlia was another story. Not her usual surly, bitch-kicking self.

Maybe it's her time of month.

At nine thirty, Carl drained the last of his Guinness. "Gotta get going. I'm opening the shop an hour early tomorrow. People have been begging me for haircuts. They want to look good for the TV cameras, on the off-chance they're interviewed."

"I've got to git, too," Bill said. "My cows don't care about TV cameras but they do complain if I don't milk 'em first thing in the morning."

"No, boys." Jacob swirled whiskey in his tumbler. "You're helping me out tomorrow. Joining the others at the Townsend farm at eight. Assuming this incessant rain stops."

Both men protested. Jacob held up his hand. "Carl, people won't be coming to your shop until later. They won't want to miss the opportunity to be on TV, shaggy hair be damned."

He turned to the farmer. "And Bill, get your cows milked fast and then haul your ass next door to the Townsends."

Jacob lowered his voice. "I can't tell you why, but it's crucial."

"Sure, Jake," Carl said. "We'll be glad to help you out."

Bill nodded.

Jacob lifted his half-filled glass to them. "Keep me company till I finish my drink."

The air behind the bar was as hot as a Swedish sauna. Dahlia's hair stuck to the back of her neck as she filled pitcher after pitcher of beer. Her skimpy, "Girls Gone Wild," rhinestone t-shirt and cutoff shorts clung to her sweaty body. She was relieved when the bar's front door opened, letting in a cool breeze from the rainstorm.

A skinny hippy limped in, his ponytail dripping rainwater onto his black jacket. The coat's sleeves were pushed back, exposing badly scarred arms which added mystery to the man. Under the jacket, he wore a white t-shirt with an Elvis Costello silhouette. His torn blue jeans covered the tops of his black biker boots.

Dahlia suspected he must be Patrick Holden, Frank Townsend's attorney. Uncle Jacob had raged on about the guy, giving an accurate but unflattering description. Holden had deep lines in his face, gray in his hair, and a goatee but he was better looking than she had pictured. He wasn't handsome like Leo; the guy had definitely sat on too many bar stools or had been in too many bar fights. But there was something fierce in his eyes. Sexy.

"Surprised to see you here," Dahlia said, as he settled on a bar stool. "Enemy territory."

"I live dangerously."

She nodded at the scars on his arms. "I see that."

He held out his hand. "Patrick Holden."

"I know who you are." She shook his hand. "Dahlia Landry."

Carrie Underwood began singing "Cowboy Casanova" on the jukebox. Three couples whooped as they pushed people and tables aside and began line dancing.

Raising her voice over the noise, Dahlia said, "What's your poison, honey?"

"I'll have a bottle of Tyranena's The Devil Made Me Do It. If you've got it."

"Why am I not surprised?" She laughed. "You're in luck, we have a few bottles." She winked and turned toward the beer cooler.

He clasped her wrist. "And the Townsend diamonds, if you've got them."

Dahlia froze. She considered playing dumb but knew he wouldn't believe her. "I've got 'em." She jerked free and went to the cooler, adjusting the pouch in her bra. The *Townsend* diamonds? Yes, one was Leo's but the other was rightfully hers. Damned if she'd let Patrick Holden take it.

Jacob stumbled on unsteady legs as he walked Carl and Bill to the door. The men laughed good-naturedly. "Rain's stopping," Bill said, and followed Carl through the mist to their cars.

Jacob turned back to the bar and scanned the room. Chief Grey and his men had left. Their booth had been taken over by Aunt Sally's grandson, Devon Hass, several of his buddies, and two of the buxom reporters. They were doing shots. The table previously occupied by Emmett and the bank board had been shoved aside to make room for line dancing to "Casanova Cowboy."

Jacob found himself swaying to the beat.

A burst of laughter came from Tom Franklin and other Endeavor High School teachers seated around a table, as a ping-pong ball splashed in Tom's beer. Jacob cringed at the thought of having to teach teenagers Monday morning after a long night of losing drinking games.

Vernon had moved to this side of the bar to talk to the third buxom reporter, his fingers twirling a strand of her long, black hair. Dahlia, behind the bar, handed a beer bottle to a pony-tailed hippy straddling a bar stool. She leaned closer to the man, exposing ample cleavage and the satiny curve of her hot-pink bra. *Maybe she'll get lucky tonight after all.*

When Dahlia placed the cold bottle of beer in front of Patrick, he motioned for her to lean closer. She obliged and, mindful of exposing the velvet pouch, displayed more cleavage, hoping this would persuade him to let her keep the diamonds.

"Dahlia." Patrick's breath tickled her ear. "You've got to return them." Quickly, he filled her in on the real estate closing set for Tuesday at the farm. "Otherwise your uncle might suspect the closing is a trap."

"I can't. Not right now." *Even if I wanted to.* "Uncle Jake's watching."

The hippy turned toward Jacob, revealing a grizzled goatee.

Patrick Holden.

Jacob swayed over. "You've got balls, I'll give you that," he said, frustrated that his words were slurred.

Holden raised his glass in a silent toast.

"Should throw ya out."

"I'd like to see you try." Holden smirked.

Jacob fumbled with his shirt, finally lifting the side to expose the handle of his concealed gun.

Holden raised his hands. "Hey, man, my money's as good as anyone's."

Jacob nodded and turned to Dahlia. "Make sure he pays." He wobbled to his office, pissed at how difficult it was to walk in a straight line.

"Shit." Patrick watched Jacob close his office door behind him. "He's going to realize they're gone."

"Nah, it's cool," Dahlia said. "He's so drunk he wouldn't notice if his dick was missing."

The closed door muffled barroom conversations and Johnny Cash now singing on the jukebox. Jacob flopped down at his desk, determined to pay some bills. He shuffled a few papers but couldn't focus because of the booze and the prospect of diamonds. Only two days, and he'd own the Townsend place free and clear.

Jacob reached for the reproduction of the *Last Supper* and was able to lift the painting off the wall and set it aside without dropping it. He tried to remember the combination. After several attempts, he pushed the correct numbers. He opened the safe, shoved aside the manila envelopes, and felt for the black pouch.

Gone.

He ran his fingers over each shelf. Searched the envelopes, the cash box. Nothing. He reached into the corners, touched every surface. No diamonds. He got down on his knees, felt every fiber of the carpet beneath the safe, under the desk, everywhere. He searched his desk drawers, the cushions of the chairs, even checked inside his granddaddy's Bible. Nothing.

Jacob shoved through the office door, the boozy fog lifting. "Vern!" he roared, startling a couple of reporters playing dice at the corner of the bar.

Vern turned away from the journalist tottering on her bar stool and lumbered over to Jake. "Yeah?"

Jacob grabbed Vern's arm. "My office."

"What about the bar?"

"Dahlia can handle it."

Slamming the office door behind them, Jacob whirled on the younger man. "Where the hell are the diamonds? Tell me you've got them!"

Vernon shook his head.

Jake slumped in the plastic employee chair.

Vern checked the carpet and under the desk, retracing Jacob's steps. He stood, hands on his hips. Finally, he said, "Dahlia."

"What about her?"

"She's the only other person who knows the combination to the safe. Told you ya shouldn't have trusted her."

"Of course I trust her. She's family."

Vern laughed. "You're the only person I know who's ever bugged their own family."

"Wasn't bugging her," Jacob said, surprised he wasn't more offended. "Was bugging Townsend. We've been so busy, I'd forgotten about that. You listened to it, right? Find anything interesting?"

"Dahlia mentions your involvement with the sex video. Nothing Leo didn't already know. Talks about her and Eddie—"

"Wait," Jacob interrupted. "When I brought Carlisle into my office earlier this evening, Dahlia was here. Caught her with tens and twenties. She claimed we were short on cash." Jacob could feel his escalating rage burning away the last effects of the beer and whiskey.

"On the tape," Vern said, "she mentions her love rock."

Dahlia gasped as the office door flew open.

"Dahlia!" Uncle Jacob bellowed.

Patrick put his hand on her arm. "Take full responsibility. Leave the Townsends out of it."

"DAHLIA!"

She nodded.

"And Dahlia," Patrick warned, his tone serious. "Don't tell him you're leaving town."

She nodded again, straightened her t-shirt over her shorts, and walked the length of the bar. She did her best to look and feel pissed off while trying to control her ankles wobbling on her spiky black heels. When she reached her uncle, she said, "What the hell?! I was with a customer."

Jacob clenched her arm, his nails digging into her elbow, making her fingertips tingle. He dragged her into the office and threw her in front of the open safe. "You've been in there. Took a few things."

"No—"

He slapped her hard. She fell back into his desk chair.

Her hand shot to her hot, stinging cheek. She tasted blood inside her mouth. Uncle Jacob had never hit her before. She fought back tears, not of pain but of rage. He'd stolen her diamond. She'd only taken back what was hers.

"Okay, yeah. I took that black bag."

He leaned closer, his face inches from hers, his breath a sickly mix of Guinness and Death's Door Whisky. "Townsend talk you into it?"

"Why would he give a shit about my love rock?" She hoped she sounded convincing.

"Tell me why you took it."

"I got to thinking about Eddie Townsend." She managed a blush, glanced at Vernon, and dropped her eyes, thinking that she should get an Academy Award for this performance. "Well, you know I… I kinda…"

"Yeah, yeah, you've got a crush on that homo and his brother. So?"

"I wanted my rock back. It's a memento from a time Eddie and I—"

Jacob snorted.

"You told me you'd hang onto it for me." She tried her best to look ashamed. "So I searched your office. Was surprised to find you'd put a rock in a safe. I took it. It's mine. It's not like I stole anything." Then she decided to play innocent. "But there were notes in the bag and another rock, Leo's mother's, according to the notes. How'd you get that stuff?"

"None of your goddamned business," Jacob said, muffled drumbeats from the bar accentuating his words. "Where's the bag?"

She shrugged.

"You got it on you?" Vern asked.

"Nah."

Vernon hooked the back of her head with one huge hand and reached down the V-neck of her t-shirt with the other.

"Hey!" Dahlia tried to squirm away from his groping hand. He grinned as he retrieved the pouch from its hiding place and handed it to Jacob.

Jacob hit her again. "What else are you lying about?"

She fell against the desk, her cheek throbbing, more blood in her mouth. "Nothing, I swear," she whimpered, wiping blood from her lip.

He raised his hand.

She cowered. When he lowered it, she felt her anger surge. "What's the big fucking deal anyway? It's not like they're worth anything."

"When you had lunch with Townsend," Jacob said, obviously trying to keep his voice steady, "did you mention your rock?"

Dahlia tried to remember when she'd discovered the bug in her purse. What part of their conversation had Uncle Jacob heard? She decided to play it safe. "Yes."

He crossed his arms. "And?"

"I mentioned you had it. That's what got me thinking I wanted it back."

"Did he mention *his* rock?"

"No. I was totally surprised to find out he had one. Surprised he didn't mention it." She prayed Jacob believed her.

"What else did you and Townsend talk about?"

"Well, we talked about his job at the paper, my shitty job here—"

"What did you say to Patrick Holden?" Jacob said through gritted teeth.

"He asked me how I liked working here. I asked him how he got his limp."

"And…"

"Right before you called me in he suggested we go away together for a couple of days."

"That's a lie," Jacob said. "I saw his girlfriend. Man would have to be insane to pick you over her."

Tears stung her eyes almost as much as his cruel words. "I didn't know he had a girlfriend." She wiped tears and blood off her face with the back of her hand, then opened her palm to Vernon. "Give me my rock."

"No," Jacob said. "If you're a good girl and keep your trap shut I'll give it back to you in a few days." He pointed toward the door. "Now get your ass back to work."

When Dahlia escaped into the hallway, the office door slammed behind her. She started for the bar and then stopped. The tipsy reporter Vern had hit on earlier had moved to the stool next to Patrick. She was laughing at something he'd said, rubbing his arm.

Dahlia rubbed her own arm, leaving a smear of blood on her pale skin. She turned and stumbled into the ladies' room, glad to find it vacant. She washed her hands, watching the diluted blood swirl around the yellowed ceramic sink and then disappear down the drain. She yanked a few paper towels out of the rusty dispenser and dowsed them in cold water. Holding the towels gingerly against her stinging cheek, the cold soothing, Dahlia looked at her reflection in the smudged mirror.

Her hair was a birds' nest of bleached-blonde straw. Her t-shirt was pulled down so that all of her cleavage and most of her bra were exposed. She lifted the towels off her face. A red welt had formed on her left cheek and her bottom lip was cracked and swollen. She cried, not caring that her sobs echoed around the small room. Then she heard voices coming from the hall—Uncle Jacob talking to Vernon as they passed the ladies' room. "Bitch deserved that."

Fucking asshole. Angrier than she'd ever been, Dahlia splashed water on her face, patted it dry, straightened her shirt, and pushed her unruly hair in place. Looking again at her swollen face, she had an overwhelming urge to bolt from Isaiah's and leave Endeavor. Forever. She resisted the urge.

No way she'd leave without her diamond.

53

"I've got a double run." Quinn laid her four cards on the kitchen table and pegged eight points on the cribbage board. "One more point and we skunk you again!" She high-fived Tali.

"You girls are on fire tonight." Mary collected the cards and handed them to Leo.

"Luck." Leo shuffled. "Pure luck. We'll keep them in the stink hole and come from behind to win, Mary."

Over the sound of rain drumming on the windows, there was laughter from Frank, Charlotte, and the Secret Service men in the living room. Griffin played a serious Beethoven piece on the baby grand piano and then Eddie countered with "Heart and Soul."

"Come on, Eddie!" Leo shouted, leaning toward the hall. "Show them what you're made of."

More laughter, deep discussion, then the happy notes of Scott Joplin's "Maple Leaf Rag."

"Can't we have pie tonight, Will?" Tali asked, collecting her cards.

With the kitchen full of the smell of baking pastry, and sweet strawberries and rhubarb, Leo had been wondering the same thing.

Will took a hot pie out of the oven. "Nope. They're for tomorrow's dinner. I've made strawberry turnovers, too, but they're for breakfast."

"But don't you need a pie taste-tester?" Tali selected a card from her hand and placed it in the crib. "To make sure it's edible?"

"Uh, oh," Quinn said, under her breath. "Now you're in trouble." She added her card to the crib.

"No." Will set the second pie on the cooling rack. "But since you're so eager to help out, you can churn the ice cream maker." He closed the oven door. "Vanilla to go with the pies."

Tali groaned. "You brought your old crank ice cream machine? I don't know why you don't get one of those automatic ones."

Quinn finished off her lemonade. "He swears the ice cream is creamier when it's made with blood, sweat, and tears."

Leo cut the deck.

"I'll churn." Tali reached for the top card. "If I get the first piece of pie."

"Deal," Will said.

Tali turned over the card. "Jack of spades. That's two points. We win!" She fist-bumped Quinn.

"Luck," Leo repeated as he put the cards away. "We want a rematch tomorrow."

"We're heading to bed," Frank called from the hallway.

"Not me," Charlotte said. "I'm going to sit on the front porch. Watch the rain. Wait for Patrick."

"We'll join you," Mary said. "Kids?"

"This may shock you," Quinn said. "But we're going to bed, too."

"Yep," Tali agreed. "Fresh air, farm chores; we're beat."

The house telephone rang as Leo turned off the kitchen light.

"Who's calling at ten o'clock on a Sunday night?" Mary asked.

"It might be Doc Stork, the vet. I left him a message earlier." Leo reached for the receiver. "Hello?"

"Frank told me you were out of town," Landry said.

"What do you want, Jacob?"

Frowning, Mary crossed her arms.

"Sell the farm to me tomorrow or your sex video will go viral."

"That won't—"

"Now that you're home, you've got no excuse to put this off."

"At least give us until tomorrow night."

"Four o'clock." The phone went dead.

"Landry's coming tomorrow at four."

The screen door creaked open. Patrick limped into the kitchen, followed by Charlotte.

"Dahlia had the diamonds." Patrick opened the fridge and selected a bottle of Ale Asylum's Bedlam. "Landry discovered them missing. Called Dahlia into his office and reclaimed them. When she came back to the bar, her cheek was red and she had a cut lip. Muttered that she'd slipped on water in the ladies' room. I think he slapped her around." He drank the entire beer in one swallow.

"Bastard!" Leo reached for the phone. "I'll call her. Convince her to leave now."

"Can't, she's stuck working at the bar." Patrick handed Leo a cold beer.

"How awful." Mary shook her head. "That's why Landry called. He's worried you'll find out about the diamonds."

Leo took a swig from the bottle. "Good."

54

Leo opened the bedroom curtains early Monday morning to sunlight fighting its way through a ground fog that obscured the fields. Fog, but no hint of storm clouds. A good morning for a run.

He turned back to Mary, still sleeping under the checkered bedspread, and considered waking her, seeing if she'd go with him. He decided against it. Let her sleep. It was going to be a long day.

Leo quietly changed into his shorts, t-shirt, and running shoes and crept downstairs to the smell of roasted coffee. *The Farm Report* with Pam Jahnke broadcasted on the kitchen's ancient a.m. radio. Eddie, always an early riser, sat hunched over *The Chicago Examiner* at the kitchen table, sipping coffee from one of their mother's colorful Italian mugs.

"I'm going for a run." Leo bent down to check his laces.

"Did you glance out the front window?" Eddie kept his eyes on the newspaper.

Leo walked down the hall and out the front door.

"GAYS GET OUT!" the mass of humanity screamed from the edge of the farm. They waved Protect Marriage Movement signs and then chanted, "NO AIDS IN ENDEAVOR! FIGHT FOUL FAGS!" Apparently Emmett Everson had brought in reinforcements.

Leo backed into the house and rejoined Eddie in the kitchen. "Okay. So the crazies have reproduced. Running was a bad idea." He took another colorful mug down from the shelf and filled it with coffee. "Where's Griffin?"

"In the study phoning his campaign manager, rearranging his schedule so he can leave after our meeting with Landry." Eddie glanced up from the paper. "Once Landry's arrested, do you think the craziness will stop?"

"First we have to put him away." Leo set the plate of Will's strawberry pastries on the table. Then he sat beside his brother. "Right now, we don't have enough evidence." He bit into a turnover. A perfect combination of fresh strawberries, sugar, and flaky crust. "Sgt. Davies should be able to trace the bugs bought in Milwaukee to Smith, but we still haven't connected those to Landry. I do have the lab results proving I was drugged, but again, that only implicates Smith and Dahlia. I'll give them my taped conversation with Dahlia, but I don't want her testifying. I'm worried about her safety as it is."

"Did you get ahold of her last night?"

"Finally. She says she won't leave until she gets her diamond back. I tried to talk her out of it, but you know how she can be." He finished off the pastry and wiped his mouth on one of his mother's blue linen napkins.

"Without her testimony, we still have the motel receipt verifying Smith was in that room Saturday night, and we have the brass plate from my computer. But to prove I was kidnapped I need something more from the hotel clerk. I'm hoping there's still a way he can connect something to Landry, but the kid's not returning my calls."

"Worst case scenario, Landry goes free." Eddie helped himself to a turnover. "But *we* might have buried treasure—the diamonds."

"It won't be enough. Not for me. And not for Aunt Sally. Landry should rot in hell.

"As far as the craziness, once you and Griffin take off on the campaign trail it'll stop here, in Endeavor. It'll follow you, though. I'm afraid this will be part of your life from now on." Leo refilled their coffee mugs. "Is Griffin worth it?"

"Would Mary be worth it?"

"Hell, yes." He set the coffee pot heavily on the table, making the mugs rattle.

"My feelings exactly." Eddie smiled. "But there's something else that *might* be a part of my life now—a part of our lives."

"What's that?"

"Diamonds." Eddie pushed his wheelchair back from the table. "Griffin will be busy for a while. Let's go treasure hunting."

"You can't do any digging," Leo said. "Not with three broken ribs."

"Nothing better than sitting back and watching you work."

Leo changed into jeans and work boots, rolled Eddie over to the pickup and helped him in, and then avoided puddles on his way to the machine shed. A spring breeze carried the angry taunts of the protestors to the yard, but this clearly didn't faze a barnyard cat who sauntered by, a limp mouse dangling from its mouth. Leo passed Johnny coming from the cow pasture. The farmhand happily reported the cows had improved. As proof, several mooed lazily.

Johnny ducked into the old dairy barn and shouted to Tali, Quinn, and Will sleeping in the loft, "Daylight's a-wastin'!"

"Daylight just got here!" Quinn shouted back. Tali and Will groaned.

Chuckling, Leo entered the shed and collected his father's crusty work gloves. He took a dented shovel and rusty metal rake from the hooks on the wall.

"Doing some gardening?" Johnny asked, as they both walked into the yard.

"Nope. Exploring." Leo winked and climbed into his father's pickup.

Several minutes later, Leo parked near the abandoned well and lifted Eddie's wheelchair out of the back. He tugged on the work gloves and maneuvered Eddie and the chair over the damp ground. The wheels sunk into the mud twice, making him glad Eddie hadn't decorated them with one of his famous painting covers. As they got close to the well, bright rays of sunlight cut through the lifting fog, making it easier for them to find their way.

Leo drove the shovel blade into the dirt, releasing a damp, earthy smell he always associated with spring. He turned over clumps of mud and debris, including a greenish-gray substance that could have been the kimberlite Professor Arsenault mentioned. Every few minutes he'd stop to let Eddie examine an unusual stone or strangely shaped rock, but they found nothing resembling Leo's crystal.

"Hand me the rake," Eddie said. "Don't worry, I'll take it easy." He sifted through the mud. "When we get back to the house, I'll call the auctioneer, postpone the auction. Hopefully, we won't be needing his services at all. Then, I'd like to spend some time with Griffin. What's your plan for today?"

"I've got to return the Camaro to the rental office in the Dells. Then, I have a few phone calls to make. The kid at the Madison motel. See if he remembers anything else. Get in touch with Doc Stork. We keep playing phone tag. I'm hoping he has some inside knowledge about Doc Krueger's relationship with Landry. Then, I plan on talking to Zach about the bugs. There's got to be a way to link Landry to them."

He dumped more dirt in front of Eddie and watched as his brother raked the fresh pile. "Anything?"

"Nope."

Leo moved to the opposite side of the well, hoping for some luck there. Despite the cool morning, he'd worked up a sweat. While this wasn't the same as running ten miles, he was glad for the exercise.

As he dropped a shovel full of the dark, wet topsoil near his brother, something sparkled. Leo put his hand out to stop Eddie's rake.

"Wait!"

He took off his gloves and sifted through the mud, his hands instantly covered in grime. *Damn, where did it go? Maybe it was just the sunlight reflecting off a water drop.* He heard a click and glanced up.

Eddie directed his iPhone at Leo and snapped a picture. "My Pulitzer Prize-winning brother playing in the mud." He examined the photo. "This will go nicely with Mary's picture of 'Leo the Farmer.'"

"Ha, ha, very funny." Leo took his hands out of the muck and shook them, spraying himself and his brother with mud. Eddie laughed, wiping a drop of grit from his cheek.

Leo positioned himself behind the wheelchair. "Okay, now you can take the picture."

"Hang on. What's that?" Eddie pointed to the spot where Leo's hand had been.

Leo bent closer. Two—no three—smooth, clear stones glittered in the morning light. He scooped them up, rubbing them clean with his thumb. "Holy crap, look at the size of this one." He handed the largest to Eddie.

Eddie whistled. "Diamonds in our backyard."

Eddie examined the five diamonds they'd found as the truck ambled down the rutted path to the farmhouse. He held them up to the sunlight, making them glow.

"Wait 'til Dad sees them," Leo said.

Their excitement dissolved the minute they exited the vehicle. Ugly chants from the end of the driveway assaulted them.

"Strangers protesting don't bother me. But I've lived in Endeavor my whole life. Most of those people," Eddie gestured toward the crowd, "know me. They know I'm not out to corrupt their kids."

"It's as if they've had a disconnect," Leo said. "Shouting about someone without putting it together that it's you."

"Fuck it." Eddie cranked on the wheels of his chair, directing it down the driveway.

"They'll eat you alive."

"I'm just going to talk to them." He clutched his side, the exertion obviously causing him considerable pain.

Leo blocked Eddie's path. "I've got a better idea. Let's get cleaned up. We'll have Will bake cinnamon rolls to bring with us as a peace offering."

Leo guided Eddie's chair down the ramp along the side of the house. Large trays of fresh bakery were stacked on Eddie's lap. The cinnamon aroma should have made Leo's stomach grumble, but worry for his brother left him with little appetite. He pushed Eddie's wheelchair toward the road and glanced back at Mary sitting on the edge of the glider and Griffin pacing the front porch. "He'll be okay," he heard Mary tell Griffin.

As the brothers got closer to County T, the noise level rose. People shoved each other to get a better glimpse. The police officers struggled to keep them off the driveway. Leo wondered if they would start throwing things. He pictured the cinnamon buns splattered with mud.

When they were within a few feet of the road, Leo handed the heaping trays of morning buns to the cops. The noise level dropped by half as the trays were passed around.

Eddie saw his opportunity. "Mr. Kenyan!" The television cameras honed in.

Carl Kenyan, holding a Fags Are Sinners sign, stopped chanting "GAYS GET OUT!" Others continued Carl's chant but the reporters turned away from them.

"Carl," Eddie continued. "You've cut my hair for as long as I can remember. Fought with me when I wanted a mohawk back in high school."

A tall man lobbed a bun at Eddie. It bounced off his shoulder, spraying frosting and crumbs all over his dark green t-shirt. The man and the people near him laughed.

Leo started for the road, ready to punch his way to the asshole.

"Don't," Eddie hissed, brushing off the mess. "I'll handle this."

Leo nodded, but his jaw and fists clenched.

"Playing hooky from teaching school, Tom?" Eddie said to the tall, glaring man. "Some things never change. Do you remember the last time I was pegged with food? It was in the cafeteria at Endeavor High School. You nailed me real good, Tom. Course that was right before I sprayed your pants with a shook-up can of Mountain Dew. Too bad I don't have any on me at the moment. Make it an even fight."

Now, people directed their laughter at Tom, whose glare softened.

Eddie wiped his sticky fingers on his pants. "Mr. Everson." He turned his attention to Emmett. "When you were promoted to Endeavor Bank president, you asked me to create a sign. You were so pleased with the results you hired me to design the bank's brochures and website. We've had a good working relationship, haven't we?"

Emmett looked down at his shifting feet.

"Mrs. Branson—Millie," Eddie said, to his longtime neighbor standing by the mailbox. "When I was eight I asked you to adopt me. Remember?"

Millie Branson tried to shrink back into the crowd but hit a solid wall of people.

"Mom told me you wanted a son but couldn't have children. I didn't think that was fair. Figured my family could spare me. When you cried, I worried that I'd made you sad, until you hugged me so tight I couldn't breathe."

Millie wiped her face. "Take me home, Hugh." Her husband guided her by the elbow, the mob parting to let them pass.

Carl watched them go and pushed his way through the crowd, dragging his sign behind him. Others followed his lead and headed for their cars.

Emmett Everson didn't budge, but he didn't look at Eddie either.

"It worked." Griffin descended the steps as Leo and Eddie approached.

"Sort of," Eddie said. "About half of them left."

"And most of those were locals," Leo said. "Those remaining are reporters, out-of-towners—and Emmett Everson."

Frank shook Eddie's hand. "I'm proud of you, son. Much better solution than my shotgun idea."

"Anyone hungry?" Will called from the kitchen. His words and the smell of bacon drifted through the open window. "I've made brunch."

"Which got him out of planting the last of the soy beans," Quinn said sleepily from the porch glider, her head resting on Tali's shoulder.

"Hey, I collected the eggs from the hen house!" Will protested.

"After breakfast and a shower," Tali said, a streak of mud on her chin, "I'm taking a nap. I'll need it to tackle Will's ice cream maker this afternoon." Her stocking feet rested on the wooden floor boards, gently rocking the glider, making it creak. Her muddy boots lay beside Quinn and Will's under the bench.

GOD ON MAYHEM STREET

"Ooo, a nap." Quinn's eyes shut as she sunk further into the glider's striped cushions.

Mary reached for Quinn's hand. "You can't be that tired. I got up when you did and worked just as hard."

Quinn let her mother pull her off the bench. "We didn't exactly go to bed as early as we'd planned. We got hooked on *Breaking Bad*, watched it on Netflix until two a.m."

Leo shifted the empty morning bun trays to one hand and held the door open. Everyone filed through to the kitchen, breathing in the aroma of bacon grease mixed with the scent of fresh coffee. There was a logjam at the doorway as Mary and Charlotte admired Will's beautiful table setting.

Blue and gold china plates, cups, and saucers, antique silverware, and crystal glasses decorated the table. Hand-painted serving plates heaped with strips of thick bacon, cut-glass bowls of berries, porcelain casserole dishes with rhubarb crumble, and stoneware pie plates filled with steaming quiches covered the rest of the embroidered tablecloth. Pots of coffee sat at either end of the table next to pitchers of freshly-squeezed orange juice.

Everyone took their customary seats with Frank at the head.

Eddie raised his water glass. "To Will, his pacifying morning buns, and this amazing feast."

"To Will!"

As Leo dug into a slice of asparagus quiche, Patrick asked, "That Camaro, how does it drive?"

"Like a giant toy," Leo said. "Seriously, it's hard not to gun it at every light."

"I'd love to try."

"How about you and Charlotte running it back to the Dells for me?"

"Exactly what I was thinking." Patrick helped himself to Will's rhubarb crumble.

"Dibs on driving the car there," Charlotte said. "You can take your bike, Patrick."

"Now, kids," Will teased, passing a bowl of raspberries and strawberries to Charlotte. "Take turns."

Patrick grinned. "You drive it halfway. Then we'll switch."

"Deal." Charlotte dished berries onto her plate.

"So Leo and I got a little muddy this morning," Eddie broke in. "Did some digging by the abandoned well and found these." He laid the sparkling diamonds on the tablecloth.

Frank whistled.

"What are they?" Tali took one in the palm of her hand.

"Diamonds," Frank said.

"No way!" Tali said.

"In Wisconsin?" Quinn picked one up and rubbed it between her fingers.

"Yep. Though we have to have them tested to be sure," Eddie said.

"Awesome," Will said.

Griffin examined the largest stone. "They look like the one Landry stole from you, Leo."

"Which explains why Landry wants this farm." Patrick examined a diamond in his hand. "Are you any closer to getting him put away?"

"No," Leo admitted. "I've hit a lot of dead ends. Our vet, Doc Stork, wishes he could help, but it's next to impossible to prove Krueger knew the cattle were poisoned. He mentioned filing a complaint with the Wisconsin Department of Agriculture, Trade & Consumer Protection. I don't know what good that would do other than alert Krueger, and possibly Landry, that we're on to them. And even if Krueger knew of the urea poisoning, there's no way he'd implicate Landry. What we need is that video…"

"What video?" Will asked.

Damn. Leo hadn't meant to tell the kids about it.

Mary touched Leo's shoulder. "Landry's niece and Vernon Smith drugged Leo, then taped him in a compromising situation. Landry emailed the tape to Leo and his editor."

"That's not cool." Will held out his hand. "Can I see your phone?"

Leo handed it to him. "But you won't find the video there. Landry encrypted the email. Wiped it out as soon as it was read."

Will smiled. "Nothing is totally wiped." He examined the phone. "It'll take a couple hours but it shouldn't be a problem." He shoved his remaining quiche into his mouth and pushed back from the table. "Is it okay…?" he mumbled through the mouthful.

"Go," Mary said. "We'll take care of the dishes."

"How will this video nail Landry?" Frank asked.

"If we can trace it back to Landry that'll connect him to my kidnapping. Felony charges. Should keep him locked away in the state penitentiary for years."

55

The late-morning sunlight streamed through the kitchen windows as Leo stacked china plates back on the shelf. Silverware clanged as Patrick emptied knives and forks from the drying rack into the drawer. Tali and Quinn finished clearing the table while Mary and Charlotte dished leftovers into Tupperware containers and organized the refrigerator. Griffin entertained them by playing Beethoven's "Pathetique Sonata" on the living room piano.

"That was my mother's favorite piece." Leo sighed.

Mary gave him a sad smile over the refrigerator door as Will bounded into the kitchen. "I've done it!" He tossed Leo's phone to him. "I've recovered the encrypted email."

Quinn high-fived her brother.

"Where you able to trace it to Landry?" Leo asked.

"Right to his email, originating from his IP address at the Endeavor Village Hall."

"No shit!" Patrick said.

"That should do it." Leo punched Sgt. Zachary Davies' number on his cell phone. "Zach, we've traced the video to Landry."

"Send me and the Marquette County Sheriff an email detailing all your evidence, the video, the receipt, witness testimony, your taped conversation with Dahlia—everything," Zach said. Leo could hear a chair scraping on a floor, keys jangling. "What time will Landry be at your place?"

"Four."

"I'm leaving now. I'll contact the Marquette County sheriff on my way. I'm sure he'll want to investigate before asking for a warrant but with this last piece of the puzzle, it shouldn't take him too long. My guess is he'll join us at your place, warrant in hand. We should be there soon after Landry."

"We'll stall him until you get here."

At a few minutes before four, Leo stood in the living room staring out the farmhouse's picture window. The afternoon had grown sticky, the hottest day of the year so far. Humidity saturated the still air and wilted the tall purple wildflowers along the driveway.

Leo felt a trickle of sweat trace down his back. His black dress shirt stuck to his skin. At least it had short sleeves.

His father had refused to install air conditioning in the old farmhouse, saying that an open window was the best way to condition the air. There were some fans in the basement but Frank wouldn't pull them out until mid-July. Leo's mother had never minded the heat. She'd spent her childhood in an eighteenth-century stone farmhouse right outside Norcia, Italy where people scoffed at air conditioning and average summer temperatures hit eighty-eight.

Leo glanced above the fireplace at his mother's face in Mary's oil painting, and wondered what Isabella would think of this mess with Landry. She'd probably think it was a gift from God. After all, this conflict had thawed his icy relationship with his father.

Looking back through the window, Leo could see two Endeavor police officers mingling with reporters, out-of-town gawkers, and a few locals who just couldn't stay away. The officers fanned their faces with their hats. Emmett Everson passed around bottles of water, no doubt decorated with the Protect Marriage Movement logo. TV and radio vans clogged County T, a sight all-too-familiar, but now news helicopters also flew low overhead. At least they provided a breeze.

"The kids are helping Johnny round up the cattle." Mary walked into the room. She handed Leo a tall glass of ice water. "The weather forecast is calling for a powerful storm."

The glass's damp sides cooled Leo's hand.

"Patrick and Charlotte are back from the Dells. Charlotte's pulling the tractor into the machine shed," Mary said.

"My Mustang's out back—"

"I gave Patrick your keys. He'll park it and your dad's car beside the tractor." She kissed him, then slid a hair tie off her wrist. "I can't believe this heat." She gathered her long blonde hair into a ponytail and secured it with the tie. The back of her neck glistened.

Leo held the cold water glass to her skin.

Mary flinched, then said, "Ooo, that's nice." She leaned into the glass and closed her eyes. "Once everything's secure, Patrick, Charlotte, John, the kids, and I are going to head to the dairy barn. We'll stay there during your meeting. Patrick wants to try out that rope swing."

Leo grinned. "Why doesn't that surprise me?"

"Sighted any evil village presidents yet?" Eddie entered the room with Griffin and the Secret Service men.

Leo turned back to the window. "As we speak."

Jacob Landry's baby blue Caddie turned into the driveway. Landry drove with the convertible's top down, Vernon Smith wedged into the passenger seat. The Caddie paused at the end of the driveway, allowing Emmett Everson to squeeze into the back for the last two hundred yards to the house. Landry handed Everson a briefcase and waved, especially at the TV cameras.

"Jacob Landry. God on Mayhem Street," Eddie said.

Leo nodded. "You got that right."

"We'll make ourselves scarce in the den," Griffin said and the two Secret Service men followed him out of the room.

Leo trudged outside as Landry parked. He kept his face grave, playing the part of a man about to lose his childhood home.

"Leo, my boy." Landry wiped his hand on his chinos and offered it.

Leo ignored the outstretched hand and walked into the house,

GOD ON MAYHEM STREET 279

muttering, "Let's get this over with." He led the men down the hall into the kitchen where Frank and Eddie were seated at the table.

"Gentlemen," Landry said.

Frank sipped ice water from a crystal glass. Eddie examined his fingernails.

When Landry got no response, he scanned the kitchen, unable to suppress a smile.

Is he picturing himself entertaining friends here, or demolishing the place?

"I'm parched. How about a little something to drink?" Landry nodded toward Frank's glass.

Leo went to the faucet and filled three cloudy Swampside Bar and Grill glasses with tepid tap water. Will had offered to make more freshly-squeezed lemonade and to prepare bruschetta and crostini using Isabella's recipes. But Leo flatly refused to serve Jacob Landry anything beyond tap water, and certainly nothing in his mother's good crystal.

"Sit down," Leo commanded, as he set the glasses on the table.

Smith growled. Sweat dampened his blue Landry Bowl Haven t-shirt.

"Please, sit down," Leo amended.

The big man took his time lowering himself onto a chair. It creaked but held him.

Everson selected a seat as far away from Eddie as possible. He took off his suit coat and laid it on the back of the chair. His cream-colored, short-sleeved dress shirt clung to his back.

Landry sat at the head of the table opposite Frank.

"Can't believe how incredibly hot it is for this time of year." Everson drew a stack of documents out of his briefcase. The top sheets stuck to his damp hands. He wiped them on his handkerchief. "This is a simple transaction," he replaced the handkerchief, "as Jacob will be paying cash."

"That's correct." Landry sipped his water and grimaced.

Everson organized the documents into two neat piles, tapping them to square the corners. He pushed one pile toward Leo's dad, avoiding the damp ring around Frank's water glass. "We'll start with you."

Frank's face glistened but he otherwise seemed unfazed by the heat. He lifted the first document off the pile and read it, turning each page slowly, peering back at the previous pages, reading some more, taking his time. Leo had the distinct impression that his father was enjoying this moment.

Landry tapped his fingers on the table.

Frank looked at him over the top of the document, one eyebrow raised.

"Sorry." Landry wiped his sleeve across his forehead. "It's just so damn hot in here. Could you read a little quicker?"

Frank finished drinking his water and wiped his hand on his pants. He re-examined the first document for a few more minutes then used the top page to blot his moist face.

"What are you—" Everson said.

Frank shoved the papers aside, spilling some of them onto the floor. He reached into his shirt pocket and tossed the five diamonds onto the table. They danced to the center, sparkling as they caught the light.

Landry drew in a sharp breath, his face going pale.

"I don't understand." Everson touched the crystal nearest him. "What are they?"

Landry clasped his shaking hands.

Smith closed his eyes.

"Diamonds," Eddie answered, coolly. "Leo and I discovered them by our abandoned well this morning."

"Diamonds?" Everson asked. "In Wisconsin?"

"It's rare," Leo said, as a door slammed in the yard. *The cavalry is here.* He glanced out the window. Johnny's truck backed away from the barn and disappeared around the side of the house.

"Did you know about this?" Everson whirled on Landry, pointing a finger.

"Certainly not." Landry's voice was steady but he kept his eyes on the diamonds.

Frank stiffened. "Now you know why I won't sell."

Landry rose, his pale face turning red. "Why in God's name didn't you tell me this on the phone?!" He batted his water glass, sending it flying at Eddie's face.

Leo's hand shot out in front of his brother. The cheap glass shattered against his hand, slicing it. "What the hell?!" Leo said, jumping to his feet and sending his chair crashing to the floor.

Frank grabbed Leo's arm and held him back.

Everson patted Landry's chair. "Calm down, Jacob. Sit."

Landry didn't move. "Why," he said, through gritted teeth, "did you insist we come here today if you had no intention of selling?"

Frank pushed back his chair and straightened to his full six feet. "You've harassed me for years trying to get this farm. I wanted to see the disappointment on your face."

Leo wrapped his bleeding hand in a napkin as he stood next to his dad. "You've poisoned our cows, bugged our home, beat my brother, and drugged, kidnapped, and blackmailed me. It ends now."

Landry turned to Everson. "I told you these people are crazy. Grab your paperwork. We're leaving."

Everson knelt on the floor to collect the documents and stuffed them in his briefcase. Smith hoisted himself from his chair and followed Landry to the hall.

Eddie blocked their way with his wheelchair. "Sorry. The chair is difficult to maneuver with three broken ribs."

Landry took note of Pablo Picasso's colorful diamond face decorating Eddie's wheels. "Get out of my way!"

Eddie made several ineffectual attempts to shift.

"Oh, for God's sake." Landry shoved the chair aside, nearly dislodging Eddie, and then stormed down the hallway. Smith lumbered after him.

Everson hesitated. "I honestly didn't know any of this was going on."

"Emmett, let's go!" Landry shouted, as the screen door slammed.

Everson dropped his briefcase, spilling several documents onto the floor. He grabbed the case and scooted after Landry, leaving the stray papers behind.

"Where are the police?" Frank demanded of Leo.

"I don't know. But both of you stay here." Leo raced down the hallway, trying to think of a way to stall Landry. He pushed out onto the porch and bumped into the wall that was Vernon Smith. The big man glanced back over his shoulder at Leo, his eyes filled with hatred and… fear.

Outside, the crowd roared. *What the hell? Are they charging the house?* Leo peered around Smith.

Landry and Everson stood frozen at the edge of the porch, Everson's case clutched against his chest. The crowd stayed off the Townsends' property but their screams and shouts magnified as a blue-and-white-striped Chicago Police squad car and a tan Marquette County Sheriff's sedan drove toward the house. They parked behind Landry's Coupe DeVille.

Zach Davies, in full uniform, exited the Chicago police car. He was several inches shorter than Leo but broader in the chest, built like a bulldog. A taller, thinner officer emerged from the second vehicle, adjusting his sheriff's cap. Both had the calm, in-control air of men who had served on police forces for years.

"Zach." Leo walked around Smith, dodged past Landry and Everson, and jogged down the stairs to the gravel driveway. "Glad you could make it."

Zach shook Leo's hand and nodded toward the other officer. "Marquette County Sheriff Brian O'Donnell."

"Brian," Landry said, his voice irritated. "What's this about?"

Smith stood next to Landry.

"I have to take you in, Jake. Judge Xavier issued a warrant for your arrest." Sheriff O'Donnell waved folded sheets of paper. "You, too, Vernon. Got a whole mess of charges—" He skimmed the paperwork and glanced at Everson. "Emmett. Glad to see you're here. We'd like to ask you a few questions, too."

"What about?" Everson's hands whitened as he clutched his briefcase tighter.

"The activities of your organization. The local chapter of," he checked the papers again, "the Protect Marriage Movement."

Smith grabbed Landry around the waist. His big hands lifted the village president's shirt.

"Vernon!" Landry struggled with Smith, yanking his shirt down.

Smith fished around in the side of the older man's slacks. Landry tried to pull away. The seams of his pants made a terrible ripping sound.

Successful, Smith shoved Landry out of the way. The village president stumbled and fell hard onto the porch floor.

"What the hell?!" Landry yelled.

Sunlight gleamed off something in Smith's enormous hand, blinding Leo for a moment. Smith raised the object. A silver revolver. He pointed the barrel at Leo's face.

Leo jerked just as the gun fired with a resounding *crack*. He felt a burning sensation graze his left cheek. Behind him, the passenger-side window of Zach's squad car shattered.

"Duck!" Zach ordered.

Leo dropped to the gravel driveway. He smelled grit and his own sweat. He heard his blood pulsing through his ears but he kept his eyes on Smith. If the man tried to shoot him again, he wanted to see it coming.

More explosive *cracks* as both Zach and Sheriff O'Donnell shot Smith.

Jacob covered his head with his hands and cowered on the floorboards.

Everson squealed and dropped his case. It clattered down the steps.

Vernon Smith teetered on the top step, curiously watching his own blood pulsate out of the bullet holes in his chest and abdomen, turning his blue shirt purple. He dropped the gun and reached for Landry. "Jacob?" Then he crumpled to the floor.

Silence.

Zach and O'Donnell hurtled the stairs. One of Griffin's Secret Service men burst out the front door and kicked the revolver aside. Avoiding Smith's widening pool of blood, Zach handcuffed him and checked his pulse. "This man's gone. No need to call MedFlight, I'm sorry to say."

Leo rose from the driveway and shakily dusted himself off. He touched his cheek and then examined his fingers. No blood. *Just a scratch. Damn, I'm lucky.*

Sheriff O'Donnell pulled Landry's arms behind his back and handcuffed him. Then, he hefted the village president to his feet. Landry stumbled but remained uncharacteristically quiet.

Zach dashed down the stairs to Leo. "Are you okay?"

Words caught in Leo's throat; he nodded.

"Close one." Zach squeezed Leo's shoulder. He jogged over to his squad car, reached through the broken window, and called the Endeavor Police Department.

Landry glanced at Vernon Smith's body then stared straight ahead with a serene expression. Leo couldn't believe a man could be so cold.

Everson cried and blew his nose on a handkerchief.

"Chief Grey is on his way. He'll contact the coroner." Zach took his cap off and ran a shaky hand through his hair. "Jesus, what a waste."

Landry continued to remain calm as Sheriff O'Donnell led him and Everson around Smith's body and the blood, down the steps, and into the squad car.

"I'm sorry it had to happen this way," Zach said.

"Me, too," Leo said. "But now it's over."

Leo avoided looking at Smith's motionless form. Instead he glanced at the crowd on County T, quieted at least for the moment by the sound of gunshots. And in the sky, above the fields, thunderheads formed.

56

"I don't think you'll need stitches." Mary held Leo's hand over the powder room sink and rinsed his cut with saline solution.

A swishing sound came from the front porch as John and Patrick scrubbed bleach across the blood-stained floorboards. Thunder rumbled overhead.

Mary dried Leo's hand and wrapped gauze around it.

"Thanks." He kissed her.

"How'd you get that scratch on your cheek?"

Leo glanced in the mirror. A red line interrupted the patch of stubble on his face. "Smith's bullet."

Mary collapsed on the toilet seat. "You could've…"

Leo knelt in front of her. "I'm okay." He wiped her tears and hugged her shaking body. "Smith's dead. Landry's in jail. It's all over."

She kissed him fiercely. "I love you."

"I love you, too."

Will poked his head into the small bathroom. "Progress report: Porch is clean. Tow company hauled Landry's car away. Aunt Sally's grandson, Devon, drove the tow truck which was pretty cool. Anyway, I thought I'd start dinner."

"Perfect." Leo rose as the house phone rang.

"Leo," Eddie called. "It's for you."

He kissed Mary again and went into the kitchen. "Hello?"

"Is it true?" Dahlia asked, breathing heavily. "Is Vern dead?"

"Yes." He adjusted the gauze on his hand.

"And Uncle Jacob, they've arrested him?"

"That's right."

Silence.

"Are you okay, Dahlia?"

"I will be. I'm packing and almost ready to go. I'd like to swing by in an hour or so."

"I'll be here."

The minute Leo hung up the phone, it rang again.

"I heard you've put that bastard away," Aunt Sally said. "Which scared the health inspector off. He won't be stopping by my diner, let alone closing it. How do I thank you?"

"Join us for dinner tonight."

"Only if I can help with the cooking."

Twenty minutes later, with the horizon an ominous blue-black, Leo stood on the front porch with an umbrella, waiting for Sally. He was pleased to see that most of the crowd on County T, and several of the television vans, had followed the police cars and coroner, hoping for some news. Now, as Sally turned her pickup into the driveway, the skies opened.

Leo met her at the driver's-side door, struggling to keep the large umbrella over their heads. She handed him a Tupperware container. "Dessert." They dashed for the house and made it inside as hail danced on the roof.

Forty minutes later, the intense storm stopped as quickly as it had begun. Leo and Mary threw open the windows, savoring a cool breeze and the smell of freshly-laundered earth. Broken branches and barn roof shingles littered the front lawn but the farm, the Bradbury Inn van, and Aunt Sally's truck had avoided serious damage. In the distance, a stream of vehicles wound their way back down County T toward the Townsend farm as protestors and TV crews returned.

"They're back. You'd think the weather would've dampened their enthusiasm." Mary stood beside him in front of the picture window.

"Not while we have a presidential candidate in our midst." Leo put his arm around her.

"Dinner!" Will and Aunt Sally called.

Leo and Mary joined Frank, John, Eddie, Griffin, Patrick, Charlotte, Tali, and Quinn at the long dining room table. Candles flickered in the evening breeze and made Isabella's gold-rimmed china sparkle. The crystal water goblets sprayed colorful prisms across the white tablecloth.

"Aren't your Secret Service men joining us, Griffin?" Mary asked.

"Nope," Will said, bringing in plates of creamy pasta. Scents of spicy Italian sausage and garlic filled the room. "One's out front, one in the back. I brought them each a plate."

"Thanks, Will," Griffin said.

"Whadya make us?" Quinn asked.

"This is Isabella's Pasta alla Norcina." Will set a dish in front of Leo.

"Oh, wow." Leo recognized the familiar, ear-shaped orecchiette pasta. "My mother made this every year for my birthday."

"Remember the year you tried to make it for her?" Eddie asked. "Used hot dogs instead of sausage?"

"She almost disowned you." Frank laughed. He opened a Sauvignon blanc, filled his glass, and passed the bottle to Griffin.

Aunt Sally strode in with a heaping tossed salad and a basket of crusty bread. As she set the basket beside Mary's plate, she said, "Your boy can cook."

Mary beamed.

When Will and Aunt Sally took their seats, Frank stood, his wine glass raised. "To family, old friends, new friends, and diamonds!"

They clinked glasses and shouted, "To diamonds!"

As Leo speared the pasta with his fork, the doorbell rang. "I'll get it." He took Mary's soft hand. "Come with me, there's someone I'd like you to meet."

Dahlia Landry stood under the porch light, biting a manicured fingernail. Her bleached-blonde hair, normally cemented in place with hairspray, was pulled back into two pigtails. She wore a Brewers t-shirt over cropped jean shorts and her feet were bare.

"Dahlia, come on in." Leo held the screen door open. A gentle breeze stroked the wind chimes. "Join us for dinner."

"Nah, thanks. I gotta get on the road. Plus…" Dahlia showed Leo the bottoms of her feet. They were caked in mud.

"Okay, then." He laughed. "We'll join you."

Dahlia smiled. The light caught a purpled bruise on her left cheek.

"Jesus!" He touched her face. "This is my fault."

She took his hand and squeezed it. "The hell with that. If it weren't for you I'd be stuck in Endeavor forever."

Mary joined them and immediately Dahlia dropped Leo's hand. She smoothed her t-shirt and tugged on her shorts. Mary looked at Leo, as if taking him in for the first time, then gave him a loving smile. She turned to the other woman. "Dahlia, I'm—"

"Mary. Nice to meet you." Dahlia held out her hand.

Mary ignored the hand and gave Dahlia a hug. "It's so good to meet you."

Surprised, Dahlia stiffened but smiled.

"I've heard nothing but good things about you from Leo and my cousin," Mary said.

"Your cousin?"

"Patrick Holden."

"He's a character!"

Mary laughed. "Definitely."

Dahlia handed a small black pouch to Leo.

Leo was surprised. He had assumed he'd never see the pouch again. "How did you manage to get this back?" He rubbed the soft velvet.

"I waited until Uncle Jacob and Vern left Isaiah's for your place. I searched his office, including his safe. Nothing. Then it hit me. Did you know Uncle Jacob kept his granddaddy's Bible on a pedestal there?"

"Sure. He had it with him at the town meeting."

"The Bible's hollow!" Dahlia laughed. "And there was your pouch."

"Unbelievable." Leo dumped the contents into the palm of his hand. A diamond and two crumpled pieces of paper. The diamond gleamed in the light.

Dahlia gave Mary a sideways glance, then reached up and hugged Leo.

"I'll see you in Chicago."

"Be safe."

They watched her climb into her Corolla. She tooted the horn and drove away, waving her hand out the window.

"In a few weeks, buy me a drink at Kasey's Tavern?" Mary asked, as he led her back into the house.

"You bet. We'll break in the new bartender."

"Who was at the door?" Frank asked, as Leo and Mary rejoined them in the dining room.

"Dahlia. She returned this." Leo handed his father the black velvet pouch and then stood over him while he read the notes. Frank looked at him and smiled, his eyes glistening.

"So how's the food?" Leo said to the group, as he took his seat.

"Horrible," Quinn said. "I'm on my second helping."

For Leo, the rich aroma of the Pasta alla Norcina brought back memories of his mother kneading pasta dough and rolling it into long snakes. She'd let him slice it and showed him how to form each orecchiette. She'd asked Bill Stevens down the road to make sausage for her, but only with spices she gave him. He'd balked until he tried it and then never went back to his original seasonings. For Isabella's funeral luncheon, he generously brought ten pounds of sausage.

"Delicious." Griffin wiped his mouth on his napkin, then glanced at his watch. "I hate to say it, but I have to leave soon. Right after dinner, in fact. I've only been off the campaign trail for two days, but according to my manager, you'd think I'd quit the election."

Eddie set his fork down, looking worse than he ever did in the hospital. "I'm glad you've stayed this long."

Griffin took Eddie's hand. "Come with me."

Eddie looked at their intertwined fingers.

"Don't worry," Griffin said. "You'll have the best medical care possible. Whatever you need to heal completely. And regarding your business, contact your office." His words came quickly. "Work remotely, like that time we took our trip to—"

"I'm already packed." Eddie gave Griffin a sly grin. "I was just waiting for you to ask."

Griffin glanced at Frank and then kissed Eddie—on his cheek.

"Who'd like some of Aunt Sally's triple-fudge brownies?" Will asked.

The room erupted in cheers.

"I'll make coffee." Sally rose from her chair.

"No!" Leo and Griffin shouted. "We mean," Leo amended. "You've already done enough. We'll make it."

The brownies disappeared quickly and soon the table was cleared, the dishes washed and put away. Everyone gathered on the front porch in the calm, cool night to send Eddie and Griffin off.

"I'm going to miss you, son," Frank said.

"I'll miss you, too, Dad."

"Don't give Griffin too much grief," Leo said to his younger brother, winking at the candidate. "You don't want to be left on the side of the road in the middle of Iowa."

Eddie laughed as he eased into the limo beside Griffin. "And you stay out of trouble. Avoid village presidents and their minions."

Leo shut the car door and the limousine eased down the driveway. A maelstrom broke out on County T as the long, black car crawled through the crowd. When the limo took off, the remaining locals in their pickup trucks and the news media in their vans pursued it, finally leaving the Townsend farm in peace.

57

Jacob woke to the sharp aroma of bleach and the stench of urine and wondered why he didn't smell Grace's frying sausage and fresh-brewed coffee. His back ached, his neck was stiff, his wrists were sore—what had happened to his pillow-top mattress? Why was his bedroom so dark? The early morning sun usually shined through their sheer curtains, something Grace had complained about for years. Where was the window?

Jake heard moaning and the distinct sound of someone vomiting into a toilet bowl. And in a rush it all came back: driving in his Caddie to the Townsend farm that was about to be his, Frank Townsend smirking as he threw diamonds onto the kitchen table, Vernon desperate for Jacob's gun, shooting at Townsend... and missing. Then holes... awful, huge, bloody holes in Vern's chest. A look of surprise on Vern's face as it turned ashen and he collapsed. Jacob watching as the man who was the closest thing to a son he had... died.

Jacob's sleepy fog was replaced by a rage unlike anything he'd felt before. It was concentrated, contained, like the fearsome energy inside a tiny atom.

Fluorescent lights burst on, stinging his eyes. He pushed off the thin, plastic mattress covering his concrete bed, his muscles complaining, and stumbled to the chrome toilet. He aimed his stream on the rim and on the floor at the base of the toilet, careful not to get any urine in the bowl itself. At the sink, he splashed water on his stubbly face, wishing for a mirror and a razor.

A door clanked open. Footsteps echoed.

Jacob ran his hands through his hair and tucked in his wrinkled shirt.

"Jacob." Sheriff Brian O'Donnell unlocked the jail cell. "Your wife contacted Judge Xavier. Called in a favor, I guess. The judge has waived your bail. You're free to go."

They walked by a cell with a haggard man passed out on his bed. And for the first time, Jacob thought about Caleb, Artie, and Buddy.

"Where'd you put Caleb and the boys?" he asked.

"Isolation. When they found out they had to sit here until a bail hearing later today, they got a little rowdy."

"What happened to Emmett?"

"He answered a few questions last night, pretty cooperative, really. Then he was free to go."

They reached the guard station. The guard passed Jacob an envelope with his watch, wallet, wedding ring, and car keys. It was 6:10 a.m., Jake noted, as he slipped his watch and ring on.

"Your gun, of course, isn't there," the sheriff said. "We're holding it as evidence."

"And my Caddie?"

"Around back." O'Donnell handed him a sheet of paper. "Your bill from the tow. Pay it now and we'll release the car to you."

Jacob's hands remained steady as he dug three fifties out of his wallet and signed the paperwork.

The sheriff walked Jacob into the sally port entrance. They stood in the small hallway while a metal-and-glass door closed slowly behind them. "I'm afraid Devon Hass didn't put the car's top down," the sheriff said. "If there's any damage from last night's hail storm, take it up with Endeavor Towing."

The metal door in front of them slid open. "Leave through the back door." He pointed at a deserted corridor. "The press is gone. They're not expecting your early release. But it won't be long before they're back. See you in court, Jacob."

Sunlight grazed the treetops as Jake trudged across the parking lot. Reaching his Caddie, his legs buckled and he swayed, but managed to stay on his feet.

The car's dimpled hood looked like someone had taken a hammer to it. The windshield was cracked and the soft leather seats were stained and caked with mud. Jacob opened the car door. Its hinges creaked. He hoisted a large tree branch off the seat and tossed it aside, then slid into the car. Water squished under his shoes. When he turned on the ignition, the car choked several times before the engine turned over.

Coldly calm, Jacob drove home.

TV vans lined the street in front of his brick Victorian home. Several had parked on the manicured front lawn, leaving deep ruts in the grass and knocking over his rosebushes. Jacob turned around before being spotted and parked in front of Mrs. Whitford's ranch house a block away. Crouching, he ignored his cramped muscles and darted to his back door, relieved not to be seen.

The house was quiet, not surprising at six thirty, but no coffee aromas greeted him. Why hadn't Grace set the automatic coffeepot the night before?

Jacob slipped his damp shoes off and walked into the kitchen. A note lay next to the pot.

Judge Xavier says this is it for him. No more. I feel the same, my dear Jake. Expect a call from my attorney.

Proverbs 12:4 came to mind, "An excellent wife is the crown of her husband. But she who shames him is like rottenness in his bones."

And yet, he was calmer than ever.

His stockinged feet left damp footprints on the cold hardwood floor as he strode through the kitchen. His feet warmed as he stepped onto the plush dining room carpet. He walked around the carved cherry wood table, running his fingers over its smooth surface, and through the living room. He paused in front of the massive brick fireplace, then reached over the mantle for his sawed-off shotgun.

58

Leo woke in his childhood bedroom early Tuesday, to the crowing of his father's rooster. He stretched, then reached for his Chicago Triathlon t-shirt and the pair of running shorts slung on his desk. As he pulled on his t-shirt, Mary stirred.

"Are you leaving me?" she teased, her eyes still closed.

"Going for a run." Leo laced his shoes, which was tricky with his bandaged hand. He fished in his leather jacket hanging on the back of the desk chair and found the red satin ribbon. He gently placed it in the pocket of his shorts. "I'll be back before you even think about leaving this bed." He kissed Mary's forehead.

She smiled and rolled away, taking the sheet with her.

Leo reached for his cell phone on the bedside table. Dead battery. He plugged it in, then went downstairs and glanced out the living room window at the lightening eastern sky. Yellow-and-orange sunbeams sprayed across the fields but the top of the sun was not yet visible. In the west, the sky remained inky black, though the stars were fading. Thankfully, County T was deserted.

Leo pushed through the creaky screen door and jogged down the steps. He ran on the puddled driveway as headlights swung around the corner and illuminated County T. *Damn, are the paparazzi back?* The lights blinded Leo as he reached the end of the drive.

"Yer up early, Mr. Townsend." Johnny pulled his truck alongside Leo.

Leo jogged in place. "I'll give you a hand with the chores when I get back." He patted the side of the truck and started down the road.

The cool morning air invigorated Leo but he held off on pushing himself too hard at first—he'd be running ten miles. Behind him, the cows bellowed a greeting to Johnny. Across Bill Stevens' field, a tractor sputtered to life.

Leo came to the stand of birch trees where he'd discovered the plastic piece from the urea bag. He was saddened to see a sapling had been uprooted by the storm and was now sprawled across the road. He gathered several newly-greened branches and dragged the small tree onto the grass.

Several miles farther, he encountered a cluster of wild turkeys sauntering across the road. They regarded him dumbly as he shooed them out of the way.

Leo crested a hill the moment sunlight burst over the treetops, warming his face. He wiped off sweat with his short sleeve and increased the pace, feeling stronger than he had in weeks. In no time, he reached the Merritt's Landing Cemetery. He slowed to a walk as he pushed open the cold metal gate, making it groan. Immediately, his running shoes were soaked from the damp grass. They squished as he passed through the older section of the cemetery to his mother's grave.

Leo traced the lettering on the fresh headstone with his finger. *Isabella Renata Salvatori Townsend, Beloved Wife and Mother. Heaven has another angel.* For the first time in his life, he wished he believed in heaven. Believed that she could hear him now as he told her all that had happened. She'd be happy to know that he and Frank were getting along.

Damn, I miss her.

Leo placed the ribbon at the base of the stone, securing it with a rock, and patted the cool marble. As he walked back through the cemetery and out the gate, a robin called and a second one answered.

He held a strong pace on the way back to the farmhouse. The sun had risen higher in the cloudless blue sky, warming the morning air. He looked forward to a cold glass of water and a cool shower.

He slowed to a walk as he came to the driveway and then stopped to take in his family's farm. A gust of wind carried the melody of the wind chimes and gently rocked the glider. The ancient oak's leaves shimmered and the branches swayed. His mother's embroidered tablecloth was clipped to the clothesline, flapping in the breeze.

Despite his father's neglect of the farm these last few months, the farmhouse had kept its beauty. Leo had to admit, this had been a wonderful place to grow up.

"I'm going to kill you, boy."

Jacob Landry's voice was as steely as the sawed-off shotgun in his hands. He stood near the mailbox, not ten feet away. His white dress shirt had armpit stains and his torn chinos were soiled and wrinkled—the same clothes he had worn the previous day. His eyes were unnaturally bright and focused as he aimed the barrel at Leo, but his left eyebrow twitched. Sweat collected on his forehead and ran down his temples.

Leo resisted the urge to charge the smaller, older man and worked hard to keep his voice steady. "Bust out of prison, Jacob?"

"Xavier let me go."

A red-tailed hawk cried overhead.

Leo raised his hands. "If you kill me, you'll rot in jail."

"Wrong. They'll arrest the gay-bashing sap I pin your murder on."

"Emmett?"

Landry smirked. "Just takes a little evidence tampering, a few words in the right ears. With no witnesses, it'll be easy. I've done it before."

"Why kill me?"

"They're my diamonds! I discovered them years ago." Spittle lodged in the corners of Landry's mouth. He stepped closer.

Leo took a step back. *Keep him talking.* "Could be. But you don't own this property, and you never will. You won't get the diamonds by killing me."

"Wrong again." Landry sneered. Somewhere down the road, a dog barked. "Finding you scattered all over County T will be the last straw for Frank. He'll beg me to buy, if he doesn't have another heart attack first. Fatal this time." He chuckled. The shotgun shook.

The hawk screeched.

GOD ON MAYHEM STREET

"And because of you, my white-trash niece took off with the only diamonds I had." Landry's voice quivered. He moved closer.

"*My* diamond." Leo shuffled backward into a puddle. The rubber sole of his shoe slid in the mud. "And Dahlia's." He managed to regain his footing while keeping his eyes on Landry.

"Thought they'd be safe in my Bible," Landry said. "Protected by the Lord. 'For the Lord God is a sun and shield: the Lord will give grace and glory: no good thing will he withhold from them that walk uprightly. O Lord of hosts, blessed is the man that trusts in thee.' Psalm 84:11-12." He shuffled forward. "I trusted her. My own flesh and blood stealing from me. Gonna kill that girl after I'm done with you."

Leo backed off the edge of the driveway onto the grass, looking for cover out of the corner of his eyes. The nearest tree stood fifteen feet away. *Too far.* "You'll have to find her first."

"But it's more than diamonds." Landry's voice was shrill. "You've humiliated me, destroyed my standing in this community. And Vernon," his voice caught, "you killed my boy." Tears began streaming down his face, adding to the sweat.

Leo began to say... what? That he disagreed? Should he condemn Smith? Apologize? Nothing he could say would help his situation.

Landry steadied the shotgun again and clicked back the hammer. "You deserve to die." He squeezed the trigger.

Leo winced, waiting for the fatal punch of slugs in his chest. He pictured his father's calloused hands, his brother's mischievous grin, and the soft blonde strands caressing his lady's cheek. *Mary, what I wouldn't give for one last kiss.* Leo closed his eyes.

And then, he heard the shot. A loud *crack* that startled a flight of swallows into the air and made the distant dog howl.

Yet, Leo remained standing.

He looked down at his t-shirt—no blood—then at Landry.

Jacob Landry stared at the bloody hole where his stomach had been. He gave Leo a perplexed expression as his shredded intestines began to fall out of the hole. Leo blanched, remembering the pig guts strewn across the porch.

Landry dropped the shotgun and placed both hands over his insides, trying to hold himself together. He stumbled backward and collapsed onto the gravel.

Leo spun around. Frank burst out of the house, carrying his high-powered hunting rifle. Mary sprinted behind.

Leo kicked away Landry's firearm and dropped to the village president's side.

Landry clutched Leo's forearm and mouthed, "Help me." He coughed up blood.

Leo peeled his t-shirt over his head and pressed it to the village president's chest. Landry began choking. Leo helped him to a sitting position. Landry recoiled, spitting up a bright-red mouthful of blood.

"Leo," Frank panted, as he and Mary approached at a run. "Are you all right?"

Leo nodded. "Call 9-1-1."

"I did," Mary said, catching her breath. She looked at Leo's t-shirt, now completely stained red. "But I don't think they'll get here in time."

Landry's eyes rolled heavenward. "Why?" He coughed up more blood. "Why have you forsaken me?"

59

Leo settled on the farmhouse's front porch glider, drinking the last of John's Italian wine, relieved that his bandaged hand holding the glass had stopped shaking. After being interrogated by Morris Grey for most of the day, Leo needed the wine to relax—and celebrate. Jacob Landry and Vernon Smith were dead and Leo's family had diamonds.

The early morning heat had evaporated, replaced by a cool afternoon. From around the corner, the tractor rumbled as Johnny steered it into the barn for the night. Cows lowed in the pasture and plates clinked in the dining room as the kids set the table. At the end of the driveway, a doe and her speckled fawn stopped to stare at the house, then trotted across County T.

The screen door creaked as Mary came out onto the porch with a wine glass and a bottle of Wollersheim Pinot Noir. The glider jiggled as she settled in and set the glass and bottle on the floor. She unbuttoned his shirt and slid her soft hand across his chest. She kissed the fading red mark on his cheek, the scar on his chin, and finally, his lips.

"Well, good evening." His voice was husky.

She'd started to kiss him again when Johnny drove by in his truck. "Headin' home," the farmhand said, waving. "See ya tomorrow."

There was laughter from the dining room and good-natured teasing from the kitchen.

Sighing, Mary put her arm around his shoulders and watched the truck disappear down the driveway. "It's really beautiful here."

Leo poured her a glass of wine. "This was my mother's favorite spot. On weekend mornings and during summer vacations, I'd join her here. I'd read her my latest article or she'd tell me about her childhood—horseback riding in the Piano Grande or selling her father's prosciutto at the National Black Truffle Festival in Norcia."

"Did she miss Italy?" Mary sipped her wine.

"When I'd ask her that, she'd always say, 'Yes, but not as much as I love living here with my boys.'"

"Did she go back to visit?"

"Never. They'd talk about it but there was always some issue with the farm that ruined their plans. Crops to harvest or calves to birth. I think that's one of my dad's deepest regrets."

They rocked the glider gently and listened to Patrick tuning the kitchen radio to rock and roll classics. Bob Seger sang about night moves.

Leo kissed the palm of her hand. "Do you have to leave tonight?"

"I've been neglecting my town, completely worth it, of course." She kissed him. "There's good news in Carpe Diem. The new family who publicly spanked their children has relocated to Minneapolis.

"But we've got to do something to avoid similar situations. I'm meeting with Patrick and the city council tomorrow afternoon. Rather than draft rules of conduct, I'd like to create an unschooling information packet. We'd give it to prospective families before they decide to move to Carpe Diem." She swirled the red wine in her glass. "And then there's the inn. The plumbing repairs are finished, so we're officially open for the tourist season. Our first guests arrive on Friday. My concierge tells me we're completely booked."

"Sounds like you'll be busy."

"Always." She smiled. "John needs to get back, too, and he's our ride home. And the kids will be leaving for Italy in less than two weeks. They've got lots to do before then. Besides, you really don't need us now that your father will be able to pay for additional crew. Right? Seriously, a possible diamond mine? Incredible."

"The farm doesn't need you, but I do. How about staying another night? The kids can go home with John tonight. I'll drive you back to Carpe Diem tomorrow in time for your meeting. It's on the way to Chicago."

Mary laughed. "No, it's not."

He tucked a strand of blonde hair behind her ear, kissed her ear lobe and then her jaw line.

"Okay," she sighed, as he pushed open the collar of her blouse and worked his way down her neck. "When you put it that way…"

"Plus," he continued between kisses, her hands running through his hair. "We have two tons of Aunt Sally's triple-fudge brownies left. You can't leave until they're gone."

"Mmm, hmm."

He kissed her beautiful mouth just as Frank walked out.

"Oops," Frank said, last Sunday's *Chicago Examiner* in one hand, a bottle of Spotted Cow in the other. He turned back to the door.

"Don't go." Blushing, Mary straightened her blouse and rose from the glider. "I need to check in with the kids. Make sure they've packed everything." She gave Leo a gentle kiss, her hand lingering over his chin, and went into the house.

Frank took Mary's seat.

"How are you doing, Dad?"

"Good, great if truth be told. Honestly, I've felt more remorse killing a ten-point buck than shooting Landry. Maybe it hasn't sunk in yet."

"Or maybe it's because you saved my life."

Frank nodded. He opened the paper and pointed to Leo's article. "I reread it. It's really good."

"Thanks."

"It's going in my book." Frank took a swig of the beer.

"Your what?"

"Since your first published article almost thirty years ago, I've kept all your stories in scrapbooks."

"You never mentioned this."

"Over the years, I've learned that if I complement you on your achievements, you stop doing them and do the opposite. Just to spite me."

Leo laughed, remembering the time his father complimented his pitching arm. Soon after that, Leo quit the baseball team and tried out for football.

He watched two teenagers trot their chestnut quarter horses on County T, a barking border collie chasing behind. "If it's okay with you, Mary and I'll stay one more night. Leave for Chicago tomorrow morning. I should get back to *The Examiner*. But if you need me, I could talk to my editor. Stay through the weekend."

Frank waved to the horseback riders, then turned to Leo. "Hell, no. You get your ass back to that paper. Write the next great story." Then his smile faded. He took a big slug of beer. "There is this issue with your brother dating a..."

"Man?"

"Well, that too, but I was thinking 'politician.' If Griffin becomes president of the United States, what will Eddie's life be like?"

"He'll travel the world. Meet heads of state."

"I wish your mother were alive. She'd be so proud of her sons." Frank studied Leo's face. "I'm proud of you, too. And... well... I love you."

"I love you, too, Dad." Leo hugged his father.

"What do you think Griffin's chances are of winning?" Frank asked.

"Anything could happen between now and the election. We'll just have to wait and see."

ACKNOWLEDGEMENTS

Many thanks to my parents, Clyde and Elizabeth Oakley, for promoting me shamelessly; to my older daughter, Caitlin Podemski, for telling me to pick up the pace; to my younger daughter, Jessica Podemski, for eagerly awaiting this book's release; to my sister, Lisa Schroeter, for her valuable feedback on draft six; and to my niece, Jamie Schroeter, for creating a website that would make even Will jealous.

Thanks again to my insightful critique partners: Catherine Conroy, Mary Lamphere, and Kathleen Tresemer—you don't let me get away with anything, ever. Special additional thanks to Mary Lamphere for her help with the book's cover design and loaning me "Leo's" jacket.

Leo and I are both city people, but unlike Leo, I didn't grow up on a farm. Thanks to Jackie and Marcel Batista for the tour of their beautiful Irish Grove Farms in northern Illinois and to Jackie for her review of the second draft. Thanks also to small town veterinarian Dr. Bill Stork who tutored me on the best way to poison cows.

My good friend Rich Brandt gave me keen insights into the lives of gay and straight men, Dr. Harvey Thorleifson passed along his expertise on diamonds in the Midwest, and Sheriff Kim Gaffney explained Marquette County police procedures and what a shotgun blast from 200 yards would do to a man. Thank you!

Karyn Saemann, my editor at Inkspots, Inc., is the female version of Ted Nelson—without the scarred biceps. She pulled this story out of me in a way that only a great editor can. Thank you!

And thank you to all the members of In Print and the Chicago Writers Association—you inspire me every day.

ABOUT THE AUTHOR

Kristin A. Oakley's debut novel, *Carpe Diem, Illinois*, is the winner of the 2014 Chicago Writers Association Book of the Year Award for non-traditionally published fiction and a finalist in the Independent Author Network 2015 Book of the Year. Kristin is the president and co-founder of In Print, a professional writers' organization, a board member of the Chicago Writers Association, and the editor of *The Write City Magazine*. As a writing instructor at the UW-Madison Division of Continuing Studies, Kristin critiques manuscripts and offers an online course on cliffhangers. She has a B.A. in psychology and a J.D., both from the University of Wisconsin-Madison. You can find her online at: kristinoakley.net.

Read the first book in the Leo Townsend Series:
Carpe Diem, Illinois!

Carpe Diem, Illinois is the winner of the 2014 Chicago Writers Association Book of the Year Award for non-traditionally published fiction and a finalist in the Independent Author Network 2015 Book of the Year.

"*Carpe Diem, Illinois*, (A Leo Townsend novel) by Kristin A. Oakley, provides us a glimpse of the homeschooling experience while delivering a gritty story of murder and intrigue in small town America. Leo Townsend, Oakley's protagonist, is a tough guy reporter whose best piece of journalism has ironically been ghost written by an anonymous source. Determined to find out who is playing him and why, Leo sets out to unravel a mysterious murder in an otherwise sleepy town. Ms. Oakley ends the novel with the promise of more Townsend in the future, which is wonderful news for those who enjoy great mysteries. I selected *Carpe Diem, Illinois* from all of the great books I read this year because the hero has both an edge and a playfulness that proved to be highly engaging."

– Jay Rehak, The Chicago Writers Association 2014 Book of the Year Finalist Judge

"With a fascinating look at unschooling, Oakley combines classic Chicago dirty politics with small town charm, murder, mystery, and political intrigue... Carpe Diem left me not only entertained, but wanting to seize the day and apply some unschooling principles to my kids' summertime activities."

– Susan Kaye Quinn, author of *The Mindjack Trilogy, The Dharian Affairs Trilogy, The Debt Collector, and Faery Swap*

"A unique combination of small-town chronicle and political thriller that's likely to draw in fans of both genres." – Kirkus Reviews

"In *Carpe Diem, Illinois*, Kristin Oakley weaves a tale of local political intrigue into a fascinating lesson in unschooling. Through the eyes of broken Chicago reporter Leo Townsend we begin to see the secrets that lie behind the fictional commune-like town of the title where there are no schools and the children are mostly left to their own devices. Ultimately, this satisfying debut novel teaches us that if we open our eyes and our minds, there is much to learn and those mysteries to us are not so mysterious at all."

– Randy Richardson, author of *Cheeseland and Lost in the Ivy*